**Meet Poppy Blake, the resilient sister of
Lake News's Lily Blake, in Barbara Delinsky's
unforgettable bestseller**

AN ACCIDENTAL WOMAN

"Delinsky has strong characters in Blake, whose disability never impedes her work, and Hughes, who looks past his lover's disability to the woman within."
—*Baltimore Sun*

"The twisty plot and icy late-winter backdrop . . . will keep you chilling on a hot afternoon."
—*People*

"A good story in an idyllic and lovingly rendered setting."
—*The Calgary Sun*

THE WOMAN NEXT DOOR

"An achievement. . . . Adept and compelling. . . . One of her best books to date."
—*Booklist*

"Delinsky peers into the dark corners of ideal marriages . . . and makes you realize that 'the woman next door' could be you."
—*Roanoke Times* (VA)

"*The Woman Next Door* . . . will stir everyone who reads it."
—*The Anniston Star* (TX)

THE VINEYARD

"High drama, beautiful scenery, and resilient yet sensitive characters make this a must for all Delinsky fans."
—*Booklist*

"Another enjoyable novel."
—*Library Journal*

LAKE NEWS

"[An] engaging tale."
—*People*

"[Her characters] . . . become more like old friends than works of fiction."
—*Flint Journal* (MI)

COAST ROAD

"Heartwarming."
—*Star Tribune* (Minneapolis)

"A remarkable journey."
—*The Cincinnati Enquirer*

THREE WISHES

"Touching and delightful. . . . A story of genuine love, sacrifice, redemption, and the cohesiveness of life in a small town."
—*Chattanooga Times* (TN)

"Delinsky's prose is spare, controlled, and poignant."
—*Publishers Weekly*

BARBARA DELINSKY

LAKE NEWS

POCKET BOOKS

New York   London   Toronto   Sydney

Pocket Books
A Division of Simon & Schuster, Inc.
1230 Avenue of the Americas
New York, NY 10020

This Pocket Books paperback edition January 2008

POCKET and colophon are registered trademarks of Simon & Schuster, Inc.

For information about special discounts for bulk purchases, please contact Simon & Schuster Special Sales at 1-800-456-6798 or business@simonandschuster.com

Hand lettering by Iskra Johnson
Illustration by Thomas Woodruff

Manufactured in the United States of America

10   9   8   7   6   5   4   3

ISBN-13: 978-1-4165-6428-7
ISBN-10:   1-4165-6428-4

Acknowledgments

So many people to thank. Where to begin? It started with a double bill—shopping for a lake house and researching a book. I succeeded on both counts, thanks to the warmth and generosity of people like Chip and Tina Maxfield, Susan Francesco, and Sid Lovett—and to Doug and Liz Hentz, who've made it such fun!

My sister, Helen Dempsey, was a tireless resource when it came to all things Catholic, for which I thank her from the bottom of my heart. If I've taken literary license and made mistakes, the fault is solely mine.

For newspaper information, I am indebted to Maria Buckley and Ron Duce of the *Needham TAB*. For apple-cider-making information, I thank Julie, Andrew, and Jo of Honey Pot Hill Orchards. For miscellaneous other bits and snatches, I thank Martha Raddatz, Barbara Rosenberger, and Phyllis Tickle. I also owe a well of gratitude to Robin Mays, who passed away shortly after I finished writing this book.

She's watching us, though. I know she is. Robin, the birdhouses are yours!

As always, my agent, Amy Berkower, and her assistant, Jodi Reamer, were there for me, as was my own assistant, Wendy Page. To my editors, Michael Korda and Chuck Adams, I offer heartfelt thanks and future promise.

I dedicate *Lake News* to my husband, Steve, who really got into the plotting of this one, and to our kids, always a boundless source of pride—Eric and Jodi, Andrew, and Jeremy and Sherrie.

Finally, to Ellyn's Lily, here it is!

Nothing so fair, so pure, and at the same time so large, as a lake, perchance, lies on the surface of the earth. Sky water. It needs no fence. Nations come and go without defiling it. It is a mirror which no stone can crack, whose quicksilver will never wear off, whose gilding nature continually repairs; no storms, no dust, can dim its surface ever fresh;—a mirror in which all impurity presented to it sinks, swept and dusted by the sun's hazy brush,—this the light dust-cloth,—which retains no breath that is breathed on it, but sends its own to float as clouds high above its surface, and be reflected in its bosom still.

from Walden, *by Henry David Thoreau*

LAKE
NEWS

Chapter 1

Lake Henry, New Hampshire

Like everything else at the lake, dawn arrived in its own good time. The flat black of night slowly deepened to a midnight blue that lightened in lazy steps, gradually giving form to the spike of a tree, the eave of a cottage, the tongue of a weathered wood dock—and that was on a clear day. On this day, fog slowed the process of delineation, reducing the lake to a pool of milky glass and the shoreline to a hazy wash of orange, gold, and green where, normally, vibrant fall colors would be. A glimpse of cranberry or navy marked a lakefront home, but details were lost in the mist. Likewise the separation of reflection and shore. The effect, with the air quiet and still, was that of a protective cocoon.

It was a special moment. The only thing John Kipling would change about it was the cold. He wasn't ready for summer to end, but despite his wishes, the days were noticeably shorter than they had been two months before. The sun set sooner and rose later, and the chill of the night lingered. He felt it. His loons felt it. The foursome he watched, two adults and their young, would remain on the lake for another five weeks, but they were growing restless, looking to the sky lately in ways that had less to do with predators than with thoughts of migration.

As he watched now, they floated in the fog not twenty feet from his canoe, not ten feet again from the tiny fir-covered island in whose sheltered cove they had summered. The island was one of many that dotted Lake Henry. Between the clarity of the water, the quiet of the lake, and the abundance of small fish, those islands lured the loons back year after year— because they didn't do well on land. Their feet were set too far back under large, cumbersome bodies. So they built nests on the very edge of these islands, where they could more easily enter and leave the water. John found it painful watching them lurch even those precious few inches from water to nest.

In all other respects, though, the loons were a sight to behold. Since the chicks' birth, in July, he had watched their plumage go from baby black to toddler brown to a rather drab juvenile gray, but they had their parents' tapered beaks and sleek necks, and a promise of future brilliance—and those parents, ahhhh, those parents were brilliant indeed, even in fall, with their plumage starting to dull, even this morning, through the veil of an ashy mist. They were beauties, with crisp checkerboards of white-on-black backs, white-stripe necklaces around black necks, solid black heads, distinctive pointed beaks. As if that weren't impressive enough, they had riveting round red eyes. John had heard that the red enhanced underwater vision, and he could believe it. Those eyes didn't miss much.

The birds lay low in the water now, swimming gently around the cove, alternately rolling and contorting to groom themselves and submerging their heads to troll for fish. When one of the adults compressed its body and dove, a webbed power propelled it deep. John knew it might fill its belly with up to fifteen minnows before resurfacing a distance away.

He searched the fog until he spotted it again. Its mate continued to float near the island, but both adults were alert, those pointed bills tipped just a little higher as they scoured the fog for news. Later that morning they would leave their young, run laboriously across the surface of the lake, and lumber up into the air. After circling a time or two until they gained altitude enough to clear the trees, they would fly to a neighboring lake to visit other loons. Breeding was a solitary time, and with two fledglings to show for months of vigilance and work, this pair had done well. Now they had to refresh their social skills in preparation for wintering in larger groups on the warmer Atlantic coast.

For an eon, loons had repeated this ritual. The same intelligence that had assured their survival for so long told the current crop of birds that September was halfway done, October would bring colder days and evening frost, and November would bring ice. Since they needed an expanse of clear water for takeoff, they had to leave the lake before it froze. And they would. In all his years growing up on the lake, then returning as an adult to watch again, John hadn't seen many ice-bound loons. Their instincts were good. They rarely erred.

John, however, erred—and often. Hadn't he done it again this morning, setting out in a T-shirt and shorts, wanting it to be summer still and finding himself butt cold now? He sometimes had trouble accepting that he wasn't twenty anymore. He was over forty—and, yes, still six three and fit, but his body didn't work the way it once did. It ached around the knees, wrinkled around the eyes, receded at the temples, and chilled in the extremities.

But cold or not, he wasn't leaving. Not yet. There might not necessarily be the makings of a big bestseller in it, but he hadn't had his fill of the loons.

He sat rock still in the canoe with his hands in his armpits for warmth and his paddle stowed. These loons were used to his presence, but he took nothing for granted. As long as he kept his distance and respected their space, they would reward him with preening and singing. When the world was eerily quiet—at night, at dawn, on mornings like this when the fog muffled other noise that life on the lake might make—the loons' song shimmered and rose. And it came now—breathtaking—a primitive tremolo released with the shiver of a jaw, so beautiful, so mysterious, so wild that it raised the hair on the back of his neck.

It also carried a message. The tremolo was a cry of

alarm. Granted, this one was low in pitch, which made it only a warning, but he wasn't about to ignore it. With the faintest rasp of wood on fiberglass, he lifted his paddle. Water lapped softly against the canoe as he guided it backward. When he was ten more feet away, he stabilized his position and quietly restowed the paddle. Hugging his elbows to his thighs for warmth, he sat, watched, listened, waited.

In time, the loon closest to him stretched his neck forward and issued a long, low wail. The sound wasn't unlike the cry of a coyote, but John would never confuse the two. The loon's wail was at the same time more elemental and more delicate.

This one was the start of a dialogue, one adult calling the other in a succession of haunting sounds that brought the distant bird gliding closer. Even when they were ten feet apart, they continued to speak, with their beaks nearly shut and their elongated throats swelling around the sound.

Goose bumps rose on his skin. This was why he had returned to the lake—why, after swearing off New Hampshire at fifteen, he had reversed himself at forty. Some said he'd done it for the job, others that he'd done it for his father, but the roundabout truth had to do with these birds. They signified something primal and wild, but simple, straightforward, and safe.

A loon's life consisted of eating, grooming, and procreating. It was an honest life, devoid of pretense, ambition, and cruelty. The loon harmed others only when its own existence was threatened. John found that totally refreshing.

So he stayed longer, though he knew he should leave. It was Monday. *Lake News* had to be at the printer by noon on Wednesday. He already had material from his staff correspondents, one per town. Assuming that the appropriate bins held articles promised by local movers and shakers—"movers and shakers" being a relative term—he would have a wad of reading and editing, keystroking, cutting and pasting. If those articles weren't in the bins, he would call around Lake Henry and the four neighboring towns serviced by the paper, take information on the phone, and write what he could himself—and if he still ended up with dead space, he would run more Thoreau.

There wasn't a book in that either, he told himself. A book had to be original. He had notebooks filled with ideas, folders thick with anecdotes he had collected since returning to town, but nothing sparked an urge to hustle—at least, not when it came to writing a book. He *did* hustle when it came to *Lake News*—but mostly between noon Tuesdays and noon Wednesdays. He was a last-minute kind of guy. He wrote better under the threat of a deadline closing in, liked the rush of a newsroom filled with action and noise, liked the perversion of keeping the managing editor on edge.

Of course, he was the managing editor now. And the production editor. And the photography editor, the society editor, the layout editor. *Lake News* wasn't the *Boston Post*. Not by a long shot, and there were times when that bothered him.

This, however, wasn't one.

His paddle remained stowed, and the loons continued to call. Then came a pause, and John dared mimic the sound. One of the loons said something in return, and in that brief, heady instant, he felt part of the team. In the next instant, with a resumption of the birds' duet, he was excluded again, a species apart.

But not cold. He realized he was no longer cold. The fog was burning off under a brightening sun. By the time patches of blue showed through the mist, John guessed it was nearly nine. He straightened his legs and, easing back, braced his elbows on the gunwales. Turning his face to the sun, he closed his eyes, took a contented breath, and listened to silence, water, and loon.

After a time, when the sun began to heat his eyelids and the weight of responsibility grew too heavy to ignore, he pushed himself up. For a few last minutes he continued to watch and absorb the whatever-it-was that these birds gave him. Then smoothly and silently, if reluctantly, he retrieved his paddle from the floorboards and headed home.

The beauty of a beard was that it eliminated the need to shave. John kept his cropped close, which meant occasional touch-ups, but none of the daily scrape-and-bleed agony that he used to endure. Same thing with a necktie. No need for one here. Or for a pressed shirt. Or for anything but denim down below. He didn't even have to worry about matching socks, since it was either bare feet and Birks in summer or work boots in winter, and then he could wear whatever socks he wanted and no one would see.

He still felt the novelty of showering, dressing, and hitting the road in ten minutes flat, and what a road. No traffic. No other *cars*. No horns. No cops. No *speed limit*. The road he drove now was framed by trees just shy of their peak of fall color. It wove in and out in a rough tracing of the lake and was cracked by years of frost heaves. Most other roads in town were the same. They imposed speed limits all on their own, and Lake Henry liked it that way. The town didn't cater to tourists as many of the surrounding lake towns did. There was no inn. There were no chic little shops. Despite a perennial brouhaha in the state legislature, there was no public access to the shore. Anyone who went out on the lake was either a resident, a friend of a resident, or a trespasser.

At that particular moment in time, with summer residents gone and only year-rounders left, the town's population was 1,721. Eleven babies were due, which would raise the count. Twelve citizens were terminally old or terminally ill, which would lower it. There were twenty-eight kids currently in college. Whether they would return was a toss-up. In John's day they left and never came back, but that was starting to change.

He made what he intended to be a brief stop at the general store, but got to talking national politics with Charlie Owens, who owned the store; and then Charlie's wife, Annette, told him that Stu and Amanda Watson's college junior, Hillary, was home for a quick day after a last-minute decision to spend the semester abroad. Since Hillary had interned for John two summers before, he had a personal stake in her success, so he detoured to her house to get the story, take her picture, and wish her luck.

Back in the center of town, he turned in at the post office and continued on to the thin yellow Victorian that stood between it and the lake. Climbing from the truck—a Chevy Tahoe, one of the perks of the job—he reached across the seat for his briefcase, shouldered its strap, and scooped up the day's editions of four different newspapers, a bag of doughnuts, and his thermos. With the bag clutched in his teeth he sifted through his key ring as he crossed the dirt drive to the Victorian's side door.

He was still sifting when he shouldered open the screen. The door behind it was mahogany, highly varnished, and carved by a local artist. Between swirls on its bottom half were a dozen slots identified by small brass plaques. The first row, politely, was devoted to the neighboring towns—*Ashcroft, Hedgeton, Cotter Cove,* and *Center Sayfield.* The lower rows were Lake Henry–specific, with slots assigned to things like *Police and Fire, Congregational Church, Textile Mill,* and *Garden Club.* Eye-high on the door, with no slot attached, was the largest plaque. *Lake News,* it read.

The door moved even before John inserted his key. As he elbowed it the rest of the way open, the phone began to ring. "Jenny?" he called. *"Jenny?"*

"In the bathroom!" came the muted yell.

Nothing new there, he thought. But at least she had come.

Tossing his keys on the kitchen table in passing, he took the stairs two at a time, past the second floor and

on up to the third. There were no dividing walls up
here, which made it the largest room in the house.
The addition of a slew of windows and skylights also
made it the brightest. Most important, it was the only
one with a view of the lake. That view wasn't nearly as
good as the one from John's house, but it was better
than no view at all, which was what the lower rooms
in the Victorian offered. Three willows, arm in arm
and more fat than tall, saw to that.

The attic room had been his office since he had returned to town, three years before. It was large enough
to house the newspaper's sales department, the production department, and the editorial department.
Each had a desk and a view of the lake. That view kept
John focused and sane.

The phone continued to ring. Letting the papers
slip to the editorial desk, he dropped the bag from
Charlie's on top, stood the thermos nearby, and
opened the window wide. The lake air was clear now.
Sun spilled down the slopes of the east hills, setting
fire to foliage in its path before running out over the
water. A month before, it would have hit a dozen
boats captained by summer folk who were grabbing
precious last minutes on the lake before closing up
camp for the year. The only boat on the water today
was one of Marlon Dewey's prized Chris-Crafts. The
sun bounced off its polished oak deck and glittered in
the wake spreading behind.

He picked up the phone. "Morning, Armand."

"Took you long enough," his publisher said in a
rusty voice. "Where you been?"

John followed the course of the handsome Chris-Craft. Marlon was at the helm, along with two visiting grandchildren. "Oh, out and around."

The old man's voice softened. " 'Oh, out and around.' You give me that every time, John, and you know I can't argue with it. Damn lake has too many bends, so I can't see what goes on around yours. But the paper's my bottom line, and you're doing that okay. Long as it keeps up, you can sleep as late as you want. Did you get my piece? Liddie put it in the slot."

"It's there," John said without checking, because Armand Bayne's wife was totally reliable. She was also totally devoted to her husband. What Armand wanted done, she did.

"What else you got?" the old man asked.

John clamped the phone between shoulder and ear and pulled a handful of papers from the briefcase. He had dummied the week's pages at home the night before. Now he spread out the sheets. "The lead is a report on the education bill that's up before the state legislature. It's a thirty-inch piece, across the top and down the right-hand leg, photo lower left. I'm following it with opinion pieces, one from the local rep, one from the principal at Cooper Elementary."

"What's your editorial say about it?"

"You know what it says."

"The natives won't like it."

"Maybe not, but we either put money into schools today or into welfare tomorrow." The source of that money was the problem. Not wanting to argue it again with Armand, who was one of the wealthiest of the landowners and would be soaked if property taxes doubled, he pulled up the next dummy. "Page three leads with a report on Chris Diehl's trial—closing arguments, jury out, verdict in, Chris home. I have a piece on profit sharing at the mill, and one on staff cutbacks at the retirement home. The newcomer profile is on Thomas Hook."

"Can't stand the guy," Armand muttered.

John uncapped the thermos. "That's because he has no people skills, but he has computer skills. There's reason why his business is worth twenty million and growing."

"He's a *kid.*" Spoken indignantly. *"What's* he gonna do with that kind of money?"

John filled his mug with coffee. "He's thirty-two, with a wife and three kids, and in the six months he's been here, he's tripled the size of his house, regraded and graveled the approach road, built another house for an office in the place where a god-awful eyesore stood, and in doing all that, he's used local contractors, carpenters, masons, plumbers, and electricians—"

"All right, all right," Armand's growl cut him off. "What else?"

Sipping coffee, John pulled up the next page. "There's an academy update—message from the head of the school. New year starting, one hundred twelve kids, twenty-two states, seven countries. Then there's police news, fire news, library news." He flipped open the *Wall Street Journal* and absently scanned the headlines. "There's the week in review from papers in

Boston, New York, and Washington. And ads, lots of ads this week"—he knew Armand would like that—"including a two-pager from the outlets in Conway. Fall's a good time for ads."

"Praised be," said Armand. "What else?"

"School news. Historical Society news. Tri-town soccer news."

"Want some breaking news?"

John always wanted breaking news. It was one of the city things he missed most. Feeling a twinge of anticipation, he sank into his desk chair, brought up a blank screen, and prepared to type.

Armand said, "They just read Noah Thacken's will, and the family's in a stew. He left the house to daughter number two, so daughter number one is threatening to sue, and daughter number three is threatening to leave town, and none of them is talking to the others. Look into it, John."

But John had retracted his hands and was rocking back in his chair. "That's private stuff."

"Private? The whole town'll know by the end of the day."

"Right, so why put it in the paper? Besides, we print facts."

"This is facts. That will is a matter of public record."

"The will is. Not the personal trauma. That's speculation, and it's exploitative. I thought we agreed—"

"Well, there isn't a hell of a lot of *other* excitement up here," the old man remarked and hung up the phone.

No, John thought, *there isn't a hell of a lot of other excitement up here.* No fascinating book material in an education bill, a computer mogul, or a family squabble; and Christopher Diehl's bank fraud trial was a far cry from the murder trials he used to cover.

His eye went to the wall of framed photos at the far end of the room. There was one of him interviewing a source on Boston's City Hall Plaza, and another of him typing at his computer with the phone clamped to his ear in a roomful of other reporters doing the same. There were photos of him shaking hands with national politicians, and of him laughing it up with colleagues in Boston bars. There was one of a Christmas party—he and Marley in the newsroom with a crowd of their friends. And there was a blowup of his *Post* ID mug shot. His hair was short, his jaw tight, his eyes tired, his face pale. He looked like he was either about to miss the story of his career or severely constipated.

The photos were trappings of an earlier life, like the deactivated police scanner that sat on a file cabinet beneath them. Listening to police or fire reports had been a way of life once. No bona fide newsroom was without one. So he had started his tenure at *Lake News* by setting one up, but static without voices for hours on end had grown old fast. Besides, he personally knew everyone who would be involved in breaking news. If anything happened, they called him, and if he wasn't at his phone, Poppy Blake knew where he was. She was his answering service. She was the answering service for half the town. If she didn't find him one place, she found him somewhere else. In three years, he hadn't missed a local emergency. How many had there been . . . two . . . three . . . four?

Nope, no big best-seller would ever come from covering emergencies in Lake Henry.

With a sigh he dropped the phone into its cradle, pulled a doughnut from the bag, added more coffee to his mug, and tipped back his chair. He had barely crossed his feet on the desk when Jenny Blodgett appeared at the door. She was nineteen, pale and blond, and so thin that the big bulge of the baby in her belly looked doubly wrong. Knowing that she probably hadn't eaten breakfast, he rocked forward in the chair, came to his feet, and brought her the bag.

"It isn't milk or meat, but it's better than nothing," he said, gesturing her around and back down the stairs. Her office was on the first floor, in the room that had once been a parlor. He followed her there, eyed the papers on the desk, thought he detected what may have been separate piles. "How's it going?"

Her voice was soft and childlike. "Okay." She pointed to each of those vague piles in turn. "This year's letters to the editor. Last year's. The year before's. What do I do now?"

He had told her twice. But she worked sporadic hours, hadn't been in since the Wednesday before, and had probably lived a nightmare since then—or so the rationale went. She wasn't exactly competent, had barely made it through high school, and was trained for nothing. But she was carrying his cousin's child. He wanted to give her a break.

So, gently, he said, "Put them in alphabetical order and file them in the cabinet. Did you type out labels for the files?"

Her eyes went wide. They were red rimmed, which meant she had either been up all night or crying this morning. "I forgot," she whispered.

"No problem. You can do it now. What say we set a goal? Labels typed and stuck on file folders, and letters filed in the appropriate folders before you leave today. Sound fair?"

She nodded quickly.

"Eat first," he reminded her on his way out the door and went to the kitchen to collect the contents of the bins.

Up in his office again, he ate his doughnut at the window overlooking the lake. The Woody had disappeared and its wake been played out, but the water had lost its smoothness. A small breeze ruffled it in shifting patches. Beneath his window the willows whispered and swayed.

Shoving up the screen, he ducked his head and leaned out. Corned beef hash was frying at Charlie's. The breeze brought the smell across the street and down to the water. On his left, half a dozen old men fished from the end of the town pier, which jutted from a narrow swath of sandy beach. On his right, yellow-leafed birches angled out over low shrubs that led to rocks and then water. There were houses farther on, year-round homes too stately to be called camps, but most were tucked into coves, hidden around bends, or blocked from view by islands. He could see the tips of a few docks, even a weathered raft still anchored to the floor of the lake. It would be hauled in soon, and the docks taken apart and stored. The lake would be bare.

The phone rang. Letting the screen drop, he waited to see if Jenny would answer it. After three rings, he did it himself. *"Lake News."*

"John, this is Allison Quimby," said a bold voice. "My place is falling apart. I need a handyman. Everyone I've used before is still working up at Hook's. Is it too late to put in an ad?"

"No, but you want the sales desk. I'll transfer you." He put her on hold, jogged across the room, and picked up the phone at the sales desk. "Okay." He slipped into the chair there and began at the computer. "I'm pulling up classified ads. Here we go. Do you have something written?" He suspected she did. Allison Quimby owned the local realty company and was the quintessential professional. Of course she had something written.

"Of course I have something written."

She read. He typed. He fiddled with the spacing, helped her edit it to make it work better, suggested a heading, quoted her a price, took her credit card number. As soon as he hung up the phone, he made a call of his own.

A tired voice answered. "Yeah."

"It's me. Allison Quimby needs a handyman. Give her a call?" When he heard a soft swearing, he said, "You're sober, Buck, and you need the work."

"Who are you, my fuckin' guardian angel?"

John kept his voice low and tight. "I'm your fuckin' older cousin, the one who's worried about the girl you knocked up, the one who's thinking you may not be worth the effort but that girl and her baby are. Come on, Buck. You're good with your hands, you can do what Allison needs done, she pays well, and she's got a big mouth if she likes what you do." He read the phone number once, then read it again. "Call her," he said and hung up the phone.

Seconds later he was back at the window by the editorial desk. Seconds after that he had a grip on his patience. All it took was a good long look at the lake and the reminder that people like Buck and Jenny didn't have that. They had the Ridge, where houses were too small, too close, and too dirty to uplift anyone, much less someone battling alcoholism, physical abuse, or chronic unemployment. John knew. He had the Ridge in his blood as well. He would hear it, feel it, smell it until the day he died.

A movement on the lake caught his eye, the flash of red on a distant dock. He focused in on it; then, half smiling, took a pair of binoculars from the bottom drawer of the desk and focused through those. Shelly Cole was stretched out on a lounge chair, all sleek and oiled in the sun. She was a well-made woman, he had to say that. But then, Cole women had been sorely tempting the men of Lake Henry for three generations. For the most part they were kind creatures who grew into fine wives and mothers. Shelly was something else. She was heading back to Florida in a week, when the weather here became too cool for her to flaunt her tan. John wouldn't miss her. He might be as tempted as any man around, but he wasn't touching her with a ten-foot pole.

With a slight shift of the binoculars, he was looking at Hunter's Island. Named after its first owners, rather than any sport there, it was another of the tiny islands that dotted the lake, and it did have a house, albeit a seasonal one. The Hunter family had summered there for more than a century, before selling it to its current owners. Those owners, the LaDucs, were teaching their third generation of children to swim from its small pebbled beach.

Strange family, the LaDucs. There were nearly as many scandals woven through its generations as there were Hunter scandals. Growing up, John had heard rumors about both families. Returning as an adult who knew how to snoop, he had done research, asked around, made notes. They were locked in his file cabinet now, along with the rest of his private stuff, but none were crying out to be a book. Maybe he hadn't read them in the right frame of mind. Maybe he needed to reread them. Or organize them. Or chronologize them. Maybe something would hit him. After three years he should have come up with something.

The phone rang. He picked it up after the first ring. *"Lake News."*

"Hi, Kip. It's Poppy."

John grinned. How not to, when conjuring up Poppy Blake? She was a smiling pixie, always bright and upbeat. "Hi, sweetheart. How's it going?"

"Busy," she said, making it sound wonderful. "I have someone named Terry Sullivan on the line to your house. Do you want me to patch him through?"

John's eye flew to the wall of photographs, to one of the prints in which he was partying with other reporters. Terry Sullivan was the tall, lean, dark one, the one with the mustache that hid a sneer, the one who always stood on the edge of the crowd so that he could beat the rest out if a story broke. He was competitive to the extreme, self-centered to a fault, and wouldn't know loyalty if it hit him in the face. He had personally betrayed John, and more than once.

John wondered where he found the gall to call. Terry Sullivan had been one of the first to blow him off when he decided to leave Boston.

Curious, he told Poppy to make the connection. When it happened, he said, "Kipling here."

"Hey, Kip. It's Terry Sullivan. How goes it, bro?"

Bro? John took his time answering. "It goes fine. And you?"

"Aaah, same old rat race here, you know how it is. Well, you used to. It must be pretty quiet up there. There are times when I think I'll retire to the sticks, then I think again. It isn't me, if you know what I mean."

"I sure do. People up here are honest. You'd stick out like a sore thumb."

There was a pause, then a snort. "That was blunt."

"People up here are blunt, too. So, what do you want, Terry? I don't have long. We have deadlines here, too."

"O-kay. Chuck the small talk. I'm calling journalist to journalist. There's a woman named Lily Blake, born there, living here. Tell me all you know."

John slipped into his chair. Lily was Poppy's sister, the elder, but barely, which would make her thirty-fourish. She had left Lake Henry to go to college and had stayed in the city for a graduate degree. In music, he thought. He had heard she was teaching. And that she played the piano. And that she had a great body.

Folks around town still talked about her voice. She had been singing in church when she was five, but John wasn't a churchgoer, and long before she would have been old enough to sing at Charlie's back room Thursday nights, he had left town.

She had been back several times since he had returned—once for her father's funeral, other times for Thanksgiving or Christmas, but never for longer than a day or two. From what he heard, she and her mother didn't get along. John might not know Lily, but he did know Maida. She was one tough lady. For that reason and others, he was inclined to give Lily the benefit of the doubt when it came to who was at fault.

"Lily Blake?" he asked Terry, sounding vague.

"Come on, Kip. The place is tiny. Don't go dumb on me."

"If she doesn't live here, how in the hell am I supposed to know about her?"

"Fine. Tell me about her family. Who's alive and who isn't? What do they do? What kind of people are they?"

"Why do you want to know?"

"I met her. I'm thinking of dating her. I want to know what I'm getting into."

Thinking of dating her? Fat chance. Lily Blake was a stutterer—much improved from childhood, he understood, but Terry Sullivan didn't date women with problems. They demanded more than he wanted to give.

"Is this part of some story?" John asked, though he couldn't imagine what part Lily could play in a story that interested Terry.

"Nah. Purely personal."

"And you're calling *me?*" They might have been colleagues, but they'd never been friends.

Terry missed the point. Chuckling, he said, "Yeah, I thought it was pretty funny, myself. I mean, here she comes from this tiny town in the middle of nowhere, and it just happens to be the same place where you're hiding out."

"Not hiding. I'm totally visible."

"It was a figure of speech. Are we touchy?"

"No, Terry, we're pressed for time. Tell me why you *really* want to know about Lily Blake, or hang up the goddamned phone."

"Okay. It's not me. It's my friend. He's the one who wants to date her."

John knew a lie when he heard one. He hung up the phone, but his hand didn't leave the receiver. Waiting only long enough to sever the connection with Terry, he snatched it back up and signaled for Poppy.

"Hey, Kip," she said seconds later in her sassy,

smiling voice. "That was fast. What can I do for you now?"

"Two things," John said. He was on his feet, one hand holding the phone to his ear, the other cocked on his hip. "First, don't let that man speak to anyone in town. Cut him off, drop the line, do whatever you have to. He's not a good person. Second, tell me about your sister."

"About Rose?"

"About Lily. What's she been doing with her life?"

Chapter 2

In the weeks to come, when Lily Blake was trying to understand why she had been singled out for scandal, she would remember the soggy mess she had made of the *Boston Post* that rainy Monday afternoon and wonder if an angry newspaper deity had put a curse on her as punishment for her disrespect. At the time, she simply wanted to stay dry.

She had waited as long as she could at the foot of Beacon Hill, under the high stone arch of the small private school where she taught, thinking that the rain would let up in a minute or two, but it fell steadily in cool sheets, and those minutes added up. She couldn't wait forever. She was due to play at the club at six-thirty, and had to get home and change.

" 'Bye, Ms. Blake!" called another of the students who passed her, dashing from the shelter of the school to a waiting car. She smiled and raised a hand to wave, but the student was already gone.

"So much for Indian summer," muttered Peter Oliver, coming up from behind. A history teacher, he was tall, blond, and worshiped by nearly every female in the upper school. He scowled at the sky. "We're fools, is what we are, you and me. Dedicated fools. If we worked the kinds of days most teachers did, we'd have left two hours ago. It was sunny then." He grunted and glanced at Lily. "Where ya headed?"

"Home."

"Want to catch a drink first?"

She smiled and shook her head. "I have to work."

"You always have to work. What fun's that?" He opened his umbrella. *"Ciao."* Trotting down the steps, he set off down the street, looking perfectly dry and content.

Lily envied him the umbrella. It occurred to her that she should have accepted his invitation, if only to have cover for some of the walk home, not to mention the possibility that the rain might stop in the time it took for a drink. But she didn't drink, for one thing, and for another, she didn't do Peter. He might look terrific in his deep blue shirt and khaki shorts, but he knew it. Peter loved Peter. Lily had to listen to his stories in the faculty lounge. His self-absorption grew tiring.

Besides, she really didn't have time. Pulling the *Post* from her briefcase, she opened it over her head and ran down the steps into the rain. She hurried along the narrow cobblestone streets on the flat of the hill, then turned onto Beacon Street and trotted on paved sidewalk. Hugging the briefcase to her chest, she made herself as small as possible under the newspaper. Given that she was small to begin with, it should have been enough, but the *Post* was quickly a soggy mess around her ears, and the tank top and short skirt that had been perfect in the morning's heat left far too much skin exposed to the cool rain.

She pushed on with her head down, turning left on Arlington and right on Commonwealth. Despite the shelter of the trees here, the gusting air had a straight shot in from the west and was even cooler. She hurried against it down one block, then a second, third, and fourth. By the time she reached the end of the fifth block, she might as well have tossed the paper away. Her hair was as wet as everything else.

Entering the outer lobby of her apartment building, she held the dripping paper off to the side while she fished in her briefcase for keys. Seconds later she was inside, and what had felt stuffy that morning was suddenly welcome. Pushing wet hair off her face, she went past the elevator to the trash closet and dropped the sodden *Post* in the paper bin. She hadn't read it yet, but doubted there was much to miss. Other than Archbishop Rossetti's elevation to Cardinal, which had been covered in depth the weekend before, the city scene was quiet.

She turned into the mail room—and immediately wished she hadn't. Peter Oliver didn't intrigue her, but Tony Cohn did. He lived in one of the penthouse suites, was a business consultant, and as dark as Peter was blond. Classically, Peter was the better looking of the two, but there was something about Tony that was foreign and daring. Lily wasn't a big talker under the best of conditions, but when Tony was in sight she was positively tongue-tied.

Of course, Tony never asked her out, not for drinks, not for dinner. Other than the nod of his head or a short word of greeting if they were stuck in the elevator together, he didn't talk to her at all.

He did look at her now, though. How could he not, with her all wet and bedraggled—wasn't it always the way?

As unobtrusively as she could, she plucked the wet of her tank top away from her breasts. They were her best asset, but this was embarrassing.

Not that he seemed impressed. "Got caught, huh?" he said in a voice that was just deep enough, just amused enough to cinch her humiliation.

Nodding, she concentrated on unlocking her mailbox. She wondered where he would be thirty minutes later and why she couldn't bump into him then. She would look good then. She would look *gorgeous* then.

But now? She slipped the mail from her box and was trying to think of something witty to say, knowing that even if she did think of something, even after years of speech therapy, she would probably mess up getting it out and be even more embarrassed than she already was—when he closed his mailbox and left the room.

Releasing a breath, she listened for sounds from the lobby. After a minute she heard the whirr of the elevator door opening, then shutting.

He could have waited for her.

Thank God he hadn't.

Resigned, she left the mail room and looked through what she had in her hands while she waited for the elevator to return. There were two bills, two contracts for her services, and four pieces of junk. With any luck, the contracts contained deposits that would take care of the bills. She knew just what to do with the junk.

She left the elevator at the fourth floor, just as one of her neighbors was about to board it. Elizabeth Davis owned a hot PR agency and had the breathless lifestyle to prove it. As always, she was dressed to the hilt. Her suit was red and short, her lipstick high gloss, her umbrella black and long. She had been using the mirror on the elevator panel to put on large gold earrings. Slipping into the elevator to finish up with the mirror there, she held the door open with a foot.

"Lily. Good timing." Head tipped, eyes on the mirror, she worked at fastening the second earring. "I'm doing a bash for the Kagan for Governor Committee and need a pianist. It would be background music, not much singing, but I've heard you at the club, and you're perfect." She did look at Lily then, giving her a dismayed once-over. "Oh dear. You're wet."

"Slightly," Lily said.

"Well, you clean up good. I've seen you at work, understated elegance all the way, which is what we want. The fund-raiser is two weeks from tomorrow night. We can't pay—the budget is pathetically low— but I can almost guarantee you'll get another job or two out of the gig because important people will be there and important people give parties, so it wouldn't be a total loss from your point of view. Besides, Lydia Kagan would be *the* best thing for women in this state, so it's in your best interest to do it. What do you say?"

Lily was flattered to be asked. Rarely did a week go by when Elizabeth's name wasn't in the *Post*. She ran top-notch functions. Lily knew she wasn't her first choice for this one, not at this late date, but that was fine. She liked playing at political functions. The more people there were, the easier it was to lose herself in the song. Besides, she agreed with Elizabeth's assessment of Lydia Kagan.

"I'll do it," she said.

Elizabeth smiled broadly and removed her foot from the door. "I'll put it in writing, but mark your calendar now. It's a go. I'm counting on you." The elevator door closed.

Lily was running too late to feel more than a passing satisfaction. Hurrying down the hall, she let herself into her own apartment. It was a small one-bedroom that she rented directly from an owner who loved green, her favorite color, and had a kind heart, which was the only reason she could afford the location. The living room was small and dominated by an upright piano against one wall and a stuffed bookcase against another. The only other furniture was a sofa with its back to windows overlooking the mall and an upholstered chair done in a matching flowered fabric of green, beige, and white. At the shoulder of the chair, more in the tiny front hall than the living room, was a glass table that held a telephone, a lamp, and the CD player that, with the touch of a button now, picked up in the middle of a flowing Chopin. The kitchen was one wall of the living room, and the bedroom was just big enough for a double bed, but the whole apartment had been renovated, which meant that she had a modern marble bathroom with a glassed-in shower.

That was where she headed, pulling off wet clothes, warming up under the hot spray, soaping, shampooing, and turning off the water well before she was ready, but the clock was ticking. In record time she applied makeup and blew her chin-length hair dry to give it a lift. She ate a quick peanut butter and jelly sandwich, then slipped into a plum-colored dress that worked with her fair skin and dark hair, stepped into black heels, and clipped on silver earrings that glittered and flowed. Grabbing a purse and an umbrella, she set off.

Naturally, when she reached the lobby, Tony Cohn was nowhere in sight, but at least the rain had stopped.

The Essex Club thrived in a large brownstone on the opposite side of Commonwealth Avenue, an easy three-block walk from her apartment. It was a private dinner club, elegantly decorated and skillfully run. Relieved to have made it with time to spare, she checked in at the office, where Daniel Curry, the club's owner, was taking a last-minute reservation.

A square-built man of forty-five with perpetually ruddy cheeks, he acknowledged her arrival with the hitch of his chin and finished up on the phone. By that time she had stowed her things in the closet.

She glanced at the reservation book. "Good?"

"Very, for a Monday. There are a few empty tables out there now, but we'll be full in another hour. It's an easy crowd. A lot of old friends." He named a few, couples Lily had come to know in three years of playing there.

"Any special requests?" she asked.

"One thirtieth wedding anniversary, Tom and Dotty Frische. They'll be arriving at eight, table six. He's arranged to have a dozen red roses there and asked if you'd play 'The Twelfth of Never' when the champagne is uncorked."

Lily loved doing that kind of thing. "Sure. Anything else?"

When he shook his head, she left the office and climbed the winding staircase to the main dining room. It was decorated in the club's trademark dark wood and nineteenth-century oils. The color scheme was hunter green and burgundy, carried through table linens, china, carpeting, and draperies. The effect was rich and Old World, which made her feel part of something with a distinguished history.

She greeted the maître d' and smiled at those patrons who caught her eye as she crossed the carpet. The piano was a baby grand, a Steinway, beautifully polished and tuned. There were times when she felt sinful being paid for playing it, but she wasn't about to tell her boss that. After taxes, what she earned at the Winchester School teaching music appreciation, coaching singing groups, and giving piano lessons barely paid for rent and food. Without her work here and at private parties, she wouldn't have money for much else. Besides, this job was what had brought her to Boston. The club was far nicer than the one she had played at in Albany.

After settling comfortably on the bench, she warmed up her fingers with soft arpeggios. The keys felt cool and smooth. Like early morning coffee, those first few touches were always the best.

Her hair fell forward as she watched her hands. Swinging it back when she raised her head, she slipped into the mildest of New Age work, variations on popular songs to which she gave a different beat, a gentle flow. Patrons might recognize the song, but even the most frequent diners at the club wouldn't hear the exact same rendition twice. Playing by ear, she just let loose and did what felt right at a given moment. She rarely used books or sheet music other than for learning classical work or, on occasion, the words to a collection of songs. More often, she simply bought CDs. Once she knew a tune she could play her own version, giving it whatever slant was appropriate to the audience. Some of the parties she played at called for soft rock, others for Broadway hits, others for Brahms. Adapting the same song for different audiences was one of the things Lily did best. It kept her fresh and challenged.

The piano stood on a platform in the corner, allowing her to look out over the room as she played. She smiled in greeting to familiar faces, smiled generically at new ones. Dan had been right. The crowd was mellow. Granted, early diners were usually older and milder, but the club had its share of aged loudmouths. She didn't see any tonight.

Based on the patrons she did see, she segued into a set of smooth oldies, leading with "Autumn Leaves" and "Moon River," moving on to "Blue Moon" and "September." Twice she played requests passed on through the maître d'. She kept going until seven-thirty, when Dan brought her a glass of water.

"Any questions?" he asked while she took a drink.

She was careful not to look at the diners now. "Davis just seated a foursome at table twelve. They look familiar but . . . members?"

"No. The men are the governors of New Hampshire and Connecticut, in town for the conference that just ended. You probably saw their pictures in the paper."

That explained the familiarity, but it raised a new question. Lily definitely recognized the man at table nineteen. There was no mistaking that dark mustache. He was a reporter with the *Post*. "Is Terry Sullivan here watching the governors?" she asked.

Dan smirked. "Not to my knowledge, or I wouldn't have let him in." The club protected its members. Journalists were welcome when they were guests of a member, as Terry Sullivan was. Few had the sponsors, much less the funds, to join themselves. "He must like the place. This is, what, his third time in as many weeks?"

"Yes," Lily said. She had counted, too.

"He likes you."

"No." But she couldn't deny that she might have been the reason Terry was there. "It's business. He's doing a series of profiles of Boston performers and wants to do one on me."

"That's nice."

Lily didn't think so. "I keep refusing him. He makes me nervous."

"Must be the mustache," Dan said and glanced at the door. Cheeks ruddying up, he grinned as he straightened. "Ah. There he is." He set off.

Lily broke into a smile of her own at the sight of Francis Rossetti. Archbishop Rossetti. Newly named *Cardinal* Rossetti. Saying the last would take some getting used to. Lily and the Cardinal went back a ways. She was every bit as proud of his elevation as Dan, who was married to his niece.

Lily wasn't Catholic. She wasn't much of anything, but for several minutes, sipping her water, she marveled at the power of the man. He wore no elegant robe, no red hat. Those would come in four weeks, when he went to Rome for his first consistory. But he didn't need robes or a hat to be charismatic. He was a tall man who stood straight and wore his crisp black clerical suit, pewter pectoral cross, and thick silver hair with style.

This wasn't the first time Lily had seen him since his elevation. A frequent pianist at archdiocesan events, she had played at a lawn party at his residence last night, but this was the first time he had been to the club. Without conscious thought, her hands found the keys and began playing the theme from *Chariots of Fire.*

He heard it, looked over, and winked.

Pleased, she finished the song and moved on to others. Fran Rossetti and she had played side by side often enough for her to know which songs he liked. He was a man who appreciated the fullness of life. His taste in music reflected that, in church and out.

She played "Memory" and segued into "Argentina." She played "Deep Purple," the love theme from *Dr. Zhivago,* and then "The Way We Were."

Promptly at eight, a couple was seated at the table with the red roses. Soon after, when the wine steward uncorked a bottle of champagne, Lily turned on the mike and played "The Twelfth of Never," singing in the rich alto that went so well with the club's decor.

Dotty Frische took a visible breath. She glanced briefly at Lily—then positively beamed at her husband. It made Lily's night.

There was soft applause at the end of the song, so Lily did a medley of other Johnny Mathis hits before returning to singing more Broadway. By the time she was done, it was eight-thirty and time for a break.

"Fifteen minutes," she told her audience, and turned off the mike to scattered applause.

Dan was talking with the maître d' in an alcove just beyond the dining room entrance. He gave her a thumbs-up when she approached. "You did good. He was in seventh heaven."

"You didn't *tell* me your uncle was coming," she scolded.

Dan glanced behind her. "I'm telling you now. Here he comes."

She turned with a wide smile. When the Cardinal gave her a hug, she hugged him back. No matter that the man was a church icon; he came from what he was the first to describe as a large family with an earthy style. It had taken Lily a while to get used to it, but the sheer innocence of his physicality was a delight.

"Thank you," he said now.

"For what?"

"For playing my song. For playing *all* my songs. For playing last night—and for coming back with that music." He grasped Dan's shoulder. "Do you know what she did? After playing for three hours straight, she drove home and then all the way back with a book of music I wanted." He told Lily, "I was up playing until two in the morning. It's a wonderful collection."

"How's your table?" Dan asked.

"Great. Great food. Not what Mama used to make," he hedged, winking at Lily, "but a close second." He gave her arm a squeeze and returned to the dining room.

Lily climbed the curved staircase to the third-floor ladies' room. She came out just as the *Post* reporter was leaving the men's room. He wore a blazer and slacks, and was tall, slim, and pleasant looking, but the mustache remained his most compelling feature.

"You have a wonderful voice," he said.

He had told her that before, twice at the club, once when he called her at home. Not that *she* had given him her phone number. It was unlisted. But the school directory had it. Terry had wheedled it out of Mitch Rellejik, a writer friend of his who moonlighted as faculty adviser to the school newspaper. Mitch had phoned her himself to tell her what a great guy Terry was.

Lily wasn't convinced. Reluctant to encourage conversation, she gave him a smile and a quiet thanks as she headed for the stairs.

He kept pace. "You never disappoint. Whether it's here or at parties, you're good. Beautiful, too, but you must hear that all the time. By the way, you didn't seem nervous."

Lily tucked away the "beautiful" part—which she did *not* hear all the time, and being human and female, rather liked—and said, "I do this for a living."

"I mean, playing for the Cardinal. He's an important guy. Don't you get a little shaky playing for him?"

She chuckled. "Oh, no. He's heard me play too many times for that."

"Huh. That's right. I did hear that he likes music."

"He doesn't just like it. He's good at it."

"Sings? Plays instruments?"

"Both."

"A Renaissance man, then?"

Wondering if he was being sarcastic, Lily stopped at the bottom of the stairs to search his face. "Actually, yes."

He smiled and held up his hands. "No offense meant. I'm as much a fan as the next guy. He fascinates me. I've never met a man of the cloth quite like him. He inspires piety."

Lily relaxed some. "Yes."

Terry narrowed an eye. "Half the women I know are in love with him. He's a virile guy."

Lily was embarrassed even *thinking* about Fran Rossetti that way.

"Don't tell me you haven't noticed?" he asked.

"In fact, I haven't. He's a priest."

"And you're not even a little bit in love with him?"

"Of course I am. I love him as a person. He's insightful and supportive. He hears and listens and responds."

"Sounds like you know him well."

She was proud to admit it. "We have a history. I met him when he was Father Fran, just about to be appointed Bishop of Albany."

"No kidding?"

Something about his nonchalance was a bit much. It reminded her that he was a reporter. She nodded and checked her watch. "I have to get back to work."

"How late do you play tonight?" he asked, walking beside her.

"Ten-thirty."

"Without dinner?"

"I ate before."

"Can I buy you a snack when you get off?"

He had offered something similar when he called her apartment. At the time, she had thought it an attempt to make the idea of an interview more palatable. Now, with him standing there in person—the right height for her, the right age, and maritally free, Mitch Rellejik had said—it almost felt like something else.

Almost—but there was still that mustache, which was alternately dashing and hard. And there was an intensity in his eyes that didn't hit her right.

She wasn't *that* desperate for a date.

At the dining room entrance now, she smiled and shook her head. "Thanks, anyway," she said and went on inside.

Back at the piano, she began playing the kind of music that this later crowd would enjoy. She sang "Almost Paradise," "Candle in the Wind," and "Total Eclipse of the Heart." She did some Carly Simon, some James Taylor, some Harry Connick, Jr. She loved every song she played. If she didn't, she wouldn't be able to perform with feeling, but the feeling came easily with these songs. They were her generation's favorites.

Playing without effort, swinging her hair back from her face and leaning forward to sing into the mike, she blotted out the audience and let her heart take over. Singing had always been her salvation, the only time when she was naturally free of a stutter. Though time and training had freed her to speak, singing remained special. She might not have been able to make it on Broadway, but when she was lost in a song this way, she could just as well have been there. The feeling of pleasure, of success, of escape was the same.

Halfway through the second set, the Frisches came over to thank her for helping make their anniversary special. A short time after they left, another patron, Peter Swift, sat beside her on the piano bench and sang harmony. He had a beautiful voice and often joined Lily in a song or two when he and his wife ate at the club. The spontaneity of it never failed to please the crowd. Soon after Peter returned to his table, the Cardinal took his place. She was playing "I Dreamed a Dream" from *Les Miz* at the time. He played along in the lower registers through the end of it, then joined right in with the more throbbing chords of "Red and Black." When it was done, he gave her hand a squeeze, rejoined his waiting guests, and left the dining room.

All told, it was a good show. Lily was tired but satisfied when she finally closed the piano lid. A handful of guests lingered over second or third cups of coffee, but the rest of the tables had been cleaned and reset. Half of the wait staff had left. The chef, George Mendes, who had trained in New York and was just Lily's age, had changed from his whites into jeans and was waiting for her in the office.

He held out a bag. "You like risotto. Tonight's was great."

She was touched that he remembered. He hadn't been at the club for long, and she was only one of many who raved about his food. "Thanks," she said with feeling and took the bag. "This'll be tomorrow's dinner. Are you walking home?" He lived in her direction.

"Not yet. I have to run a few menu changes past Dan. He's upstairs."

The third floor of the brownstone held private

dining rooms, the fourth held overnight accommodations. Lily knew from experience that Dan could be a while, and she was too tired to wait.

"Then I'm off," she said, and called over her shoulder as she left, "Thanks again for the risotto."

She was thinking that if George had been straight, she could be seriously interested in him, when she reached the street and found Terry Sullivan leaning against the wide stone stoop. He looked innocent enough in the gaslight's glow, but a part of her was starting to feel harassed. She had refused him three times. He was annoyingly dogged.

She went quickly down the steps and hit the sidewalk in something just shy of a trot, in the hope that he might take the hint.

"Hey, hey." He fell into step with her. "Where're you running to?"

"Home."

"Mind if I walk along?"

"That depends. I haven't changed my mind about your interview."

"But it doesn't make sense. The publicity would be *great* for you."

Lily might have agreed several years before, but she had been struggling then. Now, between teaching and the club, she received two fixed monthly paychecks. Add what she earned playing at private functions, and she was content. She didn't need more work, hence didn't need publicity.

"Is it me?" Terry asked. "Does something about me offend you?"

"Of course not," she said, because it wasn't her way to hurt people. "I'm just . . . private."

"It's the public you I'm interested in—the one who rubs hips, so to speak, with people like Cardinal Rossetti." He made a whistling sound. "That was amazing, the two of you playing tonight." He took a long breath. "I really want to do this interview."

They reached a corner. She shook her head, waiting only until the traffic cleared before trotting across the street.

He kept pace. "Are you sure it isn't me? Would you talk to one of my colleagues?"

"No."

"Ah. You hate the press. You're afraid someone will misuse your words. But I'm a good guy, Lily. How can I not be, especially with you? I'm Catholic, and you're Cardinal Rossetti's pal. Would I dare do anything bad, knowing it'd get back to him, knowing I might risk eternal damnation if it did?"

Lily didn't believe in eternal damnation, but if Terry Sullivan did, that helped. She slowed down a notch.

"I feel like I should know everything about the guy," Terry said conversationally. "I mean, my paper's covered him from head to toe, and the *Post* is good." He looked at her, earnest now. His voice was lower, almost confidential. "Listen. The Fourth Estate has taken a lot of flak lately. Some of it's deserved. Most isn't. It's like everything else. There may be a few bad apples, but that doesn't mean we're all rotten, and since I've already confessed my fear of eternal damnation . . ."

She had to give him credit for being upfront.

"What's so fascinating," he went on, seeming caught up in it, "is the way the Cardinal is so *normal*. I mean, there he was, sitting beside you, playing the piano. I half expected him to start belting out the words."

Lily smiled. She couldn't help herself. "Oh, he's done that too."

"You're kidding."

She shook her head.

"In *public?*"

"In private, in small groups. He used to do it more, before all this."

"You mean, before he was named Cardinal?"

She nodded again.

"So you met him in Albany. What was he like then?" He sounded genuinely intrigued, not at all grilling as a reporter would be, but more personally involved—and Lily was a sucker for fans of her friend.

"Warm," she said. "Vibrant. But I actually met him in Manhattan."

"What was he doing there?"

"Visiting the Cardinal there. They both went to a reception at the mayor's house. I was playing."

"You played at the mayor's house? I'm impressed."

"Don't be. I was a Broadway wannabe and taught piano to pay the bills. His kids took lessons. That's how he knew me."

"A Broadway wannabe," Terry said, still sounding impressed. "No more?"

She shook her head.

"Were you in anything?"

"A few ensembles. Nothing major."

"Do you dance, too?"

"Not well enough."

"Ah. I understand." He let her off the hook. "So you met Cardinal Rossetti in the city and followed him to Albany?"

She didn't answer. After another minute of walking, she felt him looking at her. When she met his eye, he said, "Why the frown?"

"This feels like an interview."

"It's not. It's just me, interested in you."

If she was frowning now, it was in skepticism.

"I've never met a religious groupie before," he teased.

She sighed. "I'm not a religious groupie. I didn't follow Cardinal Rosetti to Albany. I followed the *mayor* there." She caught herself. "Ooops. That came out wrong." She felt a tiny tightness at the back of her tongue and focused on relaxing it. With a single, slow, calming breath, it dissolved. Flawlessly, she explained, "My relationship was with his kids. They loved me, and they'd been shaken by the divorce. When he was elected governor, he had to move to Albany, and the kids went with him. He figured that if I kept teaching them, it would be one thing that didn't change in their lives. When a position opened up in a private school there, the timing seemed right."

"So you gave up on Broadway?"

"It gave up on me," she said and slid him a wary look. "You're smooth."

He tipped his head. "How?"

"Getting me to talk after I said I wouldn't."

"This is what's called a social conversation." He held up his hands. "No pen, no paper. Strictly off-the-cuff. Like I say, the Cardinal intrigues me. So—he was the Bishop of Albany when you moved there?"

Social conversation or not, Lily didn't want to talk about herself *or* the Cardinal to Terry. But he did look intrigued. And Mitch Rellejik had vouched for him. And the question was innocent enough.

So she said, "He was."

"And that's where you really got to know him?"

She nodded.

"Did you ever dream he'd be a Cardinal one day?"

She shook her head. "But I'm not surprised. Father Fran gets it."

"Gets it?"

"Understands people."

"You saw that?"

They had reached another corner and were waiting to cross. Traffic leaving the city sped by in a blur of lights and chrome. "He understood me," she said. "I've been grappling with things. He's been—" How to describe Fran Rossetti in a word? Friend? Adviser? Therapist? "He's been a comfort."

"So you followed him to Boston?"

Her eyes flew to his. Here was the reporter again, more prodding than casual.

Terry winced. "Sorry. Nothing untoward meant. Asking questions is a habit. I was always doing it as a kid, so I went into journalism. No other field would have me. It's the tone. Hard to turn off, but I'll try."

He sounded so sincere that Lily relented. "I followed him to Boston only in the sense that I moved here soon after he did."

Terry didn't say anything. When the light changed, they crossed the street and walked on.

Still feeling guilty for overreacting, she volunteered, "Father Fran told me about the Essex Club. It was a step up from the club I played at in Albany, and Dan's regular had just given notice. When I found a teaching position here, it was like it was meant to be."

Terry looked thoughtful, walking with his hands in his pockets and his eyes on the brownstones ahead. "Neat club, the Essex. Isn't it pricey for a Cardinal?"

"Not when his nephew owns the place," she said.

"Is that kosher?"

"Usually the people he's with pick up the tab. Big donors to the church."

"Is *that* kosher?"

"Why not?"

"Bribery. Favor seeking."

"From a *Cardinal?* What does a Cardinal have to sell?"

"Political clout. A good word to the gov, or the prez." He wiggled his brows. "Maybe a kiss."

She leveled him a look. "I don't think so."

"I'm *kid*-ding," he chided.

She wasn't sure she liked the joke, but then, she tended to take things too literally. At least, that was what the last guy she dated had said when they called it quits. Actually, he had used the word "dour," and though she didn't believe she was that bad, she made an effort now to go to the other extreme. "A kiss?" she kidded back. "Why not a weekend? Auctioned off for charity."

Terry laughed. "Warmin' up, Lily Blake. It'd bring in a bundle for his favorite cause. I'm telling you, dozens of women would bid."

She smiled. "Can you imagine some woman telling a friend, 'The Cardinal and I are having an affair'?"

"A *passionate* affair?" Terry asked in the voice of that startled friend.

Lily played along. "What other kind is there? Forget the auction. We've been doing it for *years.*"

He put back his head and laughed.

She laughed, too, then said, "Cute. But not Father Fran. If anyone gets anything from those dinners, it's the church. This is it," she said, coming to a stop in front of her building. She turned to him, thinking that the laughter had been nice.

"You're an interesting person," he said, grinning. "Think you could fit me in between dates with the Cardinal?"

She grinned back. "I don't know. He takes a lot of my time." She made a pretense of mental calculation. "I could probably fit you in some time next week. I'll have to check." As she moved past him, she tossed him a dry "You have my number."

She went into the building without looking back and slipped into the elevator feeling buoyed. She didn't know if she liked Terry Sullivan, didn't know if they had another thing in common besides admiration for the Cardinal. She hadn't felt an instant attraction to the reporter, but things like physical attraction sometimes took time. She did know that she wasn't interested in Peter Oliver, Tony Cohn wasn't interested in her, and she wasn't getting any younger.

She had never dated a reporter before. If nothing else, it might make for an educational dinner or two.

She never dreamed that the education would come so soon, and at her own expense.

Chapter 3

Since Lily worked nights and rarely had an early class, she usually took her time waking up. This morning the phone jolted her out of bed at eight. Her first thought was that something was wrong back home.

"Hello?" she asked, frightened.

"Lily Blake, please," said a man she didn't know. His voice was all business. Poppy's doctor? Her *mother's* doctor?

"Speaking."

"This is George Fox. I'm with the *Cape Sentinel*. I wonder if you would comment on your relationship with Cardinal Rossetti."

"Excuse me?"

"Your relationship with Cardinal Rossetti. Can you tell me about it?"

She didn't understand. The newspapers had already covered almost everything about the Cardinal that there was to cover. She was irrelevant, only one of many of his friends, and the one least equipped to talk with the press. "You'll have to call the archdiocese. They'll tell you anything you want to know."

"Are you having an affair with the Cardinal?"

"A what?" When he repeated his question, she cried, "Good God, no." It was a prank call, but not a blind one, since she did know the Cardinal. Cautious, curious, she said, "This number is unlisted. How did you get it?" Terry Sullivan was the only reporter she knew, and yes, he had her number. She didn't want to think he was passing it around.

"Were you having an affair with Cardinal Rossetti in Albany?" the reporter asked just as her call waiting beeped. She was unsettled enough by his question to switch right to the second call.

"Yes?"

"Lily Blake?"

"Who is this?"

"Paul Rizzo, *Cityside*." *Cityside* was a renegade daily that had come from nowhere to rival Boston's mainstream press. "I'm looking for a comment on the *Post* story."

Her heart was pumping faster. *"What story?"*

"The one saying that you and the Cardinal are sexually involved."

She hung up. On *both* calls. After waiting a minute for the dial tone to return, she lifted the receiver and dropped it in the bedding. She didn't believe there was any story in the *Post*—how could there be one, with no substance?—but after two calls, she had to see for herself. Slipping on a coat over her nightshirt, she took the elevator to the first floor and had barely started for the outer lobby where the daily papers were left when she saw someone waiting. He had a tape recorder hanging from his shoulder and a microphone in his hand. At the sight of her, he came to life.

She slipped back into the elevator seconds before the door closed, and quickly pressed her floor. For good measure, to hide her destination, she pressed every floor above her own on the panel. As soon as she was in her apartment again, she linked her laptop to the phone line and accessed the *Post* on-line.

She didn't have to go past the home page. It was right there in big, bold letters—the lead story.

CARDINAL LINKED TO CABARET SINGER

Beside it was a picture, apparently taken the night before, of the two of them, arm to arm, hip to hip on the piano bench, smiling at each other, in vivid, crystal-clear color.

Horrified, Lily began to read.

Less than a week ago, Archbishop Francis P. Rossetti was elevated to Cardinal amid an out-pouring of praise for his humanitarian achievements and religious devotion. With the celebration barely over, the Post has learned that Cardinal Rossetti has led a double life. In an exclusive story, the Headline Team reveals a long-term relationship between the Cardinal

and Lily Blake, 34, a cabaret singer at the posh
Essex Club on Commonwealth Avenue.

Bewildered, she clicked on to the rest of the story.

Blake and the cardinal met eight years ago at
a party in New York City. They were introduced
by then Mayor William Dean, who had first
spotted Blake on the Broadway stage. As soon
as the mayor and his wife separated, Blake became a regular guest at Gracie Mansion. It was
there that she met the Cardinal.

Lily was incredulous. She read now with a kind of
morbid fascination.

Two years later, when the mayor was elected
governor of New York and moved to Albany,
Blake went with him. Between twice-weekly visits to the Governor's Mansion, she sang at a
nightclub not far from the State House. In addition, the governor set her up entertaining at
private parties.

"No, he didn't," she cried. "Those bookings came
from my work at the club!"

Francis Rossetti, then Bishop of Albany, often
attended those parties. He began inviting
Blake to play at similar events at the Bishop's
residence. Within months, she became a fre-

quent visitor. One employee of the diocese, who asked to remain anonymous, said it was obvious that Rossetti and Blake cared for each other. She was often seen leaving the residence in the early morning hours.

"With other people!" she told the screen in outrage. "The *two* times we might have been alone were when we were playing the piano after a party and lost track of the time!"

Three years ago, when the Bishop was named to lead the Archdiocese of Boston, he secured a job for Blake at the Essex Club, which is owned and managed by his nephew Daniel Curry.

Scrolling farther, she cried out in disbelief when three more pictures appeared. One was of the Cardinal hugging her in the Essex Club lobby. The other, taken with a night lens, showed her as a lone figure running up the steps of the Cardinal's residence. The third, taken through a window at the residence, showed the Cardinal with an arm around her shoulder.

She was sick to her stomach, but she couldn't stop reading.

Blake teaches part-time at the Winchester School on Beacon Hill. She entertains at private parties and political fund-raisers, and is a regular pianist at archdiocese events. She is often seen arriving at those events in the Cardinal's company. Phone records show a pattern of late-night phone calls between the Cardinal's residence and Blake's apartment.

A native of Lake Henry, New Hampshire, Blake studied at NYU and the Juilliard School. Though she repeatedly auditioned for leading roles on Broadway and occasionally served as an understudy, she never made it out of the chorus line. She was twenty-eight when she left Broadway and moved to Albany.

Blake's relationship with the Cardinal has been a well-kept secret. Vatican sources have told the Headline Team that the Pope did not know of this relationship before elevating Rossetti to the position of Cardinal. When contacted by the Post, a spokesman for Cardinal Rossetti denied the allegations.

Blake was more forthcoming. "The Cardinal and I are having an affair," she confirmed.

Lily gasped.

"I love him. We have a history." She described the Cardinal as a warm, vibrant man, and admitted that she followed him to Boston.

The article closed by saying,

Governor Dean of New York has denied having a sexual relationship with Blake.

Incredulous, she returned to the start of the piece, but there was the headline—CARDINAL LINKED TO CABARET SINGER—larger and bolder than ever. This time, though, she read the byline. The article had been written by Terrence Sullivan.

She felt totally and utterly betrayed. And *furious.* Disconnecting the laptop, she grabbed the phone book from a closet shelf, found the number of the *Post,* and called it. After several menu choices, she reached the newsroom. Terry Sullivan wasn't there. He would be in later, they said, though they didn't know when.

Frustrated, she pressed the disconnect button. With her hand hovering over the keypad, she shut her eyes and tried to remember the Cardinal's number, but even if she called it often—which she didn't—her mind was in too much of a muddle. Scrabbling through the phone book again, she located the Boston Archdiocese and ran a finger down the list of numbers until she found a familiar one. It went to the Cardinal's secretary. Father McDonough was the one Lily dealt with when she played at church events.

His line was busy. She tried it again but couldn't get through this time either. Feeling stymied, she went to the window. There was a van parked right in front of her building, with sun glinting off the satellite dish on top and the markings of a local television station on its side.

It was insane. *Insane.* Surely a mistake. And easily corrected, once she reached the right people. In the meantime, she had lessons to give and classes to teach.

After showering, she put on a soft, soothing Schumann while she dressed, but she was too dismayed to feel any comfort. She tried the Cardinal again; the line was still busy. She tried Terry again; he hadn't yet arrived. She pushed cereal around in a bowl until she was too late to delay longer, but she knew not to leave the elevator when it reached the ground floor. The brass panels that housed the doors reflected the outer lobby. Even allowing for distortion, there looked to be a whole *handful* of reporters out there now.

Appalled, she took the elevator down to the garage and slipped out the back unnoticed. Hurrying down Newbury Street, she cut through the Public Garden and reached school in record time. The teachers' lounge was empty when she arrived, but she had barely poured a cup of coffee when a bell rang to mark the end of the first period. Within minutes, several faculty members wandered in. Since they weren't ones she knew well, the murmuring among themselves was normal. Reasoning that if they hadn't seen the *Post,* they might never be the wiser, she ignored their glances.

Peter Oliver was something else. She was stirring powdered cream into her coffee when he walked in and stopped short. "Whoa. The lady of the hour." Sidling up until they were shoulder to shoulder, he reached for a cup and spoke under his breath. "You had me worried there. I was starting to think I'd lost my touch when you kept refusing me. Now it makes sense."

Lily felt a sinking in the pit of her stomach. Her tongue tightened up.

"The *Post* story?" he prompted. "Is it true?"

She shook her head.

A different voice said a low "Lily."

Her eyes flew to the door. Michael Eddy, headmaster of the school, was short, with a gentle paunch and a normally round, friendly face. The friendly part was strained now. He motioned her to follow.

Leaving her coffee where it stood, she crossed through the reception area to the headmaster's office. Michael had barely closed the door when he said, "Is it true?"

She shook her head, shook it fast and hard.

"*Any* of it?"

She swallowed and forced her throat to relax. "No."

"You're quoted there."

"Out of context."

"Did you say those things?"

"Not like that. And not on the record." When Michael closed his eyes in a gesture of defeat, Lily's anger reared up. "I've ttttt . . ." She took a breath, focused on untying her tongue, said more smoothly, "I've tried calling the man who wrote it. He'll have to retract it. It isn't true."

Michael raised his head and sighed. "Well. As long as you've denied it, I'll be able to answer the parents who call. Several already have. I wish you hadn't given the paper the name of the school."

"I didn't!"

"Then how did they get it?"

"I don't knnn-know." Another breath, and the

return of control. "I guess the same way they learned that I went to NYU. I graduated with honors. They didn't sss-say that. Or that I got a degree from Juilliard. Or that the only reason I went to the Governor's Mansion twice a week was to give piano lessons to his kids. Or that the governor was never there when I was." She pushed a hand into her hair. It stopped midway and hung on. The reality she had been trying to ignore was finally taking root. "This is all over Boston. All over the *state*." She was feeling the horror of it when her eyes met Michael's. "I have to reach the Cardinal."

He gestured toward the desk, offering her the phone.

She punched out the number she had called earlier. It was still busy. "Oh God," she breathed, frightened. "This could ruin him." She looked at Michael. "What do I do?"

"Hire a lawyer."

"But this is just a mistake." She didn't want to think it was malicious—couldn't believe that Terry Sullivan would go to this kind of extreme just because she had refused to be interviewed—couldn't *believe* that he would deliberately slander *the Cardinal* this way.

"Hire a lawyer," Michael repeated.

"I can't. I don't have money. Besides, why do I need a lawyer? I haven't done anything wrong."

"You need a spokesperson. Someone to issue a denial. Someone to challenge the *Post*."

She took a breath and tried to remain calm. "Governor Dean denied it. So did the Cardinal. He'll do it again. It'll be over and done." Lifting the phone again, she tried the *Post*. This time when she reached the newsroom, she lucked out.

"Sullivan here," she heard, and something about his cold voice, something about the image she conjured of a slick, mustached man who appeared to have wooed her with lies, made her snap.

Fury alone kept her tongue fluid. "This is Lily Blake. Your story is wrong."

His voice stayed cold. "Wrong? No, it isn't. I check out my facts."

"There's nothing going on between the Cardinal and me."

"It sure looks that way."

"You *made* it look that way," she charged. "*You* were the one who kept talking about the Cardinal being appealing to women. You led me into a hypothetical discussion, then took my words out of context. That's really . . . ssss-scummy! You *also* said our conversation was off the record."

"I never said that."

"You *did*."

"I said 'off the cuff.' That's different from 'off the record.' "

"You knew what I meant!" Looking straight at Michael Eddy, she said, "You also knew my phone number was unlisted, so you got it from Mitch Rellejik, who had no right to give it to you in the first place. Now two other nnn-newspaper people have it. That's a violation of my privacy!"

"Look, Lily," he said with a sigh, "I'm sorry if this

upsets you, but the truth sometimes does. I saw the way you looked at the guy last night at the club. And then you gave me quotes on a silver platter."

She was livid. "You twwwwisted what I said! That is *the* most shoddy thing! And you lied to me. Over and over, you lied. Now you've lied in the paper, and people *all over* are reading it. I want a retraction."

He laughed. "Are you kidding? This is the hottest story in town."

She didn't understand his complacence. "Why are you *doing* this?"

"It's my job."

"To *smear* people? You said you *loved* the Cardinal."

"No. You said that."

"You talked about eternal damnation."

He laughed again. "Honey, I was eternally damned long before *this* story."

There had to be a method to his madness. "Do you have something against the Cardinal?"

He was suddenly impatient. "Look, in my business, you get wind of a good story, you run with it. If you hit a wall, you back off. If not, you keep going. I'm going, baby. I'm going right to the end."

"But this is a lie!"

"Tell it to the Pope. Hey, there's my other line. Take care."

The phone went dead. Lily stared at the receiver. Floored, she looked at Michael.

He held up his hands. "I've already given you my advice. I don't know what more to say. My concern is this school."

Lily tried the Cardinal's number again. It was still busy. Carefully, she replaced the receiver.

"This is unreal," she said, more to herself than her boss. "But it's all right. The Cardinal has power in this city. He'll clear everything up. That's probably why his line is busy." She glanced at the clock. "I have a class."

If any of the fifteen students taking music appreciation were aware of the *Post* article, none mentioned it. They were as blasé as ever. By the time fifty minutes had passed and the bell rang to end the period, Lily had convinced herself that, Terry Sullivan's treachery notwithstanding, the article was nothing more than a bad judgment call on the part of the *Post,* that the Cardinal would raise Cain and get a retraction printed, that the whole matter would be quickly forgotten.

She tried to call him again, but the line was still busy.

With five minutes to spare before a piano lesson, she went to the cafeteria for a cold drink. The first lunch period was under way. One step into the large, high-ceilinged room and she heard the sudden drop of conversation, felt the force of dozens of pairs of eyes.

It isn't true, she wanted to say, but her tongue was tight. So she simply shook her head and gestured no, got her drink, and left. By the time her student arrived at the practice room, she had recomposed herself, but she knew what his curious look meant.

"The *Post* article," she told him, "is wrong. The Cardinal is a friend, nothing more."

"I believe you," the boy said. He was sixteen, a lacrosse player struggling to fulfill an art requirement by taking piano lessons that he hated, but he did sound sincere.

So she set the *Post* story aside and tried to focus on his lesson and two others that followed, but she kept expecting an office assistant to cut in with a message from the Cardinal saying that everything was fine, that he would handle it, that she shouldn't worry.

The door remained shut for everything but the departure of one student and the arrival of the next, and when the three lessons were done, she tried the Cardinal again, still with no luck.

Fortunately, she wasn't hungry. She didn't want to face a cafeteria full of stares until a retraction appeared, an apology was issued, and the *Post* had egg on its face. She might laugh along with the rest then, but not now—nor at two-thirty, when her girls' a cappella chorus met. Each of the twelve was sober and staring. Clearly they knew about the article.

She stood before them, aware that her shoulders were drooping but unable to help it. She was starting to feel the strain. Quietly, she said, "Questions?" When the girls were silent, she said, "I'll answer the one you won't ask. The Cardinal is a man of the Church. He would no more have an affair with me than I would have one with him." She looked from one face to the next until she saw a modicum of acceptance, then she reached for printouts of a new song and handed each trio of voices its part.

The practice went well. At other times Lily coached

a larger mixed chorus, of freshmen and sophomores, but the small, upper-class groups, one male and one female, were her favorites. Some of the students had wonderful voices. The idea that she could train them was a gratifying one.

By the time the hour ended, she was starting to feel like herself again. Then she got through to the Cardinal's secretary.

Father McDonough was a young priest who had landed the plum assignment in Brighton as a result of his attention to detail and his endless good nature. The Cardinal relied on him heavily. As for Lily, she knew the man only by name and voice.

After identifying herself, she said with relief, "Thank goodness. Your line's been tied up. What's going *on?*"

"I take it you saw the story."

"Yes. The reporter was at the club last night. He told me he was a fan of the Cardinal. We got to talking. He took words here and there and fabricated a story."

"Well, it's made an awful mess."

"But it's all false." And nonsensical. "Does the Cardinal *know* Terry Sullivan?" Maybe their paths had crossed. Maybe there was some personal enmity.

"He knows him now. We've had calls from everywhere."

"Has he demanded a retraction?"

"Our lawyers have," came the reply, and for the first time Lily realized that the voice was cooler than usual.

"Oh. Shhh-ould I hire a lawyer?" She wanted him to say, in his normally good-natured way, that there was no need, that the Cardinal's team would resolve the matter, that it was already nearly done.

Instead, he sounded distant. "I can't advise you on that. Our concern is protecting the Church. We're trying our best to do that. But it might be better if you didn't call here again until everything is straightened out."

Lily felt as though she'd been slapped—as though she had sinned and in so doing had single-handedly caused a deep embarrassment for the Church.

Stunned, she said, "I see. Uh. Thank you." Quietly, she hung up the phone.

Things went downhill from there. After suffering through one more private lesson, she packed up her briefcase and headed home. She had no sooner breathed a sigh of relief that the front steps of the school were clear than she hit the sidewalk and, seemingly from nowhere, a woman with a microphone appeared.

"Ms. Blake, would you comment on the *Post* story?" Lily shook her head and hurried on, but the reporter kept pace. "The archdiocese has issued an official denial. Doesn't that contradict your quotes in the *Post?*"

"The *Post* lies," Lily muttered, keeping her arms around her briefcase, her head bowed, her eyes on the cobblestone underfoot.

A male voice said, "Paul Rizzo, *Cityside*. You were

seen leaving the Cardinal's residence late Sunday night. Why were you there?"

He was a balding man whose baby-smooth skin suggested that the hair loss was premature. His eyes were unblinking. His chin jutted forward. He reminded Lily of the hook stuck in the mouth of the very first trout she had ever caught for herself at the lake. Then and now, she was repulsed.

I was hired to play the piano, she wanted to tell him, but her tongue was tight, and she knew she would never get the words out. So she lowered her head and kept her feet moving fast.

"When did you break up with Governor Dean?"

"Was the Cardinal aware of your relationship with the governor?"

"How do you explain the late-night phone calls?"

"Is it true that you were in the Cardinal's arms at the Essex Club last night?"

When Lily looked up to say an angry "No," a cameraman snapped her picture. Ducking her head again, she hurried on, but the questions got worse.

"Where did you do it?"

"What kind of sex?"

"Has the Church tried to buy your silence?"

"What does your family think of this?"

Lily shuddered to think what her family thought. She shuddered to think that they even knew, period.

But they did. She learned it soon after she reached home and listened to the messages on her machine. There, sandwiched between calls from what, to her horror, seemed to be every major newspaper and television station in the country, was the voice of her sister Poppy.

"What's going *on,* Lily? The calls are coming in hot and heavy, even more after the noon news. I've been deflecting as many as I can, but Mom is *furious!* Phone me, will you?"

The noon news? Lily's stomach turned over. But, of course, television would pick up the story. Isn't that what the man in the outer lobby this morning had been about?

So maybe it had been naïve of her to think that the story would be contained—but did the media have to call her *mother?* Lily's relationship with Maida Blake was precarious enough. This wouldn't help.

Needing to hear a friendly voice, she sank into the chair by the phone and punched in Poppy's number. Poppy was barely two years her junior, and the sweetest, most upbeat person Lily knew, despite circumstances that might have caused her to be anything but. Poppy Blake was a paraplegic, confined to a wheelchair since a snowmobile accident nearly a dozen years before. If anyone had a right to self-pity, she did, but she refused to waste energy on it. As soon after the accident as she was able, she had moved into her own place on the lake and started a telephone answering service for Lake Henry and neighboring towns. Now she had state-of-the-art equipment, with sophisticated computer hookups and an increasingly large bank of phone buttons. The business had grown so fast that she even had a roster of part-timers who covered for her when she went out, which, bless her, she often did.

She had caller ID, which enabled her to say the instant she picked up the call, "Lily! Thank goodness! What's happening?"

"Nightmare," Lily said. "Total nightmare. When did you hear?"

"Early today. People in town either read it in the *Post* or on the Net. Around midmorning, calls started coming in from reporters—Boston, New York, Washington, Atlanta—and then there's the tube. They're showing pictures—Lily and the Cardinal, Lily and the governor."

"Mom saw?" Lily asked in alarm.

"Mom saw. Kip called yesterday to warn me about the *Post* guy, but he didn't say why, so how was I supposed to know about the others? I wish you'd told us."

"How could I? I didn't *know.* I didn't see the paper until this morning, and was as shocked as anyone. It's a bogus story, Poppy."

"I know that, but Mom doesn't," Poppy said bluntly. "She's convinced that everything she said all along is true and that it was only a matter of time before something like this happened."

"It *wasn't*—and I don't know why it's happening now." She fought back tears of frustration. "I thought this reporter was a friend. He came on to me, you know, asked if I'd go out with him. Sss-stupid me. *Stupid* me," she cried in self-reproach, "but he was a pro, got me talking, then pieced little phrases together to create something sordid. What kind of person *does* that? Okay. He doesn't know me. To him, I'm a nothing. But the Cardinal isn't. How can he do this to the Cardinal? Or is it just that there isn't much else going on in the world and the papers are starved for sleaze? What did Mom say? What were the words?"

"They don't matter," Poppy said. "She's just in a stir. What should I tell her?"

Lily pressed shaky fingertips to her forehead. She had worked *so hard* to win her mother's confidence. The Winchester School, where she taught, had a fine reputation. The Essex Club was as upscale as a dining establishment could be. And then there was Father Fran—ah, the irony of that! Such a strong, dignified, upstanding man. She had always thought that her friendship with him would win points with Maida.

"Tell her not to look at the paper," she told Poppy. "There's no basis to any of this. It'll play itself out in a day or two." It had to. The alternative was unthinkable.

"Have you issued a denial?"

"I keep saying it isn't true."

"You need a lawyer."

"I hate lawyers."

Poppy grew gentler. "I know, honey, but this is libel. What does the Cardinal say?"

"I haven't talked with him." The hurt returned. "I called there and was told not to call again."

"Who told you *that?* They aren't going to blame this whole thing on *you,* are they? Damn it, Lily, it takes two to tango. He's the one who's always touching people."

"But it's innocent."

"Not in the eyes of the press. You have a job—*two* jobs—to protect, and a reputation. They've all but labeled you a whore. If that isn't a violation of your rights, I don't know what is!"

"But if I hire a lawyer, that says I *need* a lawyer, which I don't, since I haven't done anything wrong. I give the story one day—stretching it, maybe two." Lily paused, alert. "What was that?"

"What?"

"That click."

"What click?"

She listened again, heard nothing, sighed. "I must be paranoid."

"Maybe you should call Governor Dean."

"And have an aide tell me not to call there, either? I don't think so. Why are reporters calling Lake Henry? What are they looking for?"

"Anything they can take and twist to increase their sales. What do you want me to tell them?"

"That the story isn't true. That Sullivan is lying. That I'm suing." She paused and asked quietly, "What about Rose?"

Rose was the last of the "Blake blooms," as Lake Henry called the three Blake girls. She was a year younger than Poppy, which made her thirty-one. More relevant, she had been barely pubescent when Lily's problems had peaked, too young to have a mind of her own, too young to question what her mother said and thought. Poppy had been far stronger even back then. She had been able to straddle the fence between Maida and Lily, but Rose had been her mother's mouthpiece from the start, and life's circumstances had done nothing to discourage it.

Rose was married, with three children. She and her husband, a childhood sweetheart whose family owned the local mill, lived on the piece of land that had been her wedding gift from the senior Blakes. Always close, Rose and Maida had grown even closer in the three years since Maida's husband, the girls' father, had died.

Experience told Lily not to expect support from Rose. Still, hope lived eternal.

Apparently it lived in Poppy, too, because—as though she had tried and failed—she said an uncharacteristically cross "Rose is an old poop. She doesn't have an independent thought in her head. Don't worry yourself about Rose, and as for the rest of town, I'll tell them what to say if anyone calls. They don't take kindly to having one of their own maligned."

"It's been years since I've been one of their own," Lily reminded her. "They forced me out when I was barely eighteen."

"No. You *chose* to leave."

"Only because they made life unbearable for me."

"Mom did that, Lily."

Lily sighed. She wasn't up for arguing, not now. "I have to go to work."

"Will you keep me in the loop?" Poppy asked. "I know that Blakes have burned you, Lily, but I'm on your side."

Chapter 4

Lily refused to turn on the television. She didn't want to see whether she was in the news, preferring to think that the story was already old. But when she reached the lobby dressed for work, the crowd of journalists outside was larger than ever. Dismayed, she took the elevator to the garage, but reporters were there, too, radioing her arrival to those in front.

Resigned, since there was no other exit and she had to get to work, she lowered her eyes and walked quickly. She ignored the questions shot at her and kept her head down, letting her hair fall forward to shield her face from cameras. Still, the questions increased in volume and frequency, along with the click-and-advance of film as the media phalanx grew. The nearer she got to the club, the more they crowded in. When she was jostled so closely that it became hard to walk, she swung around with her elbows out.

"Leave me *alone,*" she cried through the whirr of snapping cameras. She spun forward and continued on, but she might as well have saved her breath. The crowd came with her in a wave, badgering her with the same questions, goading her into another outburst. She tried to blot them out by thinking of other things, but almost everything in her life just then led back to this moment, this trauma. She was close to tears when she finally reached the club.

Mercifully, Dan was at the door, letting her in, shutting the press out. She went straight to his office, sank into a chair, and put her face in her hands. When she heard him enter, she dropped her hands to her lap.

"Rough day?" he asked kindly.

Not trusting her voice, she nodded. She studied his face.

He smiled sadly. "No need to wonder. I know you, and I know the Cardinal. There's nothing between the two of you but the same kind of friendship he has with people all over the city, all over the country, all over the *world.*"

"Then why is this happening here, now?"

"Because he was just named Cardinal. That makes for bigger headlines and bigger sales of papers."

"That's *sick.*"

"Lately it's the way things work."

She took a breath, still upset from having run the gauntlet of reporters and cameras. "What happens now? They got their splashy headlines. There's no more story, so it dies. Right?"

"I hope so," he said, but without the conviction she wanted. He seemed tired, as though he'd had a rough day, too. He also looked pale, and while pallor on Lily was only a step away from her normal color, it was a far cry from Dan's.

She had the awful thought that he wasn't saying everything he knew.

"How does tonight look here?" she asked with caution, wondering if business was hurt.

"Booked solid."

She brightened. "That's good, isn't it?"

The answer was relative. Yes, the dining room was filled with paying guests, but most of them were new faces, guests of members, and they spent an inordinate amount of time watching the pianist.

Lily tried to tune them out. She often did that when she performed—used the music as an escape—and for a while she succeeded, losing herself in the fantasy of the song—until the flash of a camera broke her concentration. Dan spoke with the offending party and Lily resumed playing, but she didn't sing. No matter that she never stuttered when she sang; she was too unsettled to risk even the most remote chance of it.

Two other flashes went off during the course of the evening, and by the end of the last set, she couldn't try to pretend things were normal. She returned to Dan's office feeling shaken and scared.

"Will this be better tomorrow?" She was desperate for things to be back to normal. She liked her life, liked it just the way it had been.

"I sure hope so," Dan answered, but in the next breath he introduced her to a large uniformed man. "This is Jimmy Finn. BPD, private duty. He'll see you get home okay."

Her heart sank. "They're still out there?"

"Still out there," said the cop, without an *r* in the "there."

Jimmy Finn was a kind man, a devout Catholic who was deeply offended by the media spreading lies about his Cardinal. So he was predisposed to keep the reporters at bay, and burly enough to do it with ease. If he was rough shouldering his way through the crowd, he was nothing but gentle with Lily. He walked her to her building and saw her right to the door of her apartment, but the minute he left, she burst into tears.

There were a slew of new telephone messages, a mixed bag. A few were from friends and were uniformly supportive, but they were overshadowed by those from the media, quickly erased, not so quickly forgotten. She slept only in fits and starts through the night and woke up to a dreary day, but she refused to let her mood match it, refused to even look out the window to see whether television vans were still there. She showered, dressed in dark slacks and a sedate blouse so that she wouldn't feel so exposed. Then she forced down a banana for breakfast, all the while telling herself that things had to get better. Either there would be a retraction in today's paper or there would be nothing at all. In any case, the story was on its way to dead.

When someone knocked on her door shortly after eight, she tensed. She waited through a second knock, then crept softly to the peephole. Relieved, she opened the door.

"I knew you hadn't left," Elizabeth Davis said straight out. She wore a T-shirt over biking shorts and had her blond hair bunched in a clip. "I wasn't sure you'd open up, though. How're you doing?"

"Horrible," Lily said with a glance at the newpapers folded under Elizabeth's arm. "Are those today's?"

"Two Boston, one New York. Want to see?"

"You tell me." She wrapped her arms around her middle. "I'm hoping for a retraction."

"You didn't get one," Elizabeth warned. Unfolding the papers, she tossed them on the table one by one. "The *Post* reports that you drive a BMW and bought a slew of expensive furniture when you moved here. *Cityside* reports that you're big into Victoria's Secret shopping. *New York* reports that you favor upscale restaurants like Biba and Mistral, and that you spent a week last winter at a posh resort in Aruba that you couldn't possibly have afforded on your own."

Lily was too stunned to be angry. "How do they *know* all that?"

"Any computer buff can get the information in five minutes flat."

"But that's personal stuff!"

"Five minutes flat."

"But that's *me*. *My* life. *My private information.*

Where I shop is no one's business!" She had a chilling thought. "What else can they get?"

"Most anything."

Lily swallowed. She had to believe that some things were safe. Her mind began to spin. "I bought the BMW used, I paid off the furniture over two years' time, I mail-order more from L.L.Bean and J. Crew than Victoria's Secret, and I booked the place in Aruba on two days' notice through a travel clearinghouse. I'm being misrepresented. This isn't fair."

But Elizabeth wasn't done. Holding up a hand, she crossed to the small radio on the counter by the stove. Within seconds, Justin Barr's arrogant tenor filled the room.

". . . an insult to Catholics everywhere! Why, this woman is an insult to people of *every* faith. Catholics, Protestants, Muslims, Jews—no matter the affiliation, we should all be thinking about the values we hold most dear, the people who embody them, and the ones who try to take them down. Is there any act of disrespect more blatantly offensive than smearing the good name of a beloved leader?"

"Me, smearing a nnn-name?" Lily cried.

"No, my friends," Justin Barr ranted, "the question is how a woman like Lily Blake was able to get close enough to a man of the stature of Cardinal Rossetti to spread the stain, even indirectly, and now, Lord help us, she teaches our children. Where does it end? I have Mary from Bridgeport, Connecticut, on the line. Go ahead, Mary, you're on the air."

Elizabeth turned off the radio.

Lily was stricken. "I don't believe this."

"Justin Barr is right-wing."

"Justin Barr is syndicated. That show goes up and down the East Coast."

"Uh-huh."

"Why?" Lily cried, referring not only to Justin Barr but to Terry Sullivan, Paul Rizzo, and all the rest who were keeping the story alive. "Why this? Why *me?*"

"Because they smell weakness," Elizabeth said. "Wolves go after a wounded deer; it's the nature of the beast. You have to take a stand, Lily. A lawyer would be a great help."

"I don't want a lawyer."

"Then let me give it a try. I'll get dressed, the two of us will go down there, and I'll be your spokesperson. What do you say to that?"

Lily didn't say a word. She stood silently while Elizabeth read a statement unequivocally denying her romantic involvement with either Governor Dean of New York or Cardinal Rossetti of Boston.

The statement was simple. Elizabeth had advised her to tackle only the major allegations and leave minor misrepresentations alone for now, and much as Lily wanted to yell and scream in her own defense about the rest, she restrained herself. Public relations was Elizabeth's field. She was an experienced image shaper. Indeed, she coaxed and cajoled the media crowd into moving back and showing a little respect, and if she looked a bit too comfortable in her roll as spokesperson, a bit too pleased while working the crowd, Lily forgave her. Her own friends, mostly book people or music people, weren't equipped to help. Thanks to Elizabeth's prevailing upon the press, Lily was able to walk to school unmolested, thinking that maybe, just maybe, the scandal had begun its retreat.

Michael Eddy didn't think so. He knew exactly how much the school paid her and, even allowing for her work at the club, wanted to know how she could afford Aruba and a BMW. She told him how, as she had told Elizabeth, and when Peter Oliver asked about Victoria's Secret, she explained that she bought jeans there, not lingerie. When people stared passing her in the halls, she simply walked on. When faculty members left her sitting alone in the cafeteria, she read a book. She might have taken her frustration out on Mitch Rellejik, only he didn't come in until late. Mid-afternoon, as soon as she finished work, she left school, genuinely happy to be done for the day.

She took heart when she saw that the press contingent remained lighter than it had been the day before, and once in her apartment, dared turn on the evening news. It was a mistake. The story was covered prominently on every channel, taking parts of the morning's stories and giving them lurid twists, and there were more photographs. In one she scowled at the camera. In another she hid her face. And then there were the glamour shots.

Lily had classy publicity photos taken shortly after she arrived in Boston. She also had older ones that were beautiful and dignified. Naturally, the media didn't use those. They were painting a picture of a woman who lived above her means and paid for it by sleeping with powerful men. So they chose the most lurid shots they could find, from her earliest days in New York, in which the skimpy leotards she wore emphasized slim legs, narrow hips, and full breasts.

She felt naked and exposed. She also felt furious—embarrassed—horrified!

Worst, she didn't know what to do, and told Dan Curry as much when she arrived at the club. He gave her the name of a lawyer, which was small solace. More comforting, he had word from the Cardinal.

"He's sick about this, Lily. We're all sitting around wondering whether the Pope will reverse his elevation, and the Cardinal is sitting around worrying about you. As far as he's concerned, you didn't ask for this, you don't deserve it, you're a victim caught in the line of fire. His lawyers have told him not to be in direct touch with you, but he doesn't like it."

That was fine, she thought. Still, a call from him might have been nice. Even one made from a phone booth. Or a friend's telephone. Just to make her feel less alone. But she understood. He was in a bind.

"He's thinking of you, Lily. He told me to tell you that he knows you have the strength to weather this and come out stronger and even more sure of yourself than before."

Lily clung to those words through a difficult night of playing before an audience that stared and talked and crowded in on her. She went to bed praying that this was the worst, and after an on-again, off-again sleep, woke up feeling tired and tense. She was listening to a ponderous Tchaikovsky piece that reflected her mood when a somber Elizabeth appeared at the door with the morning *Post*. The headline read, DETAILS EMERGE ON CARDINAL'S WOMAN.

With a hard swallow, Lily took the paper, and at first there was nothing more than a recap of the allegations. Then, to her dismay, Terry Sullivan turned to Lake Henry.

Blake comes from a well-to-do family in the small, north central town of Lake Henry, New Hampshire. Her father was a major landowner until his death three years ago. Her mother lives in the family's large stone farmhouse and oversees the hundreds of acres of apple orchards that make the family business one of the region's major producers of apple cider.

The Post's Headline Team has learned that Blake grew up with a severe stutter that kept her apart from other children.

Lily sucked in a breath. Swallowing, she read on.

She turned to singing as a means of communication. Experts on speech defects confirm that this is common. "Our casebooks are filled with examples of children who are unable to complete a spoken sentence, yet can sing an entire song without fault," said Susan Block, director of speech therapy in the Boston public schools. She also confirmed that severe speech defects may create emotional problems.

In Blake's case, these took the form of rebellion. When she was sixteen, she was involved in the commission of a felony. Apprehended and charged alongside a twenty-year-old accomplice, who spent six months in prison for the crime, Blake was put on probation. She completed that sentence shortly before graduating from high school, and left town soon after.

With a horrified cry, Lily dropped the paper. Devastated, she looked at Elizabeth. She started to speak, but had to take a calming breath before the words would come out. "That file was sealed!" she finally said. "The judge told us no one would ever see it!"

Elizabeth couldn't hide her curiosity. "What did you do?"

What did she do? She'd been dumb, was what she did. She'd been dumb and young and dying to be popular.

"The boy I was with stole a car. I didn't know it was stolen, and there I was, smiling and laughing, having the time of my life because Donny Kipling was so tough he was cool. I was sixteen. I hadn't ever been kissed. I had barely *dated,* so I went out with him in that car, and he just kept saying, 'Don't worry, this is fun,' but he told the police I planned it, and witnesses said I looked like I was really into it. There was no trial. The case was continued without a judgment, and when I finished my probation, the charges were dropped."

Numb, she picked up the paper again.

Blake rarely returned to Lake Henry after that. Sources who wish to remain anonymous have told the Post that she is estranged from her mother and her sister Rose. Another sister, Poppy, refused to comment on a recent conversation she held with Blake.

"How did they know I talked to Poppy?" she asked. Then, furious, she remembered. "Someone listened in on my phone. I heard that click."

"Wouldn't surprise me," Elizabeth said. "They'll do what they have to for a story."

Hadn't Terry said as much? "But the judge *sealed* that file. How could they learn about it?" She felt violated and exposed.

"Bribery."

"That's not *fair.*"

Elizabeth was suddenly apologetic. "Neither is this. I have to cancel you out for the Kagan fundraiser."

Lily stared at her, stunned.

"Campaign manager's orders," Elizabeth said, gesturing toward the newspaper. "He called when he saw this. It's too inflammatory. Your being there would be an event in itself. Distracting from the candidate."

Lily knew there was more to it. "She doesn't want to be associated with me."

"Don't take it personally. It's politics. One bad connection can ruin a candidate."

"But I'm not a bad connection. The picture they've painted is false."

Elizabeth sighed. "It really doesn't matter, y'know? The fact is that this is on the front page of every paper in the state. It'd be suicide for Kagan if you play at her event. I can't do it, Lily. I'm sorry." She backed toward the door as the phone rang. "Don't answer it," she warned as she left, "and *don't* turn on Justin Barr."

Unbeknownst to Elizabeth, her instructions were connected, and remarkably prescient. But she wasn't there to hear what Lily heard on her machine, the pompous voice of a guy who thought he was bigger than big. "Lily? Are you there, Lily? This is Justin Barr, and we're on the air. My listeners want to hear your side of the story—"

"They do not," Lily muttered and turned off the machine. She packed up for school, went down the back way, and ran off through the waiting crowd, wearing sunglasses so that no one would see if she cried—and if she did, it wouldn't be from fear or sadness. Her jaw was rigid. She was absolutely, positively furious.

Michael Eddy was waiting for her at the large wooden door of the school. He let her in and held up a warning hand to the press, but the warning shifted her way when he said, "My office, please."

Putting the sunglasses on her head, she followed him there. He didn't offer her a seat. She didn't take one.

"I'm getting calls from parents and trustees," he said, with one hand on the back of a chair and the other at the nape of his neck. His eyes were accusing. "They want to know how we could hire someone with a criminal record to teach their children. I told them we didn't know. I want you to tell me why we didn't."

Lily's heart was pounding so hard it practically shook her blouse. With what little breath was left, she said, "I don't *have* a criminal record. The case was dismissed. The file was sealed. I was told that that protected me."

"Who told you that?"

"My lawyer. The judge. It was very clear."

"Didn't you think the parents here would care?"

She thought about how to answer, but the longer she thought, the more angry she grew. "What's there to care about? I've told the truth. I was never convicted of anything."

"Then why the probation? And why a sealed file? You're teaching *children* here, Lily. You should have said something."

She disagreed. But Michael wasn't in her shoes— and she wasn't in his. She looked at him, not knowing what to say.

He sighed. "I hired you, and I'm the head, so I'm on the hot seat. I mean, hell, Justin Barr is making us look like fools. He's riling up the same people we solicit for the annual fund." His shoulders drooped. "I won't fire you. You've done too good a job. But I'm asking you to take a voluntary leave of absence."

Her eyes went wide. She loved her work here, she needed the money, and *she hadn't done anything wrong!* Frightened, she asked, "For how long?"

"I don't know."

"Until this blows over? Until people forget?"

"That may take a while."

The way he said it, the way he stared at her without blinking, told her more. "A permanent leave of absence," she said, because the whole situation was so absurd, why not that?

"An indefinite leave. Just until you find a job somewhere else."

She stared right back, angry at him now and not caring that he knew. He could play with words all he wanted, but yes, he *was* firing her. She tried to see it from his side. All she saw was a man who didn't have the courage to stand up for someone he believed in.

The bottom line, of course, was that he didn't believe in her.

Fitting her sunglasses to her nose, she left the office. She refused to think about the a cappella groups that she had brought so far, refused to think about the soccer player who couldn't play the piano for beans but was learning something about music. She refused to think about the dozens of students she had taught and enjoyed in the last three years, and instead let her anger carry her to the front door; but sentimentality welled up anyway.

It died the minute she saw reporters on the steps. They came to life, surging toward her as she walked.

"Why are you leaving so soon?"

"How does the Winchester School stand on this matter?"

"Have you been in touch with the board of trustees?"

She tried to blot them out, but the questions were too close, too loud, too galling.

"Is the stutter the reason you won't talk with us?"

"Is it true that the New Hampshire charge was for grand theft?"

"Were you having sex with your accomplice?"

Revulsed, Lily shot a look at the man asking that question, wondering what hole he had slithered from. "That's disgusting," she murmured and walked quickly on, ignoring another round of questions until a familiar voice said, "Are you prepared to apologize to the parents of Winchester students? They feel deceived."

It was bald-headed, baby-faced Paul Rizzo. She eyed him sharply. "How do you know?"

"I've interviewed them. They're paying big bucks to educate their kids, and they think it's inappropriate for someone with your history to be teaching here. Would you comment on that?"

She shook her head and returned to ignoring the questions, but she couldn't shake a sense of hurt. Yes, those parents were paying a lot of money, but if the point was a good education, she had delivered—and she hadn't been overpaid, that was for sure, not given her salary, not given the hours she put in. Those parents had a good deal.

They should have known it, should have appreciated it, should have felt even a small measure of loyalty. Same with Michael. Same with the board of trustees.

Besides, allegations were unproven charges. What about being innocent until proven guilty?

By the time she got home, she was angry again. She let herself into the lobby, all but closing the door in the face of Paul Rizzo, who had been breathing down her neck. She strode to the elevator, pressed the button hard, and listened for the clank and whirr inside that would tell her it was on its way. When the sounds grew more distant, she looked at the panel. The elevator had risen to the top floor.

Tony Cohn lived there along with five other tenants, but Murphy's Law said that he would be the one en route to the lobby, so she was prepared when the door finally opened.

He did a double take when he saw her, stepped out of the elevator, glanced at the front door, and swore. "Do you know what an imposition all this is?" he asked in a voice she had never heard. "I rent here for the prestige of it. Forget that now."

She was so taken aback that she didn't think to stutter. "I didn't ask them to come."

"No, but thanks to you they're here. Do you know that I've gotten calls? Phone calls? The *Post, Cityside,* even my own friends, wanting to know about you." He swore again, stepped back into the elevator, with her in it now, and punched the garage button before she could punch her own. She had no choice but to go down first.

She retreated into a corner of the elevator, folded

her arms on her chest, and wondered what she had ever seen in Tony Cohn. Scowling, he wasn't attractive at all—and he had never given her the time of day, not really.

He snorted and said, "When I took this apartment I had the realtor check out the other tenants. The slate was supposed to be clean."

"It *is* clean." Then it occurred to her that what he had just said was odd. "You *checked out* the other tenants? Why would you do that?"

The door slid open. "Some of us have images to protect."

He was out before she found a suitable retort, so she put a foot against the door to hold it open and called after him, "Only ones with their *own* secrets to hide!"

She let the door close, jabbed at the button for her floor, and glowered as the elevator began its ascent, thinking that every cloud did have a silver lining, and that if nothing else, this fiasco had shown her what an arrogant, egocentric jerk Tony Cohn was.

By the time she reached her floor she was regretting having wasted a single fantasy on the man. But she forgot about him completely when she opened the door to her apartment and heard the phone ringing. Dropping her briefcase, she gripped the back of the chair until the ringing stopped. She heard her own voice—then remembered that she had turned the machine off that morning. Ten consecutive rings would have turned it on again, which meant that she'd had at least one persistent caller.

"Uh, yes," said a hungover-sounding male voice,

"I'm calling for Lily Blake. I'm, uh, a writer. I ghost-wrote the biography of Brandi Forrest, uh, she's the lead singer with the rock group Dead Weight Off. Anyway, I'm sure you're getting lotsa other calls, but if you, uh, want someone to write your story, we should talk. I, uh, already called my publisher. They like the idea of sex and religion. They can get something out real fast. Uh. It's all in the timing. So if you want, call me." He left a number with an area code that she didn't recognize.

Lily erased the message, then listened to those preceding it. Justin Barr must have been the persistent one, because his call came first. He called three additional times, at twenty-minute intervals. There were also calls from reporters in Chicago, St. Louis, and Los Angeles—all leaving names and numbers, as if she would really return their calls. There were messages from two friends expressing concern, and messages from two clients canceling engagements.

There was also a message from Daniel Curry, asking her to call. His voice held an odd edge. Nervous, she punched out the number of the club. His greeting was gentle enough, but she heard that edge again. "Tell me," she said, steeling herself, and he sighed.

"You know how I feel, Lily. I know nothing happened. I believe in both of you. I *love* both of you, so this tears me apart, but here's my problem. The phone has been ringing off the hook with complaints."

"Complaints?"

"We're completely booked for tonight, large tables, mostly sixes and eights."

"Isn't that good?"

"Not this time. Regulars can't get reservations. Others complained about having to wade through reporters last night. The thing is that these people are the backbone of the club. The ones booking large tables now are fly-by-nights. They aren't the ones who'll be coming weekly, six months or a year from now. They're just jumping on the scandal bandwagon, one member inviting five, six, seven friends for the show, but that's not fair to the faithful."

Lily had a death grip on the phone. She knew what was coming.

"I could take the easy way out," Dan said. "I could blame it on money and say that the regulars will defect and then where will we be—but they won't, Lily. It isn't a matter of financial survival. It's the principle of the thing. I've always run the club a certain way. It's a quiet, private place. A classy place. That's why we loved having you play. Because you *are* classy."

She waited.

"But this whole business is sordid," he said. "Not a word of it is true, but it *is* sordid. Members are getting calls from the likes of Terry Sullivan and Paul Rizzo. Justin Barr is trashing us—not that we'd ever let that bastard step foot in the place, but he's creating a notoriety that we just don't need. Having people come to the club just to see—quote unquote—the woman who seduced the Cardinal, isn't what we're about."

Lily remained silent, her head bowed.

"This kills me," Dan went on, "because we all love

you here." He sighed. "But I think you should take some time off."

"Are you firing me?" Two firings in one hour would be a record. Maybe the papers would buy that.

"No. I'm just telling you to stay home for a couple of days until this thing dies down."

But she was discouraged. "Will it?"

"Definitely. It's like a car. No fuel, no go."

"There's *never* been fuel, but the car went! If they don't find it one place, they'll find it another." Exhausted, she ran a hand over her eyes. "Does this have to do with the felony thing?"

"What felony thing?"

"You haven't read today's paper?"

"No."

She told him so that he would know—so that he would hear her side of the story first. "The Cardinal knows all this," she said before he could ask. "Funny how conducive a clerical collar is to confession. He's off the hook now, but they're closing in on me."

"Is there anything else they can find?"

"Yesterday I wouldn't have said there was anything, period!" She sank into the chair. "That was my one and only brush with the law. There's been nothing since—not a speeding ticket, not a parking ticket, not even a late credit card payment. What's left for them to write?"

Chapter 5

They wrote about Lily's suspension from the Winchester School—it was front-page news on Friday morning. Terry Sullivan interviewed Michael Eddy, whose statements had enough force and indignation to restore his luster in the eyes of parents and trustees. Paul Rizzo focused on members of the board, with a long string of quotes expressing dismay at Lily's deceit, her immorality, and her lack of judgment. Justin Barr went wild about what he called the Lily Blake problem, inciting irate parents to call in discussing the teacher as a role model, the need for teachers of the utmost moral fiber, the responsibilities schools have to their students to protect them from those of poor character.

The *Post* offered a token quote from one parent who praised the work Lily had done with his child, but that quote was short and lost amid the others, as were Lily's denials of wrongdoing. The overall tone of the piece was one of self-righteousness that had more to do with the *Post* patting itself on the back than with any quest for the truth.

Both papers reported that Lily was taking time off from the Essex Club, but neither elaborated on that angle or gave related quotes. Lily suspected that Dan had refused to talk and that the print media, at least, was backing off from anything to do with the Cardinal. There was no further mention of an alleged affair, no further mention of shared smiles or late nights at the Cardinal's residence. Nor was there mention of Governor Dean.

The focus was on Lily, and Lily alone. She had become the story.

Another woman, one who loved the limelight, might have been pleased. But Lily had felt victimized before—as a child ridiculed for her stutter, as a teenager put on probation for a crime she didn't commit, as an entertainer losing a shot at the top after rebuffing the advances of the music director. Injustice happened. She should have been hardened to it. But she wasn't. She was so angry and upset that she couldn't play the piano, couldn't read, couldn't even play a CD, because nothing she owned was turbulent enough.

She was *so* angry that she put aside her distaste for lawyers and called the one Dan had recommended. His name was Maxwell Funder. Articulate and experienced, he was among the most visible attorneys in the state. She had seen him on the news many times and, cynically perhaps, wondered if his promise to be at her apartment within the hour had to do primarily with the publicity attached to the case. But beggars couldn't be choosers. Given that she could only afford to pay him for a consultation, she was grateful when he agreed to come.

In person, he wasn't nearly as impressive as the television cameras made him out to be. He was older. He was also shorter and broader, and without makeup, more mottled.

But he was pleasant and patient. Sitting on the sofa, he listened while she vented. He frowned in dismay, widened his eyes in disbelief, shook his head from time to time—and she didn't care if he was pouring it on for her benefit. The sympathy felt good.

"How can this happen?" she asked after working herself into a fury. "How can so many lies be printed? How can my whole life be put on display? How can *sealed* files be *un*sealed? I've lost two jobs, the press sits outside waiting to pounce, Justin Barr is tearing me to shreds, my family is being hassled. When I think of going out, I think of being stared at by people *I* don't know who know personal things about *me*. I feel totally helpless. How do I make it *stop?*"

The lawyer sat straighter. "For starters, we can go to court, file papers, and initiate a suit. Tell me. Who's the worst?"

"The *Post*," she said without pause. Terry Sullivan had started it all. He had used her and lied.

"The *Post* it is," Funder said. "Our suit will be the vehicle to get your side of the story out. We'll expose all the falsehoods. We'll get affidavits from the Cardinal and the governor corroborating your side of the issue. I'll call a press conference and lay it all out"—his passion rose—"calling this the worst kind of shoddy journalism, the most *reckless* example of bad press. I'll demand an investigation of the *Post* for first printing this slander and demand an immediate retraction."

Lily latched on to the last. "A retraction. That's what I want. Will I get it?"

"Now?" The rhetoric cooled. "No. They're too far into this. They'll fight to defend the basic integrity of the paper. Maybe years down the road . . ."

Years? "How many years?"

He thought for a minute. "Realistically? From now to the time a jury hears the case? Three years. The thing is"—he raised a cautioning hand—"in order for you to be really vindicated, you need a big verdict. Token damages won't do. So we'll sue for, say, four million, but I have to warn you, the *Post* will fight hard. They'll fight dirty, and you'd better know right now what that means. They have on retainer some of the toughest First Amendment lawyers in the country. They'll put your life under a microscope, and they'll do it under oath. They'll take depositions of your family, your friends, schoolmates, teachers, boyfriends, ex-boyfriends, neighbors—and that's nothing compared to what their private investigators will do. They'll sift through your life with a fine-tooth comb. They'll get phone records, credit card records, school records, motor vehicle records, medical records. They'll interview people you didn't know you knew, looking for anything, even the tiniest little hint of something, that can help their client show that you're a disreputable person. That you have a *history* of being a disreputable person. If you think your privacy has been violated now, it's nothing compared to what they'll do."

"Gee, thanks," Lily said. It was either sarcasm or tears.

"Don't think I'm kidding," he warned, harder now. "I know these people. They're animals. If there's anything out there, they'll find it. They'll try to prove that your reputation is so bad that even if they made a mistake and libeled you, it doesn't matter, because no damage has been done. They'll try to prove that your life has been filled with lies."

Lily was beginning to panic. "What about my rights? Why do they come last?"

"They don't come last. But the First Amendment guarantees freedom of speech."

"What guarantees do *I* have? The media has no right to do this to me."

"That's why we sue."

"All I want is a retraction. I don't want money."

"Well, you ought to. This kind of case can cost upwards of a million dollars."

She nearly choked. "Cost *me* a million dollars?"

"Between legal fees, court costs, jury consultants, experts, private investigators."

She felt weak in the knees. "I don't have that kind of money."

"Few people do." He studied her, inhaled loudly, laced his fingers. "Look. I don't normally take cases unless the client has the full ability to pay—I mean, I have to live, too—but what's happening to you is a disgrace. So this is what I can do. I'll handle the case for two fifty, plus an additional fifty for expenses, plus twenty-five percent of what you recover."

"Two fifty."

"Two hundred and fifty thousand."

She gulped in a breath that went down the wrong way. It was a long minute of pressing her chest and trying not to cough, before she was able to say, "I don't *have* that kind of mm-money."

"Your family does."

She drew back.

"I read there was a family business," he said.

"It's a working business. There isn't cash lying around."

"There's land. That would be good collateral for a loan."

"I can't ask that," Lily said. Cash, a loan—it didn't matter. She couldn't ask her mother for money. Nor could she imagine Maida giving it. She was the greatest disappointment of Maida's life—the daughter who went bad, the one who played with fire and got burned. It didn't matter that Lily led a truly honest, upstanding life. Maida saw her through a different pair of eyes.

The lawyer sat forward, hands still laced, a little too relaxed now, a little too slick. "I understand your hesitance—"

"No, you don't," she interrupted angrily. "This is *my* life. I haven't taken a cent from my family since I was eighteen, and I won't do it now."

"I understand your hesitance," he repeated in a tone—and with a look—that said she would be wise to let him finish, "but if family's good for anything, it's for coming to the rescue in time of trouble. I did read that you don't get along with your family, but if they have money that can get you out of this mess, my advice is to take it. Good lawyers don't come cheap. You won't get a better deal than the one I'm offering."

But Lily *couldn't* ask her mother for money. And even if she had the money herself, she couldn't conceive of spending it all on this. She hadn't done anything wrong!

Quietly she stood. "I need to think. Thank you for coming. I appreciate your time." She headed for the door.

He followed, but his face was more mottled when she turned to him next. "I won't offer this again," he warned. "If things heat up and get worse, I'll have to charge you more."

She nodded her understanding.

With one foot in the hall, he turned back, pleasant again. "No need to make a decision now. My offer stands for another day or two. Let me warn you, though. You'll get calls from other lawyers who'll offer to take the case on contingency alone, and it'll be mighty tempting for you to do that, but you won't get the quality. Given the out-of-pocket costs that a case like this will demand if it's done right, no good lawyer will work on contingency."

"Thank you," she said again and, as soon as he withdrew his foot, closed the door.

★   ★   ★

Lily went to the window to see if the lawyer would stop and talk to the press on his way out, but one of the horde spotted her first, and suddenly faces and cameras were all looking up. Jolted, she stepped quickly back and stood frozen in the middle of the floor, gazing blindly out across Commonwealth Avenue—until she realized, with horror, that a telephoto lens in a window of one of the buildings *there* could see her *anywhere* in her apartment.

She quickly closed the blinds in the living room, ran, and did the same in the bedroom. That left her in a small dark apartment, with no job, no freedom, no prospects for a speedy return of either, much less her good name. She sat in the armchair, but still she couldn't concentrate to read. She moved to the piano and let her fingers roam the keys, but they picked out depressing tunes. So she put Beethoven on the CD player—somber perhaps, but appropriate—and she walked from bedroom to living room to bedroom and back, not knowing what to do with herself. She finally ended up at the phone.

Lifting the receiver, she started to press in her mother's number, hung up, and tucked her arms to her chest so that she wouldn't try again—and it wasn't about money. She didn't want money, didn't want to sue, because the process Maxwell Funder described was heinous. Three years of media speculation, of stories twisting the facts of her life—three years of feeling used and exposed. She couldn't survive that.

No. She wouldn't have called Maida for money.

She would have liked to call for the comfort of it. Maida was her mother. Lily was feeling the need to bury her head somewhere warm and sympathetic until the storm passed. She was feeling the need for shelter, certainly for a compassionate ear.

But Maida wouldn't give either. So Lily called Sara Markowitz instead. Sara was a friend from Juilliard who taught at the New England Conservatory. They met for lunch every few weeks. Sara's had been one of the messages left on the answering machine.

She felt instant relief when Sara picked up the phone, all the more so that despite the bad press, Sara was avid in support. "I've been so worried. What *is* this *mishegaas?* False charges—a total twisting of the truth—it's *way* out of control. They're even calling *me,* would you believe, asking intimate questions, not taking no for an answer, pushing and pushing. What's with Terry Sullivan? Where does reporter stop and gossipmonger begin? And Justin Barr? He's worse! Neither *one* has a clue about what it means to be a mensch. Did you know either of them before this began?"

"Justin Barr, absolutely not."

"Good. He's a hypocritical idiot. He was too ugly to make it on TV with his fat face and beady eyes, so he turned to radio. He just loves to hear himself talk—the Champion of Home and Hearth—but what's with Sullivan?"

"He'd been after me to do an interview about my work. I kept refusing him, so maybe he's annoyed." It hit her then. "He didn't want to know about my work.

It must have been about the Cardinal all along." Feeling *doubly* used, she dragged in a breath. "My life is falling apart, I don't know why, and I'm stuck in this apartment with nowhere to go."

"Meet me at Biba—uh, no."

Lily knew why Sara caught herself. Biba was one of the restaurants the papers had mentioned as an example of Lily living high off the hog. She and Sara often had salads there, which made it a fun, low-cost treat. But not fun anymore. Not fun ever again.

Wisely, Sara said, "Stephanie's in thirty minutes?"

Stephanie's was a restaurant on Newbury Street. Lily didn't know anyone there. It sounded like heaven. "Thirty minutes is great."

She put on jeans, a blouse, and a blazer. Tucking her hair under a baseball cap, she put on dark glasses, took the elevator to the garage, and hit daylight at a brisk walk, looking as nonchalant and anonymous as she could.

The press spotted her instantly. Reporters swarmed from behind trash cans, telephone poles, and parked cars, shoving microphones in her face, yelling to get her attention.

"Ms. Blake! Ms. Blake! Where are you going?"

"What did Funder say?"

"CNN here—can you confirm that Funder is representing you?"

"Are you suing the Winchester School?"

Staring straight ahead, she continued on up the alley, but reporters tripped over one another in an effort to get questions in, the pack growing with each step. She could feel and smell its heat and hustle, waves of hot breath, stale body scent. Even if she hadn't been shorter and more slight than almost every reporter there, she would have been frightened by the sheer mass.

"Are you looking for work?"

"What about the felony conviction?"

"Is the Essex Club still paying you?"

When she turned onto Fairfield, she collided with reporters coming around the block on the run from the front of her building. She couldn't continue forward without shoving bodies and equipment out of the way, but she wasn't physically strong enough for that, and when she looked back, they were a solid block there, too. She imagined them closing in and crushing her.

"Is it true you slept with Michael Crawford—"

"—that you were a go-go dancer in Times Square—"

"Justin Barr said—"

"—apologize to the Cardinal?"

The questions came fast, overlapping and rising in pitch until she was on the verge of panic. She saw it all then, saw herself fighting her way down Newbury Street and trying to have lunch with Sara with the press hovering and interrupting and disrupting the entire restaurant. And she couldn't do it—not to Sara, not to those others, not to herself. The whole point had been to have time alone with a friend.

Whirling around, she swung her arms out in anger

until there was a semblance of a path, and barged back down the alley. For an instant, when she used her key to open the door beside the garage, she feared they would push their way in, but she was able to slip through and close the door behind her—close it tight and then stand on tiptoe and peer through a small, dirty window on the top of it in time to see the vultures, looking deflated, back off and turn away.

Safe now, she shook with fury. Storming through the garage, she took the elevator to her floor, ran into her apartment, lifted the phone, and called Stephanie's. It was all she could do to keep her voice calm when she said, "My name is Lily. I'm supposed to be meeting a woman named Sara, about five-six, curly brown hair, glll-lasses. Can you tell me if she's there yet?" According to the hostess, Sara wasn't. "Well, she'll be getting there any minute. Will you have her call Lily?"

Two minutes later, the phone rang. "God, Sara, I'm sorry," she said without introduction. "I can't get there, they won't let me through. They crowded me all the way down the back alley, so I turned around and came back. It'd be an *obscenity* leading them to that restaurant, and we wouldn't have any privacy at all. I'm so sorry to have dragged you there."

"Who's Sara?" asked a nasal male voice.

"Who's *this?*" she asked, appalled.

"Tom Hardwick. I been reading about you in the paper, and, y'know, it seems to me that since you can't see the Cardinal anymore, you may be, y'know, on the prowl, y'know? That was a neat picture in *City-*

side. Real sexy. I been with someone but we just broke up, so, y'know, I'm thinking I'm free and you're free. Got your number from my sister. She's your doctor's receptionist. I'm only twenty-three, but I love older women—"

Lily hung up. Nauseated, she stared at the phone, praying that he wouldn't call back, thinking that he wouldn't have the *gall* to call back. But he'd had the gall to call the first time, so she didn't know what to expect now, and besides, her sense of expectation had been shattered in the last few days. Anything could happen. Absolutely anything. She was as poor a judge of people now as she had been at sixteen, out joyriding with Donny Kipling—she'd certainly shown that.

The phone rang once, twice, three times. The machine came on. When her own greeting was done, she heard Sara's higher-than-usual voice. "Lily? What's happened?"

Relieved, Lily picked up the phone and told her. As she talked, the reality of the situation sank in. "I'm a prisoner here," she concluded, dazed. "A prisoner."

"Then I'll come over," Sara offered. "We'll talk there."

But Lily had to think about being a prisoner. She had to think about what to do next and how, and she had to do it alone. So she thanked Sara, promised to call her soon, and hung up the phone.

She spent the rest of the day wandering around the tiny apartment, letting strains of a strident Wagner drown out the ringing of the phone, feeling alternately caged, terrified, and numb. Also utterly powerless. And angry. Very, very angry. Angry at Terry Sullivan, Paul Rizzo, and Justin Barr for playing with her life. Angry at the *Post, Cityside,* and WROT-AM for allowing it. Angry, even, at the Cardinal for freeing himself from the mess but leaving her in it up to her ears.

She couldn't stay in Boston. That much was clear. Even if the story died the next day, she would be stared at for months. She couldn't bear that—couldn't bear knowing that millions of strangers knew private details of her life, couldn't bear being fodder for talk shows, couldn't bear the humiliation or the sense of injustice. And then there was the issue of a job. Who would hire a woman with the morals of a snake? No one offering the kind of work she wanted, that was for sure.

Her college roommate lived in San Francisco. They talked several times a year, but Debbie had a husband and three kids. Lily was afraid to call her now, much less show up on her doorstep, lest the media lunge at new bait. Same with friends in New York and Albany. Lily was afraid of tainting their lives. If she couldn't stay with a friend, she would need an apartment, but without income? What she had in the bank was finite. It wouldn't last long if she couldn't get work.

She could cut her hair short, dye it blond, and go somewhere new. She could waitress. She had put herself through college waitressing. She could do it again. But without knowing a soul? Having to use a phony name and lie to every person she met? That was no life.

What she wanted most was justice, but she didn't see it coming in the next day or two. Second to that, what she wanted was to dig a hole and climb in. She was tired of reporters and cameramen. She was tired of being a spectacle. She wanted silence, and privacy. She wanted to become invisible.

But human beings didn't dig holes and climb in. They went to places where they could hide, places like Lake Henry.

Not Lake Henry, she protested; but the idea stuck in her mind like a burr. She had a place to live there. She owned it free and clear. It had been a bequest from her grandmother, a small place on the lake that was separated from the world by a long dirt road and acres of trees.

Not Lake Henry, she cried; but it was as close to a hole in the ground as she was apt to find. It was familiar. Her cottage was well stocked. She paid a local woman to clean it each month, and she stayed there whenever she was home.

Maida wouldn't be happy. She wouldn't want Lily there, wouldn't want the scandal so close to home, but what choice did Lily have? Of her options, hiding out at the lake made the most sense. She could think there. She could monitor the media frenzy, and decide whether to fight it and how. She could breathe fresh air there. She could spend time with Poppy.

The phone rang. She turned and stared at it. Feeling a startling longing, she imagined it was Maida telling her yes, to go to the cottage. She imagined Maida bringing over her specialty, a steaming pot roast that was slow cooked and savory with bay leaves and sage, along with fresh mushrooms and carrots and a slew of the tiny red potatoes that Maida's friend Mary Joan Sweet grew in her garden. She imagined Maida feeling so terrible when she learned the truth about the scandal that she would insist Lily stay at the big house. She imagined that they would talk, cry, become friends.

Dreams. Lily sighed. Just dreams.

So she didn't answer the phone, and listening to the message, she was glad. This one, like others earlier, was from no one she wanted to know.

She had given up wondering how her phone number had spread. "Unlisted" seemed to have gone the way of "civil rights." She could call the phone company to protest, but to what end? She could curse Mitch for giving her number to Terry, and Terry for giving it to whoever else, but that was like trying to close the door when the horse was already out of the barn.

Besides, she was leaving. In another day she wouldn't hear this phone. She wouldn't shower in her beautiful glassed-in shower, walk through the Public Garden to school, or sing her heart out to people who loved her voice. She wouldn't do any of those things, because Terry Sullivan, Paul Rizzo, and Justin Barr had taken away her life.

Pacing the floor as the day wore on and the minutes crept by more and more slowly, she felt a raw fury toward all three. There were moments of wavering, moments when she reversed herself and vowed, on principle alone, not to leave town, but that bravado inevitably passed, leaving the stark truth. She couldn't work, because she had no job. She couldn't see friends, get fresh air, or buy food, because she couldn't leave her apartment—and even if the press weren't waiting to tail her wherever she went, going out, for her, now, in this town, meant embarrassment and acute self-consciousness. It wasn't fair. She wanted justice. But she couldn't initiate a lawsuit because she didn't have the money. Nor did she have the heart to launch a three-year war. Certainly not the kind Maxwell Funder described.

The only thing she had the heart for just then was escape. She'd had it with feeling out of control. She needed to take back her life—some life, *any* life. For that, she needed sleep. She needed freedom. She needed counsel, and if the spirit of her grandmother was the only counsel around, that was fine. Celia St. Marie had been a saint. She would know what to do next. She would know how to search for justice.

When darkness fell, Lily packed up the car, locked the doors, and left the garage. She fully expected a few diehards to be left outside, even one or two following in a car, but she figured she would lose them once she hit the Pike. Indeed, figures emerged from dark shadows, hoisting equipment, shouting questions, motioning her to roll down her window, as she started down the alley; and, yes, a pair of headlights fell in behind her. What she hadn't expected, though, were others that came on the instant she turned left onto Gloucester. Rechecking her door lock, she made a fast right onto Newbury. To her horror, a large satellite van parked at the corner revved up and joined the chase.

She sped up in an attempt to bury herself in traffic, but the street was too narrow. Her chasers easily kept pace. Hoping to shake them, she veered right at Hereford, then right again—through a yellow light—onto Commonwealth. She thought that her tail would be stuck at the red. But the big van sailed through it. By the time another red light stopped her, when she was waiting to turn left on Fairfield and head to the Pike that way, not only was the big van on her bumper, but a motorcyclist with a press pass around his neck started knocking on her window.

When the light turned green, she gunned the gas and, if she hadn't immediately slammed the brakes back on, would have hit a reporter who was rounding the front of the car to get to the driver's side.

Deeply shaken, she revised her plan. Driving slowly and carefully, she went all the way around the block until she reached the opposite end of the alley from the one she had left minutes before. She inched her way down the narrow stretch and turned in at her building. When she lowered her window to key open the garage door, the motorcyclist came up close and pulled off his helmet. The security light triggered by her approach gleamed off the bald head of none other than Paul Rizzo.

"I can guarantee you safe passage," he said, "if you give me an exclusive on where you were going and why."

Lily was incensed. "No exclusive. I'm going into thhhh-is garage"—she fought the stutter for all she was worth—"and *it* is private property. If you come in while this door's open, I'm callll-ling the police." She turned the key and quickly rolled up her window. As soon as the garage door was high enough, she rolled forward, but she stopped the car the instant it cleared the door and turned to see whether anyone would come inside.

She didn't see anyone. The door closed. She drove on to her parking space.

For a time, she just sat. She didn't try to leave the car, didn't even unlock the door. She waited for someone to approach her, someone who may have slipped inside without her seeing. When no one came, she turned and looked around. Granted, cars were perfect things to hide behind, and the garage was full of them, but she didn't see a soul.

She got out of the car, loaded her arms with as much as she could carry, and took the elevator to the fourth floor. Rather than going to her own apartment, though, she went to Elizabeth's. When Elizabeth didn't answer the door, she slid down and sat on the floor with her back to the wall. It was nine. She didn't know when Elizabeth would show up, but she could wait. She had nothing better to do.

Nine became ten, and she actually put her head on her duffel bag and dozed off. She had barely slept for three nights and was exhausted. But she came awake at the touch of a hand.

"Why are you out *here?*" Elizabeth asked.

Immediately cogent, Lily sat up. "I need your help." She explained what had happened with the car. "I can't stay here, Elizabeth, and the problem isn't just a small dark apartment. It's the whole thing. There's no point in my being here. The media won't let this die. The problem is how to get out without their following."

Elizabeth tipped up her chin. "I know how."

Lily held her gaze. "So do I. Will you do it?"

Actually, they had two different plans. Lily's plan was for Elizabeth to smuggle her out in her luxury SUV, then take a cab back into Boston and use Lily's BMW for the day or two it took until Lily could arrange to return the Lexus. Elizabeth's plan started out the same way but involved dropping Lily at the nondescript Ford wagon that Elizabeth's brother Doug had left sitting in his Cambridge garage while he was teaching in Brussels for the year.

Since Elizabeth's plan allowed more flexibility as to when and how Lily returned the borrowed car, they chose that one, and it went off without a hitch. Lily and her belongings successfully hid under piles of *Kagan for Governor* banners in the back of the Lexus, and even Lily saw the poetry in that. She wondered if Elizabeth was carrying it too far, though, when she stopped to chide the two reporters who were doing the graveyard shift in the alley.

Did they *really* think Lily would be leaving this late? Elizabeth asked with audible wryness. For what? A late-night rendezvous with the Cardinal? Puleeze.

Wasn't it time they gave the poor woman a break? And where was *she* going? For drinks at the Lennox Lounge. Did they want to come? They ought to. It would be her treat.

Lily nearly died at the last, but Elizabeth knew what she was doing. The reporters wouldn't take her up on the invitation. They thought it was a setup to lure them away so that their quarry could escape.

"You can't fool us," one said, and that was that.

Elizabeth drove off down the alley and around the block, heading toward Cambridge free and clear. When they reached Doug's house, she pulled right up to the garage and killed the lights.

"It's battered but trusty," she said as they stowed Lily's things in the wagon. "Here's the trick. Step on the gas twice—pause—then once more, then turn the key. Works every time."

Lily couldn't afford to be fussy. Sliding behind the wheel, she took a minute to see where everything was, then rolled down the window, pumped the gas twice, paused, then once more, and turned the key. Her heart tripped when the engine sputtered, but it started up in the next breath and purred a little noisily, but purred nonetheless.

"You're the best," she told Elizabeth by way of thanks.

Elizabeth was leaning down at the window. "Nah. If I was, I'd have insisted they keep you on for the Kagan event. Or I'd have let you take my Lexus." She patted the old wagon. "This is no skin off my back. Want me to get your mail or anything?"

"Actually, I would." Lily took her mailbox key from her key ring and handed it over.

"Where should I send it?"

"Just hold it."

"Where'll you be?"

She wasn't sure she should say. It wasn't that she didn't trust Elizabeth—yes, actually it was, which was another thing she despised Terry Sullivan for. He had taught her that unless she knew someone very, very well, she had to be on her guard.

So she simply smiled. "I'll let you know."

She rolled up the window and waved as Elizabeth stepped away. Backing out of the driveway, she shifted into drive, put on the headlights, and set off.

The trip took two hours. Lily spent the first hour watching her rearview mirror to see if she was being followed. Supercautious, she even left the highway once, reversed direction, went back an exit, reversed direction again, and continued on north. But no car followed.

She had escaped. She had one-upped the press in a small victory, made large by the context in which it occurred. The pleasure of it carried her into the second hour, across the Massachusetts border into New Hampshire, and steadily north, but thirty minutes shy of Lake Henry, ebullience gave way to qualms. She wondered if she was trading one set of problems for another, jumping from the frying pan into the fire— and that totally apart from the possibility that the press might yet find her here. If that happened, she had no idea what she would do, what the townsfolk would do, what her *mother* would do.

But she was committed. She checked her rearview mirror when she left the highway, and again when she drove through the center of Lake Henry, but everything was dark, closed up tight for the night, and no car followed, not then or when she turned off Main Street onto the road that circled the lake. Bumping around familiar curves, with an evergreen scent seeping into the car, she felt a mellowness that the lake always brought. Oh yes, there were qualms, but they had to do with people. Not with the lake. Never with the lake.

She turned off the loop road onto a narrower one that led to the shore at Thissen Cove. Several hundred feet from the water, she turned again, this time onto a rutted dirt path. Following it to its end, she killed the engine, then the lights.

At first glance, the lake was pitch black. Gradually her eyes adjusted to the absence of headlights, and she began to make out things. The cottage was a small structure of wood and stone on her left. On her right, tall trees were dark silhouettes against a sky that was only a tad less dark.

Slipping silently from the car, she stood and inhaled. The woods smelled of pine, of dried leaves, of moss-covered rocks and logs burning in a neighbor's woodstove. They were smells common to Lake Henry in fall, but in Lily they conjured up childhood images, good images involving her grandmother. She crossed the small clearing between cottage and lake, walking over pine needles that had been years gathering and gnarled tree roots that had been decades growing. Down a short stairway of railroad ties and she reached the water's edge.

The lake was still. She listened to the soft slap of water against shore, the faint crinkle of fall foliage in the night breeze, the distant sound of a barn owl. She made out layers of clouds in the sky, but as she watched they broke open to patches of stars and, minutes later, a crescent moon—and then—and then came the deep, hauntingly melodic tremolo of a loon.

She was being welcomed home. She felt it as clearly as she felt her grandmother's presence, and suddenly the contrast between the hell she had left and the beauty of this cottage, this lake, this town was so stark and heartfelt that she knew she was right to come.

Feeling stronger than she had at any time since before reading the *Boston Post* on Tuesday, she returned to the car, pulled the key to the cottage from her purse, climbed the steps to the old wood porch, and let herself in the door.

John Kipling sat utterly still in his canoe. The same something that had kept him from sleep had drawn him here in the wee hours, to the shadow of Elbow Island, opposite Thissen Cove. Call it instinct, a hunch, or a sheer lucky guess. Lucky? Hell, no. It was common sense. If her life in the city had become the hell he imagined, where else could she go?

Still, he didn't know for sure until the light went

on in the house, but there it was. He whispered a satisfied "Yesssss."

When a soft yodel came in response, he smiled. Only male loons yodeled. This one wasn't from the pair he called his own, but, man to man, it understood the satisfaction he felt. He had read the *Post* story and knew firsthand how deceitful Terry Sullivan could be. He had talked with Poppy, who was dismayed at what her sister was enduring, and had talked with townsfolk, who had differing opinions on the matter. He wondered what the truth was. It was the journalist in his blood. Now that Lily Blake was back in town, right here on *his* turf, he could pursue it.

Smiling in anticipation, he drew his paddle through the water and headed home.

Chapter 6

Lily slept deeply and awoke disoriented. It was a full minute before she realized where she was, and seconds more before she realized why. Then everything came back in a rush—the lies, the embarrassment, the anger, the loss. She squeezed her eyes shut and willed the images away, but they were an indelible part of her now, redefining her life in ways she had never envisioned. A slow trembling started inside. She tried to stay calm by reminding herself that she was safe. Only Elizabeth knew she had left the city, and no one at all knew she was here. Still, the trembling remained.

Thinking that the images wouldn't be as vivid if she was upright and actively looking at something, she slipped from bed and went to the top of the spiral stairs that led down from the sleeping loft—and it worked. Comfort was instantaneous. The magic, of course, was in these four walls. For Lily, this cottage was filled with warm memories. Practically from birth, she had visited her grandmother here.

Celia St. Marie wasn't a native of Lake Henry. She had spent her first fifty years in a remote Maine town seventy-some miles to the northeast. Widowed early, she had supported herself and Maida by doing book-keeping for a paper mill. When she wasn't working, she was bailing out her brothers, an irresponsible lot. But Maida married well. Not only did George Blake have a successful family business that he ran for his aging father, but he had a good heart. Soon after his marriage to Maida, he bought a piece of land for Celia and built her the cottage where she would spend the rest of her life.

It wasn't a large cottage. Celia hadn't wanted any-thing large. Having always lived in cramped quarters, she would have been overwhelmed by many rooms. It was enough to have her own home—something she had never had before.

So when George asked, she requested a simple cottage. She felt that if she was to be a landowner, with her own beautiful lakefront, she would enjoy open space outside and be snug and cozy inside.

Coziness was definitely what Lily associated with the cottage, which was made of dark wood top to bot-tom, with plenty of exposed beams, built-in book-shelves, and wide-planked floors. The ground level was a single large room divided into parts by the appropriate furniture. The living area was marked by a large sofa upholstered in a deep red floral print, a pair of over-stuffed chairs in a deep orange floral, two floor lamps with yellow floral shades, and a square pine coffee table that had been battered and loved. The dining area contained a wood trestle table that on occasion had sat half a dozen grandchildren, Celia's and those of her friends.

The kitchen was small but surprisingly modern. Celia St. Marie might have been parochial, but she was smart. She had arrived in Lake Henry with a small savings account that grew considerably over the years, allowing her the financial freedom to upgrade as needed and add conveniences that made her little cottage absolutely perfect.

But her savings account wasn't all that grew. Celia herself grew, spreading out, becoming a part of the community. She made friends in town. She joined the Garden Club and the Historical Society, and played bingo Monday nights at the church. In her seventies she took to wearing baseball caps and red sneakers— respectively (she claimed) to cover thinning hair and to make her visible in the dark. But Lily suspected, as did almost everyone who knew her as she aged, that she simply had come into her own. How else to explain the wide-mouth bass she had caught in a contest on the lake, then stuffed and hung on the kitchen wall? Or, on a living room wall, the huge macramé piece that was both exquisite and remarkable, since she had taken up the craft only after moving to Lake Henry? Or the hat tree that held not only an assortment of baseball caps but a wrangler's cap, a golf cap, and an old fashioned, wide-brimmed lady's lawn hat?

How else to explain, for that matter, the sleeping loft with its wrought-iron bed and profusion of birdhouses—sweet pastel ones hanging from the rafters, a diaphanous pair mounted as light fixtures on the sloping roof above the bed, a scenic one holding tissues, an oversized one used as a wastebasket? Or the political posters shellacked to wood walls, proclaiming support for Teddy Kennedy, a woman's right to choose, and Hillary Rodham Clinton?

In her golden years, Celia St. Marie had blossomed. For the first time in her life she had spoken her mind, and that included standing up to Maida on the matter of Lily. What little self-confidence Lily took from childhood had come from her grandmother's ever-open arms.

Celia had been dead for six years, but Lily felt those arms around her as she sat on the stairs at the edge of the loft. It helped that she wore one of Celia's old nightgowns. It was long and soft, and incredibly, smelled faintly of the jasmine bath oil that Celia used.

Lily wondered what her grandmother would think of the goings-on in Boston. She wondered what those goings-on would be today. There was neither a television nor a radio here, not because Celia couldn't afford it but because she had made a deliberate choice to listen to loons rather than white noise. And in winter, when the loons were gone? She listened to records, old LPs, right to her dying day.

Lily had much of the same music on compact discs. They were outside, locked in her borrowed car along with her CD player and her clothes. She would get them later. There was no rush. She was in hiding. She didn't have much else to do.

It was nine in the morning. Pale dapples of sunshine broke through the trees and spilled through the window onto the floor, a braided rug, an arm of the sofa. It was a warm, familiar sight, remembered from a childhood of overnights spent here—waking up early, legs swinging over the loft, singing softly, then a little louder, then louder still until her grandmother woke up. Lily clung to the memory as long as she could, until thoughts of Boston broke through again and brought a chill.

Barefoot, she went down the stairs, wrapped herself in the crocheted shawl draped on the sofa, and stood where a beam of sun hit the floor. The warmth of it satisfied briefly before fading. Fall was here. Once she unpacked the car, she would bring wood in from the shed.

Outside, a loon called from the lake. Pleased at the familiar sound, Lily opened the door to a world that glowed. With the morning sun behind her, the lake reflected the deep blue of the western sky. Those trees whose outer leaves had already turned color burned a fiery red and gold, all the more electric among evergreens of every deep, dark shade. She caught the scent of balsam, pine, the drying leaves of maple, aspen, and birch. The morning was peaceful and still, a far cry from the city in so many, many ways.

The loon called again, but she couldn't see it. Risking even colder feet, she darted between mossy rocks, across the pine-strewn ground, down the steps to the shore. She would have gone out to sit on the dock, but she didn't want Lake Henry to know she had come. So she tucked herself into one of the small cubbies of exposed pine roots that were characteristic of Thissen Cove, and watched and waited from there.

The lake was serene. From the woods behind her came the trill of a warbler, from the lake the whisper of water on rocks. When the loon called again, she focused in on Elbow Island, waited until her eyes adjusted, sorted through the water's reflection of trees at the island's edge until she saw it. Them, actually. Two birds were there, easily identified by their pointed beaks and the graceful sweep of their heads and necks. She wondered if there were others—perhaps the summer's brood—but she couldn't see clearly enough. Energized, she left her shelter, ran back to the house for Celia's binoculars, and returned. She was at the top of the railroad-tie steps before she saw the small motorboat that had glided to the dock.

She froze. The man in the boat wore dark glasses, but there was no question that he was looking at her. That windblown head of brown hair, a jaw so square that a close-cropped beard couldn't hide its shape, an alertness so like that of the vultures she'd left behind— she knew who he was, oh, did she ever. She also knew that he knew *her,* which made scurrying back out of sight pointless.

Appalled, heartsick, *furious* to have been found out so soon, and by a man she had reason to hate on two counts, she raced back to the house, pulled a kitchen chair to the front door, and snatched Celia's gun from the hooks above it. She reopened the door and stormed back out. By then John Kipling was halfway across the lawn. The dark glasses were gone, but he was still imposing. Large and lean, he walked like a man in command.

She had always avoided him when she was home, but she knew where he had been and what he had done before returning to Lake Henry. Poppy had told her.

"That's far enough," she shouted from the porch in a voice that shook with fury. She might have been powerless in Boston, but she wasn't in Boston anymore. "This is my land. You're trespassing."

He stopped walking. With measured movements he set a large brown paper bag on the ground not ten feet from the porch. When he straightened, he held out his hands. Slowly, not quite leisurely, he lowered them, turned, and started back toward the boat.

He was barefoot, and wore a gray sweatshirt and denim cutoffs. In other circumstances she might have admired his legs, but today she hardly noticed.

"Stop!" she ordered. She didn't want him there, but since he was, she wanted to know why. He was up to something. Newspapermen always were, as she had recently learned. "What's in the bag?"

He stopped and slowly turned, his expression wary. "Fresh stuff—eggs, milk, veggies, fruit."

"Why?"

"Because you have nothing inside but canned goods."

"How do you know that?"

"The woman who keeps up this place is my assistant's aunt."

"And you asked her? And she *told?*" Another betrayal, another fear. But this was Lake Henry. She couldn't really expect it to be any different. "Who else diii-id she tell?"

"Only me," he said more gently, "and only because I asked. I was trying to think where I'd go if I were in your shoes. I figured you'd have to come here."

She looked for smugness, but if it was there, it was hidden by his beard. "How did you know that I had?"

"Your lights were on at one in the morning. Hard to miss, with everyone else's lights off."

"But you can't see this place from the road."

"No. I live on the lake."

Poppy had told her that, too, but even without Poppy, she would have known. A Kipling on the lake, down from the Ridge, had been the talk of the town. "Where on the lake?"

There was nothing evasive about his eyes. Still, he hesitated as though he was considering another answer. Finally he said, "Wheaton Point."

Well, at least he hadn't lied about that. He might have tried, but he probably figured she knew the truth. "You can't see Thissen Cove from there," she said, not about to let him play her for a fool. "So you were out on the lake. At one in the morning?"

"I couldn't sleep."

"And now you come bearing gifts." She felt sick. Her hideout had been breached, and by the worst of enemies. "What do you want?"

"Put the gun down and we'll talk."

She lowered the muzzle but kept it at the ready. "What do you want?" she repeated.

He slipped his hands in his back pockets. "To help."

She barked out a disbelieving laugh. "You? You're media. On top of *that*, you're Dd-donny's big brother."

"Yeah, well, that wasn't my choice," he said. "I was gone when all that happened between you and him."

"And if you'd been here? You'd have stood up for your brother, just like your dad did, just like your aunts and uncles and cousins did."

"He was a troubled kid. They were trying to help him. He already had a rap sheet. He'd have gotten twice as much time if he hadn't said you'd egged him on. That was the story he gave my dad, aunts, uncles, and cousins. They believed him. They thought it was the truth."

"It wasn't."

He inhaled deeply and stood straighter. "I know that. He told me. I saw him in the hospital the day before he died."

Donny Kipling had done time for his alleged theft with Lily, and time for breaking and entering two years later. Two years after that, he crashed his car during a high-speed police chase. He died at the hospital a week later, at the age of twenty-eight. That was ten years ago. Lily had been in New York then, working on her graduate degree. When Poppy told her, she had been saddened, not because she harbored feelings for Donny but because the humiliation of her experience with him suddenly seemed all the more wasteful.

"I'm sorry," she said now, in part because Donny had been John's brother, but also because John had admitted the truth to her, which she hadn't expected.

But John seemed lost in thought. "He was a disaster waiting to happen. I don't know what went wrong. He was fine—perfect up to the age of ten. I was the bad one. So I was sent away, and Donny stayed and took my place." His eyes met hers. "For what it's worth, my father hasn't been the same since Donny died. He's a tormented man. Hate him if you want, but he's getting punished good."

I'm glad, Lily wanted to say. Only, she'd had a glimpse of Gus Kipling in town several years back. He had looked broken and old, yes, like he was suffering. She would have had to have the hardest heart to wish him even worse.

John was something else.

She glanced at the food. "Then this is for guilt?"

He made a sputtering sound, more a sigh than a laugh. "That's direct."

"I don't have time to play around. I came here to hide. You've found me out. Now I have to leave."

Immediately, he sobered. "You *do not.* I'm not telling anyone you're here."

Lily rolled her eyes.

"Why would I?" he asked.

"You're media. Media's job is to air the news. This is news."

"It's between you and me."

"You, me, and who else? The *Post? Cityside?* Or are you hoping to get a foot in the door again through something bigger, like a national wire service? Write one article, get it into dozens of papers."

John stood his ground and shook his head.

"There won't be an article in Thursday's *Lake News*?" she asked.

"No."

She didn't believe him for a minute and told him as much with a stare. Holding the stare, she drew the shawl in tighter. The shotgun remained in the crook of her arm.

"Good God," he said, exhaling loudly. "You're hard."

Dropping her guard for a minute, she cried, "Do you know what I've *been* through in the past week?"

"Yes. Yes, I do." His eyes were dark and troubled. "I've been there, Lily. I've seen what journalists do." There was a pause. "I've done it myself."

"So I heard."

"Good." Those eyes held sudden challenge. "Then let's put it all on the table. What you probably know— what Poppy probably told you, or Maida, or anyone else in town—is that I ruined a family. I did a story on a Connecticut politician who entered the presidential primary and failed to reveal that he'd once been involved with a prominent married woman. The affair had ended years before, when he got married himself, but there was the stink of adultery and the lure of lascivious details that were sure to sell papers. The man had enemies, and I loved talking with them. So the story broke, and thanks to a goody-two-shoes hypocrisy, the party withdrew its support. His political career ended, right along with his marriage and his relationship with his kids. They wanted to distance themselves from him. The public humiliation was too painful." He paused. A tic pulsed under his eye. "Did I get it all?"

"You missed the part about his little blond aide," she prompted.

"Didn't miss it. Repressed it. Turns out it wasn't true. There was no affair with a little blond aide, but that fact only came out later. By then, the wife and kids had bought into the story hook, line, and sinker."

"You left out the part about the guy's suicide," she added, intent on not sparing him a thing.

The tic pulsed again. "Yeah, well, that's what I'm living with now. If you think that suicide didn't affect my life, think again. It's haunted me since the day it happened. Afterward, when I went back to work, I was crippled. Couldn't do the hard stuff the paper wanted, because I was paralyzed by 'what if's' and 'then what's.' So I left. Let me tell you, I think about that suicide, think about it a lot. It's the single greatest influence in the work I do now." He pursed his lips, then let them go. His eyes held hers. "I do know what you went through, Lily. More than anyone else in town, I know."

She stared at him for a moment, wanting to believe him. Again she let her guard fall. "I didn't want to come back here. If I'd had anywhere else to go, I would have."

"I figured that. But people will find out you're here without my saying a word. They'll see a light, like I did. Or see smoke coming from the chimney. Or see you on the porch or down by the water."

"Or see you buying groceries and bringing them here," she charged. Even as she said it, she was startled by the way her mind had begun to work. The most innocent of acts was suddenly suspect.

But he was shaking his head. "I'm at Charlie's all the time buying stuff like this for my dad. Charlie didn't think twice when I bought these things this morning. So you don't have to worry about me. But Lake Henry is Lake Henry. You won't stay a secret for long."

"That's fine," she announced with a show of bravado. "I won't be *staying* for long. Once the story dies, I'm going back to Boston."

He gave her a doubting look, his brow arched subtly.

"Or somewhere else," she said, though Boston remained the goal. It wasn't fair that she should be banished for good. It wasn't *believable*. Besides, she couldn't see herself spending the rest of her life in Lake Henry. Celia was dead, Poppy was her only sure champion, and even aside from the long-ago business with Donny, there were too many heartaches for her here.

But if not here, where? she wondered, suddenly frightened. "Oh God," she murmured, beginning to feel overwhelmed by the predicament again.

Correctly reading the emotions in her face, John said, "I have today's *Post* in the boat. It isn't as bad as it's been."

Lily didn't want to know. But she couldn't afford not to. "What does it say?"

"That you're holed up in your apartment," he remarked, definitely smug this time. "Then the story shifts to Maxwell Funder. He's quoted ad nauseam on First Amendment rights, the difference between a public person and a private person, the nature of libel cases. There are quotes from other lawyers, so-called experts. Speculation on possible legal action that you may bring. Did you retain Funder?"

She shook her head.

He scratched an eyebrow. "He implies you did. Doesn't say it directly. Just leaves it wide open. Maybe you should."

"I can't afford him. Besides, me against the *Post*?"

"How about you against Terry Sullivan?"

Lily stilled. She hadn't mentioned that name to John Kipling.

"You need to know one other thing about me," he said, all teasing gone now. "I know Terry Sullivan. We went to college together, then worked together at the *Post*. He saw me as his competition and screwed me good."

"How?"

"The little blond aide? She was Terry's connection. At the time, I was surprised when he gave me her name instead of using it himself, but he said that it was my story and that he respected that. I'm not saying that he put her up to it, but he knew all along that she lied. That means he deliberately set me up. Don't get me wrong. I'm not blaming him for the damage I caused.

The blonde was only one piece of the pie. If I'd been less eager and checked her out better, I wouldn't have printed her story. No, all I'm saying is that I hold a grudge against Terry Sullivan. So we share that, you and me." He turned to leave.

"I don't hold a grudge," Lily told him, meaning every word. "It's worse than that. If this gun had been loaded and you'd been him, I'd have shot you on sight."

With his back to her, John hung his head. When he turned, she saw a crooked smile—and for a second, just a second, she felt a connection.

Then he turned again and walked off. He was at the steps to the beach when he yelled back, "I have ammo! Call if you want it!"

John started up the motor and glided away, but the emotions churning inside him belied the lazy pace. Three years ago, returning to Lake Henry, he'd had a plan. Turning out *Lake News* each week would pay the bills while he moonlighted writing a book that would bring him fame, money, and the justification for having left Boston—and he had tried. He had written the beginnings of a *dozen* books. Only, none interested him enough to keep on.

This one would. It had the potential to be big. The more he thought about it, the bigger it got. Lily's situation was the microcosm of a large and increasingly frightening phenomenon. The media was out of control. Individual rights—in her case, the right to privacy—were being trampled. Admittedly guilty of doing trampling in his day, John knew the media mind. That made him the perfect one to write this book. The subject matter went to the heart of what worried, angered, jaded so very many people.

There was Lily's story.

And there was Terry's story. Terry was a good writer. He was actually a *great* writer—a master with words—and he knew it. He was arrogant and he was ambitious. But ambition alone couldn't explain the kind of meanness that ruined innocent people. John had known enough reporters to separate those who were conscientious from those who were driven. The driven often had cause that went beyond the professional.

John was a perfect example. His driving force was a need to stand out that went back to childhood. When he was young, it had manifested itself in petty misdeeds in school and minor run-ins with the law. When he left Lake Henry, his drive took the more positive path of competitiveness in sports, in school, in work. The last culminated in the debacle at the *Post,* however, after which his need to make a name for himself had been muted.

With the prospect of writing this book, the drive was back. Yes, he wanted to make a name for himself. What journalist didn't? But he had a conscience now. At least, he assumed conscience was behind the restraint he felt when he pictured Lily Blake standing there on her porch, in her long ivory gown and her grandmother's shawl. He *did* understand what she felt. If he could help her exact revenge at the same time that he redeemed himself—both as a writer and a human being—what could be better?

John had taken care on his approach to Celia's cottage, meandering along the shore in a show of looking for loons, and he returned the same way, with the kind of nonchalant motoring that lakefront residents knew him for. He moseyed along until he was four properties down the shoreline, then he headed for the middle of the lake, picking up speed.

Ten minutes later he guided the boat back to shore and tied it up beside his canoe, at the ratty patch of wood he called his dock. One day he would tear it down and put out a handsome planked dock. At the end would be a big square with a canopy roof to provide shade for a desk, a chair, and a typewriter. He would write there while the sun streamed in over the water and loons floated nearby. If it rained, he would unroll an isinglass window or two.

It was a Hemingway image, he thought, not entirely unfitting for a guy reputed to be a distant cousin of Rudyard Kipling.

Securing the boat, he removed a second bag of groceries, put it in his truck, slid in behind the wheel, and set off. The air was brisk but he kept his windows down. It was another stellar fall day, another day to appreciate the brilliance of foliage whose height of color was yet a week or two away. He passed private roads that led to Mully Point and Seizer Bay, then, farther on, to Gemini Beach and Lemon Cove. Thissen Cove came next. He was acutely aware of passing the narrow drive that led there, and for the briefest instant wondered if Lily would flee.

He had taken a calculated risk in going to see her. But if the look on her face meant anything, he had figured correctly. She had nowhere else to go, and she knew it.

Satisfied, he drove on around the lake. Lake Henry center was buzzing. If people weren't fetching mail at the post office, they were buying supplies at Charlie's or pulling in at the end of the parking area behind it. There sat the police station, the church, and the library, left to right. All three were of white wood with black shutters. Each played multiple roles. The police station was a long, single-storied frame structure that also housed the town clerk, the town registrar, and social services. The library, a square Federal, rented out its generous third floor to the Lake Henry Commission. The Historical Society worked out of the basement of the church, which stood tall, venerable, and proud.

Today the Historical Society was having a plant and shrub sale, which meant that there were many cars and trucks backed up to the church, and they would not be quick to leave. Plant and shrub sales in Lake Henry—like bake sales, or art sales, or garage sales—were for socializing as much as anything else. There were as many people standing outside their vehicles, chatting in clusters, waving to friends, as there were buying plants and shrubs.

John scanned the cars and trucks, picking out an unfamiliar one or two. Tourists passing through? he wondered. The media in disguise? He skimmed the crowd for cameras but didn't see a one. Not today. Not yet.

Relieved, he drove on out of the center of town to the fork where Ridge Road broke off from the main. Symbolic, it was, that break. The road was different from there on. The same frost heaves had cracked it as had cracked the rest of the town's roads, yet these cracks seemed deeper, the resulting bumps larger. The ground was no drier here than in lower Lake Henry, but his tires kicked up dirt that put a tired look on everything in sight. Maples here were more burnt than orange, birches more jaundiced than yellow. Even the hemlock boughs sagged, as though they had too much weight to bear.

The lake might smell of autumn, the town center might smell of whatever was hot on Charlie's grill, but the Ridge inevitably smelled bad. If it wasn't a plumbing problem, it was a trash problem or a fire problem. Something was always burning out—a fan belt, a fuse, an insignificant little motor that stunk up the place—and the smell lingered, because the air didn't circulate well here. With the lake on one side and the hill on another, odors just sat.

The Ridge was actually a long, broad ledge etched into the hills several hundred feet above the lake. A road marked the lakeside. On the hillside were rows of small, tin-roofed, three-room homes, built at the turn of the century by the owners of the mill to house their employees. Back then, it hadn't been a bad place to live. The Winslows, who owned the mill, were kind and conscientious. They had kept the homes painted and repaired, added insulation, removed debris, kept bracken cleared to make way for grass so that the children would have a safe place to play. The fourth generation of Winslows running the mill were kind and conscientious, too. In the late sixties, when freedom became a national watchword, they were one of the first businesses to give its employees a piece of the profit. As part of the plan—considered extraordinarily altruistic at the time—they sold those little homes to their occupants for a dollar apiece.

The Ridge went downhill from there. The pride that initially kept things going gradually went the way of interest and money. Increasingly, broken windows were covered with boards, broken stairs were walked around. Tin roofs rusted, paint peeled, shutters slipped, cars stopped running and lay where they fell—and none of it for lack of know-how. After automation cut employment at the mill, the small homes had been taken over by menial laborers. They were paid to keep Lake Henry running smoothly, but by the time they reached home, their energy was spent. In its place was an ugly brew of boredom, frustration, and anger at the limits of their lives. So these men who were good with their hands put them to crueler use here. The bulk of the efforts of the Lake Henry Police Department was spent responding to domestic violence on the Ridge.

There was a book in the Ridge. John knew that. Between past and present there were several books. But there wasn't one he could write. He was too close.

Cresting the rise now, he could barely see the rows of ramshackle homes, hidden among the trees like ticks on a dog. But the dog was mangy. And mean. John had barely passed the first of the people sitting on crooked porch steps when they turned to stare.

He had betrayed the Ridge by moving to the lake. No matter that one of their own had moved up in the world. No matter that he tried to help those who remained. No matter that he used the paper to lobby on their behalf. The sight of him reminded them of everything they couldn't be. Out of sight was out of mind, and the feeling was mutual. John had begged his father to live with him down on the lake, but Gus Kipling had nixed that idea with the same disdain he showed for everything John did. So John bit the bullet and visited him here twice a week, more often if there was a problem and Dulcey Hewitt called.

Dulcey lived next door to Gus. She had three young children and a hard shell. She had to have that to put up with Gus, even though John paid her to do it.

Girding himself, John pulled up at his father's home. It had been his home once too, but memory hurt. So, as with the Ridge itself, he distanced himself. As he saw it now, the house was all Gus's. Neither John nor his mother nor his brother lived here. John had gone so far as to change its looks, painting it a steel blue, adding a wraparound porch, planting the front yard with hardy shrubs that wouldn't die of Gus's neglect.

With the grocery bag in his arm, he left the truck, crossed the porch, and opened the front door. The place was a mess, but that was nothing new. Gus liked clutter. John was forever amazed that a man who had trouble walking could create so much havoc in such a short time. Dulcey was forever telling John about it, full of apology, since Gus made it look like she was never in, when, in fact, she neatened up twice a day. At least the place was clean under the clutter.

"Gus?" he called. Setting the bag down in the tiny kitchen, he checked the bedroom and the bathroom. Returning to the kitchen, he opened the back door and something inside him twisted and pulled. His father was at the very back of the tiny yard, a bent bean-pole of a white-haired creature shuffling through knee-high grass, carrying a fieldstone that medical science said he should no longer be able to lift.

"Christ," John whispered, trotting down the steps and across the yard. Loudly, he said, "What are you doing, Dad?"

Gus eased his stone down on a ragged wall of similar stones, pushed and shoved until it was turned one way, then another, finally hauled it up, and started limping back through the tall grass. When John tried to take it from him, he pulled it in close and shuffled off in another direction.

"You're supposed to be weak," John reminded him. "You're supposed to be letting your heart recover."

"Fa what?" Gus grumbled in a cracked voice. He stopped at another patch of wall and deposited the stone with the kind of thunk that would have been unthinkable in his heyday. "If I cahn't lay stone, I'd as soon be dead."

"You retired two years ago."

"*You* said that, sonny. Not me. You painted my house. You bought rugs an' a sofa. You bought a microwave. A television. A compu-tuh. I don't want none a it," he growled with the wave of a gnarled hand. "All's I want's my stone." With an effort, he turned around the one he had carried. He pushed it to the left, then the right. Then he swore and muttered, "Damned thruf-tuh don't fit."

John had watched his father enough to know how a stone wall was built. Two rows of stones determined the depth of the wall. To enhance stability, every six feet along the length, masons added a single larger stone that spanned the depth. That stone was called a thrufter.

"Useta get it right the feust time," Gus spewed under his breath. "Now cahn't do it a-tall. Not the feust time, not the tenth." He lifted a leg and kicked the wall with a booted foot. The recoil set him back on his butt on the grass.

John hurried to help him back up, but it was a slow process, as physically painful for Gus as it was emotionally painful for John. He remembered a hardy man, a tireless one who worked from sunup to sundown, picking just the right piece of stone for a particular part of a wall, positioning it, moving it to a better spot, finding the best possible arrangement with the rest both for fit and for looks. Gus Kipling's stonework was more artistic than stonework had a right to be.

Now he was a grizzled old man, wrinkled from sun, snow, and scowls, scarred from years of physical work. He had been handsome once, but his face had settled crookedly with age, leaving one eye higher and more open than the other. Most people backed away from the orneriness of it. John thought it made him look sadder.

It was a minute before Gus was steady on his feet, another before he yanked his elbow free of John's grasp.

John went to the stone that wasn't right. "Tell me where you want it."

"You cahn't do it!" Gus bellowed. "It's *my* job."

John backed off while Gus fussed over the stone, but the nudges he gave it were weaker now, his head and shoulders more bent. He was clearly unhappy, not with one rock alone, but with life as a whole. His doctor called it borderline depression and said it was common among the elderly, but that didn't make it any easier for John to watch. Gus had been this way for a while.

"How about a beer?" he asked after a while of watching Gus's back. The old man was facing the wall and didn't look to be doing much of anything but stewing.

He grunted. "One a day's all I get. If I have it now, what's fa latuh?"

"You can have two today," John decided. He took off for the house and returned with two long-necks from the fridge. He handed one to Gus and sat nearby on the wall.

Gus stood in the tall grass. His feet were planted wide, minimizing his sway when he tipped back his

head and took a long guzzle. He hitched the bottom
of the bottle toward the wall. "You can walk on that,
y'know."

"I know."

"Cahn't walk on everyone's wall. Some'd fall
apaht."

"Yup."

"Too bad you nevuh could get the hang a this
kinda weuk."

John could never get the hang of it because Gus
would never show him. He was either too involved,
too impatient, or too rushed. So John had watched
from a distance, and even then had picked up a lot. He
knew which stones came from where by their color,
knew that the best stones had flat areas and angles,
knew that the laying surface was as important to stability as the showing surface was to looks, knew not to
ever, ever split a stone.

"This is aht," Gus announced. "What you do with
that papuh ain't aht."

John let the dig go. "Did Donny ever work with
you?" he asked. The doctor had suggested getting the
old man to talk, and the issue of Donny needed airing.

Gus made a noncommittal sound and took another swig of his beer.

"He said he would have liked to go into the business with you."

"He was dyin'. What else's he gonna say?"

"He could've said he hated your guts. Instead, he
said he wanted to work with you. I'd call that a compliment."

Gus shot him a cockeyed look. "What uh you up to?"

"Nothing."

"You nevuh done anythin' in life for nothin'."

"That's not true."

"Always aftuh somethin'. Always wantin' to be big-guh 'n' bettuh."

John looked off to the side. They'd been through this before, he and Gus. It went nowhere, at least no-where John wanted to be. Quietly, he said, "I think about Donny a lot. That's all."

"What's the point? He's dead."

"Yeah, well, I'm sorry about that."

"I find that hahd to b'lieve."

"Because I bullied him? Well, I'm sorry for that, too."

Gus grunted. That, and the cry of a baby several houses over, were the only sounds of life. Birds didn't sing here. They seemed to sense they'd be shot long before they'd be given a crust of stale bread.

"Have you been following the Lily Blake thing?" John asked.

Gus made a sputtering sound, meant to be a de-nial, but John wasn't buying. For a man who claimed not to watch television, Gus occasionally betrayed himself with a comment that was a little too knowing.

"Do you remember her when she was little?" John asked.

"Wouldn't tell *you* if I did."

"Why not?"

"Don't know what you'd do with it."

John was good for the first dig or two. More than

that and he bristled. "Do you always have to be so negative? Maybe I want to help her. Did that ever occur to you?"

"Nah."

"In the three years I've been back here, have I used anyone? Abused anyone?"

"The leopud don't change his spots."

"Give me a *break*."

"You'uh waitin'."

"Jeez, you don't give an inch." John looked away. Seconds later he set his bottle down on a top stone and pushed off from the wall. "Someday," he said, holding his temper, "someday it would be really nice to have a civilized conversation with you."

He strode off before Gus could hand him either another jibe or more silence, and kept going until he was back at his truck. His jaw stayed tight until he had left the Ridge behind, until fresher air blew in through the windows and anger gave way to sadness.

Gus was eighty-one. Standing out in that grass, none too sure on his feet, with his white hair jutting out, his body bent and frail under a too-big plaid shirt, and a heartful of angst in his eyes, he looked positively ancient.

John didn't want to have to remember him that way. He wanted to see different things in those eyes and hear different words from that mouth. But he didn't know how to make it happen.

Chapter 7

Poppy Blake's home, like Lily's cottage, was small, surrounded by trees, and on its own little patch of the lake, but that was where the similarities ended. Poppy's land was on the west shore rather than the east, a wedge shaved off the end of her parents' property and given as a gift to her after the accident, in the hopes of keeping her close to home. Poppy had acceded to that, but she refused to allow the direct road that Maida and George would have cut through the property from their house to hers. So the only access was off the main road, on a road that was narrow but paved.

The cottage itself comprised three connected wings on a single level. The left wing housed the bedroom, the right housed the kitchen and a weight room, but Poppy spent most of her time in the center wing. It held an arc of desks facing windows on the lake. On one end was a computer, on the other an open writing space. In the middle, with a picture-perfect view of the dock, the lake, and the fall foliage, were the multiple banks of buttons connected to the telephone that was Poppy's stock in trade.

"Boudreau residence," she said into her headset in response to a blinking light.

"Poppy, it's Vivie." Vivian Abbott, the town clerk. "Where *are* the Boudreaus?"

"On their way to see you," Poppy told her. "Not there yet?"

"No, and I'm leaving in two minutes. If they don't get here before then, they'll have to register to vote next Saturday. Nine to eleven, that's what I told them. Oh, wait! Here they are! Thanks, Poppy!" As fast as that she was gone, and another light began to blink.

"Historical Society," Poppy said.

"Edgar Cook here. My Peggy wants to know how late the sale's running."

"Till four."

"Hah. That's what I told her, only she didn't believe me. Thanks, Poppy."

"You're welcome." Another light blinked, this one on the main telephone unit, her own private line. "Hello?" she said, still smiling at Edgar.

"Is this Poppy Blake?"

Her smile faded. She recognized the voice. "That depends."

Terry Sullivan made a sound that might have been a chuckle if it hadn't been so tight. "I recognize your voice by now, too, love. Is your sister around?" he asked nonchalantly. Like Lily was right there—which she wasn't. Like Poppy would put her on if she was—which she wouldn't. Like Poppy even *knew* where she was—which she didn't, at least not for sure.

"Is she?" Poppy asked right back.

"I asked first."

"But you're the smart one. Far's *I* know, she's in Boston." The words were barely out when she knew better—because, physical resemblance notwithstanding, there was no way that the slight figure who had suddenly appeared on her deck, dressed in a baseball cap, an old plaid hunting jacket, baggy shorts, and high-top sneakers, was the very dead Celia St. Marie.

Poppy sat higher and vigorously waved Lily inside.

"She tried to leave last night," Terry said. "Didn't make it. Or let us think that. I'm just trying to imagine what I'd do if I were in her shoes."

When Lily didn't move, Poppy waved with both arms and jabbed a finger in the direction of the deck door. Into the speaker at her mouth, she said, "And you imagined she'd come here? Why would she do that?"

"By default."

"What default?" She put a finger to her lips. Lily very quietly opened the door.

"Where else would she go?"

"Manhattan? Albany? *I* don't know," Poppy said, but her bewilderment ended at her voice. Grinning, she held out an arm to Lily and gave her a tight hug.

"Would you tell me if she was there?" Terry asked.

"I wouldn't have to." She mouthed his name to Lily, whose eyes registered instant horror. To Terry, she said, "You'd hear it in my voice. We're not good liars up here. It goes against the grain."

"I'm watching her friends in Manhattan. NYU, Juilliard—I have lists. She's not there."

"Did you check her theater friends? She was on Broadway with people from all over the country. If I was in her shoes," she echoed his words, "I'd be with one of them."

"Is that a lead?"

"No. I don't have names."

"Would you give them to me if you did?"

"No."

"Would you let me know if she shows up there?"

"No."

That hard little chuckle came again. "That's my girl."

"Not—on—your—life," Poppy vowed, and with the sweep of a finger disconnected the call. The other arm still held Lily. She grinned broadly. "I had a hunch," she said, hugging Lily with both arms again, but she didn't like what she felt. Poppy had always thought of Lily as vulnerable, even fragile, though she realized she never saw her at the best of times—Lily was understandably tense whenever she returned to Lake Henry. But the fragility was tactile now. Lily was thinner than Poppy remembered, and shaky. Holding her back, Poppy saw smudges under her eyes that hadn't been there when they had seen each other last, at Easter, five months before.

"You don't look so good," Poppy said. "Beautiful"—which was the truth—"but tired."

Lily's eyes filled with tears.

Poppy pulled her close again and held her longer this time, thinking that "beautiful" was an understatement. On paper, Poppy and Lily looked very much alike—same dark hair, same oval face, same slender build—but Poppy was the best buddy, Lily the siren. Maybe it was the breasts that did it. Lily was more endowed there, but she was also quieter, more dignified, more mysterious. People knew where they stood with Poppy. With Lily they were never quite sure. That element of mystery added to her allure.

Poppy had spent a childhood following Lily around, suffering when Lily stuttered, taking pride when she sang. She hadn't always agreed with what Lily had done—going with Donny Kipling had been just plain dumb—but she knew for a fact that Lily didn't have a mean bone in her body. She hadn't asked for a stutter, or for the impossible standards that Maida set for her firstborn. There was something inherently unfair about Lily's lot in life, and the unfairness kept right on going.

Lily seemed to underscore that thought with an uneven intake of breath. The stricken look she gave Poppy when she drew back added to it.

"How'd you get away?" Poppy asked.

"A friend, a borrowed car. Does Terry think I'm here?"

"Not yet."

"They'll come," Lily said, looking haunted. "Sooner or later."

"Sooner," Poppy said. She hated to make things

worse, but Lily needed to know. "Camera crews have already come through. A few reporters."

Lily sank into a chair. "Asking questions?"

"Trying to. No one's talking."

"They will. Sooner or later. Someone'll offer money. Someone'll take it." She clasped her hands, clamped them between her thighs, and rocked back and forth. "John Kipling saw my lights last night. He pulled up at the dock this morning. He says he won't tell anyone. Can I believe him?"

Poppy liked John. She knew about the trouble-maker he'd been growing up and about the ruthless journalist he'd been in Boston, but she hadn't known him personally until he returned to Lake Henry. In those three years, she had seen nothing but decency in the man.

"I'd believe him, if it were me. Besides, what's your choice?"

"I don't have one. They'll follow me wherever I go. At least here I have a place to stay. What do I do about Stella? She'll be over to check the cottage next week."

"I'll handle Stella."

"The cottage is a haven. I can feel Celia there."

Poppy nodded. She glanced at the cap, the jacket, the sneakers, all so very Celia.

Lily looked down at herself. "I didn't bring much. Didn't know how long I'd be here." She raised bleak eyes. "John told me about today's paper. They're still at it, Poppy. They're not stopping at anything. I feel powerless. It's like I have no rights."

"You *do*. That's what we have courts for. You need to talk with a lawyer."

"Obviously, *you* haven't seen today's paper. I *did* talk with a lawyer."

"And? Doesn't he agree that you have a case for libel?"

"Yes, but the problem is the process. It'll drag the whole thing out. It'll get worse before it gets better, and it'll cost a fortune." Lily's expression turned wry. "He told me to borrow money from Mom."

Poppy might have shared the wryness, if she hadn't been flooded with guilt. Maida had given *her* so much—land, the house, a van equipped with everything she needed to get in and out and drive herself around—and she was always sending over clothes, flowers, and more food than Poppy could eat.

Poppy's problems were physical. Maida could deal with physical things. Emotions were something else.

Lily pulled off the cap and shook out her hair. She frowned at the bill of the cap. "Is she ss-still angry?"

Poppy's heart broke at the stutter. It came out now only at times of stress, but she remembered when it was virtually a constant thing, with facial contortions that were painful to watch. She couldn't begin to imagine the pain Lily had felt as the one actually doing it in front of friends, schoolmates, *boys*. Poppy knew what it was to have people stare, but she was an adult. Lily had been a child, not only stared at but mocked.

Maida might have helped, but she had always seemed paralyzed where Lily was concerned. And Lily? God bless her, she came home for holidays and special events, always hoping it would change. Poppy wasn't sure that it would. Maida was a difficult woman, and not only toward Lily. She was hard on the orchard crew, hard on the cider crew. She had even grown hard on Rose. Had Poppy had the use of her legs, and the height and physical stature to confront Maida, she would have shaken a little common sense into the woman.

"I haven't talked with her since yesterday," she said now. "Be grateful it's harvest time. She's preoccupied with work. Are you going over there?"

Lily looked at the lake. "I haven't decided. Think I should?"

"Only if you're a glutton for punishment."

Lily's eyes found hers, beseeching now. "Maybe if I explain it to her—tell her my side of the story."

Poppy wished it was that simple. Maida was a complex woman, layers and layers of emotions fifty-seven years in the building.

"But what if she hears it from someone else? She'll be hurt."

"I won't tell," Poppy promised.

"But John said people would find out—see lights or wood smoke—and he's right." She glanced at the bank of telephone buttons. "Tell me they're not all talking about me."

"I can't. It's news. But don't assume that they're critical of you. They're refusing to talk with the press."

"John is press. They're talking with him." She let out a breath, looking close to tears again. "I thought I could come here and be invisible for a while. Until I see what happens in Boston. Until I decide what to do. But now he knows I'm here."

"If he said he won't tell, he won't," Poppy assured her.

"Why not? What's in it for him?"

"Self-respect."

"He brought groceries."

"A peace offering?"

"Or a Trojan horse."

That gave Poppy pause. "You never used to be cynical."

Lily pushed a hand through her hair. "Funny how fast things change."

Poppy wanted to hug her sister again, but Lily seemed isolated, separate. The best Poppy could do was to say, "Lily, you can't leave. This is the safest place there is for you right now."

"Maybe. I'll stay near the cottage, I guess. See how things play out."

"Stay here," Poppy suggested, loving the idea, but Lily sighed and shook her head.

"No. The cottage is mine. Everything else has been taken away. I need that."

"Is there *anything* I can do?"

Lily's expression was suddenly pointed. "More of what you did just now when Terry called. Let him try to locate all the people who were in shows I was in. I don't even remember their names."

"Do you want me to call Mom?"

"No."

When a light on the bank of phones blinked, Poppy adjusted her mouthpiece. "Lake Henry Police Department. This call is being recorded."

"This is Harvey Ellman. I'm researching an article for *Newsweek* and need information on Lily Blake's criminal record. Can you fax me a rap sheet?"

Poppy held her sister's eyes. "Lily Blake has no criminal record."

"There was a conviction for grand theft."

"No. No conviction. The case was continued, then dropped."

"That wasn't what I was told."

"You were told wrong."

"Who are *you?*" the man asked impatiently.

"I'm the dispatch officer, and I know what I'm talking about. You're not the first one calling about this."

"I'd like to talk with the police chief."

"Sorry. It's me or no one. For the record, again, you are Harvey Gellman—"

"Ellman."

Poppy spelled it out. "With *Newsweek*. Good. I'll tell the chief why you called." She grinned at Lily. "We have a recording of this conversation, but I'll keep your name handy so we'll know who to blame if the facts in your article are wrong. You see, Lily Blake is well liked in this town. If you print lies, we'll have to call you on it. And we have a forum to do it, what with other press people calling. I mean, we have to protect our own tails here, don't we?"

*   *   *

Lily left Poppy's feeling marginally better. Poppy was a powerful ally. She answered phones for the most influential residents of Lake Henry, which put her in a position to lobby on Lily's behalf. She also had insisted that Lily take her cellular phone, since there was no active line in Celia's place.

Wearing the baseball cap and sunglasses again, Lily drove the borrowed wagon back to Celia's the same way she had come—around the opposite end of the lake from the center of town. Lake Henry noticed strangers. Granted, there were other cars with Massachusetts plates passing through—leaf peepers looking for foliage, newspaper people looking for dirt—but she suspected that people in town were starting to wonder if she would return. The less she tempted them with a familiar nose and chin, the better.

She held her breath when she turned onto the road to Thissen Cove, half expecting to find a strange car parked at the cottage. With a hand on the phone she prepared to call Poppy, who would call Willie Jake, the police chief, who would race around the lake in his all-terrain vehicle and arrest the intruder for trespassing. But trespassing was a minor offense, which meant that the offender would be free within hours and on the phone announcing Lily's whereabouts to all, which would bring a swarm of press people to Lake Henry, which was the last thing Lily wanted.

Of course, John Kipling might already have made those calls.

But there were no cars by the cottage. She looked around carefully. She even turned the car and parked it heading out, all the better for a speedy getaway. Then she climbed out and, watchful of the surrounding woods now, ran to the door.

There was no one around. She went from window to window, peering out, then made the rounds again, this time opening each window to allow for the mild midday air to enter. When she was certain that no one lurked on land, she opened the door to the lake. There was one boat in sight—a classic thing that looked like one from Marlon Dewey's prized collection—but it was distant and growing more so by the minute. No threat there. And no sign of John Kipling.

Everything in sight was crystal clear and serene. Breathing it in, she let herself relax, and once she'd done that, exhaustion hit.

Within minutes she was asleep on the big iron bed.

Chapter 8

While Lily slept, John was busy, as much for his own peace of mind as for anything else. He never felt good when he left Gus. There was always frustration, always remorse, always guilt. It was worse than usual today, because Gus was clearly declining, and John knew he shouldn't have walked off that way. But along with all else he felt for his father, there was anger. Gus had kept him at arm's length throughout his childhood, then had sent him away. Sure, John might well have ended up like his brother if he'd stayed. Still, the hurt from that early banishment stung—not that there was anything John could do about it now. It was ancient history. But keeping busy kept his mind off the ongoing ache.

Intent on picking up gossip for *Lake News,* he returned from the Ridge through the center of town, pulled in at the plant and shrub sale, and mingled with the townsfolk. There was talk about the play that the

Lake Henry Players had chosen for their winter drama, talk about the sale of two poems that the town librarian had made to *Yankee* magazine, and from the same librarian, talk of the litter of six kittens that the library's cat had just given birth to behind the biography shelves. Approaching a large wood cart filled with pumpkins, John caught talk of the season's bumper crop, but he had little time to make notes on that or any of the rest before people turned the questions on him.

"Paper says she's hiring that lawyer," remarked Alf Buzzell. He was the director of that winter drama, a sixty-year resident of Lake Henry and treasurer of the Historical Society. "Think there'll be a big TV trial?"

"Beats me," John said.

"Don't know's I'd like that," the man remarked, leaving John to wonder whether it was the focus on the town that he would mind or its competition with the Lake Henry Players.

"How'd they find out about the stutter?" asked the librarian. Leila Higgins was in her thirties. She had been a year ahead of Lily in school, a bookworm even back then. Though married now, she made no secret of having been a teenage wallflower. When she talked about those years, there was a bruised look in her eyes, just as there was as she asked about Lily.

"They must have seen medical records," John answered.

"But how? Who would have let the public see those?"

John didn't know for sure. He planned to look

into it. "There was probably mention of the stutter in the court file."

"But who would have let the public see *those?*" Leila insisted. It was another thing John planned to look into.

From the owner of the pumpkin cart came, "I keep wondering if she'll come here." Like the others, he felt no need to qualify the "she." There was only one "she" the townsfolk were talking about. John didn't pretend not to follow.

But since there wasn't a question, there was no need of an answer. Grateful to be spared evasiveness, John ran his hand over a rounded pumpkin. "This is a beauty," he said, taking an appreciative breath. Between the smells of sweet junipers, rich loam, and ripe pumpkin, fall was definitely in the air. It was worth lingering over, and he would do that, but not just now. Tucking his notebook into the breast pocket of his flannel shirt, he crossed the parking lot to the general store, because he knew that Charlie would be breaking for lunch.

Charlie Owens was a contemporary of his. He had grown up in a well-heeled lake family but had been John's friend through school, which was to say that Charlie had been a bad boy, too. Their favorite place had been No Man's Island, smack in the center of the lake. At twelve they had paddled there to smoke pot; at thirteen they had gotten drunk there; at fourteen they had lost their virginity there, one right after the other, to a very willing, very buxom girl two years older.

Charlie had returned to the fold straight from college, thanks to the dual incentive of a stagnant family business and the love of a woman with the ideas, energy, and style to revive it. He served as the front man at the general store, the one who knew how to communicate with Lake Henryites, but Annette was the one responsible for bringing the store toward the new millennium. She overhauled the grocery department, introducing a deli and a bakery, updated the home supplies department, and established a crafts department that brought browsers. She also was the brains behind the café, a bright, glass-enclosed room at the far end of the store.

John headed there now. When he crossed in front of the kitchen pass-through, he ducked his head and winked at Annette, who was back there ladling up something that smelled like a wonderfully fresh fish chowder. In the café, he slid into his favorite window booth, a spot that looked out at a stand of white birches. With the sun noon high, the curling bark was whiter and the fall leaves more yellow than ever.

He wasn't there for long before Charlie set down a tray with, yes, fish chowder, plus Western club sandwiches and coffee, all for two. After he emptied the tray, he slid in across from John and grinned. "Thought you'd never get here."

John reached for the coffee. The taste brought immediate relief from the lingering aftertaste of beer. "Long morning?" he asked, holding the cup for its warmth.

"Busy is all," Charlie said, but he didn't look any

worse for the wear. His thinning hair had gone white, and he already had Charlie Senior's crow's-feet, but there was an ease in his eyes and his smile that attested to something working well in his life. His wife adored him, as did their five kids, three of whom worked at the store. John might tease Charlie about the kids giving him that white hair, but John did envy him the fullness of his life.

"I won't ask what they're talking about out there," Charlie mused, gesturing around the café with his spoon. "They're talking about it in here, too. Town's obsessed with it."

"What do you remember about her?"

Charlie ate a big piece of fish from his chowder. That was all the time it took for him to decide. "The voice. She was singing in church by the time she was seven. Outside of church, she was invisible. A quiet thing."

"She stuttered," John reminded him. That would explain the quietness.

"Not when she sang. She used to sing Sundays at church, and from the time she was ten or eleven, Thursdays here. I was away when that started, but to hear my dad tell it, she kept the place packed. They used the big room in back for live music even then, though it wasn't much more'n walls of barn board, with benches round a potbelly stove and a raised platform at one end."

"Did she sing every week?"

"Near to," Charlie said and took another mouthful of chowder. He had barely swallowed when he pointed the spoon at John's bowl. "Eat. My kids caught the fish—white perch and bass from the lake." He opened a bag of oyster crackers and dumped them in.

John ate. The chowder was light and buttery, not too thick, just savory enough.

Charlie said, "But there were fights aplenty about Lily singing here. George liked it, Maida didn't. Far as she was concerned, if singing in church was a sure road to salvation, singing here was a sure road to hell."

"Then why did she allow it?"

"George insisted. So did Lily's speech therapist. They both said she needed something to feel good about."

John was trying to picture it. "A singing ten-year-old is precocious and adorable. What about a four-teen- or fifteen-year old? Was she provocative?"

"Omigod, no. Maida wouldn't let it go that far. No matter the weather, no matter her age, the girl was buttoned from throat to ankle."

"That can be provocative," John pointed out. He was trying to imagine Donny's interest.

Charlie worked at his chowder for a minute. Then he set down the spoon. "Well, Lily wasn't. She'd just stand there and sing, no swaying, no come-hither looks, just the gentlest, most unpretentious smile at the end. She'd close her eyes singing love words, like she was either in dreamland or in dire fear that her mother would show up any minute and whisk her off the stage. Only, Maida didn't. On principle alone, she wouldn't go listen. She didn't come to the store for *months* after Lily left for New York. Far as she was concerned, we were the ones who corrupted the girl."

"Not Donny?" John asked.

Charlie wiped his mouth with a paper napkin. "That was a nothing case. So's this. You think she had an affair with the Cardinal?"

"No."

"Right. Anyone who knew Lily knew she wasn't capable of doing much bad. Your brother—he was another story. Not," Charlie added, arching a brow, "that I told that to the fellow stopped in here this morning."

John felt a twinge. "What fellow?"

Charlie took a business card from his pocket and passed it over. "Said he was a TV pro-du-sah from New Yawk. Y'ask me, he looked too young."

According to the card, the man was with *Dateline NBC*. "They're young," John acknowledged. "Shows like this have half a dozen producers. A lot of what they do is dirty work, like scoping out Lake Henry and trying to decide whether to run something or not."

"I told him not," Charlie said without a trace of an accent now. "I said there wasn't any story here, and that even if there was, he wouldn't get it from us."

But John knew how the media worked. There had been strangers at the plant sale just now. Everyone assumed that flatlanders passing through town on a Saturday would stop, particularly during foliage season. In the absence of a camera, there was no instant way of differentiating a leaf peeper from a reporter. "What did he look like?"

"Us," Charlie remarked, but added a knowing "I rang the 'listen up' bell and announced to everyone here who he was, so he wouldn't have to introduce himself. Then I walked him over to the plant sale and introduced him to everyone there, so folks'd know we had someone from *Dateline NBC* in town. Then I shook his hand, wished him luck, and left him on his own."

John knew why he liked Charlie. "That was good of you."

"I thought so," Charlie said. Lifting his soup mug, he downed what was left of his chowder in a single long glug. Then he set the mug down and sat back with a satisfied smile.

John didn't know why Charlie wasn't twice the size he was. Before John could finish what was in front of him, Charlie had downed seconds of chowder and an order of long, skinny french fries that he brought to the table with the chowder refill. Happy as a lark, he went back to work in the store, leaving John feeling stuffed.

Needing to move now to wear off what he'd eaten, John walked back through the milling crowd. He kept an eye out for strangers who might be media, warned people he saw that they might be around, even walked right up and listened in to ongoing conversations between unfamiliar faces and locals that might have been interviews. But he heard nothing untoward.

So he walked across the lot to the police station to talk with the chief, who just happened to be sitting on the front porch bench, watching the goings-on with a leg up on the rail and a toothpick sticking out of his mouth. Willie Jake was nearly seventy. He had been police chief for twenty-five years, and second in command for another twenty before that. No one complained that he had slowed down. Few even saw it. John was one who did, but only because he had been gone from town long enough to see the difference— and maybe because the demands of the police chief's job were so different in Boston.

Willie Jake always had been tall. He couldn't run far now, and he was jowly as he hadn't been when John was truant, but he still walked straight and with authority, still wore his uniform crisp enough to make an impression. What he had lost over the years in physical speed he made up for in mental agility.

"See anything interesting?" John asked.

"Some," the chief said in a low voice and shifted the toothpick to the other side. He didn't take his eyes from the crowd. "There's a few no-names mixing in out there. I'm making a picture of them in my mind. They show up elsewhere in town, I'll remembuh."

John didn't doubt it for a minute.

Willie Jake adjusted his foot on the railing. "Think she was involved with the Cahdnal?"

"No."

The chief spared him a quick glance. "Why not?"

"I used to know the guy who broke the case. He makes things up. What about you?" John asked, because he had his own agenda. "Do you think she was involved with the Cardinal?"

Willie Jake was chewing on his toothpick, looking out at the town again. The toothpick went to the side. "Hahd to say. Hahd to know the woman she's become since she left."

"Do you remember the business with my brother?"

Another glance his way, this one sharper. "I put the case togethah."

"Donny told me she wasn't at fault. Deathbed confession."

"He wasn't sayin' that at the time it happened. We had a good case. She was braggin' to a friend about goin' with Donny Kipling."

"Bragging?"

"Well, telling, and when they were drivin' around in that cah, she looked to be havin' a grand old time. She coulda got up 'n' left if she didn't like what he was doing, but she didn't say boo."

"She hadn't ever done anything wrong before that."

"Dud'n' mean a thing," said Willie Jake. "She was ripe to act up."

"Why?"

"Maida."

"What about Maida?"

"She was a stiff one. Kids rebel against stiff ones."

"But George was around, and he wasn't stiff. Didn't Lily have a good relationship with him?" George Blake was in John's files as fourth-generation Lake Henry. From what John had gathered in interviews, he was a gentle man.

"Did'n' matter what kind of relationship Lily had with him. Maida was in charge of the kids."

"You don't like Maida, do you?"

Willie Jake shrugged. "I like her just fine now. Did'n' like her much then. Not many in town did. She wasn't bad right aftuh she married George. Then she got uppity. Don't think she liked us much either." He darted John a look. "Didn't tell that to the reporter from Rhode Island who came by this morning, though. Didn' tell him a *thing*. I don't like outsiders snooping around my town. Told him that. Told him I'd be watchin' him. Told him I'd take him in if he goes anywhere he's not s'posed to go. This town's got posted land. Signs say no huntin', no fishin', no trespassin'. I add no *badgerin'*. I won't have flatlanduhs tryin' to get good people to talk about their neighbuhs. We talk about each othuh, and that's fine, but we don't tell stranguhs what we learn. Don't know what's wrong with you guys. Think you can write whatever you want. You decide what's news and what isn't. Dud'n' matter if it's true."

"Hey," John said with a hand to his chest, "I'm not the bad guy here. If I were you, I'd be trying to find out who leaked the business about the arrest."

Willie Jake scowled. He yanked the toothpick from his mouth. "Emma did it." Emma was his wife. She often answered the office phone. "Said someone called from the State House in Concahd tryin' to straighten out files. I called the State House. They didn't call us. They wasn't straightenin' out any files, but they did get a call on Lily Blake. The clerk who took it was a young thing who bought the line about the calluh bein' a shrink needin' background infuhmation on his patient. Guess is good it was press doin' this."

Guess is good it was Terry Sullivan, John thought.

Willie Jake took his foot down and sat straighter, suddenly looking at John as he had in the old days, as if John were a worm covered with dirt. "Why do you *do* things like that?"

John held up both hands. "Hey, *I* didn't do it."

The chief pushed himself off the bench. "Well, it's wrong. Somethin's *wrong* in this country. People don't know about respect. Take yuh small town like Lake Henry. Ain't no privacy he-uh. We all know what we're all doin', but we don't use it against each othuh. Out they-uh?" He shot a thumb toward the rest of the world. "No respect." He aimed his finger at John. "I'm tellin' you, leave it be. It dud'n' mattuh if Lily was innocent or guilty back then. It dud'n' mattuh if Maida was too tight. That's Blake business, and no one else's."

But it sure would make for interesting reading, John thought as he shook the chief's hand and walked off.

Chapter 9

Lily slept until four in the afternoon. She awoke famished and made an omelet and a salad, which she ate on the porch looking out on the lake. She might not trust John Kipling, but she was surely grateful for his food. Fresh things were better than canned any day, and everything he had brought was Lake Henry fresh. Eggs from the Kreugers' poultry farm; salad fixings from the Strothermans' produce farm; milk from cows two miles up the road, pasteurized, homogenized, bottled, and on sale at Charlie's within hours—there was reason why everything tasted so good. Not that the air didn't play a part. The scent of fall was a fine seasoning.

She ate every bite, sating her hunger, but not her mind. She kept thinking about John having ammo and wondering what he meant by that. There was no sign of his boat on the lake, which brought her some relief. A second visit would be a dead giveaway that she was here.

So, did Maida know she had come? Suspect it? At the very least, *wonder?*

Lily debated calling, decided not to. Again debated calling, again decided not to. Phone in hand, she went down to the lake, tucked herself in a pine root cubby, sat very still amid the smell of rich earth, and debated some more. In the time she was there, only two boats moved on the lake, but they were far out and headed away. The only movement in the cove came from a pair of ducks swimming in and out along the shore, and the scurry of chipmunks through brush.

The sun fell steadily toward the western hills, silhouetting the evergreens that undulated along their crests, spilling shadow down the hillside, and still she sat. The earth retained more heat than she did, keeping her warm when the air began to cool. In twilight she heard the hum of a distant boat, fragments of voices from down the shore, the call of a loon.

She had no sooner located the bird in a purple reflection off Elbow Island when the call came again. It was a long, steady sound with a dip at the end that gave it a primitive air. She had fallen asleep many a night to that sound, both here and across the lake, because the loon's cry carried far. As a child sleeping over with Celia, she had been fascinated by the idea that her mother could hear the very same cry she did.

Lily wondered if Maida heard it now. She wondered if maybe Maida was sitting out on the front porch of the large stone farmhouse on the hill thinking of Lily sitting down here. From the house Maida wouldn't be able to see if lights were on in the cottage.

Elbow Island was in the way, and behind it, as Lily looked now, Big Island.

In daylight Lily could see the crown of apple trees climbing the hills. Their leaves were a softer green in summer than that of evergreen or hardwood, and they were khaki rather than fiery in fall, but impressive nonetheless. Acre after acre, several hundred in all, flowed in waves over the hillside. They were beautifully kept and smartly worked. Even the ancient cider house, with sun glinting off its tin-paneled roof and history reeking from its hardy stone sides, was a sight to see.

Maida still talked about the very first time she had viewed her husband's inheritance. She had been twenty at the time, and as awed by the land as by the man. Up until that meeting she had been a clerk at the local logging company, coming home to her mother's cramped apartment in a town where even the smallest pleasures were few and far between. A chance meeting when George Blake had come to buy old equipment from her boss had been her ticket to grace. Fifteen years her senior, he was the sole heir to his father's land. He offered her a home that was not only breathtakingly beautiful but large, spacious, even idyllic. How not to find pleasure in that? Marrying him had been the simplest choice of her life.

So the story went, as Lily the child had heard it— a fairy tale, and it went beyond the marriage itself. Maida had been in heaven that first year. She loved not working, loved spending fall days sampling cider and baking the best of her husband's apples into pies that were the very best ones at church sales. That first winter, she had loved reading by the fire or skating on the lake, often with George, who had little to do between the last of the cider making in December and the first of the tree pruning in March. She loved the spring orchards, when apple blossoms were a riot of white and the buzz of pollinating bees filled the air. She loved sitting on the front porch in a welcome sun, looking down over the expanse of lawn open to the lake. Come May, when the ground was warm, she nursed iris and lily, morning glory, hyacinth, and roses, tending them daily, weeding, watering, and pampering them until her garden was the best one in town.

The best garden, the best apple pie, the best children. Lily had learned at a tender age that those things mattered to Maida. She could still see the smile on her face in describing the bounty of that first year. With the Garden Club her entrée to the world of prosperous women, Maida made friends among the elite. She invited them to the big stone farmhouse to see her flower arrangements, and served them dinner while they were there. She went right down the list of everyone who was anyone in Lake Henry, from the owners of the mill to the town meeting moderator to the local representative at the state legislature. She was in her glory.

Then the second year began, and something went wrong. What it was, Lily never knew for sure, since Maida always stopped her story at that point. She did know that heavy spring rains took a toll on the apple crop that year, which made for fiscal strain. That was also the year that Maida was pregnant with her.

So which was it that turned things sour for Maida—money worries, or pregnancy? By the time Lily was old enough to be curious, Maida was short-tempered enough with Lily for her not to risk worse, and by the time Lily had the courage to risk worse, she feared the answer too much.

She still did, sitting there tucked into the cubby of roots, but now there was something new to fear. John was right. It was only a matter of time before someone else on the lake saw signs of life at Celia's. Then word would spread that Lily was back, and Maida would know. Lily didn't want her learning it from someone else. She would be badly hurt—and that wouldn't help Lily's cause in the least. Nor would it help Poppy, who was sure to be questioned and take at least some of the heat.

Fast, before she chickened out, Lily returned to the house, cleaned up, changed clothes, and drove the borrowed wagon out around the lake. It was night now. Moonbeams slanted through the trees from time to time, but her headlights were otherwise alone on the road.

Her heart began to race when she neared the stone wall that marked the Blake Orchards entrance. Slowing the car, she carefully turned in and started up the gravel road that cut between acres of stubby apple trees. After half a mile, the land opened and the house loomed in the dark. Only one side of the first floor was lit, but Lily knew every inch of the place by heart.

Her imagination filled in two stories, a fieldstone front, shingled overhangs, and eaved windows.

Pulling in under the porte-cochere, she climbed the stone steps, opened the screen door, and slipped into the large front hall. Quiet classical music came from the direction of the library, a sure sign that Maida was there. Taking a steadying breath, Lily raised her eyes up the winding staircase, past oil paintings of flowers, to the mahogany-railed balcony. The stair runner looked more worn than she remembered it being the Easter before, but the elegance of the hall was impressive nonetheless.

On her left was the large dining room, shadowy with its Chippendale table and chairs. Turning in the opposite direction, she entered the living room. A single lamp was lit there, casting a glow on elegantly upholstered sofas and chairs, mahogany tables, an Oriental carpet. Maida had good taste. Lily couldn't fault her on that. If some in Lake Henry felt that Maida had decorated the stone farmhouse with more elegance than was appropriate, Lily had to admit she had done it well.

When her eye fell on the baby grand in the corner, she felt an ache. She missed her piano in Boston, and it had nowhere near the memories of this one. Lily had learned to play here. She had felt strong and competent sitting at those ivory keys on that claw-footed bench. She had discovered her voice here.

"I thought I heard a car," Maida said in a quiet voice.

Lily's eyes flew to the far end of the room. Her

mother was backlit in the library doorway, hands at her sides, shoulders straight. Not knowing what to say, Lily remained mute.

"I figured you'd be back," Maida went on. "Poppy was evasive when I asked."

"Poppy didn't know mm-my plans," Lily said, hating even that small hesitation, but Maida distracted her. Time hadn't changed that, nor did the current situation help it. But what Lily had feared most was anger, and she didn't hear it or see it. In further defense of Poppy, she said, "I couldn't tell her on the phone. I didn't trust the lines. Someone was tapping into my calls."

"Who would do that? Did you report it? Isn't it illegal to listen in on someone's line without their knowing? Maybe it was the police who did it. Is there a reason why they would?"

Lily shook her head. She folded her arms on her chest and tried to think of something to say, but all she could think was that Maida looked remarkably good. At thirty, she had looked her age. At forty she had looked her age. Now, at fifty-seven, after she had lost her husband three years before and taken over the family business, something seemed to be working for her. She actually looked younger. She was slim and stood as tall as her five-five height allowed. Her hair was dark, short, and stylishly cut. She wore jeans and a sweater much like Lily's.

Lily hadn't often seen her in jeans.

"You look good, Mom."

Maida grunted and withdrew into the library. Lily

watched her settle into her chair, retrieve her reading glasses, and turn to the computer on the side of the desk. She was shutting Lily out, typical when she couldn't deal.

Lily debated leaving. In the past, that had been her only recourse. Then, though, she'd had things to do and places to go. She had neither now. What she did have was a need to talk with her mother.

Slowly she walked the length of the living room and stood in the doorway that Maida had just left. The library was filled with maple bookshelves, in turn filled with leather-bound classics, nondescript aged volumes, and more contemporary books brightly packaged. It was all part of Maida's fairy tale. She saw an air of aristocracy in it. The books were taken down and dusted each spring, but Lily knew that few had actually been opened and read. It was a library for show.

The desk was another matter. Lily remembered her father working there many a night. He was a stocky man, more comfortable wearing overalls and picking apples than shuffling papers, but shuffle them he did, determined to keep his family's business in the black. The computer had come only after his death. Lily was impressed at the time. She hadn't taken Maida for a computer person. But then, she hadn't taken her to be heading the business, either, and she wasn't alone. Everyone had assumed that the good-natured, easygoing, hale and hardy George would live forever.

Now Maida clicked her mouse, studied the screen, riffled the papers at her right hand until she found what she wanted, typed something in. "Bills," she murmured, sounding resigned. "I'm getting good at juggling, paying a little here, a little there. I thought things'd be better with the season being good and production up, but greater production puts strain on equipment. The press needs parts, the piping, the refrigeration units—they're all showing their age at the same time. So there's that, then there's the backhoe, bucking and starting, not much different from an old ornery horse." She sat back and leveled an accusing stare at Lily. "Your father left me with a mess that keeps me busy dawn to dusk, and then there's the telephone. Calls are pouring in from people wanting to know about you—people from town, people from other towns, people from cities where I've never been nor care to be. I don't need those calls, Lily. Especially not at harvest time."

"I'm sorry," was all Lily could say.

"Poppy takes most of them, but a few sneak by. Do you know what they ask? Do you know what they *know?* Where you shop, what you buy—did *you* tell them all that?" Lily had barely shaken her head when Maida said, "The business about the stutter, the business about that no-good Donald Kipling—do you know how *embarrassing* this is for me?"

Lily hugged her middle. She felt a stab of anger, but it was quickly tempered by common sense. If Maida had to vent, it was just as well she do it now and get it done.

"Do you?" Maida prodded.

"It's worse for me."

"Welllll," her mother said with a dry laugh, "that's what you get when you play with fire. You wanted to be onstage. You wanted to be an entertainer. But scandal comes with that kind of life. People see you onstage, and suddenly you're a public person. You're fair game for gossipmongers. I read *People* magazine. This one's having an affair, that one's having an affair. If you're in that world, people assume that your morals are loose—and you fed right into them, Lily. What was in your *mind?* Late-night tête-à-têtes with the Cardinal, hugs and kisses—didn't it occur to you that people might get the wrong idea? At least, I *assume* it's the wrong idea."

Her voice stopped, but not her eyes. They were direct, demanding an answer.

Surprised and decidedly pleased to be given the benefit of the doubt, Lily said quickly, "It's the wrong idea. Nothing happened. Father Fran is a good friend. He has been for years. You know that."

"I didn't know you were running in and out of his residence at will."

"Not at will. Never at will."

"And why did you say those things? Why did you say you loved him?"

"Because I do. He's a close friend. That's what I told the reporter. He took my words out of context. He did it over and over again. Mom, I didn't ask for this."

"Then why did it happen?"

"Because some reporter, some newspaper wanted to sell papers," Lily cried. "The media needed a scandal, one reporter created one, and the others jumped in. If there had been a high-profile mm-murder somewhere else, they wouldn't have dreamed up this, but things were quiet, and then Fff-ather Fran was named Cardinal, and someone's imagination went to work."

"You set yourself up for it," Maida declared. "You let it happen."

Lily was astonished. "What could I *do*? I denied every allegation. I demanded a retraction. I talked with a lawyer."

"And?"

"What?"

"The lawyer. What's he doing?"

"I couldn't hire the lawyer."

"Why *not?*"

"He wanted a quarter of a million dollars."

That silenced Maida. Her eyes went to the computer screen, then to her papers. Her mouth flattened, corners turned down.

Lily was about to say that she wouldn't take the money from Maida even if she had it, when she heard a noise behind her. She turned to see Rose's oldest child, Lily's ten-year-old niece, Hannah, coming toward her on bare feet. A huge T-shirt hid her chubbiness. Long brown hair, more out of a ponytail than in it, framed a round and serious face.

Lily didn't know her nieces well, but Hannah had been the firstborn of them and held a special place in her heart. She broke into a smile. "Hi, Hannah!"

Hannah stopped just out of arm's reach. "Hi, Aunt Lily."

Lily closed the distance and gave her a hug. The one she got back felt hesitant, but it was better than nothing. "How are you?" she said, keeping an arm around the girl.

"Fine. When'd you get back?"

"Late last night. I slept most of today. What're you doing here so late?"

"She's sleeping over," Maida said in a businesslike voice. "What happened to the movie, Hannah?"

"It was boring."

"I thought we rented two."

Lily felt a shrug under her hand. Hannah said, "I heard voices."

"Your aunt and I have to talk. Go on back up and watch the other one."

Hannah shot Lily a quick look before pulling away.

"Don't forget to rewind the first," Maida called after her.

Lily watched her until she had disappeared into the hall. Then she turned back to Maida. "Does she sleep over often?"

"Saturday nights, when Rose and Art want to go out."

"Where are Emma and Ruth?" They were Hannah's younger sisters, ages seven and six respectively, certainly too young to stay alone.

"A baby-sitter. It's easier for the sitter if Hannah is here." In a lower voice, she asked, "Why did the newspaper imply that you were hiring that lawyer?"

Fearing Hannah could hear what they said, Lily spoke more softly, too. "The lawyer was the one who implied it. But it wasn't only the money that bothered me. He said a lawsuit would take years, and that they'd pick at my life even more than they already have."

Maida sat back and pressed laced fingers to her lips.

Lily said, "I can't live through this for three years."

Maida dropped her hands. "Is there an alternative?"

"The story is a lie. Everyone will know it once the Cardinal gets a retraction."

"And you'll get your teaching job back?" Maida asked. "I think not. Smears linger even after the facts come clear. You put yourself in a vulnerable position. A single woman, having a close friendship with the Cardinal?"

Lily felt accused by the one person whose mistrust hurt the most. She lashed back with more force than she had dared once to show to Maida, but she was an adult now, and Maida was *wrong*. "It wasn't that close. I never visited him just for the heck of it. We used to talk at parties, but there were always other people around. Sometimes I stayed, playing the piano after events at the residence, and there were times when he'd call on the phone to see how I was, if a month or two had gone by and we hadn't bumped into each other. That's no different from what I did with other friends."

"He's a priest."

"He's a friend."

"People don't *touch* priests."

"*Everyone* touches Fran Rossetti."

"And there—there—such a show of disrespect, calling him by his first name."

"All his friends call him Fran. He tells us to. I would never do it in public."

Maida took another tack. "If you'd been married this wouldn't have happened. I've been after you to marry for years, and I was right. A husband would give you stability. Same with children. If you'd listened to me and done that, you'd have looked more settled."

"And that would have made a difference?" Lily shot back. "If one story is based on lies, another would be, too. Terry Sullivan wanted a scandal. He'd have made it happen even if I was married; only then they'd have called me an adulteress or an unfit mother."

"When did you become so jaded?" Maida had the gall to chide. Poppy had done much the same, but more as an observation. Maida was being critical, and Lily grew livid.

"When someone else's lies tore my whole life apart!"

"You should have been married," Maida insisted, but the flatness in her voice said she was done with the argument. "I take it you're staying at Mother's?"

Lily didn't bother to say that the cottage was legally hers. Tired, she simply nodded.

"For how long?"

"I don't know."

"You'll lead them here, you know."

"Not if you don't let it out. Will Hannah?"

"No."

"She'll tell Rose," Lily feared. "Rose will tell Art. Art will tell his mother, and she'll spread it around the mill." It wasn't paranoia on Lily's part, but reality. Lake Henry just worked that way.

But Maida insisted, "Hannah won't tell Rose. She doesn't tell Rose anything. I'd worry about other people who notice that you're at Mother's. Word will spread that way, and the media will come, sure as day. Is that fair to us?"

"Where else can I *go*?"

Maida threw up a hand, upset again. "Well, I don't know. All I know is that I don't want them here. You don't want them looking at you for three years? Why should we have them looking at us for three *weeks*? They'll be nosing around even worse than they've already done, and that isn't fair. You aren't the only one involved here, Lily. Leading them back here—it just goes on and on. Why are you doing this to me? What do you *want* from me?"

Lily lost it then. Tears sprang to her eyes. Years of yearning loosened her tongue. "Support," she cried. "Sympathy. Compassion. Welcome. This is my home, and you're my mother. Why can't you give me those things?" She might have stopped there, but after the emotional battering of the last few days, her defenses were down. "What did I do—what did I *ever* do to offend you so much? People like me, Mom. I'm a nn-nice person. I have friends who like me, colleagues who like me, students who like me, even a Cardinal who likes me and thinks I'm someone ww-worthy of calling his friend. Why can't *you*?"

Maida looked taken aback, but Lily couldn't stop. Tears rolled down her cheeks, but long-pent-up thoughts kept the words pouring out. "My stutter embarrassed you. It said that I wasn't perfect, one of your children wasn't perfect. But did I *ask* to ss-stutter? Do you think I *like* doing it? I made one mm-mistake—*one* mistake, with Donny Kipling. Have I burdened you since then? Have I asked anything of you? No. But now I'm asking for understanding. Is that so much? Do you think I *wanted* any of this to happen? I wake up nights shaking with fury"—she shook with it now—"because I worked *so hard* to build a good ll-life, and they've taken it away, and *I don't know why*! I don't know ww-why Terry Sullivan did this to me, or why the *Post* went along with it, and I don't know why my own mother can't ff-feel for *me* for a change!"

Whirling around, she stormed from the house.

Lily cried all the way home, alternately furious at Maida's insensitivity and ashamed of her own outburst. She parked the car without bothering to turn it around, half wishing she *would* find a media person skulking in the woods. She would take him on. She was in a fighting mood. But no one jumped out as she stalked down to the lake. Anger carried her right out onto the old wood dock, where she sat herself down, daring Lake Henry to see.

No one was about to. The night was dark, the water idle. She fumed for a while, then simmered. But the setting was too peaceful to sustain ill will, and in time she calmed. When the call of the loon came, she thought of Celia—dear Celia, who had loved her the way a mother was supposed to love a child. Had it not been for Celia, Lily might have gone on believing that she was unlovable.

That was what Maida had taught her. At least, that was what Lily had taken from Maida's frustration with her. Father Fran had said it wasn't so. He had said that mothers always loved their children but circumstance sometimes prevented its expression. All Lily knew was that the frustration was constant. Lily couldn't do anything right. George had been more supportive, but he picked and chose his fights. He insisted that Maida let Lily sing at the general store because he saw that as a larger issue. Typically male, he didn't see the smaller emotional needs that a growing girl had, needs that were going unfulfilled.

Celia had filled the void. She had given Lily the self-confidence that not even the applause of the most appreciative audience could give. She had taught Lily to go after her dreams.

What were Lily's dreams now, sitting out in the dark of the lake, with the air chilled, the water barely moving against the rocky shore, and the primal call of a loon echoing through the night?

She wanted her life back—work, freedom, privacy.

The dream was more vivid than ever when Lily awoke Sunday morning. Tamping down the urgency she felt, she waited until nine, then did the unthinkable and called John Kipling. He knew she was there, knew the situation, knew the media. He had also invited her to call, she reasoned. Besides, given how extensively she had been used by the media, she saw no harm using John in this very small way.

"It's Lily. I was wondering if you've seen the morning paper."

"Just picked it up."

"Is there anything?"

"A small blurb on the front page," he said. "Hold on. I'll check inside."

While the rustle of newsprint came over the line, she stood at the lake window with Celia's shawl wrapped around her and a tight grip on the phone. It seemed forever before his voice came again. It was preceded by a sigh.

"Okay. Not too bad. The front page has a quick recap of the week's events. Most of what's inside has to do with other people."

"What other people?"

"History."

"History?"

"Sex scandals."

Her stomach turned. "What do you mmm-ean?"

"They're talking about prominent people who've had highly publicized affairs, but this is good, I think. If they're moving away from you, it means they've run out of things to say."

Lily didn't see it quite so benignly. "But they're grouping me with those people!"

"Yeah, but anyone with half a brain knows the

situations aren't the same. There's no comparison between Cardinal Rossetti and a philandering president
caught with his hand in the cookie jar, or a high-level
diplomat caught in bed with a spy, or a Hollywood
icon who can't keep his fly zipped."

"Maybe the people reading that don't *hh-have* half
a brain."

"People are usually smarter than we give them
credit for," John said in a calmer voice. It might even
have been reassuring, if he hadn't been part of the
media. Media knew how to manipulate. Lily had
learned that firsthand. "Yes, it's offensive digging into
the past for cases like this. And yes, there's the impli-
cation that those cases are like this one. But the comparison will backfire. People will read this and see that
the allegations against you and the Cardinal are flimsy,
compared to these."

"The problem," Lily argued, catching in a shallow
breath, "is that comparisons have an effect if they're
mmm-ade often enough. People will forget the details
of the allegations against me. They'll forget they're
flimsy. The thing will take on greater weight."

"Then you need to fight back."

"How?" she cried.

After a pause, he said, "One way is through the
courts. The newspapers will hear that."

She bowed her head, shut her eyes, pressed a fist
to her temple. "So will the rest of the world. I hh-have
to go," she whispered and ended the call.

Chapter 10

Lily spent much of Sunday detesting the helplessness she felt. She reconsidered taking legal action, even envisioned a triumphant scene outside a courtroom after a jury had ruled in her favor. The vision included total vindication, with the kind of mega-settlement that would make the media think twice before again recklessly ruining people's lives. She pictured a victorious return to Boston that included the Winchester School headmaster being fired for caving in to the media frenzy and the owner of the Essex Club begging, just begging her to return to work. She imagined Terry Sullivan losing his job, Paul Rizzo crashing his motorcycle, and Justin Barr being run out of town.

Inevitably, reality returned the minute she thought of the emotional price of taking the case to court. Things would get worse before they got better. She wasn't ready to sign on for that.

What else to do? Saturday morning, John had said he had ammo. He hadn't mentioned it again on Sunday, but she may have hung up too soon. She wondered what his ammo was, whether she could trust him to share it, whether he would turn right around and use her the way Terry Sullivan had.

Issues of trust notwithstanding, she knew that John saw the papers each morning. In the absence of television and radio at the cottage, fearful of calling Boston and risking having the call traced to Poppy's number, and loath to call Maida, she bit the bullet and phoned John again first thing Monday morning.

"You're my link to the outside world," she said in an attempt at levity. "What's out there today?"

"Nothing on the front page," John replied. "The story is on page five. The Vatican cleared the Cardinal of suspicion and condemned the irresponsibility of the paper. The *Post* countered by issuing an apology to the Cardinal."

Hope came so quickly that Lily could hardly breathe. "They admitted the story was wrong?"

"No. But they apologized to the Cardinal." His statement hung in the air.

"Yes?" Lily asked. There had to be more.

"That's it. It was a small piece."

Her hopes wavered. "Was I mentioned?"

"Only at the very beginning."

Uneasy now, she swallowed. "Would you read it to mm-me, please?"

In a level voice, John read: " 'After conducting its

own inquiry, the Vatican has announced that newly named Cardinal Francis Rossetti has been cleared of all allegations that he had an improper relationship with nightclub singer Lily Blake. The Vatican inquiry involved extensive interviews with personnel closest to the Cardinal, as well as with the Cardinal himself. A statement issued from Rome last night cited a "total absence of evidence to suggest that any of the allegations made in the past week contain even an iota of truth." The statement went on to condemn the atmosphere of "carnival journalism" that exists in this country today and that threatens "irreparable harm even to men of the impeccable character of Cardinal Rossetti." ' "

Lily held her breath, waiting.

"More?" John asked.

"Please."

" 'A spokesman for the Archdiocese of Boston praised the speed and thoroughness of the Vatican investigation. "This timely action clears the way for Cardinal Rossetti to immediately resume his work with the poor, the troubled, and the needy of the archdiocese," he said.' "

John paused.

Lily waited.

" 'When reached by the *Post*,' " he read on, " 'the Cardinal reiterated that thought. "There is precious work to be done," he said. "It would have been unfortunate for that work to suffer because of spurious charges and irresponsible reporting." ' "

Again John paused.

"Is that *it?*" Lily asked.

"One more sentence. 'The *Post* has issued a formal apology to the Cardinal and to the archdiocese.' "

Lily waited for him to tack on a final phrase. When the silence dragged on, her dismay grew. "That's all?"

"Yes."

"No apology to me?"

"No."

She was dumbfounded, then irate. "But I'm the one who's suffered most. I'm the one who's out of work. I'm the one whh-who who can't walk around in public without being followed like a cat in heat. I deserve an apology, too. What about exonerating mmm-*me?*" Her jaw was clenched, her heart pounding. She was as angry as she had ever been. "Who wrote that piece?"

"Not Terry," John answered. "David Hendricks. He's a longtime staff reporter."

"Terry Sullivan is a coward," Lily seethed. "What about the other papers?"

"Same thing. Small piece. That's it."

"Will this be the end?"

"Possibly."

Through her fury, Lily managed only a quick "Thank you" before disconnecting the call. Then she called Poppy and asked to be put through to Cassie Byrnes.

Like many of its neighbors, Lake Henry had a town-meeting form of government. For two nights every March, the church was filled with residents gathered to vote on issues pertinent to town life in the coming year. Every other year, a moderator was elected. He determined the meeting's agenda and should have been the most powerful person in town.

It wasn't so in Lake Henry, where a town meeting was more a social experience easing the monotony of mud season than a policy-making body. In reality, as they arose, the everyday details of town life were handled by the police chief, the postmaster, and the town clerk. The more weighty matters at millennium's end, though, had to do with ecological interests. These were handled by the Lake Henry Committee.

The committee had first formed in the 1920s, when the growing influx of summer residents made the year-rounders edgy. Committee members focused on preserving the beauty of the lake and its land. Over the years, as ecological interests gained prominence, the committee's power grew.

It had no size limit. Anyone could belong. The only qualification was that attendance at monthly meetings was mandatory. When an emergency meeting was called, usually in reaction to a move by the state legislature that locals considered intrusive to their rights, members were expected to attend unless they had good reason not to. At any given time there were thirty members, give or take. Each January they celebrated the new year by electing a leader from their ranks.

Cassie Byrnes was in her fourth year as chairman of the Lake Henry Committee. She was the first woman to hold that position and, thirty-five now, still the youngest person ever, but her selection had been unanimous. A lifelong resident of Lake Henry, she had left town only to attend college and law school. The ink was barely dry on her degree when she returned to town to hang out a shingle. In the ten years since, she had become something of a local activist.

Lily waited for her on the porch. The lake was foggy today, but peaceful. It helped keep her nervousness in check. When she heard the sound of a motor, she walked around to the front of the cottage. She was waiting there when Cassie pulled up in a compact car that was every bit as worn as the old borrowed wagon. Crammed into the back along with what looked to be heavy jackets, a hockey stick, and a fast food bag were two child seats.

Cassie was a working mother, but the only frazzle about her was her curly blond hair. Slipping the strap of a leather pouch on her shoulder as she climbed from the car, she looked fully composed. Her long legs were encased in jeans, her slender upper half in white silk. She wore a blazer, a flowered scarf, and boots.

"Thanks for coming," Lily said.

Cassie smiled. "We were wondering if you'd come back. Speculation is second nature to Lake Henryites. No one knows I'm here, though. Your secret is safe with me as long as you want it kept." She extended a hand. "It's been a long time."

Lily took her hand. Cassie had been a year ahead of her in school, and light-years more popular. Her handshake now was confident and firm. Lily hoped she had the legal ability to match it.

They might have talked on the porch with the fog assuring confidentiality, but it was too cool and damp to stay outside long. So Lily led her into the cottage and offered her coffee. They sat in the living room, Lily in the armchair, Cassie on the sofa.

"You've followed the story?" Lily began.

"Oh, yes. Hard not to, what with a local involved."

"Have you seen today's papers?"

"I have. The Vatican cleared the Cardinal, and the *Post* apologized to him but not to you," Cassie said with a quickness that encouraged Lily. "It doesn't surprise me. The press has legal eagles on retainer. They tell editors what the law requires, and those editors don't go one drop beyond that. The *Post* issued an apology but not a retraction. It could be that unless the Cardinal demands one, it won't be offered. Or it could appear later in the week. There are statutes covering retractions, where they should be, how big. I'd have to look at the Massachusetts statutes to know how things work there."

Lily didn't care about statutes. She was talking sheer common sense. "But how could I not have been included in an apology? If I was half party to an alleged sexual affair, and the other half has been exonerated and given a public apology, how can I be ignored? How can charges be made on the front page, and apologies issued somewhere back inside?"

"That's how it works," Cassie said on a note of disgust.

Angry, Lily hung her head. She swallowed, trying to organize her thoughts. When she was ready, she looked up. "What's been done to me is morally wrong. That won't change. But laws have been broken, too. That's what I need to talk with you about."

"You're not working with Maxwell Funder?"

"No. He wanted the case for the publicity, and for the money." She told Cassie the figure Funder had tossed out.

Cassie rolled her eyes. "No surprise there, either. He's with a fancy firm. There are people who will pay his fees. So he may be giving you a cut rate on those hourly fees, but they're still out of sight. Did he give you the spiel about out-of-pocket costs?" Lily had barely nodded when Cassie said, "Court costs aren't much in a case like this. At least, not up here."

That was a new thought. "Can I use the New Hampshire courts?" Lily asked.

"Why not? The papers in question are all sold here. That means you've been libeled in New Hampshire as much as in Massachusetts or New York."

Lily took heart. "Libel *is* what it is. They've said things about me that are lies, and what they didn't say, they implied."

Cassie held up a cautionary hand. "What they implied will be harder to prove." She took a pad of paper and a pen from her bag. "Let's start with what they said."

"They said I was having an affair with the Cardinal. That is not true."

Cassie made notes. "Okay. That's point one. What else?"

"They said I was having an affair with the governor of New York."

"Said, or implied?"

"Implied, but strongly."

Cassie rocked a hand. "That's a maybe. What other
direct accusations were made?"

"That I said I was having an affair with the Cardinal. That I was in love with him. That I followed him
to Boston."

"Didn't you say those things?"

"Not the way he implied," Lily said, angry and
embarrassed at the same time. "We were talking about
a hypothetical woman saying she was having an affair
with the Cardinal. So Terry reported it like it was *me*. I
said I loved the Cardinal like many other people love
the Cardinal. It was generic. And I did follow him to
Boston chronologically, but not for the purpose of following him there."

Cassie was frowning. "Those are all maybes. You
said those words. He took them out of context. He's
apt to claim it was an innocent misunderstanding on
his part. The case won't make it to court unless we
can prove malice. Do you know him?"

"No," Lily answered, frustrated now. "He had
been approaching me for a piece he was doing on performers, but I kept turning him down. The first time
we did any real talking was at the club the night before he broke the story. He led me into those statements, Cassie. But then there's the rest of what they
printed." She raced on, because it was all so wrong, so
infuriating, so humiliating. "I didn't tell them where I

shop or where I go on vacation, and I didn't tell them about the incident here when I was sixteen. Those charges were dropped. The file was supposed to be sealed."

Cassie had been rapping her upper lip with her knuckles while Lily talked. Now she made a note on the pad. "Someone leaked it. The AG here should investigate that. The problem with the rest—where you shop and vacation—that information is available to the public. It shouldn't be, but it is. Anyone with a rudimentary knowledge of the Internet can get it."

Lily was discouraged. "Then there's nothing I can do?"

"Not on that score."

"But they broke laws, too. Someone tapped into my phone."

"Do you know for sure?"

"No, but I heard a click when I was talking to my sister, and something from that conversation appeared in the paper the next morning."

Cassie made a note on her pad. "For that we lodge a complaint with the AG's office in Massachusetts."

Lily noted the "we" and spoke with greater hesitance. "I don't have much money. I'll give you what I have."

"Hold your money," Cassie said. "We'll discuss it as I incur costs." She turned to a fresh sheet of paper. "I want to know everything about your relationship with the Cardinal, everything about your talk with Terry Sullivan, everything about what's happened to you since the story broke."

Lily talked for the next hour. It was cathartic. Her voice rose and fell with emotion, but she didn't stutter once. Though Cassie injected an occasional question, she mainly listened and made notes. Finally Lily finished. Cassie sat quietly reviewing her notes. When Lily couldn't bear the suspense, she asked, "What do you think?"

"I think," Cassie said, "that you do have a case for libel."

"But?" Lily could hear it in her voice.

"But there are several issues. A major one is whether, by any stretch of the imagination, you can be considered a public figure. If legal precedent says that you are, a libel case becomes harder to prove. That's when malice becomes the major issue. In any event, the first step is to send a retraction demand to the *Post*. It's required by law before we file a suit. We have to give the newspaper an opportunity to offer a retraction—and in our case, an apology—before we involve the courts."

"How long do we give them?" she asked. She hadn't forgotten Funder's warning about a long, drawn-out, excruciatingly personal experience.

"A week. They don't need more. Want me to go ahead?"

One week wouldn't be bad. Lily had anger enough to go for that. She suspected that if the *Post* either refused or ignored their demand, her anger would carry her further. Besides, she felt strong with Cassie there, felt empowered thinking that there might be a righting of wrongs. As Poppy had pointed out, it was her life, her work, her name. If she didn't fight for it, no one else would.

"Yes," she said calmly. "I want to go ahead."

While Lily and Cassie talked, John rocked back in his office chair with his feet on the desk, his hands around his coffee mug, his eyes on the foggy lake, and his mind on why the *Post* had ignored Lily. It was no sweat off his back; his book would work either way. But the more he thought, the more annoyed he grew. On impulse he picked up the phone and punched out a familiar number.

"Brian Wallace," mumbled a distracted voice at the other end of the line. Brian had been John's editor at the *Post*. He continued to be Terry Sullivan's editor.

"Hey, Brian. It's Kip."

The voice picked up. The two men had been friends. "How're you doin', Kip?"

"Great. You?"

"Busy. It never lets up. There are times I think you had the right idea, chucking the daily grind. So now you're up there in the sticks. Who'da known a big story would break right in front of your nose?"

"It's in front of *your* nose. It happened in Boston."

"But she's from your town. Terry says you're clamming up on us."

"Terry wanted information I didn't have. And even if I'd known something, I wouldn't have given it to Terry," John admitted, knowing that Brian would understand. Terry made enemies right and left.

"Huh," Brian said. "That's blunt. So. Want to give that info to me?"

"What's to give?"

"She isn't up there?"

"If she is, she's hiding out good. People around town haven't seen her." Neither statement was a lie. Misleading, perhaps, but Brian Wallace had taught him well. "We're just following the story. Today's was interesting. It isn't often that the paper issues apologies."

Brian blew out a breath. "The Church was pissed."

"Now everyone up here is pissed. They're wondering why Lily didn't get an apology, too."

Brian made a harsher sound. "Lily Blake should apologize to *us*. Christ, if she hadn't said those things, we wouldn't be embarrassed now."

Not wanting to tip his hand about talking with Lily, John began treading with greater care. "Do you really think she said those things? Or did Terry manufacture them?"

"I wouldn't have run it if he had."

"Do you know for sure that he didn't?"

There was a short pause, then a cooler voice. "Is that an accusation?"

"Come off it, Brian. This is *me* you're talking to. I know what went on behind the scenes there a time or two. I worked with Terry. I also went to school with the guy. It wouldn't be the first time he's fabricated a story."

"Careful, John." They were opponents now. "Statements like that can be libelous."

"And what he's written about Lily Blake isn't? Aren't you worried she'll sue?"

"Nope."

He sounded so sure, John was more annoyed than before. "Why not? The story was false. You admitted it yourself. Doesn't that tell you Terry got it wrong?"

"Christ, John," Brian shot back, "do you honestly think we'd have run a story like that without damn good cause to believe it? Do you honestly think *I'd* have run it based on Terry's say-so? I know what he's done in the past, so I watch him closely. He'd been telling me about that relationship for weeks, right from the very first rumors that Rossetti might be elevated, and I told him I wouldn't touch it with a ten-foot pole unless he got more than circumstantial evidence. But he got it. I have a tape. A tape, John. Lily Blake said those things, no doubt about that. So maybe she's crazy. Maybe she has a crush on the guy. Maybe she's fantasized about him so long and hard that she started thinking it was true. But she did say those things. I heard it myself."

John hadn't expected that. His mind shifted gears. "Did she know she was being taped?"

"We were told she did. But, hey, we're being cautious. That's why we haven't gone public with it. We're not stupid, Kip. This tape wouldn't be admissible in court. But it justifies our running the story. Listening to the tape, we had cause to believe the story. There was no malice involved on our part. The lady's nuts."

*　　*　　*

Poppy had known about the apology issued to the Cardinal well before Lily called to get in touch with Cassie. She had heard about it early from three separate friends, all of whom had heard it on television and were shocked that the apology stopped short of Lily. Between calls from those friends, she fielded others coming in from the media. The callers' names were familiar, their voices urgent. They wanted to know the reaction of Lily's hometown to this latest turn of events.

She told the one who called looking for Charlie Owens, "We believed in Lily all along."

She patched the one wanting Armand Bayne on to Armand's house, trusting that he would handle the man with ease.

To the one who called looking for Maida, she said, "We're relieved that Lily has been exonerated," though that wasn't anywhere near the truth. But Maida was at the cider house and wasn't about to take the call, and Poppy figured that if the papers were going to print comments, those comments might as well stress Lily's innocence.

The phone rang for Willie Jake. She pressed his button and said into her headset, "Lake Henry Police Department. This call is being recorded."

"William Jacobs, please," said a voice she hadn't heard before. It was wonderfully deep and decidedly male.

When Willie Jake had called in, he was on his way to Charlie's for an early lunch. "He's not here. May I help you?"

"That depends," the man said in a good-humored way. "My name is Griffin Hughes. I'm a freelance writer putting together a story on privacy for *Vanity Fair.* I'm focusing on what happens when privacy is violated—the side effects to the people involved. I thought that the Lily Blake situation would fit right in. Lake Henry is her hometown. It occurs to me that people there may have thoughts about what's happened to her."

"Damn right we do," Poppy said with feeling.

He chuckled and went on in the same deep-throated, easygoing way. "I thought I'd start with the chief of police, but his dispatcher sounds like she might be good. So. What do you think?"

"I think," Poppy said, attempting to sound as easygoing as he had, "that I would be crazy to share my thoughts with you, because anything I say may be twisted and turned. If what's happened to Lily has taught us anything, it's that. You and your media colleagues are scum."

"Hey," he said gently, "don't group me with the others. I don't work for a newspaper. Besides, I'm on Lily's side."

"And you're not looking to be paid for your story?"

"Of course, I am. But Lily is only one of the people I'm researching, and she isn't the first. I started this project weeks ago. Most of my subjects have suffered when medical information was leaked, so Lily's situation is different. I'm doing the story on spec. The magazine may reject it when the article's done, but I think it's an important piece to write."

He sounded very nice and very reasonable. There was none of the urgency or arrogance she had heard in other media people who had called. She pictured him as a man of average height and weight, with a friendly smile and a sense of decency. He had to be a phony.

"What kind of a name is Griffin Hughes?" she asked disparagingly. "It doesn't sound real."

"Tell that to my dad," came the answer. "And to his dad. I'm the third."

"You're trying to trick me. You're deliberately sounding friendly and kind."

"And honest."

"That, too, but I don't believe you."

"I'm sorry," he said, sounding sincere. Curiously, he asked, "Are you a native of Lake Henry?"

"What does that have to do with anything?"

"You don't have an accent."

"Few people my age here do. We've spent time in the big, wide world. We're not rubes," she said more harshly than she intended, but that deep voice conjured up an Adam's apple full of virility, and she felt defensive.

He said a gentle "Shhhhh. No need to convince me. I'm on your side—uh—what did you say your name was?"

"I didn't say my name. See, you are trying to trick me."

"No," he said, sounding sorry again. "I'm just trying to imagine that we're friends. You're blunt. I like people like that. I like knowing where I stand."

"Poppy," she said. "My name is Poppy. I'm Lily Blake's sister, and I'm angry about what happened to her. So's the rest of the town. You can print that."

"I'm not printing anything yet. All I'm doing is gathering information. I mean, there you are in a small town where everyone knows what you're doing and when. Nothing's private there. So maybe you don't feel the need for privacy that city people do."

"I just said we're upset."

"Yes, but are you upset about what happened to Lily, or about people like me intruding on your life?"

"Both."

Griffin Hughes sighed. In a voice that was low and smooth, he said, "Okay. I've exhausted my welcome. I'll try the chief another time. Take care, Poppy."

"You, too," Poppy said, severing the connection with a sense of relief. She might have liked to listen to that voice more—and then God only knew what she might have been charmed into saying.

Chapter 11

John couldn't stop thinking about the tape. Its existence added a whole new twist to the story. But it was Monday, which meant that the week's *Lake News* was priority one. He had dummied the pages and scanned in photos. Now he had to add meat.

The cover story was of three families that had recently moved from big cities to Lake Henry. The Taplins—Rachel and Bill and their four-month-old daughter, Tara—had come from New York. The Smiths—Lynne and Gary and their teenagers, Allyson, Robyn, Matt, and Charley—had come from Massachusetts. The Jamisons—Addie and Joe and their two chocolate labs, plus their three grown children, who visited during vacations—were from Baltimore. The three couples ranged in age from their late twenties to their late sixties, but the search for a better quality of life was common among them.

John had conducted interviews with each family

the week before and had outlined the story by hand at home on Sunday. Pulling in his chair, he began composing on the computer. The writing was interrupted by the usual calls regarding public service announcements and classified ads. When the interruptions grew tiresome, he went down to the parlor and asked Jenny to answer the phones.

He explained to her twice what she needed to do. He made sure that the proper forms were on her desk. He highlighted in yellow the most important questions she needed to ask. When she looked terrified, he went over the procedure a third time. A third time, too, he told her that she was ready for this, that it was good training, that he knew, absolutely knew, she could do it well.

Closing the door to his office, he returned to his computer, but rather than writing about the lure of small-town life, he found himself in cyberspace, accessing the *Post*'s archives. There had always been grumbling when Terry Sullivan fabricated stories. John quickly located and printed out four such questionables that had appeared during his own final years with the paper. Then he called Steve Baker, an old pal who was still a reporter there.

"Hey, you!" Steve said with pleasure when he heard John's voice. "Your ears must be burning. You're the talk of the newsroom. We're all wondering what you know about Lily Blake."

"Not much," John said. "She left here when she was eighteen, and I left ten years before that. Me, I'm wondering what you all know about Terry Sullivan. Is this another one of Terry's cherries? Did he make it up?"

"That depends on who you ask," Steve said without missing a beat. "The official story is that Lily misled Terry. Taken with all the other stuff he gathered, what she told him had the ring of truth."

"That's the official story. What's yours?"

There was a pause, then a lower "He's been building this story for months."

"Following Lily?"

"And Rossetti. When he was named Archbishop of Boston, everyone knew he was in line to be elevated. The only question was when. The Catholic community expected it sooner. Once rumor spread that the elevation would come on or around the third anniversary of his coming to Boston, Terry got busy. That was six months ago. It was a fishing expedition. He was looking for anything he could find. He tried focusing on other women, only nothing panned out."

"Did Brian propose the story, or was it Terry's all the way?"

"Terry's."

"Does he have something against the Cardinal?"

"Terry doesn't *need* something to savage a subject. He's vicious when he smells a good story. He wanted this one for the Headline Team. Brian resisted."

That was consistent with what Brian had told John. "Okay. But the paper says Terry's work was on the up-and-up. What's the newsroom buzz?"

"Geez, Kip. I'm not exactly unbiased. Terry has stolen good assignments from me."

"The buzz?" John coaxed, then waited out a long pause. He knew how it would end. Terry Sullivan was a powerful writer who made powerful enemies.

Steve kept his voice low, but it was vehement. "He decided there was a story, only he couldn't find anything incriminating. He was out of time, and everything else had fallen through, so he wrote a piece that was half speculation, half imagination. Most of us have met Rossetti. If ever there was a decent, honest, upstanding guy, he's it. Hey, I'm saying that and I'm not even Catholic."

"But Lily Blake is quoted as saying it was true."

"Oh, yeah. We know how that works. Ask a leading question, you get a malleable answer."

"Do you know about the tape?"

Steve's voice remained low, but its monotone was telling. There was buzz about a tape, too. "What tape? If there was a tape, you'd have read about it on page one. Did you?"

"What about if he made a tape without her knowing?"

"That's a crime. If the paper knew about it and didn't do anything, they're guilty of aiding and abetting. So the *Post* is in potential deep shit here. *And"*— Steve hurried on, talking under his breath—"the shit thickens if the *Post* ran a potentially libelous story on the say-so of an illegally gotten tape. So the paper won't mention any tape. I'd say that gives Terry Sullivan the kind of protection he likes."

John agreed. So did two other old media friends he called. He made notes on these conversations.

Then he called Ellen Henderson, a college classmate of Terry's and his. The college was a small one, where students knew one another and alumni stuck around. The entire Development Office staff had been students at one time or another. That was how John knew Ellen was there. She had called him several months earlier looking for money. He had pleaded poverty at the time. Now he wished he hadn't.

"I'll make a deal," he told her right off the bat. "Send me a pledge form and I'll do what I can."

"In exchange for?" Ellen asked, sounding amused but affectionately so.

"Information on Terry Sullivan."

"Ah." Her voice grew less affectionate. "Our favorite classmate. Want to know what *he* did when I called to solicit for the annual fund? He said that everything he was now he had learned before or after college, so he didn't owe us a thing. Seems to me he's forgetting something."

It seemed the same way to John.

Ellen said, "I recall a few close calls he had with plagiarism. At least, I recall *us* talking about it. Remember the Wicker Award?"

John certainly did. It was given to a member of the senior class for excellence in fiction writing.

"I recall," Ellen went on, "some of the others who were in the running for that."

"Not me."

She sighed. "Well, me. I wanted that award. But I can name a handful of others who wanted it, too, and deserved it more than me. Deserved it more than

Terry. There was lots of talk when he got it. He'd been sucking up to the head of the English Department for months. Rumor had it that some of the professors were as upset as the students when Terry got that award."

"I need more than rumor," John said.

After a moment's silence, Ellen said, sounding pleased, "I think I can accommodate you. How much did you say you wanted to pledge to the annual fund?"

John hung up with Ellen and pulled up Quicken to make sure he could afford the pledge he had made. No matter that it was a good cause, since a large portion of the annual fund went for scholarships; he wanted to stay solvent. He had spent his childhood listening to arguments over money and had made it a point in his own adult life to live within his means.

The pledge he had made wouldn't break him, assuming he didn't incur major expenses with other research. Two fortunate things suggested he wouldn't. First, Terry rarely went places without offending people. Second, John was just the opposite.

Jack Mabbet was a former FBI agent. Ten years earlier he had been involved in the investigation of a notorious mobster working out of Boston's South End. Terry Sullivan had written a series of scathing articles critical of the investigation in general and Jack Mabbet in particular. Jack had been forty-five at the time, with a wife and four children, all of whom suffered a public tarring. The mobster was subsequently tried and convicted, with no single mention of Jack Mabbet as a potential G-man on the take. The case had gone to archive heaven with no further mention of Jack.

He resigned from the FBI soon after that. It didn't matter that his superiors had total confidence in him; he felt the doubt of his fellow agents. Worse, his family had become known for being related to "that man" and "that case." So they sold the little house they had bought in Revere and moved to Roanoke, Virginia, where he became a private investigator. His firm was a legitimate one that specialized in doing background screenings for employers hiring new help, and "due diligence" probes for corporate clients approaching mergers and buyouts.

John had come to know Jack Mabbet in the course of covering other cases on which Jack had worked, and he had the utmost respect for the man. John had argued with Terry when the incriminating articles were printed, had even argued with editors, but the situation was like many in the media. Terry hadn't made any libelous accusations. He simply made suggestions. He quoted bad guys, who loved the idea of bringing down a good guy or two with them. He used innuendo to do to Jack Mabbet what he was currently doing to Lily.

John figured that Jack would sympathize with her.

"Damn right I'll help," the man said before John had done much more than say that he was looking into the underside of the Rossetti-Blake case and wanted information on Terry. "What do you need?"

"What can I get?"

"Legally? Most anything. Just like Sullivan did

with that case. I work with information wholesalers on a regular basis. They have data banks filled with information that's right out there for public consumption. Before they get their hands on it, it's just scattered around. They collect it and put it in one place. Insurance investigators use them. Business competitors use them. Parties in contentious divorces use them. For someone like me, they're a dream. So what do you want?" he asked, clearly enjoying himself. "Credit card activity? Phone records? Bank balances? Life insurance policies, medical history, motor vehicle records? I can tell you if he had a parking ticket in the last ten years. Give me five minutes."

John knew about information wholesalers, but hearing it spelled out so bluntly was frightening. "God. I'd think the American public would be up in *arms* about the free flow of information."

"They are. At least, some people are. There are dozens of bills pending in Congress to stop the flow. Guidelines are springing up. Some database companies are even agreeing to follow them, for what good it'll do. The information is out there. And PIs are exempted. We can gather what we want and do what we want with it. There are sixty thousand of us in the country. Some states don't even require PIs to be licensed. If you want to talk scary, that's it. Me? I'm duly licensed. I have resources at my fingertips and no love for Terry Sullivan. You want information on that jackass, I'll get it. No charge."

They were the magic words. But John wanted to be involved. This was his story, his revenge as much as Lily's. So he had Jack teach him how to get information himself. When Jack sounded disappointed, he added Paul Rizzo and Justin Barr to the search. Jack could work on those. Terry was John's.

What was he looking for? Anything and everything. He knew surprisingly little about Terry, given that they'd been friends—a relative term, there—for nearly twenty-five years. He wanted little mistakes and big mistakes. He wanted things that didn't add up. Ideally, he wanted a reason why Terry had gone after Francis Rossetti with the kind of vengeance that people like Steve Baker described.

Steve had dismissed the possibility that Terry held a personal grudge against the Cardinal, and John knew Terry would deny it. So he picked up the phone and called Rossetti directly—or tried to. The closest he got was to his personal secretary, a nice enough man, well versed in his answers, who said that the Cardinal knew Terry only in a media context and that, prior to the current problem, there had never been contention between the two.

John had barely hung up the phone when Armand called asking about the week's paper, but the anticipation in his voice suggested he had something particular in mind.

Sure enough, John had barely outlined the lead story on Lake Henry refugees when Armand said, "What are you putting in about Lily Blake?"

"Not much," John answered.

"Why *not?*" Armand roared hoarsely. "This is the big time. It's a national story on our turf."

"It's not on our turf. The story's in Boston."

"You know what I mean," the old man grumbled. "What in the devil do we need to lead off with a story on newcomers when we have a na-tive whose name and face is known all over the country, all over the *world?*"

"Everyone's seen her there. We don't need to see her here, too."

Armand persisted. "But she's one of us. We know her. Christ, John, this is our chance to scoop the buy guys."

John rose from his chair. He put a hand on his hip and stared out at the fog. "I don't think so."

"Why *not?*"

"Because she *is* one of us. That demands a certain amount of compassion. The mainstream media is committing character assassination. I won't stoop to their level."

"I'm not askin' you to do that, but we can't just *ignore* the story. We print news, and that girl *is* news."

"The *Post* said the allegations were false. There's no more story."

"That's a story in itself."

John gave a little. "Okay. I'll do something on an inside page. Mention the story and the apology to the Cardinal." He was comfortable with that. The more he thought about it, it was actually a good thing to do. Actually, he began picturing a small piece about the apology on the front page after all. Lily deserved that.

But Armand had something else in mind. In a voice that was a little too enthusiastic to be genuine, he said, "I have a better idea. This will tie in with your lead about why people are moving to small towns in droves. I'll focus my column on the forgiving nature of places like Lake Henry. I'll talk about how judgmental and quick to accuse the outside world can be. I'll talk about how Lake Henry is more tolerant of mistakes and more forgiving of its own."

"That implies Lily Blake is guilty. Do you know that she is?"

Armand grew cranky. "She must be guilty of *something*. Otherwise it couldn't have gone this far."

"Sorry, Armand. We don't do that to our own."

"It doesn't have to be bad," Armand wheedled. "We'll just give a little local history, tell a little that only we know—"

John cut in. "I won't do it."

"I said *I* would."

"If you do," John warned, "I'm gone. If I'd wanted to do sleaze, I'd have stayed in Boston. We've had our differences, Armand, but this is as big as any. Fuel that farce with stories about Lily and you'll have my resignation in your hand so fast you won't know what hit you." Furious, he hung up the phone.

Startled by the strength of his feelings, he strode to the far end of the room, then back, then threw open the lakeside window and stuck out his head. There was something about newspaper offices that reeked. Stale smoke was a thing of the past, as was the smell of gummy white stuff from the kind of cut-

and-paste that left shoe bottoms covered with paper shred. What was left was the smell of cold coffee, pepperoni-and-onion sandwiches wolfed down at desks in open cubicles, perspiration, and messy hair when a story required late nights and early mornings.

But all that was back in the city. There was none of it here. Still, he smelled it.

John suspected that some of what he smelled was his own sense of guilt. He might not cover the Lily Blake story for the paper, but he had a drawerful of information, and it was growing by the day. Dummying up the week's paper wasn't all he'd done yesterday. He had spent hours writing up thoughts, organizing ideas, weighing approaches he could take in his book.

Sinking into his chair, he opened that drawer, pulled out his notes on Lily, along with a file he had made earlier on her father. George was newly deceased when John first returned to town. At the time, John had seen him as exemplifying the old-time town families that had made their living off local land. There was a potential book here, hence the file, but the idea had gone stale early on. Now that file held potential from a different angle.

By all accounts, George Blake had been a gentle man, in every respect more easygoing than his wife. And then there was Lily, who had overcome a debilitating stutter and made a successful life for herself. So, was she easygoing like George? Driven like Maida?

His book would focus on the big picture—the power of the media to destroy—but he needed detail and depth to make his point. Terry was the way he was for a reason. Same with Lily. The past explained things.

His certainly did. He had left Lake Henry at fifteen and gone years without seeing Gus, but he had never been free of the man. As a kid, with Gus telling him he wouldn't amount to anything, he had been determined to prove him right. As an adult remembering those words, he was determined to prove him wrong.

Frightening, how heavily Gus affected his life. There had to be a Gus in Terry's life. There had to be one in Lily's. John was curious, as all journalists are. He wanted to know how these two different people, motivated in entirely different ways, had come to cross paths.

Psyched, he put in a call to Richard Jacobi. Richard was an executive editor at a small but savvy publishing house in New York. John knew him through a mutual friend in Boston.

Richard was at a meeting, but his assistant put John through to his voice mail. Wary of saying much in a place where others might hear, John left a short, friendly greeting, followed by his phone number and the request for a call back.

Chapter 12

Lily spent the rest of Monday alternately curled in a chair by the woodstove and bundled in a chair on the porch. She remained angry, but for the first time, her anger was overlaid by the calm that came with having a focus. She had a lawyer now, which meant she wasn't quite so alone. Within an hour of their meeting, Cassie had called and read the proposed retraction demand. It had been faxed to the *Post* shortly thereafter.

Lily imagined the *Post* receiving it, calling a meeting, discussing it. She liked the idea that a bunch of egotists in an unfeeling newsroom were being forced to consider that she was a human being, not a doormat. All she needed was one sensitive soul insisting on issuing a retraction, and the matter would be done. She took perverse pleasure imagining an ashamed Michael Eddy, a regretful Daniel Curry, a smug Elizabeth Davis. She took even greater pleasure imagining Terry

Sullivan looking like the fool he had tried to make *her* out to be.

So, when would she return to Boston? She thought about that a lot, sitting on the porch by the lake, and it occurred to her that she wouldn't rush back. She missed the Public Garden, missed her piano, her apartment, her car, and her friends. But she still had no job, still had no taste for media attention, and a hasty return to the city would rekindle that.

Better to wait a few days, maybe even a week or two. The more distance she put between herself and the scandal, the better. Besides, it was nice being in Lake Henry. There was comfort in the quiet of Celia's cottage, comfort in the lake's serenity. There was also unfinished business with Maida. Once the *Post* issued its retraction, Lily wanted to talk with her. There were things that needed saying.

Fog clung to the water for most of the day, leaving the scent of wet leaves in the air. A gaggle of mallards emerged from the mist to swim past the dock at one point. At another, a loon broke through. She heard its call then and later, when the dampness had driven her inside and the woodstove was stoked. She imagined that the loon's cry spoke of strength, because that was what she felt. Strength and hope.

She woke up Tuesday morning feeling energized. She waited only long enough to give John time to buy the paper, before calling him for the news.

"The Sox won," he said.

Lily had met John face-to-face once and talked on

the phone with him twice. In all three instances, he had seemed quick and insightful. So either he had a weird sense of humor or the news wasn't good.

Gut instinct suggested the latter. Her hopes faded. "Oh. No retraction?"

"No."

"What, then?"

"Stupid stuff. It's not worth reading."

Her hopes faded more. "What stupid stuff?"

"You know what they do, Lily. They got the story wrong from the start, so now they're trying to cover their tails."

"You're being evasive," she said. When he didn't respond, she was forceful. "Www-what does it say?"

"There isn't an article, per se." He paused, sighed, said, "It's an op-ed piece by Douglas Drake. He's a regular columnist."

"Yes." She had read Douglas Drake. His columns were always well written and well positioned. She didn't always agree with him—but the *Post* editorial board did, if the unsigned editorial that usually followed by several days was any indication.

"Drake tests the waters," John explained. "He's sanctioned by the big guys to say what they're thinking but don't quite have the guts to put into print. Based on reader response to his column, they follow up with their own."

It didn't bode well for Lily. She steeled herself. "What does he say?"

"He attributes the scandal to your infatuation with the Cardinal."

She was horrified. "They're blaming *me?*"

"I told you. They need a scapegoat."

"But why *me?*" She caught herself. She hated that phrase. "What does New York say?"

"That Boston is attributing the whole thing to your infatuation with the Cardinal. Now, there's courageous reporting for you."

"And Paul Rizzo?"

John snorted. "Rizzo's still stuck in the gutter, reveling in other sex scandals. He's still trying to connect those with something that's now been disclaimed."

The energy high Lily had woken with was gone. She bowed her head.

"Lily?" he asked gently.

"Yes?" she whispered.

"Just so you know it all, Justin Barr is taking the *Post*'s angle. I listened in a few minutes ago. He's blaming the scandal on your being unbalanced. But there were as many calls in disagreement with that, and sympathy with you, as the other way around."

That was small solace. Lily hung up the phone feeling defeated. Then two things happened to boost her spirits.

First, Cassie called. Having seen the paper herself, she wasn't as much angry as determined. "Don't let this get you down, Lily. I didn't expect a fast response to our letter. They'll milk what's left of the story for whatever added sales value they can get, but the longer they wait—and the more they print stories like today's—the more the libel stakes rise. And do *not* worry about today's piece being on the op-ed page.

That won't exempt it from a suit. Doug Drake is a lackey. It's well known. If need be, we can prove that, too."

Second, patched through by Poppy, came a call from the Cardinal. Hearing from him for the first time since the scandal's start, Lily felt a tangle of emotion ranging from relief to affection to—surprisingly—anger.

"How are you, Lily?" he said in that rich voice of his. Yes, indeed, some women thought it sexy. Lily had always thought it . . . *full,* as in flush with sensitivity and compassion.

Her affection come to the fore. "I'm better. I'm feeling more in control."

"I can't tell you how sorry I am about this. You were caught in the crossfire of something that wasn't your making."

"Nor yours."

"But I was better equipped to fight it. I never fully understood the resources available to the archdiocese until I needed lawyers and spokesmen and lobbyists. Then they came out of the woodwork. And they're still at work, Lily. The paper's apology was supposed to encompass you, too. If I'm innocent of those charges, it stands to reason that you are, too."

In the space of seconds, Lily recalled every last one of those charges and was mortified all over again. Her words came in a rush. "I never said those things the way he reported them. I didn't want to talk about you at all, but he struck up a conversation and just slipped things in. He kept saying that women found you attractive, and *I* kept saying how *absurd* that was, with you a priest."

There was understanding, even a bit of humor in the Cardinal's voice. "I know, Lily. I know. You've never been anything but respectful of me that way."

"How could I *not?* You *are* a priest."

"Tell that to the little redhead who came on to me at the Governor's Ball last year." When Lily gasped, he chuckled. "It happens. And yes"—his humor faded—"I suppose there may be priests who cheat, just as there are husbands who do. I never have and never will. I've always felt you were the same. Unbalanced? Fat chance. I've been counseling you for years. I know how sane you are. Good Lord in heaven, you give *me* strength—though, of course, if I told *them* that, they'd twist it around."

"Why do they do that?" she cried. "What gives them the right? And why *me?*" She did hate that question, but it poured out with the rest. Fran Rossetti drew it out. Perhaps it was the fullness of his voice that suggested vast knowledge—more, suggested that if there was a God, this man was indeed one of His messengers. Lily wasn't religious, but she responded to him, and she wasn't alone. He had a way of reaching inside people and cleaning the dust from dirty little corners with the gentlest of hands.

So, the Lily who rarely spoke as voluminously asked, "Why this now? Why Donny Kipling then? Why my mother and my stutter? Have I done something wrong, Father Fran? Why do these things *happen* to me?"

"I don't know that for sure," he said, "but it could be because God knows you can handle them. God knows you can learn from them. Some people can't. Some people aren't strong enough. Jesus was. So are you."

Lily wanted to say that she wasn't Jesus, that she had no wish for martyrdom, and that she didn't take to being crucified—which was one word for what she felt had been done to her—but that would have been disrespectful. As frank as she had learned to be with Father Fran, there were certain lines she would never cross.

"Ach," he chided. "There I go again, forgetting that you're not sure about *any* religion, let alone mine. But I did mean what I said. You *are* strong, Lily."

"And innocent," she reminded him, feeling the anger that startled her so—startled her because it was directed at him. If he truly had been a *mensch,* to use Sara's word, he would have come out vocally and publicly in her defense. If he had an ounce of chivalry, her sister Poppy would say, he would have put her vindication before his own.

"You're also smart," he said now. "You know that self-pity accomplishes little."

With a long breath she let the anger go. Sheepish, she smiled. "I should have known that was coming."

"You should have. I am predictable. Y'know," he teased, "I always did want to get you closer to home. I've been inching you along for years. Manhattan, Albany, Boston, Lake Henry. Can't get much closer. Have you seen your mother?"

Lily had to laugh. "Predictable there, too. You don't beat around the bush." Her smile ebbed. "My mother wasn't thrilled to see me. It seems I'm the bane of her existence."

"Did you talk?"

"Not about important things."

"You need to do that."

"I know. But it's hard."

"You talk with me."

"You're not my mother. I talk with friends, but they're not her, either. Why are mothers so tough?"

"God makes them that way," said the Cardinal. "Who else can He rely on to shoulder the burdens of the world without cracking under the weight?"

"Seems like I'm the one shouldering them."

"You may think that now. Wait till you're a mother."

He said it as though it was only a matter of time—something Lily had once believed. She wasn't sure she did anymore. She was thirty-four. God had designed women to have children by the age of nineteen, at least according to her gynecologist. The Cardinal claimed that God had updated His thinking since her gynecologist had done his training and that He was confident that the female mind could compensate for the minor failings of a slightly older body.

Old-line clerics believed that the purpose of marriage was procreation. Lily didn't, but that was another line she didn't cross.

"Keep at it, Lily," the Cardinal said.

It was a moment before she realized he was referring to Maida.

"I want you to work things out with her. Will you
try?"

"I don't have much choice," she said quietly. "I
think I'm here for a little while still."

"It must be beautiful there this time of year."

"Yes." Through the window she saw the yellow of
an alder at the edge of the woods. It was flanked by a
crimson maple. Both were surrounded by the rich
green of hemlock. All this, even in the fog.

"And you have the house. Is there anything else
you need?"

Revenge, she thought, but she would no more have
told the Cardinal that than she would have argued
about the Trinity. The Cardinal was in the business of
forgiveness. He would never condone thoughts of
revenge.

John Kipling might. Lily thought about that as
morning ended. By midafternoon she was restless
and bored. She needed something to do. So she
changed into jeans and the kind of plaid flannel shirt
that half the town wore, tucked her hair under a Red
Sox cap, put a loose wool scarf around her neck to
hide her chin, and Celia's huge sunglasses on her
nose to hide whatever else could be hid, and drove
into town.

The fog hung heavy on the lake road and the foliage framing it, as well as the houses that stood closer
together as she neared the center of town. The mois-

ture made the air raw, so that few people lingered outside. That gave Lily extra coverage, she realized, driving past Charlie's in broad daylight for the first time since her return. She turned in at the post office, pulled all the way down to the yellow Victorian housing the newspaper office, and parked beside the pickup she assumed belonged to John.

No doubt which door the paper used. It was a beautiful wood thing that was riddled with slots. After ringing the bell, she let herself into the kitchen. Walking silently, leaving the hat, the scarf, and Celia's dark glasses firmly in place, she followed the sound of a voice to the front of the house. A young woman sat at a desk there. She was holding the phone to her ear, frowning, sounding confused as she studied something on the desk. It wasn't until she turned to look at Lily that Lily realized she was more girl than woman, and very pregnant.

Seconds later Lily heard footsteps on the stairs and John appeared at the opposite door. He shot her an uneasy glance, then bent over the desk to see what the girl was trying to do. Taking the phone from her, he finished getting information for what sounded to Lily like a classified ad.

"There," he told the girl when he hung up. "You did just fine with that."

The girl sounded even younger than she looked. "You had to finish it."

"Nah. You had most everything we need."

"I have to leave," the girl said. "Buck's coming at three."

"I thought we agreed you'd work till five on Tuesdays."

"He said he was coming at three."

John sighed. He ran a hand around the back of his neck. "Fine. Neaten things up. I'll take it from here."

With a single sweep of both hands the girl consolidated the papers on the desk. Then she pushed herself out of the chair and with surprising agility, given the bulk of her belly, slipped past Lily. Lily turned to watch her. Footsteps faded, the door slammed, the girl was gone. Lily looked at the desk with its ragtag pile, then at the dismay on John's face.

It was a handsome face, she realized—tanned skin, close-cropped beard, enough weathering to suggest time spent in the great outdoors. There was only a vague resemblance to Donny, though her memory was of a twenty-one-year-old, and this man was mature. She was drawn to his eyes in particular. They were a deep brown, gentle even in frustration.

"I'm trying," he said in a controlled voice. "The girl's gonna need some kind of skill after that baby's born, unless Buck gets his act together, which I seriously doubt he will."

Lily hadn't been so long gone from Lake Henry that she didn't remember the cast. "Buck, your cousin?" she asked as she unwrapped the scarf.

John nodded. "Total jerk."

"Is the baby his?"

Another nod, then a muttered "Poor thing." He looked her over. The corner of his mouth twitched. "That's a fair disguise. Not that you'd need it with

Jenny. She's too young to know you, and when she watches the tube, it ain't for the news." He glanced at his watch.

"Is this a bad time?"

"Yes." He reversed himself in the next breath. "No. It is not. I came to Lake Henry because I didn't want rigid deadlines. The paper's supposed to be at the printer at noon tomorrow. If it's a little later, no one'll die."

The kitchen door sounded, then footsteps. Lily turned fast, fearing that rather than Jenny it would be someone more apt to recognize her, when John came from behind her and touched her arm. "Go on up the front stairs," he whispered. "All the way to the top. I'll be up in a sec."

She moved quickly and quietly, turning on the second floor landing, continuing on to the third. The openness of the place struck her first, then the brightness, even under clouds. There were three desks, each with a computer, each showing signs of use. More interesting, though, were the walls. One held time-worn maps of the lake and aged photos of the town, framed in wood and exuding reverence. Another held newer photos, richer in color, taken on the lake itself, shots largely of loons. A third was black-and-white and busy.

Removing the dark glasses, she approached that one and felt a chill. Here were newspapermen at work, photos taken during John's time in Boston, if the banner on the wall was any indication. Hard to believe that a photograph could capture such focus and intensity, but there were faces with the very same ardor she had seen in her nightmares. Terry Sullivan's face jumped out at her from one print, other familiar faces from others, though she couldn't place them. There was an attractive woman in one, but mostly she saw John. He looked different from how he looked now in person, and it went beyond the beard and the tan. In glossy black-and-white he was like the others—tightly wound, frightening, definitely a man to avoid.

"Scary, isn't it?" John said from the door. He could imagine what Lily was thinking, looking at that particular wall. And his mug shot? A disaster, if the goal was to win her trust. If he'd known she was coming, he might have rethought the decor.

When she shot him a nervous look, he was doubly sorry he hadn't. The big glasses were off, exposing the fear in her eyes. She was fully dressed now—no nightgown this time—but with her hair stuck under that cap and jeans encasing slim legs, there remained a fragility to her.

She glanced at the large manila envelope in his hand.

He tossed it on his desk. "Essays and poems from the academy. I always try to print a few. I'll have to sort through later and pick."

She eyed the other two desks. "Where's the rest of your help?"

"Jenny's it."

"Then why three desks?"

"Different desks for different jobs." He pointed accordingly. "Editorial, production, sales. I have a correspondent in each of the towns we cover, and freelancers drop things off, but none of them works here. They don't do enough to warrant it."

She folded her arms on her chest, left the *Post* wall, and moved in for a closer look at his loon pictures. "Did you take these?"

"Every one," he said with pride. He had sat hours for many of those shots, waiting for trust to build so that he could paddle closer, then waiting with the camera at his eye for just the right moment to trip the shutter. "Some are last year's, but most are new."

"Did you print them yourself?"

"Yes. That's one of the perks of the job—a darkroom down cellar."

Lily went from print to print. There were nearly a dozen in all, taken at various times of day in various weather. With the exception of one of a loon on its nest, they were water shots—an adult grooming itself, a pair leaving a smooth liquid trail, a family of adults and their young. One print was of an hours-old chick. Another was of two chicks riding on a parent's back.

With Lily seemingly engrossed, John went in for a closer look himself.

"Are they the same pair of loons?" she asked.

"I think so." He pointed at the short white lines ringing the neck of one bird in each of two shots. "Two different years, but the same little break in the line right here. I imagine he has a scar that prevents the feathers there from growing smoothly."

"He?"

"I think. He's bigger. Hard to tell otherwise. They share parenting chores, take turns sitting on the nest and fishing for food." He amended the thought. "Actually, I know that's the male." He pointed to one of the other pictures. "This was taken last April, my first loon sighting of the year. See that little break in the neck marking? Males typically return a week or two before females. They scout around for nesting sights. I'm not sure if the female is the same one both years, though. Loons are monogamous through an entire breeding season, but we don't know for sure whether they mate for life."

He looked down at the top of her cap. It didn't quite reach his chin. Wisps of dark hair—shiny hair—escaped at the neck and the hole in the back. The bill prevented him from seeing her eyes, but he could easily hear her voice, soft though it was.

"When I was growing up," she said, "there was concern about a decline in the loon population."

When John was growing up he hadn't given a hoot about loons. He had been gone from Lake Henry by the time the concern had been voiced, but he had read about it since.

"The decline continued. The concern grew. Eventually people realized that big boats and jet skis were taking a toll. Too much noise for loons—they were being frightened off their nests and the eggs were lost. Too much sediment stirred up—loons rely on clear water to see the fish that they eat. Too much wake—eggs were being washed right out of nests. So jet skis

were outlawed and boat speed was limited. Lo and behold, the population rebounded."

When Lily tipped her head back and looked up,
something inside him flip-flopped. Her eyes were as
soft as her voice. He hadn't expected that.

He swallowed. "Life's solutions should always be
so easy."

"They're magnificent creatures."

"Yes." He couldn't look away. Her face was exquisite.

"They're wonderful pictures," she said.

His heart was beating faster. "Thanks."

Her eyes grew vulnerable. "You said you had
ammo. What did you mean?"

For an absurd minute, John felt like the guy with a
crush on a girl who had a crush on someone else and
wanted his advice. Like he'd just been shot down. It
wasn't betrayal exactly. More like disappointment that
business could intrude.

But business was the name of the game. So, val-
iantly, he said, "Terry Sullivan has a history of rigging
stories. It's never been proven, because he's shrewd.
He worms his way into the confidences of someone
in a higher position, someone who can protect him.
But there are a whole lot of someones in lower posi-
tions who know exactly what he does."

"Do they know why?"

"Ambition. Ruthlessness. Greed."

"Malice?"

"I'm working on malice," John said. He knew
where she was headed. "Malice" was the magic word,

where legalities were concerned. "The obvious thing is that he concocted the scandal as a personal vendetta. You didn't know him from Adam, so it wasn't against you. Rossetti's personal secretary says *they* didn't know each other. So I'll have to come at it from a different angle. For now, all I have is a growing list of times when Terry Sullivan has shown a reckless disregard for the truth, as they say."

"I'd have to prove malice in court."

"Probably."

"I could go through years of agony and still lose."

"Possibly." He sighed. "Do you know that there's a tape?"

Her startled look said she didn't.

"He taped your conversation without telling you. That's illegal. It's something to add to the arsenal."

Lily looked crushed. "A tape will show that I did ss-say those things, only I didn't say them the way he printed them."

John was thinking that he believed her one hundred percent, when she said, "I met with Cassie Byrnes."

That surprised him. "You did?"

"We demanded a retraction. That was yesterday. Today-yy's today"—he saw her blink with the stutter, a split second's bid for control—"and there's no re-traction. Cassie says not to panic, but I'm tired of doing nnn-nothing."

The phone rang. John might have ignored it, if it hadn't been crunch time for the week. He picked up at the nearest desk, which just happened to be the ed-itorial desk by the lake.

The caller was the owner of a crafts shop two towns over, wanting to do pre-Christmas advertising. John pulled up a piece of paper and took the information he needed. By the time he hung up the phone, Lily was looking at him. Again, something turned inside him.

He glanced at his watch. "Tired of doing nothing?"

"Yes."

"Got a few minutes?"

"Slightly."

Smiling, he reached for the envelope from Lake Henry Academy. His free hand guided Lily around the desk and into his chair. Upending the envelope, he shook out its contents. "Pick three."

She looked at the papers, then up at him—and he felt a twist in his chest this time. He figured it was the cap. He was a sucker for the Red Sox.

When she didn't say anything, he started to blabber. "There'll be things here from all grade levels, seven through twelve, some typed, some handwritten. Sometimes I pick three that are totally different in style, form, and content—like a poem, an essay, and a letter to the editor. Other times I pick three on one theme. So you can do what you want, whatever hits you as being the most interesting."

She looked game.

He grinned. "You're a teacher. Go to it."

Without further ado, he took the ad information, sat himself down at the sales desk, and began to build an ad. But his mind wasn't on it. He kept thinking about Lily showing up at his office asking about ammo, kept thinking that if he helped her out, he could be shooting himself in the foot if the point was to save things for his book. But he felt guilty for what his brother, Donny, had done, and guilty for what his own profession, in the guise of Terry Sullivan, had done; and there were those soft eyes of hers that felt good touching his.

So he said, "There's another way."

She looked up, brows arched.

"To fight Terry without going to court," John explained. "You could turn his own methods right back on him. Fight fire with fire."

"How?"

"Discredit him. Go public with allegations about him that may have no weight taken one by one, but that taken as a set paint an ugly picture."

"I don't know what those allegations are."

"I do."

"And you'd share them?"

Here it was. "I might."

"In exchange for what?"

He thought about that for a minute. He didn't see why it couldn't work for them both. "Your side of the story."

He was immediately sorry he'd said it. There was the subtlest shift of her shoulders, the faintest widening of her eyes. "You said you wouldn't."

"I won't without your say-so."

She looked down at the papers. Three were slightly separated from the others. She pushed them all the way out now, and stood. "There are your three." She put on her sunglasses.

He rose. "Nothing without your say-so." He knew she was thinking that he might be another Terry Sullivan. Her distrust was obvious. He had come on too fast. But it was done.

Carefully she wrapped the scarf around her neck. She started for the door, pausing to look at the loon wall a final time. He could see her taking a deep breath, even calming a little. But she didn't turn back.

"Lily?"

"I'd rather prove malice," she said and left.

Chapter 13

Poppy's Tuesday was quiet, thanks in part to the weather. When days were cold, wet, or snowy, many of her clients stayed at home. Dense fog at the end of September, keeping temperatures in the forties at night and the fifties by day, had much the same effect.

The quiet also had to do with a slowdown in media calls, which didn't surprise Poppy one bit. Blaming the scandal on Lily had been a ridiculous move. Everyone in town knew that, with an indignant handful calling to say it to Poppy. Lily Blake unbalanced? It was the final straw, a major blow to what little credibility the case had, an offense to the sensibilities of people who knew the Blakes. Poppy guessed that the press knew it, too, and, noble to the end, was backing off from the story to spare themselves further embarrassment.

Oh, there was still the occasional halfhearted

media call requesting reaction to the story's latest twist. But no such requests came from major outlets, and by late afternoon the only calls that possibly could be related came from Lake Henry's librarian, Leila Higgins, and its postmaster, Nathaniel Roy. Both had seen a tan Ford wagon with Massachusetts plates parked outside the *Lake News* office and wanted to know whose it was.

Poppy knew, though she had no idea why her sister was there. So she called Kip and said, "You had a visitor."

Kip sounded cross. "How'd *you* know?"

"I got calls about the car from Leila and Nat. They didn't know whose it was. Why was she there?"

"She wanted to say hi," he muttered.

"To you? Try again."

"She was helping me work."

Okay. It was Tuesday. He was hunkering down. She could almost buy that on his end, but on Lily's? "Why?"

"She was bored."

"And she figured that was the liveliest place to be?"

"Ask *her,* Poppy."

"I will," Poppy said. She ended the call wondering what was stuck in *his* craw, and tried to call Lily, but the cell phone was off. She tried several more times, but by then it was evening, the fog had lifted to allow a near-peak sunset to be seen over the lake, and her friends arrived.

Sigrid Dunn was an artisan who specialized in large-loom weaving and home-baked bread; she brought a loaf of warm, fresh olive bread and a bottle of Merlot. Marianne Hersey owned a small bookstore in the next town and an insulated casserole carrier; she brought hot coq au vin and a bottle of Chablis. Heather Malone was a full-time mom who devoted herself to raising two young children and vegetables; she arrived with a huge salad dotted with kernels of local sweet corn and a nutty pinot grigio. Cassie Byrnes—lawyer, mother, and wife—brought cookies from an Italian bakery in Concord, purchased after an appearance in federal court that afternoon. Poppy provided jugs of apple cider and a pot of coffee, along with all the paraphernalia needed to eat the rest.

They met every Tuesday and called themselves the Lake Henry Hospitality Committee, and they were, indeed, hospitable. When new families moved to town or old ones suffered traumas, they were fast on the scene, seeing what could be done to help. But Lake Henry being small, those kinds of events didn't happen often enough to fill up weekly meetings. So, typically, the Hospitality Committee relaxed and enjoyed itself, five friends sharing news, thoughts, and laughs. On occasion they could be downright boisterous, thanks to the wine.

They reached that point quickly on this night. Poppy, for one, needed the outlet after a week of worrying about Lily, and while she couldn't tell her friends that Lily was back, she took comfort hearing them take Lily's side. That led to a discussion of townsfolk who didn't, and why, which led to a discussion of the more repressed of Lake Henryites, which led to a discussion of the most prim characters in the town's history, which led to hearty laughter.

Poppy was feeling light-headed when the phone rang. Marianne went into the other room to reach the bank of buttons, but she was quickly back. "It's for the chief. When I said Willie Jake wasn't available, he asked for you. Griffin Hughes?"

Poppy swallowed a laugh the wrong way. She coughed, hit her chest a time or two, held up a hand, and took a deep breath. Then she wheeled herself out to the phone.

"Griffin Hughes," she said without preamble, "did you really think the chief would be here at this hour?"

"It's only seven-thirty," he answered in that smooth, low, Adam's apple voice. She remembered it clearly enough—and was pleased enough to hear it again—to want to lash out.

"This is Lake Henry," she thundered. "We don't work twelve-hour days like you folks do."

"We don't do it either," he responded genially. "At least, I don't. I thought I might catch him after dinner. I pictured this number connecting to his house, or his house being connected to the station. Isn't that how it works in small towns?"

"Not in Lake Henry," Poppy said, wishing he didn't sound so sincere.

"What are *you* doing there so late?"

"I live here."

"At the police station?"

She laughed with surprising ease. "No. At my own house. I'm Lake Henry's answering service."

"No kidding?" He sounded charmed. "Like Lily Tomlin?"

Poppy rubbed the heel of her hand against the arm of her chair. "Not . . . exactly. But you'll have to go through me to get to most of the rest of the town, and I haven't changed my mind. I'm still not talking." She didn't care how sincere he sounded. "*Especially* after the latest," she said, and let the wine carry her on. "What is *happening* down there? Calling my sister un-balanced? Blaming *her* for the trouble? That's not only stupid, it's immoral. And it's *wrong*!"

"I agree. Immoral and wrong. That's the point of my piece. But I can't just *say* that it's wrong, I have to show that it is. I need to know how it's affected Lily's life. I've been trying her number in Boston. She's not answering."

"Her number's unlisted."

"Every newspaper has it."

"Ah-*hah*," Poppy cried, as unrelated laughter erupted in the kitchen. "You *are* working with them."

"Not working with them. *Using* them. Excuse me, am I calling at a bad time? Is there a party going on?"

"I have a few friends over for dinner. We do that kind of thing up here. You know, isolation and all. Boredom and all. Backwoods socializing and all."

"Lay it on thick, Poppy," he said in a voice warm with humor, but deep, so deep and smooth. "Is Lily there with you, too?"

"Would I tell you if she was?"

"Have you heard from her?"

"Would I tell you if I had?"

"What *will* you tell me?"

Poppy thought for a minute, then grinned. "I'll tell you about James Everell Henry."

"Who's he?"

"Was. He was a logging baron who lived in this neck of the woods at the turn of the century. He came in with his three sons and built a village out of nothing—railroad, lumberyard, sawmill—all to get those logs cut and moved to market. He bought up land right and left until he had acres and acres and acres, and he logged it without a thought to the effect that would have on the land."

"James Everell Henry."

"That's right," Poppy said. "So then the effect of what he was doing started being seen. His machinery was a menace, raking entire areas clean, then throwing off sparks and starting fires in hayfields that decimated the neighboring forests. Without those trees to hold the soil in place, spring rains caused mud slides and flooding, and between fire and flood, Henry's empire grew shaky. Right about then, the locals wised up. They bought back as much of his land as they could to form conservation trusts, and they passed environmental ordinances to safeguard the rest. Henry was finally forced to sell out. He died quietly some years later, well after his fortune was gone."

There was silence, then an amused "Yes?"

"Up to that point, this town was called Neweston. Soon after his death, its was renamed Lake Henry."

"You honored a guy who stripped your hillsides bare?"

"He was an important fellow. You could say that he was the father of the local environmental movement."

"You could say," Griffin agreed, but he sounded puzzled. "Is there a message here?"

"There certainly is," Poppy said. "From perversity comes positive stuff."

Silence, again, then, "And the deeper message in that?"

"Feisty independence. New Hampshire is known for it. Lake Henryites live it out. Tell us to eat *A,* we'll eat *B.* Tell us to wear *C,* we'll wear *D.*"

"Tell you to talk about one of your own, you clam up."

"Bingo." She was pleased that he'd caught on. It stood to reason that a man with as cultured a baritone ought to be smart.

"But the thing is," that cultured baritone said, "I'm trying to help. If you all clam up, my case is weaker."

Poppy wasn't being lulled, cultured baritone or not. "Do you have a nickname?"

"A nickname?"

"Griffin Hughes is very formal. Don't they call you Griff or something?"

"Griffin."

"How about Junior? Or Trip? Aren't you third-generation Griffin Hughes?"

"Yeah, but the middle name's different three times, so I'm not even a Junior."

"What did they call you growing up?"

"Red."

"Red?"

"I have red hair."

"You're kidding," Poppy said. She had imagined sexy dark hair to go with that deep, sexy voice. Revision was in order. "Is it long?" she asked, then turned at a sound. Four faces were at the doorway, wearing curious looks.

"My hair?" Griffin asked. "No. I mean, it's longer—much longer—than a buzz cut, but you can see my ears."

She shooed her friends away. When they didn't budge, she thought, *What the hell.* "Do they stick out?" she asked Griffin.

"What *is* this about?" Cassie asked.

"Nope," Griffin said. "Guys named Griffin Hughes have neat little ears. But we hear everything. Who was that who just spoke?"

"My friend Cassie." Poppy stared at the group in defiance. "How tall are you?" she asked Griffin.

"Who *is* he?" asked Heather.

"Five ten. One seventy. Blue eyes."

"Dark blue, or light blue?"

"Dark blue during sex, light blue other times."

Poppy felt a second's dismay. "Was that necessary?"

"You asked."

She scowled. "Not about sex."

The group at the door began to titter.

"My turn," said Griffin. "Height, weight, eyes?"

"You didn't tell me your age."

"Thirty."

"That makes me older than you."

"By how much?"

Primly, she said, "A lady doesn't talk about her age."

"Or her weight. So how about height and eyes?"

"That's private information."

"Wait a minute. I told you."

"That was your choice. I choose differently. Tell you what. I'll tell Willie Jake that you called. I'll even give him your number, see if he wants to call you back."

"Think he will?" Griffin asked.

"Nope."

"Then I'll keep my number to myself."

"A-ha!" she cried. "It's okay for *you* to pester *us,* but not the other way around?"

"Poppy," Griffin said in a very mature voice, "you said he wouldn't call back. So I'll just try again another time. Go back to your friends."

Disconnecting the call, she felt a twinge of disappointment, but her friends quickly filled the void.

"Who was that?" Cassie asked.

Poppy snorted and wheeled back their way. "Some writer."

"What sticks out?" Heather asked, moving aside to let her pass.

"His ears don't."

Sigrid followed inches behind her chair. "How did you come to talk about ears?"

"He was trying to trick me," Poppy said, turning to them. "They do that, y'know, give you little tidbits, little pieces of bait, hoping you'll bite. Good Lord, if there's one thing we should have learned from what's happened to Lily, it's not to breathe a *word* to these guys."

"So how old is he?" Marianne asked. When Poppy shot her a despairing look, she said, "If you're not interested, I am."

"He says he's thirty."

Marianne was approaching forty. Her face fell. "He sounded older."

Poppy set her jaw and nodded. "Uh-huh. He also said he was five ten, weighed one seventy, and had red hair and blue eyes. What kind of person reels off that kind of information to a stranger? I sure wouldn't."

There was a moment's silence. Poppy was listening to it, thinking that there were other reasons she wouldn't reel off that kind of information, when in a sad voice Marianne said, "Too bad. He had a great voice."

Poppy sighed. "That he did," she said and let it go.

Lily sat cross-legged on her dock in the dark. She had the scarf on again, plus a wool cap, a down parka, hiking boots, and mittens—all for warmth now, not disguise. Okay. So it was overkill. But she didn't like shivering. With the fog's dissipation, the air had dried, but it was cold. Her breath made little white wisps in the light of the moon.

But she wouldn't have been inside for the world. It was a glorious Lake Henry night. The surface of the lake was mirror-smooth, reflecting the moon, reflecting the North Star, reflecting even the yellow of an autumn birch on the edge of Elbow Island. With the loon silent, the tiniest sough of water against shore could be heard. It lent a hypnotic something to the serenity of the moment.

A movement westward on the water drew her eye, and at first she thought it was the bird. She held her breath and listened, but the sound she heard wasn't loon. It was paddle and canoe, more distinct with each rhythmic stroke.

She hugged her knees and held still, watching the canoe cut through the water. It was a dark sliver in a wedge of moonlight, growing larger as it approached. When it was thirty feet from the dock, the paddle ceased its movement and held steady, a keel now, directing the boat. It glided alongside the dock with barely a bump.

"That's ESP for you," John said, grabbing the dock's edge. "Hop in."

ESP? Not quite. Lily had been thinking about the lake, not about John. But thinking about the lake had been calming, so she felt safe and in control.

She unfolded her legs and slid to the edge of the dock. Lowering her feet to the floorboard of the canoe, she shifted her weight as she had done dozens of times growing up. She was barely seated in front of John when he pushed away from the dock, backpaddled, and turned the canoe.

"Where are we going?" she asked as he headed back the way he'd come.

"To see my loons."

She felt a touch of excitement. "The ones in the pictures?"

"Yup. They'll be leaving soon. My visits are numbered." His voice turned teasing. "Think you're warm enough?"

She glanced back. He wore jeans and a sweatshirt, with a fleece vest—unzipped. His head and hands were bare. She wondered how they would feel in another twenty minutes.

"I'm not sharing my mittens," she announced. Facing forward, she felt the night air on her skin as the canoe sliced through the water, heading out from the shore. She was pleased to be dressed warmly. This way, the air was bracing rather than cold. She let it fill her lungs, one large breath after another.

John hit stride with his paddle, propelling the boat forward with a minimum of sound and effort, leaving Lily nothing to do but feel exhilarated. She raised her head, breathed in the night, and smiled. Much as she loved Boston, it didn't have this. Albany didn't, either. Nor, for all its own excitement, did Manhattan. Her visits here over the last sixteen years had been brief and preoccupied. It struck her that she had missed this leisure on the lake.

It also struck her that John knew that and was buttering her up for another bid for her story. If so, he was in for a grand disappointment—*particularly* if he ruined the night noise with his voice. That would be sacrilege, a sure sign of insensitivity, which would be a tip-off to ulterior motive.

But he didn't say a word. Apart from the occasional wisp of his breath as he paddled and the slip of his paddle through the water, they moved in silence.

Sparsely set lake homes offered gentle bits of light along the shore. There was the occasional creak of a boat against its mooring, the occasional jangle, hook against mast, but she and John were the only people out. Lily did feel safe.

They had passed a handful of small islands before John stopped paddling and let the canoe glide toward another. It was a small one, little more than forty feet long and, judging from its jagged black skyline, covered with hemlock and pine. The canoe slowed. John brought it to a standstill with his paddle.

Here the lake moved against low-growing brush, throwing off the occasional lapping sound. John put his mouth to her ear.

"The nest was over there." He pointed to a spot, but Lily couldn't make out much more than a wad of grass in the dark. "The big guy scouted out the spot in late April. His mate was here by the middle of May. By the middle of June, there was one egg. The next day there was a second."

"How did you get pictures of the eggs without scaring the loons off the nest?" she whispered back. She didn't have to turn her head. His was right there.

"Caution, and a very long lens. I sat here once for three hours waiting for one parent to relieve the other. Sit long and quiet enough, and they think you're a tree. The one on the nest hoots to the other. They don't leave the eggs exposed for more than a minute, while they change places. It's a sight to see. The one going off duty slips into the water to feed or preen or sleep. The one going on lumbers up on shore to the nest, turns the eggs, shifts the nesting material, and plops right down. Then it sits. Bugs hover, and it sits. Thunder rolls, lightning strikes, and it sits. If a predator nears, it shrieks and makes a grand show of warning with its wings, but otherwise it's like a statue. Like two statues, actually, when the lake is still and the reflection is clear."

Lily saw the picture.

"They sit for twenty-nine days, give or take," John went on. "Then one egg hatches. A day later, the other follows. The babies hit the water within hours, as soon as their feathers are dry. They may not touch land again for three years, until they're nesting, themselves."

"Really?"

"Uh-huh. Ninety-nine percent of their lives are lived in water."

Lily hadn't known that.

"They have mobility there," he explained. "They can protect themselves better there than they can on land."

There was movement from the end of the island. One bird, then a second glided into a stream of moonlight. Then came a third, then a fourth.

She caught her breath.

His voice was even lower. "The front two are the parents, the rear two the kids."

Keeping her eye on the birds, she turned her head just enough so that he could hear her whisper. "The kids are nearly as big as the parents."

"They grow fast."

"Can they fly?"

"Not yet. Give them another month. The parents leave first. They're getting ready. Their feathers have begun to change. There's a partial molt before the fall migration, and a total one before the spring migration. When that happens, usually in March, they can't fly at all. Then their breeding feathers come in. Those are the brilliant ones, the ones they're losing now. They'll look pretty much like their kids by the time they take off and leave."

The loons were swimming down the edge of the island, floating in and out of moonbeams.

Lily asked, "If they leave first, who makes sure the kids get airborne?"

"The Great Spirit of the Lake," John teased. "Not to worry. It's been happening this way for more than twenty million years."

"No." She didn't believe that.

"Yes."

"But humans haven't been here a quarter of that time."

"Nor have the lakes as we know them. Maybe that's the appeal of these birds. They've witnessed a lot of changes on this planet."

One of the loons released a long, arching wail.

Lily gasped.

"Wait," John whispered.

Sure enough, an answering call came from the east. The voice was crystal clear but distant. "One lake over," John whispered.

The Lake Henry loon repeated its call, and the distant bird answered again. The sound of it had barely died when a third call came. This one was even more distant, farther east, likely from two lakes away. But it was distinct.

For nearly ten minutes the three birds called back and forth. Lily had heard night chorusing before, but never when she was on the lake, and never when she was so close to one of the participants. It was totally eerie, totally beautiful.

When they were done and the still of the night returned, she let out a breath. John remained as quiet as she, until the loons swam around to the back side of the island and out of sight.

Still without a word, he lifted his paddle and, with a deft combination of side strokes, turned the canoe. When he set them moving again, back in the direction of Celia's, Lily grew melancholy. She wasn't sure why. What they had just seen and heard had pleased her so—but that was it. The beauty of the night, the lake, and the loons was a lush, tight-woven tapestry. By contrast, her life—the life John propelled her back to now—was a lone thread. She felt small and insignificant. Unconnected. Lost.

Tucking in her legs, she pulled her hat down, her scarf up, and her clothing closer around her, and still she felt cold. John didn't speak. She felt very alone.

When they reached her dock, he was out of the canoe before she could get herself up. He tied the boat with a line and held out a hand. She couldn't feel that hand through her mittens, didn't know whether it was warm or cold, coarse or soft, but she took it and held on tightly as he helped her out of the canoe. She was about to thank him for taking her out when he put a gentle hand at the back of her waist and began walking her up toward the house—and she felt *that* hand. Oh, she did. Right through her parka, right through her flannel shirt and the T-shirt under that. She wondered what that meant. It was just a hand.

But it did feel good. It was gentle and supportive. It was companionable.

It seemed an age since she had experienced companionship. Hard to believe that little over a week ago, she was walking down Commonwealth Avenue with Terry Sullivan, about to say things to him that would forever change her life.

John stopped at the bottom of the porch steps. She mounted one and turned.

"Thh-hanks," she said, despising the nervousness, but she didn't know what to expect or whom to trust, didn't know whether he was truly friend or foe.

His eyes held hers. In the oblique light of the moon, he looked oddly beseeching. "Thank you. I'm usually out alone. That was nice."

She nodded, buried her hands in her pockets, and hugged her arms to her body. *Go inside, dummy,* a little voice inside cried, but she just stood there, held in place by eyes that were level with hers. She wanted to call him a friend but didn't know if he would respect that.

"Life is complex," she finally said.

He smiled. "Why do you think I love these loons? They stand for simplicity."

She nodded. "Twenty million years. All on instinct?"

"Animal instinct. Funny how we pride ourselves on being one step above."

She nodded and looked away, thinking that he did understand, and how gratifying that was. Then he touched her cheek and her eyes flew back to his. His hand was already lowering and he had turned to go, but she felt something in the aftermath of that touch—a connection, a tingle, perhaps a germ of trust.

It could be real. Or deception. Or illusion. Even wishful thinking.

Not knowing which made it absolutely terrifying.

Chapter 14

John was out on the lake again early Wednesday morning. His mind was more filled than it had been in three years, which made canoeing now more an exercise in stress reduction than in loon watching. With a dawn mist rising, lake life was muted, almost surreal. He let the stillness of it seep in and focused on clearing his thoughts.

But they had a mind of their own. They hung on Lily the whole way out and back, and hung on her when he drove into town for the newspapers. His first memory of her in that long, flowing gown was replaced by last night's, of her all bundled up but innocent and exposed. He liked the feel of her skin. In later fantasies, he touched more than her cheek. He was attracted to her. That complicated things.

He wanted to write a book about her, but she wanted privacy. That put them on opposite sides. His being physically drawn to her heightened the conflict.

No matter. Back home, he was standing by the phone, waiting when her call came. "There's nothing today," he said in response to the inevitable question.

"Nothing on the front page?"

"Nothing anywhere, in *any* of the papers."

In the ensuing pause, he pictured her frowning, thinking about the retraction she wanted, trying to decide whether no news was good news or bad. Finally, sounding cautiously hopeful, she said, "That's okay, isn't it?"

John told her that it probably was, because he didn't see the point in upsetting her. Yes, indeed, the absence of Rossetti-Blake news probably meant that the story had run out of steam—and yes, indeed, if the *Post* was going to issue a retraction, it would be done as unobtrusively as possible, preferably when no one was looking for anything more on the story.

But John knew how newspapers worked. Mistakes were rarely admitted; retractions were issued only under duress. In common practice, once a story wore out its welcome, it was dropped.

John had mixed feelings about that happening now. Lily wanted her retraction, and he wanted it for her, but it was to his own advantage to see the story die. The longer it lingered, the deeper an odd reporter might dig. John wanted the diggings for himself.

There were no diggings that day. *Lake News* consumed him from the minute he arrived at the office to the minute he transmitted the last page to the printer. That happened at two in the afternoon, well past the noon deadline he usually tried to respect, but there was no harm done. The printer was an ice-fishing buddy of his. The delay cost John a dinner at Charlie's. It was a fair trade.

With six hours free before the finished paper would be ready for pickup in Elkland, forty minutes to the north, John stopped at Charlie's for supplies and drove out to see Gus. He felt the same heaviness in the pit of his stomach that he always felt approaching the Ridge, the same dismay that even at foliage time the place could look bleak, the same revulsion when it smelled of garbage, rather than pumpkin, cider, or pine. And he felt the same tugging at his heart when he entered his father's home.

Any evidence of Dulcey's neatening that morning was gone. The table in front of the sofa was pushed crooked and a lampshade was askew. The sofa itself was covered with remains of the morning paper. What might have been breakfast—a plate with pieces of egg and torn-up toast—was on the floor.

"Dad?" he called as he always did. Scooping up the plate, he went on through to the kitchen. Gus was there, a hunched figure at the table. He was pressing against a fork with hands that were gnarled and chapped.

"What are you doing?" John asked kindly.

Gus's unruly white hair shook a little, but he didn't look up. "Straightenin' it out. She bends 'em."

"Dulcey?"

"Anyone else comin' in hee-uh?" Gus barked.

The fork didn't look crooked to John. But he wasn't arguing. Rather, he put the plate in the sink, which was otherwise clean. Disconcertingly so. "Have you had any lunch?"

"Wasn't hungry."

John suspected he hadn't had the strength to make anything, and felt another tug inside. He put ice cream in the freezer, and milk, cream, eggs, and a rotisserie chicken, cut into quarters, in the fridge. He took out half a loaf of the bread that he had brought the weekend before, opened a can of tuna, and mixed it with mayonnaise. When three sandwiches were made, he refrigerated one for a later meal for Gus. After putting the other two on plates, he poured two glasses of milk and sat down to eat with his father.

"The paper just went to the printer," he said conversationally. "It's a good issue, I think." He took a large bite of his sandwich, not so much out of hunger as to suggest to Gus that he should eat, too.

Gus continued to fight with the fork.

"The lead is about new families moving to town."

"We don't need 'em."

"They need us. That's the point of the piece." When Gus didn't respond, John said, "It's about quality of life. That's a buzzword these days."

Gus snorted. "Up hee-uh?"

"The Ridge is better than an urban slum," John said, but he knew enough not to pursue that line of thinking. Inevitably it led to Gus calling him a snooty big-city man who thinks he knows so much. Wisely, he changed the subject. "Armand and I had a disagreement about how much to write about Lily Blake."

Gus set down the fork and stared at his food.

"About Lily Blake and the Cardinal in Boston?" John reminded him.

"Am I s'posed ta cay-uh?"

"Lots of people around here do, since Lily's a native."

Gus raised his eyes slowly, insolently.

John weathered his stare for a minute before gesturing toward the sandwich. "Eat." He took another bite of his own, chewed, swallowed. Then, because his father wasn't biting at gentle bait, he sharpened it. This was his own need, he knew, but it was a big one. "She was innocent in that business with Donny. You know that, don't you?"

Gus dropped his eyes to the sandwich. It was the only sign he gave that, yes, he did know and, yes, he wasn't proud of it. At least, John interpreted averting his eyes as being a sign. He didn't want to think that the man had no conscience.

"I've often wondered whether things wouldn't have been different if I'd been here," John said.

"You'da saved us all from behavin' like fools?" Gus asked.

"No. I might have saved Donny from whatever it was that he felt he needed to do. He was okay before I left. When I was the bad boy, he was the good. What happened after I left?"

Gus picked up the sandwich. A chunk of tuna fell back to the plate. He turned the bread and studied the empty spot.

"Maybe if I'd stayed," John said, "he'd have been all right."

"But you'da gone to hell. So I saved one."

"Why me? Why not Donny?"

"She had to have one."

She. John's mother—who was alive and well, happily remarried, and living in North Carolina. "But why me?" he asked.

"Ask her."

"I did. A million times." He got along well enough with his mother now, but back then their relationship had been precarious. He had always suspected Dorothy would have preferred to take her youngest—had often suspected that Gus had ruled it the other way around precisely because he knew that. She had mourned Donny long and hard. But she had never answered John's question. "She always said to ask you. I'm doing that now."

Gus shot him as much of a level gaze as he could, with one eye lower than the other. "She's the one wanted outta the marriage. I said fine, shoo-uh, go ahead. Jus' leave me the good one, an' she did."

The good one. "You didn't really say that."

"Yes suh."

John was hurt enough to lash back. "Looks like you didn't have much insight."

Gus pushed himself to his feet and tottered for an instant, but that instant was long enough for John to feel remorse. He was up in the next breath, pushing his father back down. It was frighteningly easy.

When he was sure that Gus would stay put, he returned to his own seat. "Sorry. That's a sore point with me. I always felt sent away. Exiled. Punished."

"You was," grumbled Gus.

John bit into his sandwich and chewed with some force. By the time he swallowed, he realized he was getting no further than he ever did. So, again, he changed the subject. "You knew George Blake pretty well, didn't you?"

"I did not. I only weuked f'him once."

John knew for fact that it had been far more than that. Gus had done stonework in both the big house and Celia's. John had firsthand knowledge of it. He had watched, albeit from a distance. "What did you think of him?"

"Think a who?"

"George."

"Didn't know Geawge. Maida's the one I was dealin' with. Prissy little thing," he muttered, then raised his voice. "Cold as a bass outta the lake in Mahch." With a grunt, he turned his head and scowled at the yard. "Somethin' strange about that lady."

Casually, John asked, "What was it, do you think?"

Gus's eyes met his. "How the hell do *I* know? I can't figyuh out my *own* life, let alone someone else's. But that woman wasn't right from the minute she came to town. Too smiley. Too uppity. Always expectin' somethin'. No *wunduh* the daughtuh's in trouble." The wider of his eyes narrowed on John. "She'll be back."

"Lily? You think?"

Gus mimicked him. " 'Y'think?' Whadda *you* think, smaht man? You got the big-city education. You otta know. *You* think she'll be back?"

*   *   *

John wanted to tell Gus that Lily was already back. He wanted to share the news as a gesture of goodwill, a show of trust.

Only, the trust wasn't there. Three years of regular visits, and John still didn't know what made his father tick. He didn't know how a man could send away a son and not care what happened to him, but that was just what Gus had done. He hadn't called or written once—not on a birthday, not on Christmas. Dorothy, who did write and visit Donny, had called Gus an emotional dwarf, and John had gone along. Deep inside, he had dreamed that his father thought about him a lot.

He didn't know how a man could be as angry and unfeeling as Gus seemed to be. He figured there had to be something softer inside—figured that if they saw each other enough it would come out, figured that if John could prove his worth, Gus would confess.

So when word came that Gus was failing, John had returned to Lake Henry. He envisioned a reconciliation, a meeting of minds, a détente. He imagined their talking about Donny, and about Dorothy, and about where Gus had built his longest, most beautiful walls and what stories John had written that made him the most proud. He had imagined finding a father. What he found was a man as hard and unyielding as those long, beautiful stone walls that he built.

John had no idea whether Gus liked him even the littlest bit. Without liking, there wasn't apt to be respect, and without respect, if John shared the secret of

Lily's return, Gus might well turn right around and tell it to the first person he saw. That would be Dulcey, who would tell her mother, who would tell her sister, who would tell her husband, who would tell the woman who kept his meager carpentry books, along with those of half the other small businessmen in town—and *that* woman was the biggest gossip around.

John couldn't do that to Lily.

The postmaster was another matter. Nathaniel Roy liked and respected John. He made that clear soon after John's return to Lake Henry, and their daily chats at the post office had grown in depth and openness. John often sensed that Nat placed greater value on what he had to say precisely because of the years he had spent away from Lake Henry. Given that John played down his past with the rest of the town, he could be more himself when he was with Nat. The man was seventy-five if he was a day, but they were good friends.

Needing a friendly face now to fill the emptiness he felt leaving Gus, John headed back into town for his mail.

The post office was a pretty, single-story brick building. To step inside was to be enveloped in the smell of advertisement circulars and, more faintly, if remarkably, the cherry pipe tobacco that Nat had sworn off years before.

Nat looked up from reading a magazine and immediately lit up—quite a feat for a man whose full

smile was as spare as his face. He was long and narrow, a Yankee from his thinning gray hair to his wire
spectacles to his baggy cardigan, tweed pants, and
worn deck shoes. He continually chewed on his unlit
pipe, and rarely minced words when he spoke.

"You don't have much," he said around the pipe
stem as he handed John a small, elastic-bound pack.
"A few bills, a few ads, new L.L.Bean catalogue.
There's a postcard from your mother. She and the
hubby are in Florida. Sounds like they're buying a
place."

John had known they were looking. He pulled out
the card and read the back. It described a cottage in
Naples four blocks from the beach. "Sounds good."

"She's excited. Nice lady. Even when things were
rough, she was always polite, always smiling. Sorry to
say this, but we never could understand what she saw
in Gus."

"He was taller then," John said. "Very good looking."

Nat took the pipe from his mouth. "Looks fade.
Then what's left? She came from away. That didn't
bode well."

"Maida Blake came from away," John pointed out.
"She and George were married for more than thirty
years. Do you think they were happy?"

"Actually," Nat said after a moment's pondering, "I
do. Of course, George was never good looking the
way Gus was, so it wasn't like she lost something
when he got older and wider. I have to hand it to her,
though. She stepped right in and took over when

George died. Didn't miss a beat." Clamping the pipe in the corner of his mouth, he leaned sideways, produced someone's new *People* magazine from a stack there, opened to an exact page, and pushed it toward John.

John skimmed the article. It was about the Cardinal and Lily, written prior to the apology to the Cardinal.

"She's famous," Nat said. "Can't imagine Maida liking that much. She never did approve of Lily going off to New York. Far as she was concerned, that was the worst den of iniquity on this earth. Not that I could fault the girl for wanting to leave. She got a lousy shake in that business with your brother." He leaned closer and lowered his voice, as though there were others around, which there weren't. "Think she'll be coming back here?"

John was tempted to tell him but refrained, and it wasn't a matter of trust. John had tested Nat a time or two. He could be closemouthed when asked. But something else pulled John from the other side. "She may." He saw an opening. "Does she ever write to Maida?"

"No. But then, Maida never writes to her. She isn't the kind who does that. Never did. When she first moved here, there was no mail a-tall back and forth to the old hometown."

"Where was that?"

"Linsworth, Maine. It's a little logging town northeast of here. Celia used to send and get, but not as much as you'd expect, and after a while that ended, too. They cut their ties." He frowned. "So maybe there was unpleasantness left behind. Maybe they just wanted to start over fresh."

"Was there no family back there?"

"If there was, they didn't write. I was new to the job back then, and people were asking who they were—Maida and Celia—so I kept an eye out. But there was no mail coming from anyone by the name of St. Marie." His voice sharpened. "Not that I told that to the fellow who was nosing around here yester-day. Two-bit reporter from Worcester trying to look like one of us, trying to sound like one of us, trying to make like he's on Lily's side, but he wasn't. I could see the slyness in him, asking question after question. I kept wondering why he came to me. Because I han-dle the mail? Like I'd tell him what I see. That'd be wrong. A violation of the trust the gov'ment puts in me. Almost a federal offense, like tampering with the mail."

John grinned crookedly.

Nat took the pipe from his mouth and pointed its stem at John. "You're different. You care. It's one thing for *us* to know who we are and where we come from. It's something else entirely for *them* to know it. We like each other, and even if we don't, we recognize that we're all in this together. People from the outside don't understand that. They don't know squat about community."

Had John not missed the paper's noon deadline, he would have been on the road to Elkland when Richard Jacobi called. With two hours to kill, though, he had returned to the office and was rereading files, making notes for himself, thinking about possibles and probables, when the phone rang.

Richard was interested. Several questions later and he was very interested. Several more questions and he was so interested that he offered John a large amount of money to settle the deal there and then. No need for an agent, he said. The issue is speed and surprise, he said. I can get your book out in six months, I can publish it well, you *know* the reputation of this house, he said.

What John knew was that the house was a David among Goliaths. It was small but hungry. When it aimed at the best-seller lists, it often hit its mark, and it was due for another big one. The advance being offered John was large enough to suggest that his book might be it.

He hung up the phone ten minutes later feeling breathless. Richard wanted an outline and introductory chapters as soon as possible. That meant organizing his thoughts fast.

Chapter 15

At the same time that John was pondering his options for literary intrigue, Lily left the cottage and drove around the quiet end of the lake. She bypassed the narrow road that led to Poppy's, taking the wider one that led up the hill toward Maida's, but she soon turned off onto another. Rose lived at its end with her husband, Art Winslow, and their three daughters.

The house was barely a dozen years old, built as a wedding gift from the senior Winslows to complement the gift of the land given by the senior Blakes. That Rose had chosen its design was obvious to anyone who knew Rose as Maida's clone, which meant anyone who knew Rose at all. This house was a smaller version of the one on the hill—the same fieldstone, the same porch, the same eaves. The implications of that notwithstanding, Lily thought it a beautiful house. It was particularly so now, with gaslights framing the drive and lighting the porch.

Lily had timed her visit so that she would arrive after the children were in bed. She didn't know whether Rose knew she was back, whether Hannah had told, or Maida had told. She didn't know whether there would be a scene, in any case. Never a diplomat, Rose had always been the mouthpiece for Maida's most negative thoughts.

This wasn't a visit Lily wanted to make, but there was danger in Rose finding out from someone else that she was in Lake Henry. Coming in person seemed the decent thing for Lily to do, bearding the lion in her den, so to speak.

She knocked softly on the front sidelight. The footsteps she heard a minute later were heavy ones. She wasn't surprised when the heavy oak door was drawn open by her brother-in-law.

Art Winslow claimed to have fallen in love with Rose Blake on the very first day of first grade. He had been a sweet boy then, grown into a sweet man now. That he was far gentler than Rose might have been a problem if he had been anything but a Winslow, but his family owned the mill, which gave him a vehicle for authority. That meant he could take a backseat to Rose at home, which was the only reason Lily could figure why the marriage worked. Art was the quintessential gentle giant.

Lily might not have been surprised to see him, but he was clearly surprised to see her, which answered one of her questions. Hannah hadn't told.

She smiled, raised a hand, and waved.

"We were wondering if you'd be back," he said, his

voice friendly. "Come on in. Rosie?" he yelled over his shoulder, then explained to Lily, "She's with the girls."

"I thought they'd be asleep. Mm-maybe I should leave and come back another time."

"No, no. She'll want to see you. So will the girls."

Art Winslow was kind. He was good with Rose, good with the girls, good with the mill. But no one had ever accused him of being swift. The possibility that Lily might not want everyone to know she was back didn't enter his mind.

So, by way of a hint, she said, "I'm lying low. I hate to ask the girls to keep a secret."

"They *love* keeping secrets," Art insisted, and Lily knew that Hannah, for one, did.

The foyer light suddenly came on. Rose stood at the far side with her hand on the switch. In the instant when she spotted Lily and held perfectly still, Lily was stopped as short. Same dark hair, same pale skin, same slim hips and ample breasts—looking at Rose was like looking at herself in the mirror. Granted Rose's hair was longer, cut bluntly, and tucked behind an ear, and her hips were covered with tailored slacks, standard evening wear for Lake Henry's young well-to-do. Still, the resemblance was marked.

"Well, hello," Rose said, coming to stand beside her husband. "The prodigal daughter returns. The whole town's been speculating. When did you get back?"

Lily considered lying. Then she thought of Hannah, even of Maida, and said, "Saturday."

"Saturday, and you're only now coming here? This is Wednesday. Who else knows you're back?"

"I'm in hiding."

"Does Mom know?"

"Yes."

"Poppy?"

"Yes."

Rose let out a breath and said a hurt "Thanks a lot."

"I've seen them each once," Lily reasoned. "I didn't want to put the girls in the position of lying if someone asked. I thought they'd be asleep now."

"You thought wrong," Rose murmured smartly and turned. Sure enough, three faces were at the door. "Come say hi to your Aunt Lily."

The girls straightened and ran forward—six-year-old Ruth first, with seven-year-old Emma on her heels. They were adorable little girls, with dark curly hair and sweet little flowered nightgowns that went all the way to their tiny toes. Hannah, in the same kind of over-sized T-shirt she had worn at Maida's, looked chubby and plain beside them. She hung back, even when they were done with their hugs, and came forward only when Lily held out a deliberate arm. "It's good to see you, Hannah. I like your T-shirt." She studied the cat on the front. "You don't have one, do you?"

Hannah shook her head.

"God forbid," Rose put in. "I have enough trouble keeping *her* groomed. Forget a cat."

"A cat grooms itself," Hannah said.

"Cats shed. Do you want cat hair all over you?"

Hannah said nothing. Lily was sorry she had mentioned it.

Art said to the little ones, "Show Aunt Lily your teeth."

They opened their mouths wide to show gaps, Ruthie's in front, Emma's on the side.

"Impressive," Lily said. She squeezed Hannah's hand. "Boring for you. You've been through this."

Rose sighed. "Her teeth came in crooked. She'll be getting braces soon."

"I had braces," Lily told Hannah, who raised her brows in interest.

"I didn't," Rose said. "Neither did Art. Speaking of teeth—" She looked at the younger two and pointed at the stairs. "Go brush. Daddy'll watch. I need to talk with Aunt Lily."

"What about Hannah?" cried Ruth.

"Hannah has *big* teeth to brush," cried Emma.

"Hannah doesn't need watching," Rose said. "She's ten. I can't be yelling at her for everything. Her teeth are her responsibility. If she wants to have brown teeth, that's her choice."

"I always brush," Hannah said, but she might as well have saved her breath, because Rose was looking at Art, conveying silent orders that had to do with the two little ones.

In the next instant Art was corralling them around and up the stairs. Hannah stayed beside Lily.

"Did you finish your homework?" Rose asked and, when she nodded, said, "Go on up then and read. I have to talk to your aunt."

Lily hugged her. "Go on up," she said softly. "I'll see you another time." She watched the girl plod up the stairs, sensing an ache there, wondering if anyone else saw or cared.

Rose leaned against the wall right there in the foyer. "I should have realized you were back. Mom's been in a foul mood. She's been in a foul mood since this whole thing began. Newspaper headlines, pictures, phone calls—it's been awful for us, Lily. She was terrified when you left here and went to New York. She knew no good would come of it, but never in her wildest dreams did she imagine it would be this bad. She refuses to go into town now."

"Refuses?"

"Well, she thinks twice about it. She's convinced that everyone's talking and watching, and that makes her nervous, and when she's nervous, she takes it out on me."

Lily found that hard to believe. Rose had always been Maida's pride and joy.

"Who *else* can she yell at?" Rose went on. "She can't yell at Poppy, so she yells at me. I'm the one who's here all the time. I'm the one taking care of her."

"She's self-sufficient."

Rose sputtered out a laugh. "Not as much as she thinks. I'm always bringing meals up to the house or picking things up for her in town. Fine, she runs the business, but she wasn't raised to be doing that."

"It keeps her busy."

"She's not getting any younger. She should be

relaxing. She should be traveling." The phone rang. "She should be enjoying her grandchildren."

"Wasn't Hannah over the other night?"

Rose shot her a look. "Hannah is not a child one enjoys. She'll be the death of me yet."

"How so?"

"Ornery." The phone rang again. "Headstrong. *Fat.*"

"She isn't fat."

"She's on her way."

"She'll be growing taller soon. She'll slim out then. She has a beautiful face."

The phone rang again.

"Get that, Art?" Rose yelled, then returned to Lily. "Why are you back?"

Lily knew that the edge she heard might be left over from the yell, but it sure sounded like indignation. Indignant right back, she said, "I have a home here."

"How long are you staying?"

"As long as I need to."

"What if the press follows you here? Mom will flip out."

"I didn't do anything wrong, Rose."

"If she flips out, I'll be the one to suffer." She looked around when her husband trotted down the stairs.

"That was Maida," he told her. "Two of the Quebecois were doing night work in the meadow when the backhoe bucked and overturned. She called an ambulance. I'd better go up."

"Seriously hurt?" Rose asked.

He was already taking his jacket from the closet. "One maybe. But she's frightened."

"I want to go, too," Rose said quietly, and for the first time Lily saw caring.

"I'll stay with the girls," she offered.

"They're in bed," Art said, handing Rose her sweater. "They won't even know we're gone."

"We'll be fine," Lily said and softly shut the door after them. Feeling awkward, too much a stranger to want to wander around her sister's house, she crossed the foyer to the staircase and sat on the bottom step. With her chin propped in her hands, she listened, but there was no sound from either upstairs or outside. There wouldn't be a siren, of course, no need to clear already empty roads. She imagined that the ambulance crew was only now being alerted by beepers and climbing aboard.

At the sound of a distant giggle, she considered going upstairs to check. But it was a happy sound. No knowledge of accidents there. Her presence, rather than Rose and Art's, might upset them. Better to leave well enough alone.

Then the stairs creaked and she glanced up. Hannah was there on the top step, looking hesitant and unsure. When Lily waved her down, the hesitancy vanished. Quickly and lightly, she ran down the steps and sat beside Lily.

At first, neither of them spoke. Finally, in a soft whisper and with the shyest of smiles, Hannah said, "I'm glad you're here."

For a split second, looking at that face—yes, a beautiful face—Lily was glad she was, too.

As accidents went, this one was middle of the road. Neither worker was seriously injured, though both suffered enough fractures and contusions to count them out for the rest of the harvest. Since the orchard made two-thirds of its yearly income during the months of October and November, the loss was serious. Compounding the problem, one of the injured workers was a cider house fixture.

That was why Lily rose at dawn the next morning, put on jeans and her warmest layers, and drove around the lake again. She went all the way up the wide drive this time, turned right after the big house, and followed the road around a bend.

The cider house was a squat stone building, covered with ivy and surrounded by hemlock, actually pretty for a place of hard work. The insides had been gutted and rebuilt twenty years before to shore up the structure and allow the addition of new equipment. Apart from a larger, more efficient refrigeration unit and a faster bottling system, though, the process of making cider hadn't changed much since the Blake family had bottled its first quart in this very same spot four generations earlier.

The instant Lily slipped into the cider house, she was enveloped in the sweet smell of apple. She had come here often as a child, intrigued by the working of the cider press and eager to help. By the time she was sixteen and big enough to do that, she was too

busy with music and school. Besides, her father believed that the orchard was man's work.

She pictured him, larger than life in a long rubber
apron and high rubber boots, fishing an inferior apple
from the wash bin and tossing it aside, scooping the
rest through the water toward the lift that took them
up to the chopper. Another worker, standing on a platform five feet off the ground, ushered them along the
conveyor belt and into the chopper. Two other men
stood on similar platforms, layering racks and cloths
and apple mash one on another until there were eleven
layers in all—always eleven, she remembered that.

"Oh my," came a voice from behind, and Lily
turned to the startled face of Oralee Moore. Oralee
was the widow of George's foreman. It was ironic,
given George's view of women, that Oralee was now
Maida's foreman. Tall and sturdy, with ashy skin and
wiry gray hair, she had to be nearing seventy, but she
was dressed the same as Lily, ready to work.

Lily liked Oralee. Even in the worst of earlier
times, the older woman had always had a kind smile
for her, a compassionate look. She gave both to Lily
now—but Lily's gaze quickly moved past her to the
young man entering the cider house on her heels.

In that instant, Lily realized what she'd done. She
had come here to work for many reasons, the most
urgent being that Maida needed help, but it had been
an instinctive response, with little time to ponder or
doubt. Oralee wasn't a concern; she was loyal and dis-
creet. But the young man behind her was only one of
many who would see Lily in the course of a day here.

Some lived in the dormitory. Others lived in town. Those others would go home after work and spread the word. Her secret would be out.

After an initial moment of panic, she suddenly relaxed, a bit surprised to realize that she wasn't sorry. Her stomach still knotted when she remembered the hounding of the press, but she'd had to face them on her own in Boston. She wasn't in Boston anymore. She was in Lake Henry. She had been born and raised here, and if the town had treated her poorly once, now was the time for them to make up for that. She was tired of hiding.

Besides, it was done.

"How are André and Jacques?" she asked in reference to the injured men.

Oralee's mouth went crooked. "They'll be home in two days, sitting up there in the dorm, pleased as punch to have time off with pay." She waved the young man into the cider house. "This is Bub. He's from the Ridge."

Bub was tall, solid, and not a day over eighteen. He made such a point of not looking at Lily that she knew that he knew just who she was. Trusting Oralee to tell him anything else he needed to know, she went outside to wait for Maida.

It was the coolest morning yet. A fine sheen of white, a cross between dew and frost, lay on the hillside grass. Lily leaned against the vine-covered stone, pulled her sleeves over her hands, and tucked them under her arms. Each inhalation brought a bracing reminder of fall. Each exhalation was wispy and white.

She wondered what was in the *Post* today. It had
been too early to call John when she left. She wondered if he was awake now, if he was on the lake or
driving into town. Driving into town, she decided.
Basking in the week's *Lake News*. She wondered if he
had run the pieces she had chosen. It had been fun
picking them out, thinking of the pleasure three students would have seeing their work in print. She supposed this was the upside of John's job, a positive
thing for a change.

Maida came into sight then, rounding the bend in
the road, walking up from the main house with her
head bowed. Lily straightened, but her mother seemed
deep in thought. She was nearly upon her before she
finally looked up. Startled, she stopped.

"You're short a man," Lily said. When Maida didn't
respond, she added, "I can help."

Still Maida said nothing, and Lily feared she might
actually refuse her help. That would be the ultimate
punishment, the ultimate insult.

The verdict remained in doubt when Maida resumed walking. It was only when she held the door
open for Lily that Lily had an answer.

The machines were already warming up—the
whirlpool bath, the conveyor belt, the grind, the
press—chugging away in an old familiar rhythm. Lily
thought of her father again. Hard not to, he was such
an indelible part of the scene. Maida wore the rubber
apron now, but her presence was almost jarring. Still,
she seemed fully in control.

Lily traded her jacket for a hooded oilcloth slicker,

put on oversized boots and long rubber gloves, and climbed up opposite Bub, onto the platform beside the press. She didn't tell him that she had never done this before, because it didn't feel that way. She had watched the process hundreds of times as a child, and though the old burlap cloths had been replaced by nylon ones, the latticework racks and the folding technique were exactly the same.

That didn't mean she didn't feel apprehension. But there was anticipation, too. She had waited a long time to do this. In her mind, it was as much a game as a job.

Within minutes, the bottommost rack was in place, a cloth draped over it with the corners hanging down, and the first apples came through the grind into the large funnel above them. Bub shifted a lever just long enough for the right amount of mash to fall to the cloth, which it did with a splat that made Lily laugh, but she went right to work. She folded the left corner of the cloth up over the mash, waited while Bub folded over his left corner; then she folded her right corner over, waited while Bub folded his right corner over. While he smoothed and straightened the cloth, she picked up the next rack, an identical piece of latticework three feet square. After she had placed it on top of the folded parcel, Bub spread a second cloth there, then pulled the lever, and the next portion of mash splattered down. They alternately folded over the four corners of cloth, straightened the packet, added another rack and another cloth, and let more mash fall.

The pile of racks and cloths grew. When there were

eleven in all, capped by a spare rack, they pushed the whole stack sideways on runners until it was centered under the large iron press. Bub added fat blocks of wood between the top rack and the press to tighten the fit, Maida shifted the lever to start the stacks rising, and what had been a background chug suddenly took on a bite. The gears turned with a rhythmic hum and bang. In no time juice was seeping from the cloth, spilling down the sides of the racks to the reservoir below.

Lily straightened then, looked around in self-satisfied surprise, and let out a breath. She'd done it! She felt exhilarated!

Maida was turned the other way, back to culling bad apples from the bath, but Oralee was watching. She sent her an understanding smile, then gestured her back to work, and the process began all over again. This time, before the stack of eleven could be pushed under the press, the spent stack was removed—apple dregs tossed into the backhoe at the side door, cloths dropped in a pile for reuse, racks standing against the wall.

Lily lost count of the number of stacks they built, pressed, and broke down. At one point, Maida started the pump that moved the cider from the reservoir to the large refrigeration unit at the far end of the room. At another, she used her walkie-talkie to call for more apples, then drove the small loader to raise the crates up to the bath. At yet another, she hooked up a hose and washed stray bits of apple and juice down the concrete floor to a central drain.

The cider house was clean. George had been a

stickler for that, and Maida carried on the practice. No amount of washing, though, could erase the smell of fresh apples and sweet juice. It permeated the concrete walls, the floor, the machines. Lily breathed it in deeply. It was heady stuff, conjuring up good things— which was remarkable, when she thought about it. For the most part, the memories of Lake Henry that she had carried with her since leaving were negative. But now she was remembering things like sitting with Poppy and Rose in this very room, scrunched up in the corner near the refrigerator, chomping on apples that George slipped them.

By the time Maida called a midmorning break, Lily was too pumped up to be tired. She washed off her oilskins and hung everything up, then went down to the main house. She might have used the bathroom at the cider house, but the morning paper wasn't there.

It was neatly folded on the large wood table in Maida's kitchen, a snake lying coiled and silent, with no rattle to tell if it was poisonous or not. Feeling the beginnings of a knot in the pit of her stomach, Lily skimmed the top half of the front page. There was nothing there or, when she turned it over, on the bottom half. And on the inside?

Rather than opening the paper to check, she went to the phone, and for a minute her hand hovered. *Call Cassie,* her brain ordered. Cassie was her legal adviser. She was the one who had sent the retraction demand and would surely be looking for a response.

But she didn't know Cassie's number off the top of her head. She did know John's. She tried his home first, hanging up after three rings so that she wouldn't get Poppy. She quickly tried the *Lake News* office. The phone rang three times there, too. Disappointed, she was about to hang up when he answered. He was all business.

"*Lake News*. Kipling here."

"Hi," she said, a little breathy.

His voice warmed. "Hey. I missed your call this morning."

"I left early. Mom needed help. She was one short in the cider house."

"I heard about the accident."

Lily smiled. "I won't ask how." Cautiously she said, "I haven't looked through the paper."

"Don't bother. There's nothing in it today, either."

She felt a letdown. "Nothing at all?"

"Nothing at all."

Then anger. "They still owe me an apology."

"Cassie will have to drag it out of them."

"Do you think they've left my apartment?"

"Probably. There was a murder last night. An activist in the local Republican Party was found stabbed to death in his Back Bay town house. Finger pointers are going wild, alternately accusing two ex-wives, one mistress, a disgruntled business partner, and the mob. That's a lot of ground to cover. The papers will need all their troops."

"So if I return to Boston I'm a nobody again?" she asked, making light of it, but he got the point.

"Hard to say. Are you in a rush to get back?"

"My life is there," she said. "My apartment, my

clothes, my piano, my car." But they were distant, more words than needs just then, especially when Maida wandered into the kitchen. She looked disapproving, which was nothing new. Lily had no doubt that her mother knew who she was talking to, and wondered if she'd been listening for long.

"I'd better call Cassie," she told John, and went through Poppy to make that one while Maida filled the teapot.

Cassie's paralegal answered, but Cassie came right on after that. "We give them a week," she said before Lily could ask. "One week. Then we take the next step."

"What's that?"

"We file suit for defamation of character."

Filing suit meant a trial, which would take forever. From the start, Lily hadn't liked that idea. For the first time now, with her name absent from the Boston papers for two days in a row, she wondered what would happen if two days became three, then five, then ten. She wondered if people would forget. If they did, she might be better to just let the whole thing die.

Then again, if she was destined to be stared at each time she left the apartment, or followed each time she went to work, or prevented from finding work at all, she couldn't return to Boston. Her choice would be filing suit, starting a new life incognito somewhere else, or staying here.

So, then, it was good that orchard workers would see her and spread the word that she was back. She needed to know where she stood.

Chapter 16

Anna Winslow was the matriarch of the local textile family. She had long since ceded the everyday workings of the mill to her son, Art, but she kept a seat on the board and a small office beside his. Winslow Textiles had been her life for more years than she cared to count. She first became involved with the plant's operation when her husband, Phipps, began fooling with pretty young weavers on company time, and she had stayed involved out of sheer love for the place. She had no ego. She was content to let Phipps take kudos for progressive thinking, though she was the major force behind it.

Phipps was retired now. On occasion he strutted through the mill and made noise to simulate command. For the most part, though, he spent his days working with canvas and oil, producing monstrous paintings that only he liked, and which now filled a huge barn behind the house. Anna was contemplating

building a second barn for the overflow. She didn't
expect that he would ever sell a one, but Phipps painting was better than Phipps philandering.

Art was far more Anna's son than Phipps's.
Though he was only thirty-one, he had been raised at
the mill and knew its workings well. Anna trusted him
to know when to replace a piece of equipment or retire an outdated design. She trusted his manner with
employees and stockholders, and had confidence that
if anyone could save a small textile mill in an era of
conglomerates, it was Art. She didn't have to supervise
him to know he would do the right thing.

That freed her to enjoy the sounds of the loom,
the smell of the wool, the refraction of light through
rooftop windows, the rush of the river under the aged
stone. Rarely did a day pass when she wasn't seen
walking among the looms, talking with weavers or
leaning over a designer's shoulder in companionable
delight. She had designed many a piece of fabric herself, and had even learned to do it by computer.

Anna was a round woman with a flair for dressing
that canceled out her size. Wearing tunics woven with
unique yarns, scarves done in striking patterns, flowing skirts made from the finest threads, she served as a
mobile display of the mill's wares. Art talked numbers
with flowcharts and cost sheets; Anna talked style
without saying a word. She had the kind of charm that
sealed deals, frequently over lunch, for Anna enjoyed
her meals. With Phipps holed up at the barn, she was
forever on the lookout for a lunch mate. Twice a week
there might be buyers in town; another day there

would be an employee celebrating a birthday. On this Thursday, there was no one. That was why, when John called to ask her out, she was thrilled to accept.

"Thursdays are my least favorite days," she told him as soon as they were seated in his window booth at Charlie's. "It's an in-between day, not exciting like the start of the week, or wrapping up like the end of the week. I'm *so* glad you called." Her eyes shone. She leaned in, a bubble of bridled excitement. "I got word just before I left the office." She lowered her voice. "Lily Blake is back."

John was startled. He had warned Lily that word would get out, but he hadn't heard about a leak. "How do you know?"

Anna grinned. "One of our weavers, Minna Du-Mont? Her husband works at the orchard. He saw Lily at the cider house this morning. She was working with Maida. *Working with Maida,*" she repeated, marveling. "I called my daughter-in-law to confirm it, and she did. Working with Maida. Can you imagine?"

"There was an accident—"

"I know, and Maida needed help, but she and Lily were never ones to work side by side. Not once did the two put their heads together during the celebrations when Art married Rose. There was trouble between them *way* back."

John wasn't one to look a gift horse in the mouth. Anna was all but begging him to ask. He held off only long enough for Charlie to take their orders, before saying, "How well did you know the Blakes before Art married Rose?"

"We've moved in the same circles for years—though Lord knows why," Anna added under her breath, "with Phipps and, rest his soul, George so different. But Lake Henry is small, and they had the orchard and we had the mill. Maida entertained a lot in the old days. The house was beautiful, the food was delicious. I didn't see Lily often. She was kept in the background, except in church. Singing, she had an angel's voice. But talking? Poor thing, stuttering that way. Maida was horrified."

"Horrified for Lily, or for herself?"

Anna's full cheeks grew flushed. She whispered, "Both, I'm afraid. She was convinced people blamed her for the stutter."

As well they might, John was thinking when Anna said, "It's entirely physical. Did you know that?"

He didn't. He didn't know much about stuttering at all, except that the person listening often suffered as much as the stutterer himself. Herself.

"It has to do with the coordination of the muscles for speech," Anna went on. "That isn't to say there aren't emotions involved. Tension makes it worse. It distracts the person from concentrating on controlling it. But the root of the problem is physical."

"Did Lily always have it?"

"Always. She was a late talker, didn't say much until she was four or five, and she didn't say much even then, most likely because it was hard for her. So they didn't hear the problem at first, and then they thought it was something that would work itself out, but the more they made her talk, the worse it got.

Your heart would break watching her, and when Maida snapped at her for doing it . . ." Anna took a sharp breath and sat back.

"She *snapped*?" John asked.

"Snapped, shook her finger, made apologies to everyone in sight."

He cringed. "Why didn't they get help?"

"Eventually they did." Anna looked him in the eye. "Maida didn't like that much, either."

"Why not?"

"It confirmed the existence of a problem."

"But if everyone already knew . . ."

"Therapy made it official. Therapy made it *serious*. Maida wanted the Blake blooms to be perfect, and suddenly one of them wasn't, in a very public and obvious way. It's no wonder she's been so upset by this business in Boston. The very same Blake bloom is imperfect *again* in a very public and obvious way—not," she added with an edge, "that I said any of this to that reporter." She looked up and produced a grin when Charlie arrived with food.

Anna had a Cobb salad piled high with goodies and topped with generous dollops of blue cheese dressing. By comparison, John's bacon cheeseburger and fries looked tame.

He offered her a fry, which she accepted with grace.

"What reporter?" he asked.

She finished the fry and fingered her napkin. "Sullivan. He's been calling nearly every day since this broke."

"Still calling?" John was mystified, and vaguely alarmed. Terry should have been off the story once the paper issued its apology to the Cardinal. If he was still calling, that meant he was after something.

"Still calling," Anna confirmed. "He gets me going talking about every other little thing, like he finds me so fascinating that he just can't help getting off the subject. He brings the talk around to the mill and suggests that there's enough for *three* stories in it, but I know men like him. I've lived with a sweet-talker for too many years not to know insincerity when I hear it. He's trying to get my guard down. He's trying to get me to betray one of my own." She waved her fork gently. "Tries to slip in little questions."

"About Lily?"

"And Maida. He's looking for worms under rocks, but, good Lord, there isn't a one of us doesn't have something in life he isn't proud of, some little smudge." She let the fork dangle, set her elbows on the table, and smiled. "What's yours?"

John had lots of little smudges and more than a few big ones, but in that instant, when he pushed aside his concern about Terry, a long-forgotten one sprang to mind. "Calling my father a bastard. I was twelve. He had called me a girl, because my voice hadn't changed. There isn't much worse that a boy can be called when he's twelve. So I called him a bastard. He went all quiet and hard and stalked out of the house. He didn't come back for three days. What I didn't know then was that, *A,* he was, in fact, a bastard, and, *B,* that my mother had used the word in an argument the day before."

"Had you heard her?"

"No. It was pure coincidence, but bad timing." He smiled back at Anna. "What's your smudge?"

Her eyes twinkled. "I stitched the zippers in Phipps's pants shut. Every last pair in his closet. It was quite a sight watching him struggle with one after the other."

John didn't have to ask why. "Who unstitched them?"

"Not me," she said with pride. "I figured that if working with fabric was his stock in trade, he could just do it himself—which he did, with some contrition. Mind you"—she pointed at John's heart with her fork—"if you tell anyone I told you that, I'll put in a bad word with Armand, who will then cut your year-end bonus. Now, *there's* a sweet-talker if ever there was one."

"Armand?"

"You wouldn't know," she said with the dash of her fork. "You're not a woman." She speared a piece of ham. "But you get my point on the other. We all have smudges. If we didn't, the word 'secret' wouldn't exist—not to *mention* the fact that even if you did tell someone, it wouldn't be all that bad. We like each other. We respect each other. That reporter?" She put the ham into her mouth and waved the empty fork in mimic of a slow headshake.

The only thing John could figure was that Terry was trying to shore up the blame-Lily angle. But he was stepping on territory that John considered his own, particularly now that he and Richard Jacobi had a deal. He was in a fighting mood when he returned to the office after lunch, but before he could decide what to do with it, Armand called.

Excitement livened his raspy voice. "Lily Blake's back in town. I think you ought to get yourself over there and do an exclusive."

John thought quickly. "The paper's just come out. There won't be another for a week."

"Yes, well, we put out a special supplement when this Republican town went Democratic in the last election. So we'll do a special supplement now."

"I don't think this story is quite the same."

"What's that matter? I'm saying I'll pay for it."

"But I'm the one in charge of quality control," John insisted. "What's to put in a special supplement? Do you want me to do a rehash of what everyone else has been printing for the last week? What's *new* in the story?"

"Didn't you hear me?" Armand bellowed. "She's *back*. That's news. Christ, John, this is basic journalism. People in town will want to know why, for how long, what she's doing, where's she staying."

"Everyone in town will know most of that before the day is out," John said quietly. "The only thing you'll accomplish in a supplement is to score points with the mainstream press."

"And what's wrong with *that*? If you don't interview her, someone else will. Come on, John," he whined. "What's your *prob*-lem? She's *our* girl. This is *our* story."

"Right. She's our girl, and we protect our own. Our story should be that there is no story, because that's where it stood when last I heard."

John hung up the phone feeling duplicitous on two counts. The first involved Armand and what might indeed have made a good story for *Lake News*. The second involved Lily and had more to do with John's future intentions than with anything immediate he might write. He liked Lily. The more he learned about her, the more he admired her. The more he admired her, the worse he felt about his book. Some would say he was exploiting her. He preferred to think he was simply studying her, but he found either case vaguely unsettling.

So he took the fighting mood that hadn't quite disappeared and focused on Terry Sullivan. On one side of his computer he put the list of tips Jack Mabbet had given him. On the other side he put his growing file. Several clicks and half a dozen typed responses later, he was connected to a database that, using Terry's current address, spewed up his Social Security number, his monthly rent, two bank account numbers, four credit card numbers, and ten other places of residence in a total of four states over a period of twenty-three years.

John studied the ten. The three most recent were in the Boston area, making it a total of four moves in the twelve years Terry had been with the paper. John didn't know if *he* would want to haul his own stuff in and out of as many apartments, but four in twelve years didn't raise any flags. Seven in the eleven previous years was a little stranger. He studied them one at a time.

The first two were college apartments. John recognized the Pennsylvania address. That took care of two years, with nine to go.

The next two apartments were in Connecticut— one in Hartford, one in a nearby suburb. They covered the four years immediately following college, when Terry had freelanced for several of the local papers.

He moved to Rhode Island when he was offered his first staff position. During the five years he was there, he lived at three different addresses, each within commuting distance of Providence.

John swiveled his chair and looked out at the lake. He sat back, rubbed a thumb over his mouth, tried to think of all the reasons why a man would move so often. Knowing Terry, he hadn't been able to get along with landlords, neighbors, roommates. The man could shift from charming to abrasive in no time flat.

Psychotic? Possibly. Schizophrenic? Possibly. It was also possible that he was mentally fit but simply driven by private demons.

John was wondering what those demons might be, and where eleven apartments in twenty-three years, plus hatred of the Cardinal, fit in, when the telephone rang. *"Lake News.* Kipling here."

"Kip!" It was Poppy. "I wasn't sure if you were back. Terry Sullivan's calling for you. Do you want to take it?"

For a split second, John felt guilty—like a peeping Tom caught in the act, as if Terry knew exactly what he'd just been doing and thinking. Then he realized it couldn't possibly be so, and that even if it was, Terry had been doing much the same where Lily was concerned.

With that realization, his anger returned. "I'll take it," he told Poppy. Seconds later, more coolly, he said, "What's up, Terry?"

"I hear she's back."

John chose his words with care. Figuring it would be transparent of him to ask who "she" was, he said, "I haven't heard that. Who's your source?"

"I have dozens of sources, little people here, little people there. Can you confirm it, yes or no?"

"I can't confirm it," John said, because it was the truth. He would be betraying Lily if he did. "Why are you asking? The story's done. You've been proved wrong."

"No. The paper caved in to pressure from the Church. I stand by my story."

John was incredulous. "What's to stand by? All you had was circumstantial evidence, and it was flimsy at best. Is there a reason for this? Do you have a grudge against Rossetti?"

"Don't need it to smell something fishy. He's a lady-killer. He and Lily Blake were too close for it to be innocent."

"Have you suddenly found an eyewitness to say it wasn't?"

"No, but I'm lookin'."

"You're pestering people like Anna Winslow, but she won't tell you that Lily Blake was having an affair with Cardinal Rossetti."

"Did you know she was married?"

"Of course. Her son is married to Lily's sister."

"Not Anna," Terry said. "*Lily* was married."

John hadn't heard that. Neither had anyone else in town, including—he would put money on it—Lily's family. Too many other secrets had already been printed. If Lily had been married, Poppy would have told him.

He was silent a second too long.

"You didn't know," Terry gloated. "There you are, right in her own hometown, and you didn't know. It was a quickie, done the summer after her freshman year in college. The guy was a senior, they were both studying in Mexico. A month after they got back, she had it annulled. I have proof this time, John."

"And what," John asked in disgust, "are you going to do with it? Is the paper running it?"

"No—"

"Because the story's done," he cut in. "Because *you* embarrassed the paper once and they're not letting you do it again. Because a quickie marriage years ago has absolutely no relevance to anything or anyone now!"

"That remains to be seen," Terry said, and John felt a sudden sharp loathing.

"Don't . . . even . . . try," he warned, sitting forward in his chair. "You've done her harm enough. It was wrong the first time, arguably libel. Do it this time and I'll go after you myself."

"You?" Terry laughed. "That's a good one. You don't have the guts to go after me or anyone else. You're jealous, is your problem. I'm a better writer than you'll *ever* be. I dig and you sit. I find and you drool. I'm here and you're there. Know something? I do believe that she could be right there in your own hometown, and you wouldn't even know it! You had it once, John, but you've lost it. Lost it good."

John waited. "Anything else?"

"Nah. That's it." Almost to himself, but with a hint of dismay and disgust, he muttered, "This is a waste of time. A waste of money." He hung up.

John spent the night thinking about Lily. By dawn he felt a need to see her. Knowing how early she would be leaving if she was working with Maida again, he threw on the nearest clothes, grabbed a down vest, and started the Tahoe. Five minutes later he was turning down the road to Thissen Cove. He was relieved to see the tan wagon beside the cottage.

The sun hadn't yet risen high enough to provide much warmth. Pulling on the vest, he crossed over the pine needles to the porch. He was up the steps in a single long stride and, seconds later, knocking. There was a movement at the side window, then the door opened.

For a minute, he couldn't speak. Lily looked frightened and pale—and disheveled enough, *sleepy* enough to suggest that he had woken her up. She was in her nightgown and had a hand on her chest. Well, not exactly her chest. More like her throat. There was no room for a hand on her chest what with . . . what with . . . what with those breasts.

"Has something happened?" she asked in a frightened whisper.

He cleared his throat. "Uh, no. I mean, I don't know. I haven't seen the paper." He swallowed. "Can I come in for a minute?"

She ducked out of sight and returned wrapped in a shawl. When he was inside, she closed the door and crossed to the kitchen counter. She put an old-fashioned coffee percolator under the faucet and filled it with water, put the basket inside, and began scooping coffee.

The sight of bare feet beneath the long nightgown made her look all the more fragile.

Feeling oddly inept, John stood with his hands on the back of one of the ladder-back chairs at the kitchen table. Each of the four chairs was painted a different color. His was dark green. "I'm sorry. I didn't mean to wake you. I figured you might be going to the cider house again. I wanted to catch you before you left."

She kept on scooping. "Oralee has to go to the dentist, so we're not starting till nine."

"How late did you go yesterday?"

"Four." She capped the coffee can.

"You must have been tired."

"Yes, but in a good way." She put the percolator on the stove and lit a flame underneath. Hugging the shawl, she finally turned. "It kept my mind busy." Her eyes held his. "What's happened?"

"Terry Sullivan called me yesterday. He said you were married once."

She didn't blink. The only visible reaction was a subtle tightening of the hands cinching in the shawl.

"It's really none of my business—" he began, but she cut in.

"Is he printing it?"

"I doubt it. I don't think the paper wants more, after what happened to the big story. I thought about calling his editor, but if I went to the effort of saying it wasn't true, I might have only made him curious."

"It's true," she said. Still holding his gaze, she slipped into the nearest chair—a pale purple one. He saw her inhale, then tip up her chin a fraction. "I was studying art in Mexico the summer after my freshman year. Brad was a senior. I thought I was in love. I'd been so lonely that first year at college that it seemed the perfect thing. We had fun those six weeks. Getting married was part of it. The fun ended the day we got back. He woke up and said he couldn't be married to me because he loved someone else."

John saw hurt, along with a more general embarrassment. Needing to move on, he said, "So you had it annulled."

"I paid a lawyer to do that, but there was no need. The ceremony wasn't legal. Brad knew it all along. I felt like a fool."

"Does anyone here know?"

She shook her head. When a wisp of hair stayed at her mouth, she moved it away. "We did it two days before the summer semester ended. He said we should keep it a secret for a while. That was fine with me. I was afraid of what my parents would say about the rush. Then it didn't matter."

She stopped, seeming to hold her breath, waiting. It didn't take a genius to hear the question she wasn't asking.

"I won't tell," he vowed, but she didn't look assured. So, without pride, he said, "Donny wasn't the only Kipling who stole a car—but he was the only one who did it more than once, and the only one who got caught. When I was fourteen, I wanted wheels. My dad wouldn't even let me drive his truck with him in the cab. So I stole one right from the center of town."

Lily looked cautiously curious. "Whose?"

"Willie Jake's." When her eyes went wide, he laughed. It was part pleasure, part relief. She looked adorable. "Yup. His pride and joy was a sporty little Mustang. He used to leave it parked in front of the office while he did his rounds in the cruiser."

"In *front?* How did you steal it with no one seeing?"

"Remember the fire up at the academy? No, you were probably too young, but there was a big fire in one of the dorms—someone smoking and stashing the cig out of sight when the dorm mother came sniffing. The cigarette wasn't out, the dorm was an old wood house, everyone who might have smelled smoke was either on a lower floor or playing afternoon sports. The place caught like tinder. The town center cleared out—everyone up there making sure every last boy was accounted for. So there was the

Mustang with the keys right in the ignition. I drove it all the way around the lake, then up to the mill."

"Didn't people *there* see?"

"I waited around the corner from the office until no one was around the other cars. Then I drove in the parking lot, locked the thing up, and walked off." She looked like she thought he was crazy. "Well, where would the challenge have been if I'd left it at the end of the lake? A shrink would say that I wanted to get caught, and he'd probably be right, but I wasn't caught. Willie Jake was furious. He interviewed dozens of us, but he never did find out who drove that car. I snuck in one night and buried the keys in the old stone wall back of his house. To my knowledge he's never found them. A hundred years from now, a scavenger looking for relics will spot that rock slightly out of place and put a metal detector to it."

Soberly Lily said, "So you stole a car and didn't get caught, and I didn't steal a car and got caught."

"Yes," John said. "That gives you something to tell Willie Jake."

"The statute of limitations will have expired."

"But it would hurt my credibility if that comes out. So if I tell anyone about your marriage, you can toss that out as evidence that I can't be believed."

"What about Terry? Will he tell?"

"Not so soon after the apology. He'll lie low for a while."

"Then what?"

"That depends. If we have dirt on him, he'll be neutralized."

"That sounds like blackmail."

"Oh, no. He'll be able to say whatever he wants. No one will listen. That's all."

It sounded good to John. Lily looked as though she was considering it. When the coffee began to perk, she lowered the flame and stayed at the stove with her arms around her middle and her head bowed in thought.

John didn't rush to fill the silence, what with the percolating pot doing it so well. Within minutes, the smell of coffee began filling the room. He had a modern coffee machine that he filled with beans ground fresh before each use, but his coffee never smelled like this.

It didn't taste like it either, he decided five minutes later when she poured him a cup.

Five minutes after that, he had a refill. By the time he left the cottage to head into town, he was feeling wide awake but mellow. Celia's spirit was a peaceful one, indeed.

It wasn't until he was in the truck again, driving the rest of the way around the lake, that guilt set in. Lily's early marriage spoke of a craving for love and affection—possibly the same need that made her friendship with Cardinal Rossetti so strong, certainly the same need that had her back in Lake Henry trying to patch things up with her mother. That early marriage helped flesh out the picture of who she was.

But if he included it in a book about the invasion of privacy, he would be invading Lily's privacy even more.

Chapter 17

Lily didn't trust John. She had made too many errors in judgment where men were concerned to do that. She liked the way he looked and liked the way he talked. She liked the fact that he told her things about himself that no one else knew. She liked his knowledge of loons and his appreciation of *her* appreciation of them, but she wasn't taking chances. When she called him thirty minutes after he left the cottage, it was just for the news.

"Nothing," he said with what might have been frustration.

She was relieved that there was nothing about her marriage in the paper. She wouldn't have wanted to explain that to Maida, who would be angry and hurt. They had spent the whole of yesterday together without disagreement. It was a record. Granted, what little talk there had been was about work, but it was something, and Lily hated to rock the boat now.

Unfortunately, no news meant that there was no apology or retraction either. "Nowhere?" she asked John.

"Nowhere."

"They're just dropping the story cold, leaving me as the bad guy." After three days, it was no longer a question.

"They're trying. There were actually two letters to the editor accusing them of doing just that, so you have fans out there. The papers print letters to ease their guilt—you know, show what fair guys they are."

Lily didn't think they were fair at all. After thanking John and saying good-bye, she considered calling Cassie. But Cassie couldn't do anything more for another few days. Besides, Lily had to get to Maida's.

So she put it aside, drove around the lake to the cider house, and let the smell of fresh apple mash, the demand of the work, and the rhythm of the machines keep it stashed in that distant mental compartment. It came to the fore with a rush, though, when Maida called a late-morning break. This time, when Lily returned to the main house, she called Dan Curry.

"Lily," he said, sounding pleased to hear her voice, "we were just talking about you, George and I. How are you?"

She felt a wave of nostalgia. Many a time she had stopped at the club to pick up a check and had sat over coffee and scones with George and Dan. "I'm fine. How are you both?"

"We're fine," he said brightly. "Booked every night, even with the spectacle of the scandal gone. When I see members looking wistfully at the piano, I know they're missing you. Your replacement didn't work out. We had to let him go after two nights. He just didn't know the songs. You're a hard act to follow, Lily Blake."

That was good news. But the not-so-good lingered. "It doesn't look like the papers are going to apologize to me like they did to the Cardinal. Is he— are his people still working on that?" The Cardinal had said they would. Lord knew, they'd gotten an apology for *him* quickly enough.

"Gee," Dan said, "I don't know."

"Until they do, I look bad."

"Nah," he said in a jovial way. "Anyone who knows you never thought you looked bad."

"Maybe not musically or physically, but what about mentally? Do all those people think I caused the scandal by saying those things?"

"I really don't talk about that with them. They know how I feel."

They did indeed. Dan was on her side, which meant that the general membership of the club might blame him for hiring her in the first place.

Testing the waters, she said, "Each day that passes without more in the paper, I think about coming back. Will people forget?"

"The people who matter already have. Past tense. Over and out."

Lily had always liked Dan, but she wasn't stupid. She knew that one of the reasons he was good at running the club was that he could tell members what they wanted to hear. She had a feeling he was doing that to her now. Patronizing her.

So she made the question more specific. "When do you think I'll be able to come back to work?"

"Here?" He asked with such surprise—as though the thought had never occurred to him—that her heart sank. "Oh, it's still premature. You've only been gone a week."

"But if the allegations are wrong."

"It's not only those allegations. It's the others, too."

"But they're lies."

"We need to let it die down, Lily. It won't do any good to rush things."

Quietly, she said, "This is mm-my job, Dan. The money pays my rent."

Dan sighed. His voice was suddenly bare. "I know. But the truth is that, if you return here, it'll revive the whole thing. I can't do that to the membership. I've hired another replacement. This one's really quite good."

Lily felt the blow. His words held a finality that said arguing would be wasting her breath. He owned the club. His mind was made up. "I see."

"I sent a check to your apartment for what I owe you, but if you're not there—"

"I'll get it. Thanks."

"I'm really sorry, Lily. This was a purely business decision. I feel bad. You didn't intend for any of this to come from those comments."

His statement hit her the wrong way. She was suddenly furious. Enunciating each word in a way that had less to do with controlling her stutter than with educating someone she had hoped would have been more loyal, she said, "For the record, I didn't *make* those comments as they were reported. I have never been infatuated with the Cardinal. We would never have even been friends if he hadn't set out to save my soul. *For* the record," she said, letting loose, "*he* was the force behind the friendship. I'm not Catholic! I'm not religious! I'd *never* have thought to approach him if he hadn't approached me first!"

She ended the call before Dan could apologize and, heart pounding, punched out Elizabeth Davis's number. She assumed that her neighbor would still be home, sleeping in after a late night. Sure enough, the hello on the other end of the line was groggy.

"Hi, Elizabeth. It's Lily."

The grogginess vanished, giving way to what sounded like genuine excitement. "Lily. Wow, it's good to hear from you. Are you okay?"

"I'm furious," she said, needing to vent. "The papers have left me high and dry, my job at the Essex Club is now permanently gone, and I want my own car!" She exhaled and said a quieter "How are things there?"

"You've got mail!" Elizabeth chirped. The tone was mocking, the message not.

"Much?"

"One large supermarket bag worth. It's mostly junk mail—ads and catalogues. A bunch of bills. There's something from Justin Barr. Should I open it?"

"Yes." She heard the sound of paper tearing, then a moment's silence.

"Whoa. He's offering you money to go on his show."

"That hypocrite! He always says he doesn't pay!"

"Yeah, well, what else is new?" Elizabeth murmured. "You have letters here, Lily." She started reading off return addresses. Some were from friends, others from strangers. "Want to hear?"

"If you don't mind."

Sara Markowitz had written a heartwarming thinking-of-you letter. Likewise her college roommate, several teachers and students from the Winchester School, and friends in New York. Lily was feeling buoyed by them, until the negative ones came. They stung.

Elizabeth had just finished reading a particularly mean one when she said, "While we're on bad, you might as well hear this. The condo association met last night. The media is still calling around trying to find out where you are and what you're like. Granted, it's not the mainstream media, just little local pests, and there aren't any of them stationed outside round the clock, only during rush hour, when they think you may be coming or going. Unfortunately, that's when most of the owners are coming and going, too. They hate the notoriety."

"Tony Cohn."

"Most vocally, but there are others. Me, I'm of the belief that all publicity is good publicity, but I'm in the minority. That group—whew. Pretty conservative.

They've taken the bad press to heart, and they're up in arms. They don't think it's right that a renter—a mere *renter*—should be causing them trouble."

"This mere renter probably pays more each month for the right to be there than some of them do!"

"I know that. I'm on your side, Lily. I didn't say they were right. I'm just telling you what they're saying. They want to know what's true and what isn't, where the case stands, whether you're planning to fight. They know you're not here and want to know when you'll be back."

"Are they asking *you*?"

"I'm afraid they are," Elizabeth admitted. "I made the mistake of speaking up a little too forcefully on your behalf, so they think I know something. Well, I do and I don't, if you know what I mean."

Lily did, but it didn't matter. What did matter was the sense she had, when she hung up the phone, that she wouldn't be welcomed back. Granted, she didn't see her neighbors often—and she no longer cared what Tony Cohn thought—but did she want to be stared at? *Glared* at? Talked about behind her back? Resented? If she sued the papers and won, things might change. But a verdict would be years away and would involve negative publicity that those neighbors would hate. She wondered if a more immediate public retraction would make the difference—or if all the allegations that Dan Curry had mentioned would be a permanent stain.

Maida entered the kitchen and put the kettle on to boil. She busied herself with the box of tea bags, kept her back to Lily, and gave every indication of ignoring the dilemma.

But Lily needed help. Heartsick, she pushed her hands into the back pockets of her jeans. "The Essex Club hired someone else. I can't go back there."

Maida unlatched the dishwasher. When she opened it, a stream of warm air rushed out. She began juggling the hot plates into a pile on the counter. "God works in mysterious ways."

"Why do you say that?" Lily cried, hurt by the barb. She knew exactly what Maida meant and wondered why for once she couldn't be understanding.

"Because it wasn't a good place to work," Maida said around the chink of flatwear being put away, "so it's good the job is gone. I don't care what you say, a club is a club. The newspapers called you a cabaret singer, for goodness sake! That's not a pretty image."

"The newspapers also called me the Cardinal's woman, but I'm not." She didn't know how to make Maida understand. "I had a good life, Mom. I spent my days teaching kids and my evenings doing what I love, which is playing the piano and singing. It wasn't cheap. It wasn't sleazy. I didn't do annn-ything wrong."

Maida barked out a laugh. "Famous last words. How many of us have ever said *that* in our lives?" She dropped the empty flatwear rack into the dishwasher and began removing hot mugs.

"When have you said it?" Lily asked.

Maida stood for a minute. Then, tightly, she said, "I *wallowed* in self-pity when your father died." She finally turned and stared at Lily. "I didn't know what to do with the business. It was our livelihood. But the choice was either to learn how to work, or to sell. I chose to learn. What are *your* choices?"

Lily hadn't outlined her choices, not with this newest twist. She had left Boston assuming she would return. Yes, she still had a lease. She could stay in her apartment until the end of June, regardless of what anyone in the building said. But without a job?

Terry Sullivan had a job. His byline was right there in today's paper, attached to a story about the Back Bay murder that had conveniently captured the public's heart. He had screwed up far worse than she ever had, but he hadn't been fired. That wasn't fair.

The kettle began to whistle. Lily might have turned and left the room if Maida hadn't made a show of putting two cups, two spoons, two muffins on the table—and even then, she was almost angry enough to walk right out. She needed sympathy. She needed encouragement. Maida had a history of denying her those things.

A cup of tea and a muffin weren't sympathy and encouragement. But they were better than nothing. So she stayed.

Lily did love work at the cider house. Though rote, it demanded attention, which meant that the remaining morning hours passed quickly enough. Come lunchtime, though, she was in the tan wagon, heading for town. She didn't bother with a hat, scarf, and dark glasses this time. There was no need for a disguise.

The town knew she was back. Indeed, she turned heads as she drove down Main Street. Angry enough, defiant enough, she smiled and waved.

Passing Charlie's, she turned in at the post office and drove right back to the yellow Victorian. She had barely set the brake when John came out of the house. Head down, he was sifting through keys. He looked up, startled to see her, and quickly glanced toward the road.

She rolled down her window and called, "They know." When he came closer, she said more quietly, "I need help. Can we talk?"

He rounded the wagon, slid into the passenger's seat, and shut the door. Then he faced her, stretching an arm over the back of the seat. "I'm all yours."

She might have smiled if she hadn't felt so driven. "I want to fight. How do I do it?"

He rubbed the spot under his lip where his beard was a short line. "Fight Terry? Dirty?"

"Well, Cassie's doing it clean, but that'll take time. I need to do something now, or at least feel like I am. I'm tired of sitting and waiting. What are my options?"

He thought about it a minute, studying her with eyes that were surprisingly warm. "That depends. Are you talking about revenge?"

"Let's call it justice."

He smiled crookedly. "They're pretty much the same thing."

"Justice sounds nicer."

"How bad do you want it?"

"Bad."

He was pensive for another minute, but she didn't mind the delay. She felt good with him here, like she was finally *doing* something.

"Here's the thing," he said. "Whether you call it justice or revenge, there's still a right and a wrong way to do it. You want instant gratification? I'll give you a list of questionable articles Terry's written for the paper, you call a press conference, lay them out, and, bingo, public embarrassment."

"Is that what you'd do?"

He shook his head. "I think fabricating stories is the tip of the iceberg. There were four separate instances of alleged plagiarism in college. They were investigated but never proved. My source has reports stating that fact. Other sources may produce other instances. Clearly, the more we dig up, the stronger our case. But the digging takes time. You have to decide how instant the gratification has to be."

"Not instant. But not long. This is . . . humiliating." Humiliating was the least of it, all told, but it was what she felt right then. "Terry conned me into trusting him. I can't be the only one who fell for that."

"No. I'd lay money on there being others. I'd also lay money on there being something wrong with his personal life. He moves from apartment to apartment more times than anyone I know. So maybe he doesn't pay rent and gets evicted. Maybe he trashes the place and loses his lease. Maybe he fucks his neighbors— excuse my French—and goes while the going is good. I want to know why he moves so much."

"I want to know why he went after me," Lily said.

"I want to know why he went after the Cardinal," John added, and Lily knew then that they were thinking alike. Yes, her goal was to discredit Terry as he had discredited her, but the idea of understanding the why of it felt like the right way to go, too.

Was she making a deal with the devil for this?

If so, he was a handsome one—square jaw, trim mustache and beard, hair that fell over his brow and looked great even with receding temples. He had been more rumpled at dawn, but every bit as attractive. She wondered if he knew.

His eyes were a warm cocoa. Not seductive. Just warm. They invited trust. Deceptive? She was asking for his help, asking media to punish media. Last time, he had offered his help in exchange for her story, and she had refused him outright. That felt like an eon ago.

"Is the price the same?"

He lowered his arm and studied his hands. His fingers were long and lean, forearms lightly haired, flannel shirt rolled to the elbow, its tails loose over faded jeans.

He met her gaze. "Yes."

So much for warm eyes. "My story."

He nodded. "An exclusive."

"For the paper?"

"No. I want to do a book on the media versus an individual's right to privacy. What's happened to you is an example of things run amok."

She couldn't argue with that. A book might not be

so bad. That suggested something more . . . thought-ful. "Am I the only example in your book?"

"I think your experience illustrates a widespread problem."

"That's a yes."

After a pause, he conceded the point. "Yes. Your case would be the focus. Media dysfunction is a hot topic right now. I could have a book published by summer."

"Do you know that for sure?"

"I have a publisher who wants to do it."

Ah. He had already talked with a publisher. He was ambitious. That was a strike against him. She was wise not to trust too much, too easily.

Then again, this way there would be movement, at least. Summer was nine months off. Nine months was better than the thirty-six the legal system might take.

"The book would be a major release," he said. "This publisher has a remarkable record of hitting best-seller lists. He goes out with tens of thousands of copies, gets reviews in every major outlet, bookings on major talk shows."

"I won't go on talk shows."

"I will. It's one way of getting your side of the story out."

Well, that sounded nice, but there was still the question of trust. "How do I know you're really on my side?"

Again he studied his hands. When he looked up, he was sober. "I've told you I am."

"I've been burned before, John."

"Not by me. Besides, you know my feelings about Terry, and I'll be focusing on him just as much as on you. One of you is the good guy and one the bad guy. It's a no-brainer which one."

She supposed so. "You have a personal interest in smearing Terry. Will you mention that?"

"I haven't decided."

But she had. "It's the only honest thing to do. If I cooperate, I'll need that."

"Honesty."

"And veto power," she added because it didn't hurt to ask. If she worked with him, she would be compromising what little privacy she had left.

"You don't want the business about the marriage coming out."

"No."

"Anything else?" he asked.

Because he seemed agreeable enough, she said, "I don't know. I'll tell you as I go."

"That gives you an advantage."

She shrugged. "It's the best I can do. How bad do you want that best-seller?"

The look in his eye suggested a whole other story behind the question. He turned sideways to face her fully. "You can't talk with anyone else."

"I wasn't about to. I'm not a talker."

He smiled. "You do fine when you want to make a deal."

She smiled back. "It's desperation."

"You want justice that bad?"

She thought about the mortification, the embarrassment, the humiliation, the loss. Terry Sullivan hadn't worked in a vacuum; other papers had picked up his story and perpetuated it. But his had been the lie on which they were based. For whatever reasons, he had wreaked havoc with her life.

"I do," she said solemnly.

Lily was invigorated. Upon returning to work, hidden again under rubber coverings, she worked deftly positioning racks, folding cloths, positioning racks, folding cloths. Her heart pulsed in time with the gears of press, steady and rhythmic, purposeful now.

Maida directed the work through the midafternoon break, but when it came time to transfer cider from the refrigerator unit to the bottling station, she left Oralee in charge. When two hundred gallons of fresh cider had been bottled and sent off to the warehouse, the machinery cleaned, and the cider house hosed down, Lily went down to the main house. She found Maida in a rocker on the porch, looking pale.

"Are you all right?" she asked.

Maida set the rocker in motion. "Tired. Accidents take a toll."

"How are the men?"

"Fine. The backhoe isn't. We've rebuilt it once too often. It has to go."

"Is a new one very expensive?"

Maida shot her a reproving look. "You wouldn't ask that question if you had any idea."

Obviously, Lily thought.

Maida sighed and looked out over the orchards

that flanked the gravel drive. "I can't afford a new one. There's an auction coming up north. I can get one there for less. Such a shame. It was one of the last of the small dairy farms. Just couldn't make it."

Lily leaned against a post and followed her gaze. The apple trees were a muddy green, drab in comparison to the more vibrant foliage down by the lake, but there remained a lushness to them. They were squat and full. An old wood carton sat under one. A long picker lay close by.

"The trees were larger when I first came here," Maida mused. Her voice was faraway. "That was how they did it then—bigger trees and fewer of them. Then the thinking changed, and we began planting four small trees for every large one. The yield is better that way."

Lily remembered the unsureness accompanying the transition. After generations of doing things one way, her father had borne the brunt of the responsibility for change, and that change had been gradual. Painfully so. "How is the yield this year?"

"Oh, it's good. We'll have a record year. Will we have more money to show for it? No. Costs are rising more than profit. I worry sometimes. Not that any of you girls wants the business. There are times when I wonder why I work myself to the bone. I'll die in my sleep like your father did, and the business will be sold. I should have had a son."

Lily had heard that before. Starting with the not-that-any-of-you-girls part, she had heard the whole speech. It had always made her feel doubly guilty for who and what she was. But, Lord, she was tired of feeling that way. So, sharply, she asked, "Why didn't you?"

Maida turned her head against the rocker's back to meet Lily's eyes. "I put in an order, but it came through wrong."

It was a typical Maida statement—but different. There was actually humor in the voice, in the eyes.

Lily wasn't sure what to make of that. "You could have tried again," she said more gently.

Maida smiled, shook her head, closed her eyes. "I couldn't. I'd had trouble carrying Rose. They suggested I leave it at that. So I had my girls."

Lily felt a whisper of warmth. It wasn't the words, but the way Maida said them. There was satisfaction, even peace. It was completely uncharacteristic and totally welcome.

Then came the sound of a car turning off the road onto the drive, and Maida sat forward. "It's Alice." Alice Bayburr was one of her closest friends. She rose and went to the edge of the porch.

"I'll leave," Lily said.

"Not yet. Why do you think she's come, if not to see you?"

Sure enough, Alice was barely out of the car when she called, "They were talking about it in town, but I had to see for myself! Lily Blake! You are a celebrity!"

"That's what you always wanted," Maida said out of the side of her mouth.

"No. What I wanted was to play the piano."

"And sing."

"Yes."

Alice was a brunette of average height and build who fought mediocrity by wearing pink. Lily hadn't known there were pink jeans until she had seen Alice wearing them when she was home the Easter before, and the color had had nothing to do with the holiday. Today, Alice wore pink slacks, a pink blouse, and a pink blazer that flared out as she approached.

"Good Lord, give me a fright, you look like Celia," she said, holding Lily at arm's length to look her over. "A little taller, a little thinner. But you smell of apples, just like your mom."

"She's been helping out in the cider house," Maida said.

"So I heard. That's good of you, Lily. Someone else in your situation might be doing absolutely nothing. Someone else in your situation might be afraid to show her *face,* after being called a slut." She caught herself. "Oh my, that sounded harsh. What I meant was that after going through what you have, another woman, a *lesser* woman, would be sitting at home absolutely *paralyzed.*" It was one faux pas after another. "What I meant—"

"We know what you meant," Maida said, and Lily remembered something else about Alice: she was renowned for putting her foot in her mouth.

"I do it every time," she said in quiet apology to Maida. Then she turned to Lily. "When did you get back?"

"Last weekend." It would be a week that night. Hard to believe. Boston felt at least a year away.

"And we just found out? Well, maybe it's just as well. There's been a lot of concern here, mostly churchwomen thinking back to the incident with that boy. We weren't sure what to believe when this whole thing first broke. Lily Blake corrupting a man of the Church? Some in town said they weren't surprised, others said they were. But there was no doubt you knew him. We all saw those pictures. There you were, a beautiful girl in the city, sitting hip to hip with the Cardinal. The *Cardinal*." Her voice lowered, conspiratorial now. "What's he like?"

"Alice," Maida protested.

But Alice said, "I want to know," and repeated the question.

"He's a nice man," Lily said.

"As handsome as the pictures suggest?"

"I guess."

"Definitely a ladies' man."

"Alice," Maida protested again.

Alice shushed her and returned to Lily. "Is he?"

"No."

"You don't think he's ever—?"

"Alice!"

"Well, goodness, Maida, it's a natural question." To Lily, she said, "There's the intrigue, you know. Does he, or doesn't he? After his elevation, the papers were filled with every other bit of information on him. It was only a matter of time before it turned to that. You, my dear, just happened to be there when it did."

A clamor came from around the corner of the house, footsteps on the gravel, breathless little laughs.

Rose's youngest daughters appeared, shooting out across the grass with their heels kicking up as they ran. Rose came at a more sensible pace in their wake. Looking at her, Lily marveled at the strength of certain genes. She and her sisters—all three—looked just like Maida. What set Rose apart was the natural color on her cheeks, and the way she dressed. Maida and Lily wore jeans, which were appropriate for work at the orchard. Rose wore long skirts or tailored pants, which were appropriate for marketing, chauffeuring, and socializing around town.

She climbed the porch steps, set a large pot on the rail, and gave Alice a hug. "Come sightseeing, have you?"

"Better me than all the others wanting to take a look. Since word got around your sister was back, the phone hasn't stopped ringing. Mark my word, this is one for the Lake Henry history book. There hasn't been such a buzz since . . . since . . ."

"The polygamists," Rose put in dryly.

"That was before all of our time, but you're right. Since the polygamists. It's all about morals and where this town stands. I tell you, there'd o' been half a dozen ladies up here right now if I hadn't said I'd come. But I've seen what I want, so I'm leaving now."

"No tea?" Maida asked.

"Not today. Lily, don't you mind if people stare. You're a spectacle right now, is all. No, that came out wrong. You're *different* from them right now, is all. They'll get used to you again." She was off down the stairs before Lily could say that she wouldn't be staying long enough for that.

But her job at the club was gone. Gone.

"Stay there, girls!" Rose yelled and held up an open hand until Alice had turned her car around and passed them on the drive. Then she closed her fingers to unfreeze the girls, let out a breath, and turned to Maida. "I made a chicken stew. It should last you several days. How do you feel?"

"I'm fine."

"Were you sick?" Lily asked.

"She gets headaches," Rose answered. "They're from tension."

"No," Maida said. "They're from eyestrain. I need new glasses."

"Percy DeVille died last summer," Rose told Lily, "so she doesn't know who to go to, but I do. There's an optometrist in Concord who's good. I had to take Hannah to see him just last month."

"Where is Hannah?" Lily asked.

"*Hannah?*" Rose called.

Hannah came quietly up the steps.

"We thought she needed glasses. The teacher called to say she was squinting. Thank goodness, it was a false alarm."

"I wouldn't have minded," Hannah said.

"You'd look *awful* with glasses."

"Movie stars wear glasses. Some of them look cool."

"You wouldn't have," Rose told her, then turned in dismay to Maida. "Would you believe? This is what

I'm dealing with now. She argues with everything I say."

Lily thought it might be the other way around, and she knew how *that* felt. "Actually," she said, studying Hannah's round, serious face, "you'd look good in a pair of those wire-thin Calvins."

"Lily," Rose complained, "why are you *saying* this?"

"Because it's true. And someday she may need glasses. If she does, she'll look adorable."

Rose waved a hand. "I'm not arguing with you about this. The fact is that she doesn't need glasses. Don't ask me what the squinting was about, but her eyes are fine. I thank the Lord for that. She's only ten."

"Almost eleven," Hannah said. "My birthday's a week from Tuesday."

Lily smiled. "Are you celebrating?"

Rose pressed her knuckles to her brow. "That's a whole *other* bone of contention. She wants a party. Don't ask me why. She isn't a party girl. I wouldn't even know who to invite."

"I would," said Hannah.

"Who? Melissa and Heather?" To Maida, she said, "Those are the only names I ever hear. This is not a girl with a large circle of friends. I don't see the point of throwing a party for three girls."

"I do," Lily said. Her heart was breaking for Hannah. It was bad enough that Rose was thinking those things, worse that she was saying them, *worst* that she was saying them in front of the child.

Rose turned to her and smiled. "Fine. You throw the party."

Lily was good for the challenge. She smiled right back. "I'd like that." She held out a hand to Hannah. "Walk me to my car. I need to know what kind of party you want."

In the few seconds before Hannah joined her, it struck Lily that she might be worsening the situation between Hannah and Rose, but she couldn't stand by and let the poor child feel so bad about herself. Someone had to give her a boost. Lily had had Celia to do that, but Hannah didn't seem to have anyone at all.

She closed her hand around Hannah's. Passing Maida, she said a quiet "I'll be here Monday morning."

Maida didn't answer. She seemed startled, but not by Lily. Her eyes were on Rose.

Chapter 18

Griffin Hughes of the sexy baritone tried calling the chief of police again on Friday at the exact time he had called on Tuesday, but Poppy didn't take him for being forgetful or dense. She figured he would know that if Willie Jake hadn't been in his office at seven-thirty Tuesday, he wouldn't be there now. That meant Griffin didn't really want to talk to Willie Jake, but to her.

Or so the fantasy went.

After their last talk, that fantasy had a face. Poppy conjured up red hair, blue eyes, and neat little ears. But it was still the voice that touched her most. It was low and divine.

"Well, hi there," she said brightly.

"Hi, Poppy. How are you?"

"Just fine. But if you're looking for Willie Jake, he's not here."

"Home again, huh?"

"Yup."

"That's okay," Griffin said with admirable honesty, "I was really looking for you. Rumor has it that Lily's back home. I thought you'd be the person to know."

Poppy would indeed, but she didn't care *how* sexy Griffin Hughes's voice was. "Knowing is one thing, telling is another."

"Will you tell?"

"Nope. Nothing's changed there."

His voice fell another few notes. "I am not the enemy."

"Any guy out to make money off my sister and this bogus story isn't good," she said, but good-naturedly. It was hard to be any other way with so charming a guy.

"I'm out to redeem her," Griffin argued, but before she could respond, he asked, "Are your friends there tonight?"

Poppy winked at Lily, who stood against the doorjamb. They had just finished dinner—a lemony chicken from a recipe Lily brought. It had been delicious.

Griffin, of course, was referring to her Tuesday group. "No," she answered truthfully, "they're not here."

"Then tell me how old you are."

She relaxed in her chair. "Thirty-two."

"Aye-aye-aye. Old. What color's your hair?"

"White."

"It is not."

"No. It's brown. And short. Probably shorter than yours."

"Any special reason?"

There certainly was, but she couldn't imagine he knew. "Why do you ask?"

"It's one of the trick questions we journalists use that seems simple on the surface, but can be revealing. If you wear your hair short for the ease of it, you're probably a woman who doesn't like to fuss, kind of loose and free, if you know what I mean. If you wear it short for style, you're hip. If you wear it short to show off a great-shaped head, you're vain. If you wear it short because you're just . . . right out there, if you get my drift, you're self-confident. Which is it?"

Poppy thought for a minute. "Mostly the first."

"Loose and free? I wouldn't have guessed it. You're too tight-lipped. But maybe that's something you caught, living up there in that town. I keep thinking about the story you told me last time. You know, about James Everell Henry? About feisty independence? I have a question about that."

He remembered the logging baron's whole name. Poppy was impressed. "Yes?"

"You said that the more outsiders push, the more the town will clam up. Does that mean the town believes Lily's story? Or will it clam up on principle alone?"

Poppy looked at her sister. "It means that the town believes Lily's story." She didn't know it for fact, but she refused to say anything else. And it wasn't for Lily's sake. It was for the sake of whatever Griffin Hughes might tell a friend. "I have another story. Want to hear?"

"You bet."

"Once upon a time," Poppy began, "back when Lake Henry was Neweston—I told you we were called that, didn't I?"

"Yes."

"It was called Neweston after the home port of Weston from which the original British settlers came."

"Ahh."

"So, back when Lake Henry was Neweston, there was a colony of polygamists who were looking for a place to settle."

"Polygamists?"

"Polygamists. They liked the looks of our lake, so they bought a few houses and started moving in. Well, it was a little while before the townsfolk realized what was going on inside those walls, but let—me—tell—you, when they finally caught on, they didn't like it one bit. I mean, it was unanimous—rich, poor, year-round, summer, Baptist, Episcopal, Congregational—they were united as they'd never been before. They formed an association and pooled their money and tried to buy those houses back, but the colonists weren't selling. So they stared."

"Stared?"

"Stared at those settlers at the post office, the school, the general store. They were relentless. They even lined up their boats on the water and stared from there. They made the environment hostile for the settlers without saying a word."

"Did the settlers finally sell?"

"You bet."

"And the message here for me is . . ."

Poppy caught Lily's eye. "High standards. Lake Henryites come from the kind of stock that puts certain values on a pedestal. If the townsfolk thought for one minute that Lily had truly done what your colleagues claim, my entire *family* would be ostracized, but that hasn't happened."

"This isn't hard on your mom?"

Distrust reared its head again. It was an interview type of question. She was on guard. "Why do you ask that?"

"Because I read that she doesn't get along with Lily, so it follows that she might be suffering."

"I'd think a mother would suffer, regardless, in a situation like this."

He didn't have an immediate comeback. It was a full minute before he said a quiet "Touché."

He was thinking something. Poppy waited.

Still quiet, he said, "I have one sister. Four brothers, but only one sister. So you'd think she and my mother would have been close, being the only two girls in the house, but they weren't. They fought constantly. Cindy was headstrong and wanted to do things her own way, and after a while my mom let her. She had to. A child is only a minor for so long. Cindy moved out the day she turned eighteen and then made every mistake in the book—hooked up with lousy guys, got pregnant, had an abortion, started college, flunked out, reenrolled. My mom swore that she was on her own, but she suffered each time something

went wrong. One of us would remind her of their differences, and she would nod and say we were right,
but you could see that pain in her eyes."

"Do they get along now?"

"My mom's dead."

"I'm sorry."

"Me too. Life isn't the same without her. The rest
of us are strewn all over the country, but she used to
make holidays worth coming home for."

"Is your father still alive?"

"Uh-huh. Alive and well and living it up. He married my mom when he was twenty, so he's sowing the
wild oats now that he didn't sow then. He's fallen in
love five times in as many years. Always a different
woman. Kind of makes holidays *not* worth coming
home for."

"But if he's happy . . ."

"None of them's my mom."

Poppy couldn't say anything to that, but there was
no need. He hurried on, actually sounding embarrassed. "Why am I telling you this? It has nothing to
do with anything."

"It has to do with you."

"Which has nothing to do with you or with your
sister. You won't tell me anything?"

"About Lily? No."

"About you, then?"

"I've already told you stuff."

"One thing more. Tell me one thing more. Anything you want."

She thought of telling him that she had half a

degree in forestry, but she feared he would ask why she worked inside. She could tell him that she liked the outdoors, but then he might ask about sports. She considered saying that Armand Bayne, who bankrolled *Lake News* and knew everyone of any stature in publishing, would have Griffin Hughes blackballed if he tricked Poppy into saying something revealing. Except that name-dropping worked two ways. Griffin might have the gall to call Armand, who wouldn't know not to mention, even in passing, that Poppy Blake couldn't walk.

So she told him, "My house is on the lake. I'm looking out at it now. It's a beautiful night here—not too cold. The weekend's supposed to be sunny and warm."

"I was thinking of driving up. I'm in New Jersey. I could do it easily."

Her heartbeat sped. "Not a good idea."

"Why not?"

"The crowds. The traffic. Foliage is near peak. There'll be buses all over the place. And RVs, and motorcycles. One accident and the highways are backed up for miles. It's like a *zoo* here this time of year. Besides, I'm not going to be here, and no one else will talk with you, so there's no point in your coming."

"Where are you going?"

"Away," Poppy said. It was the smallest lie she could think of.

Griffin said, "That's too bad. It might have been nice."

Yes, Poppy thought moments later when he was

gone, *it might have been nice.* But might-have-beens did her no good, so she let it go.

Only, the fantasy lingered.

Lily was free of fantasies that night, sitting again in the pine root cubby at the edge of the lake. Being with Poppy was fun but sobering. Listening to her talk on the phone—listening to her flirt—she had seen fleeting glimpses of a sorrow that Poppy kept out of her voice. Lily couldn't begin to fathom that sorrow. It cast her own life in a different light.

Or maybe it was working at the cider house. Or planning a birthday party with Hannah. Or hiring Cassie. Or dealing with John.

Maybe it was simply the passage of time. The shock was over. The upheaval in her life wasn't as new or abrupt. Oh, she was still angry. But she didn't feel as lost as she had.

Poppy was right. It was a beautiful night. A robust moon hung over the center of town, making an elegant white wand of the church steeple before shimmering gently out over the lake and its islands. The occasional window held a light along the water's edge, but that was the only sign of humanity.

Softly, the lake brushed the shore. The earth under her fingers was rich. The air smelled of wood smoke, and was comfortably cool. Celia's baseball jacket kept her as warm as she needed to be.

Lily had loved Manhattan at night, especially at year's end, when the city glittered under holiday lights. She had loved Boston nights more in summer,

when the colors had to do with the crowds on Newbury Street, and the smells were old and European.
Lake Henry nights were . . . they were primal.

She waited and listened intently but didn't hear a
loon this night. So she began humming her own song,
a chant, actually, Celtic in origin. Melodically simple,
it captured the haunting quality of the lake at night,
and it took on a life of its own, evolving into soft
words whose meaning she didn't know. She hugged
her knees and rocked gently, feeling a deep reverence
as she sang. Her thoughts flashed on childhood Sundays when she had sung in church. The feeling was
much the same.

She was connected to this place. She didn't know
whether it had to do with growing up here, having a
mother and two sisters here, or having a father and
countless other relatives buried out there under the
moon, in the graveyard beside the church. But she felt
peaceful here. Oddly content.

Then again, maybe the peace and contentment had
to do with nothing more than the song. Nine days
was a long time to go without singing, but it hadn't
occurred to her to sing before. Her mind had been too
filled with dissonant things to even think about it.

Now that the thought had taken root again, it
hung on.

John spent a good part of Saturday at the office. Every
so often he took breaks by walking up to the post office, over to Charlie's, or across to the crafts fair set
up at the town center. There were booths of baskets,

balsam wreaths, hand-dipped candles, locally woven scarves, and booths of wood carvings, small paintings, rock creatures—much to see, but John was more interested in the people around him. He knew most. Others were foliage freaks, buying mementos of their trip.

Then there were the questionables. He recognized a newspaper reporter from Concord and thought he recognized one from Springfield. He was willing to bet that another pair of strangers were in television. They were a little too coordinated in their L.L.Bean outfits to be real, plus they were being given cold shoulders by the locals.

Satisfied that Lily was being protected, he returned to the office with the small bits of news he collected and added them to the file for the next week's paper. He worked for a while on the cover story, which was the accidental shooting of a three-year-old child in Ashcroft the day before and, legislatively, the use and abuse of guns. Mostly, though, he researched Terry Sullivan. He wanted to find out why the guy moved so much.

With the windows wide open, the office smelled of the candied apples that the Garden Club was making in a huge pot hung over a wood fire on the town beach. The weather was perfect for it—cold enough to set the candy coating, warm enough for people to linger for second helpings. He might have gone down there himself if he hadn't been intrigued by the information coming up on his screen.

He moved from one link to the next and made phone calls in between. Quitting at seven, he drove home with a mind to writing some of his thoughts out by hand. As the sun grew low and amber over the woods, though, he was drawn to the lake. Pulling an old sweater on over his T-shirt and shorts, he unbeached his canoe. He slipped inside, picked up the paddle, and set off.

He had barely reached the island where his loons swam when they emerged from the shadows. The two juveniles were there, but only one parent. He guessed that the other was out visiting and would be back, standard behavior for adult loons at September's end. No matter that the weather was milder tonight than it had been earlier in the week; fall was deepening. The adult that remained was duller in color than it or its mate had been even two days before.

The more vibrant the leaves, the less vibrant the loons. It was one of nature's sad quirks. Another—not so much quirk as bare fact—was that soon the leaves would wither, drop, and die, and the loons would be gone.

Totally aside from the onset of cold, John wasn't looking forward to winter. He loved skiing, snowshoeing, ice fishing. He loved the warmth of Charlie's café, with snow swirling through the birches outside. He loved hot chocolate piled high with whipped cream. Still, winter was a lonely time of year.

Moving his paddle through glassy water, he backed away, turned the canoe, and set off for Thissen Cove. By the time he reached it, the sun had dropped behind the west hills, and the shadows along the shore were more purple than blue. Thirty feet out from shore he set his paddle across the gunwales and let the canoe drift. Then he waited for a sign.

He got three.

First came a light in Celia's window.

Second came the call of a loon from the far end of the lake.

Third came a song. At first he thought it was another loon answering the first, but this sound was sweeter and more lasting. It was a minute before he realized what it was.

Lily had never been much of a cook. As a child she had stayed out of the kitchen to avoid Maida. As a student she hadn't had the time. As an employed adult she hadn't cared enough about eating to prepare much more than perfunctory meals. Besides, there was take-out around every corner in the city.

Not so in Lake Henry, but that wasn't a problem. For the first time in her life, Lily had the kitchen, the time, and the desire to cook. It wasn't exactly out of boredom, either. It was more like curiosity.

Celia had left a notebook filled with recipes. It was covered with quilting fabric, actually more a binder for small handwritten pieces of paper than a notebook, but it served the purpose. Even apart from the fact that Lily remembered Celia holding it in her wrinkled hands, when she held it in her own now, it felt rich.

The lemony chicken that she and Poppy had made was one of Celia's recipes. Now she made two others. One was a sweet-corn chowder that was appropriate to the season and particularly practical, since Poppy had foisted on her a dozen ears of newly picked corn, foisted on *her* in turn by a well-meaning friend. The second was corn bread, made with more of that corn, plus cornmeal, eggs, butter, maple syrup, and walnuts.

Between the chowder and the bread, the smell of the cottage on Saturday evening was heavenly. Lily even had her windows open a drop so that she could hear the sounds of the outdoors, and the aromas were hardly diluted. When she heard a distant loon song, it struck her that when all was said and done, she could do a lot worse on a Saturday night. Without conscious thought, she began to sing back.

She sang while she stirred the soup and while she took the corn bread from the oven. Humming, she set the table with a pretty woven mat, picked the soup bowl and a plate that she liked best from Celia's eclectic collection, gathered three fat candles of different heights and shapes from other parts of the cottage, and lit them. Singing softly again, she opened a bottle of wine, another gift from Poppy. She had started to fill a fluted wineglass when she heard a knock on the door.

Her singing stopped abruptly, and with a gasp, she held her breath. Seconds later, her heart pounding, she exhaled with a rush of dark resignation. The town knew she was here. It had to be only a matter of time before the rest of the world found out as well.

But the voice that came through the open window, a familiar face peering at her through the screen, wasn't the rest of the world. "It's just me," John said.

Relieved enough to be giddy, she pulled open the

door. "I can't tell you what just went through my mind."

"I realized it would as soon as I knocked. Sorry. I didn't mean to scare you."

She took a deep breath. Her heart kept pounding, but she figured that was a side effect of facing someone this tall and good looking on a Saturday night. She didn't have to trust him to be pleased that he was there. Singing wasn't the only thing she had been without of late. The company of people was another.

She tucked her hands in the back of her jeans. "What's up?" she asked, but he was looking past her to the table that she had just set.

"Uh-oh. I've come at a bad time."

She laughed. No point in being coy. "Not really. It's just a party for one."

"Some party." He inhaled loud and long. "Whatever you've cooked smells incredible."

"Have you eaten?"

"No. But I don't crash parties."

With a chiding look, she stood back and waved him in.

He ran a hand across his beard and down his sweater. "I look like shit."

Granted, his sweater was stretched, his shorts frayed, and his sneakers old, but he was clean—which was more than she could say for herself. Batting at flour smudges on her T-shirt and jeans, she said, "So do I."

But she couldn't do anything about it, not with his standing there and dinner hot and ready. Leaving him to decide for himself whether to come or go, she returned to the kitchen and set a second place at the table. It was a minute before she had the corn bread cut in squares and put into a basket. By that time, John was standing in her living room, looking all around the cottage. She dished up the chowder, quite pleased with herself. It was only when she was filling the wineglasses—when he continued to look around—that she had second thoughts.

Yes, she welcomed the company. Yes, she might call it business. Yes, she wanted John to dig up every last bit of dirt on Terry Sullivan. But she wasn't ready to deliver on her half of the deal.

She straightened slowly. "Are you taking notes?"

John had been studying the loft. Now he grinned. "Birdhouses?"

She followed his gaze. "They're Celia's doing. All of this is."

He took a step toward the spiral stairs, seeming about to climb them before catching himself. "She was a character." Then he saw the table ready, food served, wine poured. His mouth formed a silent "wow."

Lily warned, "This isn't for your book. It's because you happened to come here at a time I happen to be eating."

"Not for my book," he promised, approaching the table. His eyes were wide and appreciative. "I wouldn't share this with anyone. Do you always eat this way?"

"No. I'm not a cook. That's a disclaimer. You eat at your own risk."

John didn't look worried. "Anything that smells this good can't possibly be bad. Besides, you made this for yourself. If you'd made it for me, I might have worried you'd put something in it—a little arsenic, a dash of hemlock." Brows arched, he pointed to the place setting nearest him. "Want me here?"

She had barely nodded when he ran around the table and pulled out her chair. She was impressed. Given his excitement, she might have wondered when he'd eaten his last square meal.

"Thank you," she said when he pushed in her chair.

He circled to his own, settled in, and put the napkin on his lap. Then he looked from his filled soup bowl to her semifilled bowl to the stove. "I didn't ask if you had enough."

She smiled. "I have enough for *ten* other people. I just figured you normally eat more than I do."

"You probably figured right," he said with a grin. The grin softened and he grew less clever, more serious and touchingly sincere. "Thank you. I didn't expect this when I headed over here."

"What did you expect?"

"I don't know. I was just out there on the lake checking up on my loons, and before I knew it I was hearing you sing. You have a beautiful voice."

Terry Sullivan had said the very same thing. "So do the loons."

"Yours is better. It does more than they can."

"It doesn't carry like theirs does."

"Maybe not. But it's lovely." He lifted his wineglass, proposing a toast. When she raised hers to meet it, he said, "To your voice."

But John *didn't* sound like Terry Sullivan. Was she a fool for thinking him sincere?

The wine warmed its way down her throat. "Thank you," she said when she set the glass down. "I've missed it."

"Missed working at the club?"

"Missed singing. It struck me last night how long it's been. I hadn't realized."

"You've had other things on your mind," he said. His eyes held hers. "I can't start eating until you do, but the smell of this chowder is killing me."

She sampled the chowder. In her totally biased opinion, it tasted as good as it smelled.

"It tastes *better* than it smells," John said, and helped himself to a piece of corn bread when she extended the basket.

For several minutes they ate in silence. Since the loons had stopped singing, Lily slipped away from the table and put on a CD. It was a Liszt kind of night—a major-key mood for a change. She was marveling at that when she returned to the table.

"The cottage is great," he said.

She looked around. "It could use a piano. I have one in Boston. I also have a BMW."

"Ahh," he breathed. "The infamous BMW."

She smiled at the way he said it, but was instinctively defensive. "Do you know how *hard* I had to work to find one I could afford? Same with the piano. I miss both of them. Call me materialistic, but I'm not. I didn't buy that car to impress anyone. It just represented something for me."

"What?"

She held his gaze with something of a dare. "Independence. The ability to take care of myself." She might have been made a fool of by the press, fired from two jobs, and ostracized by her neighbors, but she was no shrinking violet. She could take care of herself. She wanted him to know that.

"And the piano?" he asked.

She smiled in spite of herself. "It's like a limb." She sat straighter. "So, when can I have it back?" The answer, of course, had to do with restoring her name.

"Are we talking business here?"

"I guess." She set down her spoon. "Have you found anything?"

"Yes. I just don't know what it means." He took a bite of corn bread, chewed, swallowed. "This is wonderful," he said and put the rest of the piece into his mouth. When he had washed it down with wine, he said, "I did another property search. It confirmed all the different apartments Terry has rented. It also gave me other information, like that he drives a Honda that is eight years old and has a spotty registration record. That means he's either lazy, forgetful, or defiant. He lets his registration expire, then reregisters the car. He has a problem with parking tickets. Usually pays off a hunk of them at a time, most often coinciding with the car reregistration. He gets speeding tickets and appeals them."

"Does he win?"

"Yes. Terry's glib. He can talk his way out of a paper bag."

Lily knew that. Remembering how she had been taken in, and knowing motor vehicle problems wouldn't be worth publicizing, she was discouraged. "Is that it?"

"One more thing." His eyes held hers. "An interesting little fact. It starts to explain why he moves so much. He's been married three times."

"How old is he?"

"My age. Forty-three. I know what you're thinking, and you're right. There are plenty of guys my age who've been married three times."

No. Lily was thinking—wondering—whether John had been married at all.

"The odd thing here," he went on, his eyes a deeper brown, "is that no one knew he was married. I mean, no one. The first happened when he was in college. Terry and I were classmates, but I didn't know about a wife. I called two other people who knew him there, and neither of them were aware he had a wife. He was married the second time while he was in Providence. I know a photographer there who teamed up with him a lot, and he never met any wife, much less heard mention of one. The third marriage was in Boston. I called three guys down there, including his editor, and they all thought I was making it up. They didn't know about one wife, let alone three."

"He may be a very private person."

"But that's weird, wouldn't you say? Okay, so he

isn't a big partier. He keeps his personal life separate from his professional life. But wouldn't you invite friends to a wedding? Or tell friends the good news, even about an engagement? Most guys would want to introduce their wives to the people they work with. Or they'd make references to a wife, like, 'I have to run because my wife's waiting at home.' Not Terry. Blowing three marriages is one thing. The fact of no one knowing about any of the three is another thing. I'd say that's bizarre."

The more Lily thought about it, the more she agreed. "Do you have the names of the women?"

He nodded. "They were on rental forms. My next step is contacting them."

"Why would he keep it a secret?"

The possibilities ranged from the innocent to the damning, but it was all speculation. By the time John had gone through seconds of chowder and corn bread, Lily was tired of speculation about Terry Sullivan and curious about John. Heating apple cider, she filled mugs and led him out to the porch, but the night was too still, the lake too peaceful to say anything at first. They sat on the steps for a time, looking out, sipping cider—and she was aware of him, aware of his hands holding the mug, his bare knees, his hair-spattered legs. She let the silence linger.

"Cold?" he asked.

She shook her head. "Tell me about you."

"What do you want to know?"

She wanted to know if he was honest. She wanted to know, if push came to shove, whether he would put his own interests before hers. She wanted to know if she could trust him.

But there was no point in asking those questions. If she wasn't sure about trust, the answers would be meaningless. So she asked, "Terry's your age, and he's been married three times. What about you?"

He shot her a wry grin. "What did you hear? Not that you *asked* anyone, but people talk. Poppy told you where I live." There was a tiny rise in his voice at the end that said he was guessing that.

She didn't argue. "Never married, she said. They would say the same about me."

He tipped an imaginary hat, ceding the point. "It's fact with me. I was in a long-term relationship once. Marley and I were together for eight years. She would say we came close to getting married. I wouldn't."

"Why not?"

"She didn't like my hours."

"Didn't she work?"

"Sure did. She was an ad executive. Her hours were much worse than mine, only she wanted me free when she was. It didn't work that way often. That's probably why we stayed together so long."

"Because you didn't see each other much?"

He nodded. "We were very different people. She wasn't a schmoozer, if you know what I mean."

Lily knew what he meant. Sara Markowitz called often just to schmooze. Or used to. Right now, Sara didn't know where Lily was.

John said, "Marley wouldn't have appreciated Saturday mornings in the center of town. She wouldn't have appreciated loons. She wasn't a person who liked to relax. I do."

Wanting to picture where he did that, Lily asked, "What's your place like?"

"At Wheaton Point? Modest, but growing. When I bought it, it was a typical old lake camp. Small and musty smelling. And cold. I put in a woodstove first thing, but you can only do so much without insulation. I nearly froze that first winter. My pipes did. That was an experience. But I got it fixed, and added insulation and new plumbing that spring, and an extra room on the first floor that summer, and two rooms upstairs the summer after that."

"Did you come back here because of your father?"

He looked off into the dark. "Nah. The job offer was good."

Lily was thinking that he must have had offers other places, too, and that Lake Henry took a certain kind of person—when he reversed himself.

"Yeah." His voice was quiet. "Actually it *was* because of him. We have unfinished business, Gus and me."

"Are you getting it finished?"

"Not yet. He's a tough nut."

Lily knew about those. Maida was another. "Was it hard when you first came back?"

"Yes. I didn't fit anyplace. After a few issues of *Lake News,* people in town began to thaw." He turned his head and looked at her. "I've had some letters to the editor about your case."

Letters to the editor? Dropping her forehead to

her knees, she shivered. It was inevitable, of course, especially now that people knew she was back.

She heard a rustle but didn't identify it until she felt the weight of John's sweater settle on her shoulders. She might have protested if the warmth hadn't felt so good. Drawing the arms around to the front, she wrapped her hands in the wool and looked up. "Are they good, or bad?"

"Mostly good."

"Mostly."

"One expressed concern that the press would be poking round again once they learned you're here. The others ranged from accepting to welcoming. Do you want me to run them?"

She was startled. "Are you asking me?"

"Yes."

She hadn't expected that. "If I asked you not to, you wouldn't?"

"That's right. It's your choice."

She pulled the sweater in tighter. It smelled of John, a calming combination of clean and male. For no reason at all she smiled. "Is that because you're a nice person, or because you want to get on my better side?"

"Both. I haven't had a dinner like that in years."

"Soup and bread? It was barely dinner."

"Thick chowder, sweet corn bread, mellow wine, and a beautiful woman—it was, too, dinner."

Lily turned her head sideways. His features were barely lit, but she saw a smile. It warmed her deep inside. He might be a charmer, but she liked it just then.

A new sound came.

She raised her head and listened. It was distant, one little cry, then another. Not loons. More like squeals. Human laughter?

"What was that?" she whispered.

John chuckled and whispered back, "It's the last Saturday night in September."

"Oh my God. Still?"

"It's a Lake Henry tradition."

On the last Saturday night in September, the town's brave souls went skinny-dipping. The site was a hidden cove off a bend in the lake. The participants were usually in their teens and early twenties. On occasion, the weather was downright cold.

Not so the bodies taking part, and not so Lily's just then. Sitting with John, thinking about those naked bodies down the shore a ways, she felt a humming inside.

John moved closer. "Did you ever?" he murmured in an intimate way.

His thigh was inches from hers. She pressed her eyes to her knees and shook her head no. "Did you?"

"Oh yeah. Every year from eleven on. That was how I got my first feel of a woman's breast."

Lily tried to picture it but couldn't imagine a prepubescent John. She easily imagined a pubescent one, though. He was much like the man beside her, only naked.

"I mean," he whispered, "there you are, in the middle of all those arms and legs and *bodies,* and no one knows who's touching who. It was a curious little troublemaker's dream come true."

She couldn't help herself. "Whose breasts did you touch?"

"Don't know, but they sure felt good."

She laughed into the sweater that carried his scent, embarrassed but delightedly so. With a shaky breath she realized that she was also aroused. It had been a long while since she had felt heat in that particular spot. It was one of the evening's surprises, not bad as surprises went.

But then, just when she was wondering what he might do to fuel it, he said, "I'd better go." Before she could object, he was off the porch and eating up the ground to the lake with purposeful strides.

She thought to call out—*Here's your sweater,* or, *Thanks for coming,* or, *Don't leave yet!* But she didn't move, didn't speak. She sat there embraced by his scent and watched the moonlit canoe leave her dock.

How to sleep, thinking about that? How to sleep with a whole new realm of possibility suddenly opened up wide? It was one thing to admire long, leanly muscled, lightly haired legs, and another to want to touch them.

But that was what she imagined doing—that and more, lying in bed through long hours of darkness, feeling lonely and in need. The damn sweater didn't help. It lay on a chair, smelling of John. She fell asleep frustrated and awoke confused. She didn't know whether to trust John. She didn't know whether to mix business with pleasure. She didn't know whether to add a complication to her life at a time when there were so many others.

Ironically, setting the sexual elements aside, it was the kind of thing she might have discussed with the Cardinal. She had done just that when she was trying to decide whether to move from Albany to Boston. She had been dating someone there, and he had potential. He was exciting and romantic and very interested. He also had a problem with gambling—and it wasn't that Father Fran counseled her to abandon him. He didn't tell her what to do or to think, but was more of a sounding board. He asked questions. In thinking about them, she usually came to see the larger picture.

She wanted to see the larger picture now, but her mind was filled with too many small and conflicting thoughts. Father Fran might have helped her sort through them. He might have helped her achieve a measure of emotional peace.

But Father Fran was no longer available. So, this being Sunday morning, she decided to go to church.

Chapter 19

Seeking a measure of peace—it sounded simple, but good things rarely were. Showing up at Lake Henry's First Congregationalist Church on Sunday morning meant being seen. Part of Lily wasn't ready for that. The other part of her was tired of hiding like a timid little frog. That part said it was time to break the ice.

She showered, picturing her closet full of clothes in Boston, and dressed in the lone pantsuit she had brought with her. She put on mascara and blusher, and carefully blew out her hair, then lingered over coffee with an eye on the clock. At just the right time, so that she could slip into the back unnoticed when everyone was inside and the service was about to begin, she slid into the borrowed wagon, catered to its quirks until the engine caught, then drove around the lake.

The morning was cool but not cold. The air was

clear, the foliage glorious. It was a morning for pleasure driving, but Lily was too apprehensive to feel much more than a distant appreciation. Finding the church parking lot full, she parked near the library and walked over. Two teenaged girls were running up the broad white steps as she arrived. She didn't recognize them but she could tell they recognized her by the way they stared for a few seconds too long before disappearing inside.

Turn around and go home, the cowardly part of her cried, but she needed something more than a life trapped inside the cottage. Besides, now that the two teenagers knew she was here, if she didn't show up inside, tongues would *really* wag.

Nervous but determined, she followed them in. The foyer was empty of people but not of sound. There were organ chords, then the choir singing "Faith of Our Fathers," and suddenly a world of memory opened up, visceral images of Sunday after Sunday when she had sung in the choir herself. She had loved doing that. Maida had approved, which made it one of the few times when all of the elements of her life meshed.

Taking a shaky breath, she passed through the foyer and stood at the meeting hall door. Row after row in the large room was filled, but she spotted a small space on the aisle in the next-to-last pew. Slipping in with an apologetic glance at Charlie Owens's youngest brother, who had no doubt left the extra space for stretching, she sat with her fingers laced in her lap and her head down. She didn't need to look to know that her mother would be with Rose and the Winslows in the fourth pew on the right, or that other prominent Lake Henry families would be in the pews immediately before and after. She figured she would know many of the people sitting farther back, too, but she didn't look up. She could feel them glancing her way—could feel it as tangibly as the chill of her fingers—and didn't want to see.

So she concentrated on the sounds of the organ, the hymns, the choir. "Blessed Assurance" came next, then "Sweet Hour of Prayer." She didn't sing or participate in the responsive readings that followed, but she listened to every word. From the pulpit came talk of charity, forgiveness, and love. She focused on the strength of the minister's voice and his words, wiping frustration and confusion from her mind for this little while, at least. She concentrated on ingesting the hallowedness of this place, using it to ease the parts of her that felt bruised and beaten. And it worked. By the time closing hymns were sung, she was breathing slowly and deeply.

She slipped out of the church before the benediction, fearful of ruining the feeling of ease she had achieved by having to mix and mingle. And the sense of calm remained. It was joined by something else, something unexpected, the sense that for those few moments, sitting quietly with the rest of Lake Henry, she had belonged to a community.

She couldn't remember when last she had experienced that feeling.

*   *   *

Even before the whispers reached John, he knew that Lily was in church. Bidden by a sixth sense, he had looked up at the exact instant when she entered. He was in the far opposite end of the pew ahead of hers. No regular churchgoer himself, he had arrived just minutes before.

And why was he here? After spending the night with an erection that wouldn't die, he had felt a need to elevate his thoughts. One look at Lily, however, and his good intentions were shot. So he devoted himself to singing his heart out with every hymn and listened to the minister's sermon, listened intently to every word. By the time the service was done, he was in full control.

At that point, physical awareness became intellectual awareness, and he tipped his hat to Lily in other respects. She had shown courage coming to church, braving whispers and stares. Yes, she had left early, but he had left town events early, too, when he had first returned to the lake. The difference was that he had fully earned the wariness of the townsfolk. Lily hadn't. She should have been able to walk right up that center aisle and sit with her family. It bothered him that she couldn't.

He was grappling with that thought outside the church, watching the townsfolk stream down the steps into the warm fall sun, when he spotted Cassie Byrnes. She was standing with her husband and was holding one child in her arms. Two others hovered by her hip.

When her husband left to talk with the pastor and

she headed for the car, John maneuvered himself so that he met up with her halfway. He swooped up to his shoulders the younger of the two standing children, a four-year-old boy named Ethan, and walked alongside Cassie with the child clutching his chin.

"Did you see Lily there?" he managed to ask in an audible way, despite the pull on his jaw.

She shot him a facetious look. "How not to?"

"She said you were representing her. How's it going?"

"If you're asking for the sake of the paper, I have no comment."

"I'm asking as a friend." It was half the truth, at least.

"Lily's?"

"Yes."

She stopped and searched his eyes. He didn't know how much she saw, but a minute later she began walking again. "The answer is it's going nowhere. I sent a fax to the newspaper Friday to remind them that they have a week to issue a retraction before we file suit. The week expires tomorrow."

"Do you think they'll do it?"

"Do you?" she returned. "You know these people better than I do."

He did at that. "They'll let you sue. They'll stand behind their story. They have a tape."

"Lily told me. That's a plus and a minus."

"She didn't know it was made."

"That's the plus," Cassie said as they reached her car. "It's against the law." She slid the child on her hip into a car seat in back. Lowering the boy from his shoulders, John passed him to Cassie for similar tucking away. When the third child climbed into the car on his own, Cassie straightened and faced John. "This case sucks. Even if Lily weren't my client, even if she weren't the underdog here, I would feel for her. I remember her when we were growing up. She suffered."

"Because of the stutter?" John asked. Lily hadn't stuttered once the night before. He wanted to think that it meant she felt comfortable with him.

"Because of Maida," Cassie said. They were far enough from the nearest ears; still, she lowered her voice. "Hey, I had problems with my mother. Every girl does. She and I didn't exactly breeze through my teenage years. But I remember being very grateful— and more than once—that Maida wasn't *my* mother."

"She was that bad?"

Cassie rolled her eyes. "A perfectionist. Everything had to be done just so."

"Why?"

"I don't know for sure. I only know what my mother said."

"Which was?"

"That Maida was that way from the first, way back when she came here and married George."

"So, was her life perfect back then, before Lily was born?"

"That was the image she cultivated. Who knew the truth?"

But the truth interested John. People did things

for reasons. His mom had been raised in a family that was socially skilled, which made living with Gus a trial. Gus had never seen a functioning husband, so he didn't have a clue about functioning as one himself. Growing up, John had never had Gus's approval, so he was still seeking it at forty-three. And Maida? Maida Blake wanted perfection. He wondered why.

"Who does know?" he asked Cassie now.

"Not me, and not my mother," she said, holding the car keys out to her approaching husband. "Try Mary Joan Sweet. She knew Maida back when."

Mary Joan was the head of the Garden Club. Central casting couldn't have chosen better. A small, delicate woman with gray hair fringing her face, a dusting of blue shadow on her lids, and a smudge of pink on her cheeks, she reminded John of the pansies that the club planted in town window boxes each spring. She was quiet, reputedly saying more to plants on any given day than to humans. Indeed, she was breathing words of praise to the fiery burning bush outside Charlie's after church when John spotted her from the parking lot and loped across the street.

"We do go back," she admitted when he mentioned Maida's name. "I was in the club when she first joined. I was older than her, but we were immediate friends. When Lily ever walked into church . . ." She sent John a sad look. "Poor Maida."

"Poor *Lily*," said John.

"Poor Maida," Mary Joan insisted. "She did try with Lily. This was her greatest fear."

"Do you believe the newspapers?"

"No," she drawled, wrapping her mouth around the word. "But damage has been done. This is one more thing in Maida's life. First Lily's stutter. Then Poppy's legs. Then George's death. Now Lily again." She shook her head and, cradling a spray of bright red leaves in her hand, murmured something to the shrub.

"I'm sorry?" John asked.

She straightened. "I said that Maida came here for something better."

"Better than what?"

"What she had had."

"What was that?"

Mary Joan smiled. Bending, she gently gathered branches and pulled them toward the center of the shrub. She gestured at the dirt she had uncovered. "See those little shoots coming out of the ground? They're from the root system of this plant." She released the plant with care, then straightened and looked him in the eye. "They're suckers. I'm not. You're asking too many questions, John Kipling. You're beginning to sound like Terry Sullivan."

"He called you?"

"One of many. It was natural, I suppose—my being head of the club and Maida being a garden person. He's been the most persistent."

"What did you tell him?"

"Just what I'm telling you." She tipped up her pansy face, lips shut tight.

"Ahh," John said, then tried, "but I'm not doing an article for the paper."

"Maybe not. But Maida's my friend. I won't betray private things."

"You know private things?"

"Of course. I've known Maida for thirty-five years." Again that defiant tip of the head, those firmly sealed lips. She stared at him for a long minute while he tried to come up with an approach. When he couldn't find one his conscience could live with, she gave him a smug smile and headed off.

John tried to imagine Maida's secrets as he drove to the Ridge, but the things he came up with were all tired and worn. Still, it kept his mind off the darkness he felt as he neared. He raised a forefinger to people on porches, but he didn't meet any eyes or expect a wave in return. Pulling up to Gus's, he scooped up a grocery bag and went inside.

Gus was on the sofa, not quite upright, not quite sprawled. He wore a pair of wrinkled green pants and an orange shirt that was misbuttoned. John had instructed Dulcey to shave him every other day, but he must have put up a good fight, because the gray stubble there now was older than that. With his lopsided eyes and his messy white hair, he was the sorriest sight John had ever seen. And his socks had holes.

That galled John. Clutching the grocery bag, he approached the sofa. "What happened to the new socks?"

"What new socks?" Gus grumbled without meeting his eye.

"The dozen pairs I put in your drawer last month."

"I didn't ask for 'em."

"No, but I bought them. They were a gift to you."

"I like mine bettuh."

"Yours are torn."

Gus looked up. His lower eye was half closed. "What's it to you? If I want to wey-uh tawn socks, that's *my* business. An' you tell Dulcey Hewitt not to come. I'm tie-uhd of people tellin' me what to do. Leave me *be.*"

He looked so unhappy that John didn't know what to do. So he went into the kitchen, which was surprisingly neat. If he had to guess, he'd say that Gus had been on the sofa since Dulcey left that morning.

"Have you had lunch?" he called.

When Gus didn't answer, he poked his head back into the living room. Gus was glaring at the floor. Rather than risk another argument, John unloaded the groceries, cooked up an omelet with buttered toast, and brought it out.

Gus shifted his glare from the floor to the plate.

"It has everything you like," John said. "Ham, cheese, green peppers. The toast is from oatmeal bread baked fresh this morning at Charlie's."

"I hate green peppuhs."

John didn't believe it for a minute. This was a man who used to crush a crisp green pepper in his hand, tear off pieces, and eat them one by one. But he wasn't arguing. No point in that. "Well, they're good for you."

Gus snorted. "They-ull make me strong? Make me young again? Hah!" But he took the plate.

Figuring that he would eat better if pride didn't get in the way, John left him alone. Standing at the stove, he ate what was left of the omelet straight from the pan and washed everything up. Wanting to do more, he wiped down the refrigerator shelves. Most of the food he had brought last time was gone, though whether Gus had eaten it or Dulcey had tossed it out, he didn't know.

After a good twenty minutes, he dared return to the living room. Gus was asleep. It looked like he hadn't moved a muscle. But the plate was empty.

Satisfied, he cleared it away. Then he sat for a while in the old stuffed chair, watching, as he had forty years before, while his father slept. Gus had seemed huge to him then, a large man with large, all-seeing eyes and a large, barking voice. John remembered studying the prominent veins on his father's forearms, the scars on his fingers, the hair on the curve of his ears. They had been signs of strength to him.

He had admired Gus. Telling him that was something else, however.

John didn't know Maida's secrets, but he did know Gus's. There was the fact of being illegitimate and the fact of a failed marriage. There was the fact of a lifetime laying stone and the silence of that lonesome work.

So Gus wasn't a talker. Part of John wasn't either. That part was content to sit and write. Writing was lonesome work, too. There was even—despite what Gus said—an art to it.

Not that Gus would agree. Gus didn't think much of what he did. Rudyard Kipling wrote fiction. That was creative. But nonfiction? As far as Gus was concerned, newspapermen wrote about the news because they didn't have the brains to *make* the news. John could argue until he was blue in the face, but nothing he said would convince Gus.

A commercially successful book might do it.

The fax that was waiting at the office when he stopped on his way back from the Ridge gave him a lift. It was from Jack Mabbet and was informative on two fronts.

Paul Rizzo had launched his career on a false resume. He claimed to have an undergraduate degree in English from Duke and a graduate degree in journalism from New York University. In fact, he had started at Duke, flunked out, transferred to the University of Miami, and dropped out of that. So there was no undergraduate degree. As for NYU, he had never applied to *any* program there, much less enrolled. He had deceived employers and readers alike.

And Justin Barr, champion of home, hearth, and chastity? He had a predilection for kinky sex, as vouched for by a small ring of call girls who specialized in doing things for married men that their wives wouldn't do. They dealt with a privileged clientele that paid a premium for privacy. But there were records. There were photographs. No doubt about it. They had Justin Barr cold.

Had John been Terry, he might have begun scheming about the most shocking, most injurious way to use this information. But John wanted to be better than Terry. He wanted to be more decent. So he didn't scheme. Rather, he tucked the information away, simply pleased to know it was there should the time come when it might be of help.

Chapter 20

Before leaving for the cider house Monday morning, Lily called Cassie. There was no retraction in that day's paper, and the week was up. Cassie promised she would have a suit filed by the end of the day, but Lily was deeply disappointed. She had been praying for a faster resolution. Her life was in limbo. She needed to settle things and move on.

The rhythm of the cider press was more welcome than ever. Dressed head to toe in rubber, she threw herself into the work. She lifted, pushed, pulled, and folded, even took over hosing down the floors when Maida left to get more apples. When the others stopped for coffee, she drove the loader herself. It took several tries before she maneuvered the metal scoop in a way that would properly position the large crate of fruit at the end of the bath, but she did it—with no small amount of satisfaction. As soon as the others returned, she was back on the platform beside the press, layering racks and cloths and mash.

Come time for lunch, she knew what she needed. She cleaned herself quickly and ran down to the main house, but she didn't go to the kitchen this time. She went to the beautiful baby grand in the living room, sat down on the mahogany bench, and opened the lid.

She felt relief before she touched a single key. Here were old, loving friends. She brushed them with the pads of her fingers and breathed in their aged, ivory scent. Then she positioned her hands and began to play. She didn't think about songs, just let her fingers move on their own, and they knew her heart. They created sounds that were sweet and melancholy, like her emotions—a little lonesome, a little confused, but pleased, so pleased to be here.

Closing her eyes, she let the beauty of the chords take her away. The tension in the pit of her stomach began to dissolve. Her thoughts calmed. When she felt strength return, her hands fell still. She took a deep breath, straightened her spine, and opened her eyes.

Maida stood in the middle of the living room. With one hand on the back of her neck, and her head tipped, she seemed as taken as Lily. She dropped her hand and straightened her head with a sigh. "No one else can bring quite that sound from those keys," she said in a wistful voice. Then she took a breath and said a more neutral "Would you like lunch?"

Lily was warmed by the compliment and, yes, suddenly hungry. She started to get up.

But Maida was already on her way out. "Stay here and play. I'll bring it in."

A second compliment? Maida waiting on her?

So Lily played, choosing songs that her mother liked, in part to thank her, in part because entertaining people was what she did best. She continued to play when Maida returned carrying a large silver tray. She might have been an invited guest, for the way Maida set out ham and cheese sandwiches and poured fragrant tea.

"Thank you," she said when they were seated on the sofa.

Maida busied herself squeezing lemon into her tea. "It's the least I can do. You've been good in the cider house."

"I like the work."

"I should pay you."

Lily had raised a sandwich half. She put it right down. "Don't do that."

"I pay the others."

"They aren't relatives. I don't mind helping. What else would I do?"

"You could be over at Cassie's," Maida said. She brushed crumbs from her lap. "Are you really filing a lawsuit?"

"I don't have much choice."

Maida took a bite of her sandwich. Then she put it down and smiled. "Do you remember Jennifer Hauke? She was your year in school. She's Jennifer Ellison now, married to Darby Ellison, that dark-haired little boy. She just had a baby. It's their third. Another girl."

Lily didn't know what the connection was between Jennifer Hauke's new baby and her own lawsuit, but the baby was certainly a more neutral topic. "That's exciting. Do they live here?"

"No. They have a house in Center Sayfield. Anita Ellison died last month."

"Darby's grandmother? I'm sorry."

"She was one of Celia's good friends."

Lily remembered that. She had spent enough time at Celia's to know her friends, because Celia loved entertaining. She invited groups at a time, seeming in her element when the small cottage was filled. Lily remembered curling up in the bed in the loft while the ladies laughed themselves silly over something she didn't understand. Those somethings usually had to do with men. Lily would have liked to listen in on them now.

"I miss Celia," Maida surprised her by saying.

"Me too."

"She was a good person."

"Yes."

"Had a big heart."

"Had big *ears*," Lily mused. "I could talk to her about most anything."

That brought Maida back. She sat straighter. "You could. But your generation is different that way. My generation was never given permission to talk about certain things."

"You don't need permission. You just speak your thoughts."

Maida sputtered out a laugh. "It's not that easy."

"It is."

She looked at Lily, challenging now. "What would you have me say?"

Lily backed down. She and her mother had shared so few companionable times that she didn't want to spoil things. "I was being hypothetical."

"I'm serious. What would you have me say?"

Lily felt the old tightness at the back of her tongue. She focused on easing it, then said, "What your childhood was like. I haven't a clue."

"Why does it matter? What difference does it make? My life began when I married your father. And you're a fine one to say I should talk. What about your thoughts? You told them to Celia, but never to me."

Lily refused to look away. "I was afraid of stuttering."

"I don't hear you stuttering now."

No. She was thinking clearly. She was in control of herself.

From the other end of the house came a hollered *"Mom?"*

"In here," Maida called back. "It's Rose."

Lily knew that. Rose's voice was distinct from Poppy's, and no one else called Maida Mom.

Rose appeared in the archway and gave a startled look at the silver tray, the sandwiches, teapot, and cups. "This is nice," she said. "Elegance in the middle of a workday."

"We had to eat," Maida explained, extending the sandwich plate. Half a sandwich remained. "It's yours if you want."

Rose shook her head. "No time. I put a turkey breast in the fridge. It's cooked. All you have to do is heat it up. School got out early today. I have the girls in the car."

"Only Emma and Ruthie," said Hannah, slipping past her. "Hi, Gram. Hi, Aunt Lily."

"I asked you to wait in the car," Rose said.

"They were pinching me." She leaned against the sofa arm nearest Lily. Lily gave her shoulder a welcoming rub and was rewarded by a glowing smile. "They can come. All four of them."

"Super!" Lily said.

The deal was a movie and supper. Hannah had asked if she could invite three friends. When Lily readily agreed, she had cautiously asked if she could invite a fourth. "In case they don't come. They might not want to."

"They'll want to," Lily had said, praying it was so.

She and Hannah had written invitations up on Maida's pretty paisley stationery. Hannah had made her father drive her to the post office to mail them Friday night. Lily learned this from Poppy, who learned it from Rose, who had apparently been slightly put out.

"Pure guilt," Poppy had told Lily. "She knows she should be doing the party herself, but having said she was against it, she won't lift a finger to help."

"She's driving me crazy about this party," Rose said now.

"I'm not," Hannah told her, but her glow had faded. Nervous now, she murmured to Lily, "I just don't know what to wear."

"She has a closet full of clothes," Rose put in. "It's not my fault if they don't fit."

"You bought them too small."

"You outgrew them too fast."

"I can't help it."

"Oh-ho, yes, you can."

The words were different, but the tone just the same. Lily remembered too many such arguments from her own childhood to bear listening. "I think," she said quickly, "that I have to go shopping. I don't have many clothes here. I didn't knnn-know how long I was staying. I don't have the right kind of thing for this party."

"It's only a movie," Rose said. "What you're wearing is fine."

"It's a birthday party," Lily said right back. The moment of stuttering was past. She knew where she was headed. "Hannah can come shopping with me. We'll both get something. My treat."

"When?" Hannah said, glowing again, and suddenly Lily was as excited as she was.

They went the following afternoon. Lily had barely finished at the cider house and cleaned up when Hannah ran up the road. Her big T-shirt and baggy jeans were as unflattering as ever, and her hair was in a ponytail that exaggerated the roundness of her cheeks, but those cheeks were rosy and her eyes were alive. The part of Lily that identified so closely with Hannah was pleased—the promise was definitely there.

They drove south to Concord. Poppy had given Lily a list of stores in order of preference, but they didn't have to go far. At the very first store on the list, Hannah fell in love with a dress. It was a Black Watch plaid, cut in an Empire style, of a fabric that was soft enough to fall gently and smoothly. Hannah couldn't take her eyes off her reflection in the mirror, and Lily knew why. The dress made her look grown-up—and remarkably slim.

They bought a matching hair ribbon, a pair of dark green tights to match the green in the plaid, and a pair of shoes with the smallest wedge of a heel.

Setting those things aside, they moved to the part of the store that had clothes for Lily, and again, Hannah fell in love. Moments after she touched it, Lily was trying on a long skirt, vest, and blouse. The skirt and blouse were a soft heather blue rayon; the vest was woven of a dozen compatible colors. Lily could have looked for days and not found a better choice.

"Shoes, too?" Hannah asked, into it big-time by now.

"Thank you," Lily chided, "but I have shoes."

"Earrings, then," Hannah said, pointing to a rack.

"Thank you," Lily said in the same chiding tone, "but I have earrings." She reached for her wallet. "My credit card can only take so much." She slipped it out and handed it to the salesgirl, who went to work writing up the sale.

She didn't realize what she had done until the salesgirl went still. An adorably mod young woman, early twenties perhaps, she looked at the credit card, looked at Lily, looked at the credit card again. Her eyes grew wider.

"You're Lily Blake?" she finally asked in a tone of awe. "*The* Lily Blake?"

Lily's heart started to pound. *Deny it,* the little voice inside said. *There are other Lily Blakes in the world.*

"I *knew* you looked familiar," the girl cried with an excited smile. "We don't get many famous people in here." Her mouth went from wide to round. "Omigod. Wait'll I tell my boss. She'll be *wild* that she wasn't here when you came."

Lily felt her tongue tensing up. She held up a hand and shook her head while she made it relax. As soon as she could, she said, "Don't do that. I'm in hiding."

"Only my boss," the girl promised. "She'll *die.*"

Hannah was suddenly at Lily's side. Standing straight and tall, sounding like an imperious brat, she said, "If you tell anyone, you'll *ruin* my birthday. If you tell *anyone,* we won't ever come into this store again. Not me, not my mother, not anyone in our family, not anyone in our town."

Imperious brat? She sounded just like Rose! At that moment Lily didn't even mind. All she could think of as she quickly signed the sales slip and they hurried out of the store with their bundles was that she should have paid in cash.

Poppy's phone rang early Wednesday morning. It wasn't the first call, and it wouldn't be the last, but it was the one that interested her most.

"Hey, Poppy," said Griffin Hughes. "How's my girl?"

She loved his voice, oh, she did. "Fine. But . . . where's Willie Jake?" The call had come through the police department line; only, Willie Jake hadn't told Poppy he was out.

"He's at his desk. I asked him to switch me to you when he wouldn't talk. He said you wouldn't either, but I had to give it a try."

"I always talk to you."

"Not about Lily."

Poppy let out a breath. "Ahh. And here I was start-ing to think that you were interested in *me*."

"I am."

"But you keep asking about Lily! Everyone keeps asking about Lily! I have gotten four other calls this morning from press people asking about Lily!"

"That's because word's out that she's back. This time it's more than rumor. She was seen. So. What do you think?"

"About what?"

"Her being back."

Poppy sighed. "Griffin, Griffin, Griffin. The press has been *cruel* to my sister. What kind of person would I be if I talked?"

"I'm not the press. I'm a writer. There's a differ-ence. A press person works for someone else. Any-thing he writes is subject to editing. He works on a deadline, has to consider sales potential and manage-rial politics."

"And you don't?"

"No. I'm my own boss. I write an article the way I want to, then put it up for sale. I've done other things for *Vanity Fair*. They like me. They like my writing."

"They aren't interested in sales?" Poppy asked. "I don't believe that."

"They are. But what I write is what their target audience wants to read. It's a good fit, so to speak."

"And they don't want this article yesterday?"

"They do. A good part's done. I started writing it long before this happened to Lily. But her experience adds something. Come on, Poppy," he coaxed. "Tell me a little."

She was sorely tempted. His voice was that strong. "Why do you keep calling *me*? Why don't you call someone *else*?"

"I've *tried*. I called, uh"—she heard the rustle of paper—"a realtor named Allison Quimby, an old guy named Alf Buzzell, and the guy who runs the general store."

"Did they say Lily was here?"

"Didn't say yes, didn't say no. I have never met people more skilled at evasion."

Poppy smiled. "Evasiveness isn't a crime. We protect our own, that's all. Have I ever told you the story of the sacred gourd?"

There was a pause, then an amused "I don't believe you have."

"Well, y'see, there was a gourd once. A gourd is a hard-shelled fruit?"

He cleared his throat. "I did learn that once."

"Well, there was this gourd that grew one summer

on a farm just off the south end of the lake, and it was a beauty, all rich greens and purples, regal almost. There was something unusual about it, something up- lifting. You could stand out there in the field and look at it, and after a little while you felt better than you had when you came. If you had a headache, it was eased. If you had a dilemma, you had solutions."

"What did it do for you?"

Poppy caught her breath. "What do you mean?"

"What problems did the gourd help you with?"

An innocent question. She released the breath. "This all happened in the early fifties. I wasn't born then."

"Oh. Okay. Go on."

"So," she said, relaxing, "people *felt* something after they visited this gourd. They'd go home and tell friends in neighboring towns, and pretty soon those people were coming to see it. Word spread to the city, and once it got there, well, you *know* how word spreads there. One little bitty article in the paper, and people were coming from cities *all over New England* to see it."

"Must have been one crowded yard."

Poppy said, "Never underestimate a Yankee. They're orderly and they're shrewd. They managed the crowd by setting up stands selling local goods on the perimeter of the field. That way, people coming to visit had a diversion while they were waiting to see the gourd."

"That way," Griffin put in, "the locals cashed in."

"That, too," she admitted, "but could you blame

them? It was harvest time. They had bushels of sweet corn and apples, and gallons of cider, right on hand."

"So, if I visited there, saw that gourd, and bought that cider and went home feeling better, I'd never know whether it was because of the gourd, the cider, or a day in the country."

"Oh, it wasn't the gourd," she assured him. "It was an old ordinary gourd that just happened to have unusual coloring. The locals ruled out anything miraculous from that gourd early on."

"Then the whole thing was a marketing ploy?"

"Brilliant, wouldn't you say?"

Griffin didn't say anything during the short pause that followed, but she could hear a grin in that deep voice of his when he asked, "What happened to the gourd?"

"A pig ate it at the end of the season. Weud was," she laid on the accent, "that paw-kuh made soo-puh bacon."

He chuckled. "The moral of *this* story being that Lake Henryites are wily when it comes to looking out for their own interests."

"Right-o," she said.

"Sounds like a place I'd like. I really should come take a look."

But the fantasy was that he was her prince, and she could walk right into his arms. If he came to visit, the fantasy would be shot. "You wouldn't be welcome here," she warned. "Not with things the way they are."

"With Lily there, you mean?"

"No," she said with care. "I didn't mean that. I

never said Lily was here. But I'm not the only one tired of getting calls asking if she is."

"Tell me for fact that she isn't, and I won't call again."

For an instant, Poppy was trapped. But one of the things about losing the use of her legs was that her mind had grown sharper to compensate. Her voice grew gentler. The fantasy revived. "But I want you to call again. I like talking to you. So call again, Griffin Hughes. Anytime."

Chapter 21

John felt pressured Wednesday morning. He was scrambling to put the week's *Lake News* to bed, but Jenny was home with a cold and the phone kept ringing. The calls from outside media were handled fast; he said that he didn't know where Lily was, which was technically the truth at any given time. The call from Richard Jacobi was more demanding.

Richard had heard that Lily was back in town and was worried that if John didn't get something together fast, someone else would beat him to it. John pointed out that there were no other Lake Henry insiders on the scene. Richard reminded him that the deal was for an exclusive story to be published in book form in time for summer reading. John said that he understood, but countered that he knew for a fact that publishers could execute a one-month turnaround from manuscript to bound book if they chose. Richard argued that a turnaround like that made things harder—

especially with a book so legally sensitive, written, he might point out, by someone with no track record— and that he had already gone out on a limb offering John the deal he had. John reminded him that he didn't have a contract yet. Richard said it was in the works.

They ended on an amiable note, but John hung up the phone feeling a churning in his stomach the likes of which he hadn't felt since he was the stressed-out journalist seen in the mug shot on the wall. Part of the problem was time; good books weren't dashed off in a handful of days. And of course, part had to do with Lily; he liked her too much to push for information she wasn't ready to give. He even felt guilty when he thought about nosing into Maida's history in that little logging town in rural Maine.

Part of the problem, though, was *Lake News*. This was still his real job. It might only be a small-town weekly, but there was much work and great responsibility—and he took pride in it. Since his name was prominent on the masthead, he wanted each issue to be good.

So he wiped all the rest from his mind and focused on inserting post-deadline community service ads, rereading his major stories one last time, rewriting a poorly done piece from Center Sayfield, and finalizing the placement of photos with regard to local town and sports news. He sent the last page off to the printer just before one, then sat back in his chair, closed his eyes, and pinched the bridge of his nose, trying to ease the feeling of pressure in his head.

His stomach was slow in settling, and he sat there remembering that he had returned to Lake Henry to escape this feeling. He was thinking that maybe he wasn't cut out to be writing books after all, when Terry Sullivan called.

So John wasn't starting off in the best of humor. It didn't help when Terry said a smug "Your girl was seen with her niece in a store in Concord yesterday. Are you still playing dumb about where she is?"

Irritated, he sat forward. "Why are you calling me? Why are you even *thinking* about Lily Blake? The story's done. I told you that last time you called, and it's still done." He was disgusted. "It was a lot of hot air that amounted to nothing. You blew it, Terry."

"Not me. My story stands."

"Because of that tape?" John charged. "She didn't know about any tape. That's illegal."

"Ahh. So you did talk with her. That means she's back."

"Illegal, Terry. I'd be worrying about that, not about whether she's here. What is it to you, anyway?"

"I'm doing a follow-up story."

John was incredulous—and it had nothing to do with his competitive streak. "For what paper? In case you haven't noticed, the *Post* dropped the story. Besides, what in the hell would you do a follow-up *on*? Journalists who create bogus scandals?"

"Try nightclub singers who get carried away and confuse the lines between fantasy and reality."

"Yeah. Right. You gonna prove that with an illegal

tape?" He had a sudden thought. "How about a tape that's been edited?"

There was a pause, then a cold "You have nerve."

"Not me, pal," John said. He could feel the tiny pulse throb under his eye. "It takes nerve to pursue something that's already been discredited. But here you are, calling me again. I'm just letting you know there's another side to this story. Last time we talked, you said I'd lost it. Don't you wish. For starters, I know who called the wife of the chief of police here under false pretenses and tricked an innocent old lady into mentioning a case whose file was sealed eighteen years ago. Know how I know? There's a tape. Funny, isn't it? What goes around comes around, pal. Only this tape's legit, because it's an official police line, and it has your voice on it. If you don't trust my recognizing it, we'll take it to an expert. I also have a growing collection of articles you may have plagiarized during college."

"You're investigating *me*?"

John wasn't about to defend himself. Was he pulling a Terry Sullivan? No way! He wasn't going public with allegations, wasn't smearing for the sake of the smear. Like the information on Rizzo and Barr, this was just good to have. "What kind of writer cheats?"

"In college? College is ancient history. Besides, you have no proof."

"The thing is, I don't think you want the debate. It could hurt your career. And then"—John was on a roll—"there's the weird personal stuff, like three wives. I thought we were friends back when, Terry, but I never knew you were married *once,* let alone three times. We were together in college. None of our other friends was married. None knew that you were. Not then, not the other two times. Why the big secret? *Three times*—why the big secret? What do you do to them, Terry? Keep them tied up and gagged? Something stinks about those wives—I'll bet they have stories to tell. And then there's the Cardinal. What the hell is Cardinal Rossetti to you?" There had to be something, *had* to be something. "Do you have a personal grudge against him? Or against the Church? Are you another little altar boy who was molested by a priest?"

Terry's voice was icy. "I was never an altar boy."

"Maybe a choirboy, then? There has to be a reason why you battered an innocent woman in an attempt to bring down the Cardinal."

"What's she to you?" Terry threw back. "Are you fucking her, Kipling? Trying to make me look bad to make you look good?"

John rose from his chair. "I don't make anyone out to be something he isn't, but I'm warning you. You look into her life, she'll look into yours."

"She will, or you will?"

"Same difference," John said and slammed down the phone. Seconds later, he picked it back up and called Brian Wallace at the *Post.* "Quick question," he said when Brian didn't sound thrilled to hear from him. "That tape Terry made of his conversation with Lily Blake?"

"If you're thinking about reporting it to the AG,

you won't be hurting us. We have no proof she didn't know. We ran the story on the belief that she did. I've checked with our lawyers on this. The paper is covered legally. They bring a case against us, and it'll fail."

He sounded a bit too defensive to John—and that wasn't even why he was calling. "Have you checked the tape's authenticity?"

"What do you mean?"

John thought his meaning was perfectly clear. "Have you checked the tape's authenticity?" he repeated.

"Authenticity—as in, was that really Lily's voice?"

"I hadn't thought about that, but it's a good point. What I meant was whether the tape had been artificially manipulated."

"What in the hell does that mean?"

"Cut and spliced, Brian. You know how it's done. Words are shifted around or removed entirely. TV does it all the time. It's called editing an interview— only, the end result often conveys a very different message from the original. Do you think Terry did that? Anyone with a rudimentary knowledge of an editing machine could have helped. Hell, Terry's a crafty guy. He might have done it himself."

"Why do you think that?"

"Because the lady in question denies saying the things he quotes her in the paper as saying. I'm assuming that if you heard that tape, it must sound pretty much the way he reported it, or you wouldn't have printed it that way."

"Have you talked with her?"

"That's not the issue," John said with waning patience. "The issue is whether Terry doctored that tape."

There was a groan. "Now, when do you suggest he did that? He didn't have time, Kip. You forget fast. It was late, and he was working on deadline to get that piece done."

"Ten to one, he had the text written days before, all but the quotes."

"Yeah, and he left Lily, raced back here, and was on the phone with me by eleven, playing the tape. So when would he have had time to edit it?"

"Did you hear the whole thing?"

"I heard the incriminating parts."

"But how do you know he didn't skip around? How do you know he didn't take those parts out of the context that would have made them a joke?"

"Because I played it myself the next day."

"When? Morning? Afternoon? He could've played excerpts for you over the phone at night, then had it edited before you listened to the whole thing in person. Think he did that?"

Brian grunted. "How in the *hell* would I know?"

"You could have the tape checked."

"Why would I *want* to?"

"To cover your butt," John suggested. "The story Terry wrote doesn't jibe with what the lady claims she said."

"She lies."

"Or he lies. His story's already fallen apart. Are you condoning shoddy journalism?"

Brian sighed. "I'm not gonna take that personally. I'm gonna remind myself that Terry wasn't real nice to you and that maybe, just maybe, you'd like to see him fall. But my interest is this paper, and *it* ain't gonna fall. Trust me on this, John. That tape is real."

Typically, on a Wednesday afternoon, John visited Gus, but he didn't today. His exchange with Sullivan had fired him up. He spent the afternoon making phone calls. Following a trail of rental applications, he located two of Terry's wives with frightening ease. The most recent one still lived in Boston. Her name was Maddie Johnson, and she had been tipped off.

"He said you'd call. I have nothing to say."

"Why not?"

"I have nothing to say," she repeated.

"Did he threaten you?"

"He warned that you'd push me."

"Push you about what?" John asked, keeping his voice even and reasonable. "Hey, I don't want to know anything about you. Terry's the one who interests me."

"Yeah, well, we were married," she grumbled.

"But you aren't anymore. Why would you protect him?"

"Because he's dangerous! I tell something about him, he tells something about me. I have secrets, just like the next guy. And you're media, like Terry. You know exactly what I mean. You're *all* dangerous."

John expected her to hang up on him. When she didn't, he grew gentler. "I don't know what Terry did to you while you were married—I truly don't want to know—but he ruined an innocent woman in this Lily Blake thing. I'm just trying to understand why."

"Ego. He wanted headlines. He always wanted headlines."

"And that's it? No deeper motive? No grudge against the Catholic Church?"

"Why are you asking *me*?" she cried. "You think he only lies in his work? I was married to him for four years and I never knew he was married before until his ex-wife called on the phone. So he told me the marriage had been so bad that he had to pretend it never happened or he'd go crazy, but then I called someone at the paper, and he didn't know about *me*. How do you think I felt then? I kept asking Terry why we never did anything with people. He just wanted me home. Didn't want me to work, nothing. He'd get angry when I saw friends, and I was the one who lived here even before *he* came to town. He said he wanted kids. Hah! I bought into the bit about waiting until we had enough money saved up, only we weren't saving a whole lot. He was sending it to his mother—a woman I *never even met* because he said she was crazy and totally out of his life. But she was *dead*. I learned that during the divorce. I mean, after a while you start to wonder what's real and what isn't!"

In the sudden silence, she must have realized what she'd said. "Fu-uck. He's going to kill me."

"No, he won't," John assured her. "He'll never know you talked to me."

"You'll print what I said."

"I won't. I told you, Terry's the one I want. My guess is that any one of his other wives would say the same thing you have."

"There was only one wife before me."

"There were two."

She swore again. "He's crazy."

"I'd say so, but I'm not a psychiatrist. I'm just a writer who's wondering why he went after Francis Rossetti. Have any thoughts on that?"

She gave a sarcastic laugh. "I am the last one who'd know. A week after we met we were married in a no-name town in the middle of the night by a justice of the peace whose shingle was hanging in front of his house. In the four years we were together, Terry insisted he knew from nothing about religion. Considering all the other lies, I'd say he probably lied about that, too. If there's an answer to your question, I'd be real interested in hearing it."

John ended the call feeling that he was inching toward answers. He came even closer with Terry's first wife. Rebecca Hooper sounded like an even quieter and simpler sort. She, too, recognized John's name.

"He said you'd call," she said in a timid voice. Based on when they were married, John guessed she had to be at least forty, but she sounded half that.

Gently, he asked, "Did he say why?"

"He said you'd try to blackmail me into telling things about us. But there's nothing to tell," she said quickly. "Honest."

John wasn't pushing her on that, any more than he

had pushed Maddie. "Did he tell you that I went to college with him?"

"Yes."

"You must have recognized my name from that."

"No. He never talked about school when he was home."

"Why not?"

She was slow in answering, and then she said, "I don't want to talk with you."

"I won't hurt you. I'm only trying to understand Terry a little."

"Good luck."

John chuckled. "Yup. He's an enigma. He only lets you get so close. I figure something happened when he was a kid to make him that way."

"Do you know where he grew up?"

"No." No one did, not even Ellen Henderson, who had checked Terry's college files for John. They showed a Dallas address for the last two years of high school only. He had called the high school there, but it was a large one. He had been passed from office to office, to no avail.

"Do you?" he asked Rebecca now.

"Meadville."

"Pennsylvania?" John asked.

"Yes."

It was a start. "I appreciate your telling me that."

"I only knew him in Lancaster." The college was there. "But you're right."

"About what?"

"Something happening in Meadville."

"Any idea what?"

"No. I have to go."

She hung up the phone then, but that was fine. John turned to his computer and began to browse. Meadville was workable. It was a fraction of the size of Dallas.

In no time he had the phone number of the assistant principal at the high school in Meadville. The man seemed delighted that John had called and was more than happy to talk. "Terry left here well before I arrived, but you can be sure all of us newcomers know about him now. Our current principal actually taught him when he was here. He was the one who tipped us off that Terry had broken that story. I mean, what do *we* know about reading bylines, and in the *Boston* papers? Never would have known a thing if the principal's sister wasn't living in Boston and recognized the name from Al talking about him all those years ago."

"Was he that memorable?" John asked. A lot of time had passed since Terry's high school days.

"To an English teacher he was," the assistant principal answered. "He was an anomaly among sixteen-year-olds. He could write. His brother couldn't. That one was a total loss in the literary department, but he was smart, peoplewise, the nicest guy in the world."

John hadn't known there was a brother, as he hadn't known there were wives. "How many years between them?"

"Oh, a good four or five. Maybe more. Like I say, I wasn't here then. Someone mentioned it the other day, but mostly they're talking about Terry. Al had him for freshman and sophomore English. He was a stand-out, light-years above the others. Are you doing a story on him?"

"I am," John admitted. "Did he have friends?"

"Well, I couldn't tell you about that, not being here myself at the time. We've only been talking about his writing. He did some wonderful pieces for the school magazine. One that he wrote as a sophomore won all sorts of awards. It was even reprinted in the *Tribune*."

"The *Meadville Tribune*?"

"The same. I have a copy of it sitting right here on my desk. We circulated it when we learned of Terry's role in exposing the Rossetti-Blake affair. I'd be happy to fax it to you, if you'd like."

Five minutes later, John was reading a copy of the article. It was about life in an Italian neighborhood in Pittsburgh in the aftermath of World War II. The piece wasn't long. Reading it, John saw germs of Terry's current style and skill. Even back then, Terry didn't use three adjectives when a single potent one would suffice, and he did choose potent ones. He described local personalities in ways that made them come alive. Not that John wanted to cross paths with any of them soon. The piece wasn't flattering. Its villain was the local Catholic church.

The view was surprisingly dark to have been written by a sixteen-year-old. But it wasn't surprising at all, if that sixteen-year-old had a gripe.

John was on the right track. He could feel it in his gut. He needed to know what that gripe was.

But later. *Lake News* was ready for pickup. Satis-

fied to put Terry on hold at such an optimistic point,
he drove up to Elkland, loaded three thousand copies of the paper into the Tahoe, then delivered them
to post offices there, and in Hedgeton, Cotter Cove,
and Center Sayfield. All of the towns but the last
had general stores, so he delivered additional copies
to those, and to the small family restaurant in Center Sayfield; and inevitably he saw people he knew
and stopped to talk, even caught dinner with a friend
in Cotter Cove. It was well into evening by the time
he returned to Lake Henry. He dropped a bale of
papers at the post office, at Charlie's, and finally at
Armand's, and through it all, there was enough to
distract him that he didn't think about Terry again
until he was heading around the lake road toward
Wheaton Point.

Then it hit him.

Lily was out on the dock with her legs folded and her
elbows on her knees. There was a loon out on the lake
tonight. She had heard a single call, then nothing. She
peered through the darkness, trying to spot it, but the
lake was an inky mass of shadow and flow.

The whisper of a paddle broke the silence, the approach of a canoe. She held her breath, thinking it
might be John, but it passed her dock without turning in.

A night rower? A gawker? She might have worried, now that word of her being here had reached the
outside world, if she hadn't known that the outside
world couldn't get onto the lake. A few more locals

than usual had boated past the cottage of late, but if they were hoping to catch sight of her, they were respectful enough not to stop.

Sure enough, this canoe was soon out of sight and sound. Not John, then. He would have stopped. She might have liked that. He wasn't all bad.

But being without him was fine, too. It was a mild night for early October. She wore jeans and John's sweater, which was miles too big but a comfortable substitute for the sweaters she had in Boston. The shore smelled of pine. It blended with the jasmine oil—Celia's jasmine oil—that she had poured into her bath after work. She felt clean and fresh, comfortably tired, oddly content.

She began to sing softly, hoping to coax a loon into song, but the night remained still. After a time, she returned to the house, put on a CD, and sat on the porch listening. It was a Harry Connick, Jr. kind of night, smooth and rhythmic, a little lazy, sexy perhaps. She was humming to "Where or When" when she heard tires on gravel. She stopped, turned her head, held her breath.

Was she found out?

The engine stopped. A door opened and shut. It was a heavy sound, from either a van or a truck.

"Lily?" John called.

Relieved but cautious, she rose and went to the porch rail. He spotted her the minute he came around the side of the cottage.

"Good news," he fairly sang, taking the first two stairs in a single stride.

Lily was afraid to hope.

He hooked his wrists over her shoulders. His face was nearly level with hers, lit by the lamp in the window behind her. It gave his eyes an excited glow and added warmth to his mouth.

Sounding triumphant, he said, "Terry Sullivan grew up in Meadville, Pennsylvania. The family moved away before his junior year, but up until then he wrote for his high school literary magazine. His most renowned piece was about life in an Italian neighborhood in Pittsburgh in the late forties." He paused, clearly waiting for her to react.

She didn't follow. "Yes?"

"Sound familiar? *Feel* familiar?"

Bemused, she shook her head.

He beamed. "Cardinal Rosetti grew up in an Italian neighborhood in Pittsburgh. It was one of those things that was buried in all the material written about the man after his elevation to Cardinal. How many Italian neighborhoods were there in Pittsburgh back then?" He held up a lone finger in answer. "So, is this a coincidence? It could be."

Lily could see his excitement. "But you don't think so."

He shook his head. "The same Terry Sullivan who so recently tried to skewer Francis Rossetti wrote—at the tender age of sixteen—a vividly detailed essay about the Cardinal's hometown. It wasn't Terry's hometown. So how did he know details?"

"Maybe he visited? Or spent summers there? Maybe someone he knew came from there?" She was getting into it, catching the excitement. "Someone who knew Father Fran?"

"I don't know. The essay didn't mention him."

"He'd have told me if he knew Terry."

"They don't have to know each other personally for there to be a connection," John said, and Lily bought into it. How could she not, with him so sure? His eyes held a glow. It warmed Lily inside, warmed her until she burst into a grin. If they could prove a personal connection between Terry and the Cardinal, there would be a solid case for malice, and a solid case for malice would make her own case open-and-shut.

She couldn't stop grinning. Needing even more of an outlet, she locked her hands around John's neck. "This is good."

He was grinning right back, straight white teeth forming a crescent in that close-cropped beard. "Yup," he said. Before she knew what he was up to, he slipped his arms around her waist, swept her right off the porch, and whirled her around in a jubilant circle. When he set her down, he pulled her into a hug.

Lily loved it. She couldn't remember the last time anything had felt so good. Not even that hot bath in Celia's jasmine oil had felt quite as fine. And it wasn't done. When Harry Connick started in with "It Had to Be You," John began to sway with her on the pine needles. With the night dark, the air fresh, and his body firm and supportive, she was entranced.

Letting go was easy, because he led well. Lily had seen everything in her line of work, but John ranked with the best. He felt the beat and moved with it, holding her hand to his heart, later anchoring it at his thigh. For a while she felt the soft brush of his beard when he hummed at her ear. Then he buried his mouth in her hair, and the warmth of that was wonderful, too. They covered ground in a smooth, lazy way, at the porch now, at the lake then, and the one thing that came to her through the headiness was that every step was coordinated, his body to hers.

Then he kissed her. It came in a space between songs and was part of the moment, all smooth and lazy, nothing to cause alarm. But it was delicious, indeed. She welcomed seconds and thirds, might even have considered fourths, because he knew how to kiss as well as he knew how to dance. But he was dancing again.

Only it was different now. She was aware of his body in more intimate ways, aware of his legs, his chest, his belly. And her own? On fire with a sudden wanting.

He felt it, too. Even if his body hadn't betrayed that in such a virile way, she would have known it by the kiss he gave her when the song was done. It was deeper and more hungry. Wrapping her arms around his neck, she let it carry her away. She gave herself up to sensation and floated.

Then something intruded. At first she thought it was the ragged breathing at her ear. It was a minute before she realized that it was a car. Seconds later, headlights cut a swath of light right past them.

She gasped and tried to leave John, but he held her immobile against him. "Wait," he whispered hoarsely. "Wait."

The car stopped. A familiar voice called from the window. *"Lily?"*

"Poppy," Lily whispered and, suddenly frightened, looked up at John. "It's too late at night. Something's wrong."

When she pulled away this time, John let her go, but he was right beside her, running up to the spot behind the Tahoe where Poppy had stopped. She had her door open, so that light filled the van. Lily's thoughts were on Maida, but Poppy's eyes were on John.

"I played a hunch when you didn't answer your phone," she told him. "Lily didn't have the cell phone turned on, so here I am."

"What's wrong?" John asked.

"Gus had a heart attack."

Chapter 22

The hospital was in North Hedgeton, easily a thirty-minute drive from Lake Henry. John drove faster than was safe, but he had visions of Gus dying before he got there—dying out of sheer spite. He couldn't let that happen. He and Gus had to talk. If the old man died on him, it would reduce much of the last three years to a farce.

Had he been alone, he would have driven even faster, but Lily had insisted on coming, and he hadn't been of a mind to argue. He was feeling a sense of déjà vu—unhinged, a little as he had been at fifteen when he and his mother left the lake. Then, he had hidden his fear behind a wall of bravado, but fifteen-year-olds did that, not forty-somethings.

Lily reminded him of the here and now. She anchored him somehow.

"I'm okay," he assured them both every few minutes, and she would nod, or touch his arm, or say a soft "I know" in response. It worked, making him feel more in control.

Pulling up at the hospital, John was grateful for small favors. Had he been in Boston, he'd have had to waste precious time parking. Here he left the Tahoe at the emergency entrance, took Lily's hand, and hurried inside. As soon as he gave his name to a passing nurse, he was directed to the second floor, and once there, he made a beeline for the trio of doctors conferring at the door to one of the rooms.

Gus was in that room, but he was outnumbered by machines. One delivered oxygen, another medication; one monitored his heart, another his oxygen level. Two others waited silently, on call. Gus, himself, was positively ashen. He was long, thin, and utterly still under the sheets—either sleeping or unconscious.

Without taking his eyes from his father, John asked the trio, "How is he?"

"Not good," Harold Webber answered. Gus had been under his care since an initial attack shortly before John had returned to town. Since then, John and Harold had worked together to try to get Gus to live more gently, but it had been a futile effort, and physical lifestyle was the least of it. What physical stress they had relieved by making him retire had only heightened his emotions.

"It was a bigger one this time than last," Harold said quietly. "It doesn't look good."

"Can you operate?"

"Not now. He's too weak. We'll have to wait until he stabilizes. Then, if he agrees . . ." Bypass surgery was becoming commonplace, but that didn't mean there weren't risks involved. The last time Harold had suggested doing it, Gus had flat-out refused. That was four months ago.

"What happened?" John asked.

"Dulcey saw lights on later than usual and went to check. She called the ambulance. It could have been worse. His brain wasn't deprived of oxygen. It's still functioning. He's just very, very weak."

"Is he conscious?"

"In and out."

John tightened his fingers around Lily's. "Can we go in?"

Harold said, "I don't see that it would hurt him any. He's ornery by nature. You won't upset him more than he'd be anyway."

John started forward. He was at the door when Lily pulled back. Apprehension was written all over her face. It hit him that seeing Gus had to be difficult for her—that *feeling* for Gus had to be even harder.

"Maybe I should wait here," she whispered.

"He's probably the last person on earth you want to see."

"I was thinking about Gus. He won't want to see me. I'll remind him of Donny."

It was a possibility. Selfishly, though, John needed her there. He felt empty, thinking about Gus. *It doesn't look good.* They had never been at that point before. "Come with me? Please?" he asked, and she went, as he knew she would. She was a more decent human being than any Kipling, that was for sure.

Feeling a deep fear along with emptiness, he approached the bed. He let Lily stand a bit behind him, but he kept a grip on her hand.

"Gus?" he called quietly.

Gus didn't respond. His eyelids lay perfectly still.

"Dad? It's John. Can you hear me?" When there remained no sign of awareness, John said, "I always see him on Wednesdays. I skipped today. Figured I'd go tomorrow. I shoulda gone. I *shoulda* gone." He snorted. "There you have it. My relationship with Gus in a nutshell. Forty-three years of 'shoulda done's.' "

Lily rubbed his arm, and it settled him some. He put his elbows on the bed rail and studied his father's face. It seemed frozen in anger, as though whatever was eating at his insides had such a deep hold that it shaped even the unconscious mind.

"I haven't a clue," he said quietly.

"About what?" Lily asked.

"The anger that makes him scowl that way. I used to think it was me. Do you know, I can only remember one time in my entire life when I saw him smile in response to something I did."

"What was that?" she whispered.

"I went to bed with a stone. He used to carve them."

"Stones?"

"He'd chisel out little faces—eyes and noses and mouths. He gave me one when I was six."

"For your birthday?"

"No. He didn't believe in birthdays. Just gave it because he felt like it, I guess. I never knew why." He grunted. "Another one of those never-knew-why things." He drew up two upholstered chairs that had been pushed to the wall. "Mind sitting a little while?"

An hour passed. A startling number of doctors and nurses came and went for such a small hospital, but then, Gus was their only patient in critical condition. As they monitored him, John kept watch, alternately sitting back in his chair, coming forward with his hands between his knees, and standing. Gus didn't move, didn't blink, didn't make a sound.

At one point when they were alone, seemingly out of the blue, Lily said, "All families have them."

"Have what?"

"Those never-knew-why things."

"You and Maida?"

"Especially."

"You're lucky she's in good health. There's still time." But time was running out for Gus. John felt it as keenly as he'd ever felt anything. Looking back, the signs had been there. Hell, the last few times John had seen him, Gus hadn't moved from the sofa.

He shoulda known.

John was feeling a sense of futility by the time Wednesday became Thursday. Lily was curled in the chair beside his. Her eyes closed from time to time, but as soon as he suspected she had fallen asleep, she opened them and gave him an encouraging smile. She didn't say a word, didn't have to. She just smiled in a way that said he was absolutely where he should be.

And she was right. Gus was his father. John hadn't been around when bad things were happening to Donny, and he would go to his own grave regretting that. Now bad things were happening to Gus. He couldn't not be there.

Lily didn't have to be there with him, though. Making her stay through the night was being selfish in the extreme.

So the next time she closed her eyes, he touched her hand. Her eyes opened immediately. "You don't have to stay," he whispered. "You're exhausted."

"I'm fine."

"Take the Tahoe and go home and sleep. I just can't leave."

"Would you rather be alone?" she asked gently.

No, he would not. He shook his head.

She smiled. Tucking up her legs, she settled into the chair.

Watching her, John felt an incredible fullness swell his heart. That was the moment when he guessed he was in love.

Lily dozed off.

John might have, too, but he wouldn't let it happen. It was the middle of the night, the room was dim, and the beep of the heart monitor was hypnotic. His eyes grew dry and gritty, a tic pulsing under one, but he refused to sleep. When an angel in scrubs brought hot coffee, he drank every drop. He kept watch on the machines and on what the nurses did, but Gus didn't wake up.

* * *

Lily did. She had barely slept an hour when she came awake with a gasp. Her eyes went to John, then, in alarm, to Gus.

"He's the same," John said.

She let out a breath. "I'm sorry. I dreamt it was my mother." She bent forward and pressed her forehead to her knees, then turned so that her cheek was there and her eyes were on him.

"Does she talk while you're working together?" he asked.

"Not about what we need to discuss."

"You mean you talk, but you don't say anything?"

She nodded.

He turned back to Gus. When he thought he saw the flicker of an eyelid, he came out of his chair and leaned over the rail. He reached for his father's hand, but drew back just shy of a touch. Their relationship wasn't physical. His voice, however, held raw urgency. "Gus? Talk to me, Gus."

Lily appeared at his side. "Maybe you should talk to him," she suggested softly.

John opened his mouth to speak, looked for words and found none, so he closed it. He was that fifteen-year-old again. It was all he could do not to squirm. "I can't."

"Why not?"

It was like touching. "We just don't."

"Then talk to me."

"About Gus?"

"Yes. What do you love about him?"

Absolutely nothing, was John's first thought. He could more readily have said what he hated. Or what he resented. Or what he didn't understand. There were lists and lists of all those things.

But there had to be the other, too. If not, John wouldn't be feeling the fear he did now. He wouldn't be feeling the frustration or the emptiness. He wouldn't be here at all, but would be at home, sleeping until the hospital called to say that it was done. Hell, if there wasn't feeling, he wouldn't be in Lake Henry at all.

What was there to love about Gus?

"He builds beautiful stone walls," John said. "Has probably built hundreds of them. They'll still be standing long after you and I are gone. I was always in awe of those walls."

"He's an artist," Lily said.

John nodded. He imagined that the frown on Gus's face had eased a little, and took heart from that. "He spent a lifetime working with stone. Never did anything else."

"How'd he learn?"

"He never told me. He told my mom that the woods were where he did things right. He dropped out of school when he was fourteen. For months no one knew where he went during the day. Then they found him helping an old stonemason. He was doing fine, keeping out of trouble and learning a trade, so no one dragged him back to school. Huh. I missed a *day* of school and he hit the roof!"

"He wanted better for you."

"Better than being an artist?" John asked. He couldn't imagine that. "I could have been perfectly happy working with him, but he wouldn't hear of it. Not for me *or* for Donny. Said we'd mess things up. He was a perfectionist. Took pride in what he built."

"Don't you take pride in what you write?"

"I suppose."

"Then you're like him in that."

John wanted to think so, but writing was different from building stone walls. Stone walls were functional and aesthetic. They didn't have the power to ruin people. Writing did. That was the part of it that stuck in John's craw. So maybe Terry was right. Maybe he wasn't tough enough to hack it, if hacking it meant wielding a poison pen.

Yes, he took pride in what he wrote. He had left Boston when that ceased to be the case. He took pride in *Lake News*. It was well written and served a positive purpose—was functional and aesthetic.

It was—yes—like Gus's stone walls.

Shortly before dawn, Gus's eyelids flickered and opened. John was quickly up, leaning over the bed. "Dad?"

Gus focused on nothing at all, then on John, but if there was awareness or thought, he didn't let on. When his eyes slipped shut, John looked at the heart monitor. The beat took an erratic turn, then steadied.

He stepped back when a nurse arrived. She checked Gus, checked the monitors, and withdrew.

John didn't know whether to try to get Gus to

wake up again or not. Waking up was a good sign, definitely cause for hope, but if it caused erratic cardiac activity, he could do without seeing Gus wake up yet. The lines were more even now. More peaceful.

So he stood quietly for a time, studying Gus's face. Many a night, as a child, he had done this while Gus slept in the big chair by the woodstove. He had been less threatening asleep than awake. Dorothy had been calmer then, too, even affectionate, as she watched Gus and warned John to be still.

Dawn brought a gentle, flattering light that enhanced the memory. When Lily stirred and came up to stand beside him, John said, "He really was a handsome guy. You can see some of it now." He saw a full head of neatly cut hair, a clean shave, straight shoulders, strong hands. "My mother still talks about it. He was antisocial but handsome."

"How did they meet?"

"Over a flat tire. She was driving through the hills with a friend, looking at foliage, just about this same time of year. He was a good-looking outdoorsman, who came right out of the woods to give them a hand when it looked like they'd be stranded. A month later, she came back looking for him with three tins of her mother's coffee cake. She was infatuated. Hung around watching him work and baking him things, until he realized that she was his single best shot at settling down. He was nearing forty. She was young and pretty and eager."

John sighed. "I never dared mention her name, the few times I saw him after they split."

"You saw him here?"

"During college. I thought he'd be proud that I'd got that far. He wasn't. He didn't want to look at me. So I never stayed long. I left, and then it ate at me, all I had wanted to say but didn't."

A nurse came in with two mugs of coffee. She checked on Gus, adjusted the rate of a drip, and went out.

John welcomed the warmth of the mug in his hands. Having Lily beside him was a help, but the winds of his history with Gus were cold. Oh, yeah, a lifetime of "shoulda done's."

"I wanted to tell him," he said quietly, "that I understood what happened between my mother and him. That it wasn't all his fault. She made him out to be something he wasn't. She was the one who went after him and then couldn't hack it when life in the Ridge wasn't romantic. He never made promises. She was the one with the expectations, so she was the one let down. I can't blame him. Not for the marriage, not for the divorce. I wanted to tell him that."

So you have, he could practically hear Lily say. But she simply nodded and remained close.

Lily had never sat vigil with a dying man before. A month ago, had someone told her she would be doing it for Gus Kipling, she would have shuddered. But right now she couldn't picture being anywhere else. A psychiatrist might have said she was making up for not being in town when her father died, but she didn't think so. Her being here had nothing to do with Gus and everything to do with John.

She wanted to be with him. It was as simple—and easy and natural—as that.

Hard to explain to her mother, though, when Lily called her shortly after seven.

"But why are *you* there?" Maida asked. There was enough of an edge in her voice to trigger a conditioned response in Lily. A rush of white noise started to build.

Lily fought it. She closed her eyes and forced herself to think clearly. "Because John's here. He's having a hard time."

"Gus Kipling won't thank you."

"I'm not here for him. John and I were talking last night when he learned about Gus. I couldn't lll-let him come alone."

"Kiplings have a history of using you. First Donny, now John. This feels familiar, Lily."

"It's different," she said and reminded herself that she was a big girl. She didn't have to ask Maida's permission. "I'm only calling to see if one of the orchard hands can cover in the cider house, so that I can stay here."

"Are you sure you want to do that?" Maida asked. "Word will spread. Do you want the town to know you're there?"

Lily was suddenly exasperated. "Well, why not?" she cried boldly. "It adds an interesting twist to the story, don't you think?"

★   ★   ★

Morning ripened. Harold Webber came, as did other staff doctors. The general reaction to Gus's condition was one of surprise, but it stopped short of optimism. All signs pointed to a further weakening. While they agreed that Gus was holding on better than they had expected he would, they predicted that the next hours would be crucial.

John allowed himself to hope. He envisioned Gus waking up and being mellowed by having a near brush with death. He imagined the two of them having a few months, maybe more, of quality time. John could be satisfied with that.

As morning became afternoon, Gus did wake up occasionally. Each time, he pulled himself from disorientation to focus on John—and he did recognize him. John knew it. He didn't know, though, whether the recognition was helping or hurting.

Then, come midafternoon, the beat of the heart monitor shifted. Doctors and nurses came on the run, and after a medication change, Gus's heart steadied, but it wasn't a good sign. There was talk of a secondary attack, worsening color, fluid in his lungs.

John waited in the hall with Lily while the doctors worked, but as soon as the bedside was clear, he was back again at the rail. Desperate enough to do something, with Gus looking waxy now, he took his father's hand. It felt awkward in his—uncomfortably limp and cold—but he couldn't put it down now that the connection was made.

"Come on, Gus," he murmured. "Come on. Don't leave me hanging here. Don't you dare leave me hanging here." When Gus didn't respond, he said, "I'm trying to help. For Christ's sake, I'm trying to *help.*" When still there was nothing, he got angry. "You can hear me, Gus. I know you can. You always could, just turned away and made like what I had to say wasn't worth your while, and maybe it wasn't back then. I let you down. I'm sorry I did that. I let you down, and I let Donny down, and if I could turn back the clock and change that, I would. But I'm here now, and I want a chance."

His anger faded. How to sustain it, without Gus's sneer?

Defeated, he opened his hand and studied those old, scarred fingers. They seemed vulnerable in ways Gus himself never had. More to himself than to Lily or Gus, he murmured, "How to ask forgiveness from a man who won't listen?"

Those fingers moved then—not much, but enough to suggest life. John looked up to find Gus looking straight at him. The sound the old man produced was hoarse and broken, but every blessed word came through.

"You gut it ass backwuds," he said. His eyes closed, then reopened. " 'T's me let you down . . . 't's me failed . . . 't's me was . . . nevuh good 'nough . . . not f'y' muthuh . . . not fuh Don . . . not fuh you . . ."

John was a minute taking in his meaning. "That's not true," he said, but by then Gus had closed his eyes, and something was different this time. It wasn't until Lily was touching his arm and the room was filled with doctors and nurses that John realized the monitor had gone flat.

They tried to resuscitate him. They shocked him once. When that did nothing, they tried a second time and a third. There was a moment's pause, then a reluctant exchange of glances. In the next instant what little hope there had been seeped away, like air from lungs that had finally ceased to work.

The doctors and nurses left.

"He said what he needed to say," Lily whispered, then she, too, left, and John didn't try to stop her. For a final few minutes, he needed to be alone with his father.

He didn't say anything. He didn't even think anything. He just stood there holding Gus's hand in both of his now, studying the face that he had both hated and loved. When the time seemed right, he gently put Gus's hand down on the sheet. He bent, kissed his father's cheek, and started to leave.

But something drew him back to the side of the bed. So he stood with Gus a little longer, and it was a peaceful time. When he was sure that his father's soul had passed to wherever it was headed, he gave Gus's shoulder a last gentle touch and left the room.

Lily had waited and watched from the hall. She straightened when John came toward her. He looked exhausted but managed a sad smile. Without a word, he took her in his arms and held her so tightly that his arms trembled, but she wouldn't have complained for the world. Giving him comfort pleased her more than she would have imagined possible.

When he finally drew back, his eyes were moist. He raised them to the ceiling and took a shaky breath or two. Then he looked at her and said, "I'll drop you home. I have to go to the Ridge."

They drove back to Lake Henry in silence. When he pulled up at the cottage, he thanked her. "It meant a lot having you there."

She pressed a finger to his lips, then shook it to suggest that he shouldn't say another word. Feeling that same incredible fullness in her heart, she climbed out, watched him turn and drive off. When the Tahoe was gone from sight, she walked slowly around the cottage.

It was nearly five in the afternoon. The lake mirrored Elbow Island, the far shore, and the sky, all seeming calm and reverent in the wake of Gus's death. Needing to commune with it—with Celia, with a loon or two—she crossed the pine needles, went down the railroad-tie steps, and out to the very end of the dock, all the while wondering whether she was crazy to feel what she did.

But all the wondering in the world couldn't stop the feeling, nor did she really want it to.

Chapter 23

John felt a loss the minute he left Lily at her cottage, but the need to go to Gus's place was great. Gus's place? It was his place, too. But had it ever really been his home? He had grown up there. No amount of repainting, relandscaping, or refurnishing could change that fact. Driving along Ridge Road now, with Gus dead and gone, he had to acknowledge the connection.

He parked beside the tiny house and walked inside as he had thousands of times as a kid. The small living room was the bedroom that he and Donny had shared. Dropping into the sofa, he heard the sounds of those years—yelling, but laughter, too. Gus wasn't happy by nature, but John's mother was. And Donny. He and Donny had fun times.

John put his head back and closed his eyes. He felt weary in ways that went beyond the physical—weary in ways that had to do with being the only surviving male in this house, the head of the family, so to speak. Arguably, he had borne that responsibility for the past three years. But bringing food, paying a maid, and repairing the house were physical things. What he felt now was emotional.

The weight of it was too much after a night without sleep. He dozed off in no time, sitting right there on the sofa as Gus had done so often of late. A muffled cry brought him awake with a start.

Dulcey Hewitt stood just inside the front door with a hand over her mouth. She pressed it to her chest. "You *scared* me," she breathed. "Here I'd just heard about Gus and I was comin' over to straighten up so's you wouldn't find a mess, and there you are, sitting just the way he was."

For a minute, John was groggy enough to be confused. Then he remembered that Gus was dead, and felt a sinking in the pit of his stomach. With an effort, he pushed himself forward.

The light was on. Dulcey must have done that. It was dark outside.

He ran a hand over his beard and into his hair. "What time is it?"

"Eight. I'm sorry about Gus."

John nodded. "Thanks for coming by last night. I wouldn't have wanted him to die here alone."

"Were you with him?"

Again he nodded. He looked around. "Nothing much is messed. He didn't have the strength at the end. Go home, Dulcey. Be with your kids."

John watched her go. Totally aside from grogginess,

he was feeling confused about things he couldn't put his finger on. He wanted to be alone.

Dulcey had no sooner left, though, than a neighbor came from across the street to offer condolences. She didn't come inside. Nor did any of the others who came by in short order. They just stood at the door, told John that they were sorry about Gus's death, and left.

He was touched. Gus hadn't been any warmer to his neighbors than he had been to his family, yet these people found it in themselves to come by. They made him feel guilty for every negative thought he'd had about the Ridge, which only added to his confusion.

Needing to do something, knowing that he had a funeral to plan and that he wanted Gus looking good, he went to the bedroom closet. It was a total mess. Either Dulcey had drawn the line here or Gus had forbidden her to touch it. There was an overcoat that John remembered from childhood, and a couple of shirts that weren't flannel or plaid. There were—incredibly—a few dresses that had belonged to John's mother. And there was a suit. John pulled it out, thinking that he might bury Gus in it. Apart from needing a pressing, it was in fine shape. He brushed at a place where the jacket bulged.

Feeling something there, he pulled back the lapel. Suspended from the hanger on a string was an opaque plastic bag. He laid the suit on the bed, removed the bag, and opened it. Inside was a collection of clippings. Some were old and yellow, some more recent. They were arranged chronologically and neatly, as though a hand had carefully pressed them flat before filing them away.

John looked at the clippings, one after another, until the heartache was too great. Here was a collection of his work, preserved by a father who had never once, *never once* told John that he loved him.

Feeling intense inner pain, John straightened, arched his back, and pressed his hands to his eyes. He moaned, but that brought little relief. He ran a hand around the back of his neck, stared at the papers, moaned again.

Unable to stand still, he went out the back door and paced the yard in the dark. He walked the length of the stone wall that Gus had been busying himself with so recently, then walked back as he tried to sort through his thoughts. From nowhere came the image of Gus falling on his butt, of John trying to help him up and being shaken off.

Then came a weak and gravelly voice. *It was me who let you down. Me who failed. Me who was never good enough. Not for your mother. Not for Don. Not for you.*

Understanding then—feeling a gut-wrenching sorrow for a man who had suffered, an illegitimate child born at a time when illegitimate children were marked, a man who had grown up believing himself unworthy, a man John had loved for no other reason than that he was his father—John sank to his knees on the grass. Hunching his shoulders, appalled but unable to stop, he cried softly for everything that he hadn't seen, hadn't known, hadn't done.

He couldn't remember the last time he had cried,

couldn't remember the last time he had let go quite this way. After a while, he might have been able to stop, but the release felt good. So he let the tears flow until they ran out.

Slowly, he rose from the grass. He dried his eyes on his sleeve, went inside, and threw cold water on his face. By the time he straightened, he was thinking clearly.

Carefully, he returned the packet of clippings to the bag where Gus had kept them, and rehooked the bag on the hanger, to be buried along with the suit and Gus. He collected a clean shirt, a tie, underwear, socks, and shoes, and brought everything out to the truck. Then he drove home, hung Gus's clothes in his own closet, and took the shower that he badly needed after a day and a half without.

His body was still damp when he set off in the canoe, and the cool air was chilling, but a strong, steady stroking warmed it quickly. When he reached his loons, he stowed the paddle. All four birds were here this night, swimming slowly, diving occasionally, raising their voices in the night, in a sound so primal that it shot straight to his soul.

There was timelessness here, a sense that death was no more than a progression of life. There was history here, a returning from season to season, and survival—two young successfully raised to perpetuate the species. Yes, the years had seen losses when nests were flooded or young lost to predators. But there was reason, order, and meaning.

Breathing that in, feeling at the same time loss and

gain, John put his paddle in the water and set off. The call of his loons followed, carrying smoothly across the water and around a series of bends to Thissen Cove.

Lily was sitting at the end of her dock. She stood when he neared, as though she had been expecting him. When the canoe glided alongside, she took the line from him and tied it to a cleat.

Seconds later he was on the dock, taking her in his arms, and it was the most natural, most right thing he had ever done. He wasn't thinking about writing a book. Wasn't feeling duplicitous or exploitative. His mind and his heart were in total sync.

He held her close, then closer still, while the lake flowed around them and the loons called. He kissed her once, then again—sweet, then deeper. By the time the third kiss was done, there was hunger as well.

At Lily's urging they went up to the house, up the stairs to the bed in the loft, and again it was the most natural, most right thing—removing clothes, touching private spots, rushing toward consummation. John's dreams had been dominated by Lily's body, and he found it even more beautiful than he had imagined, the full expanse of warm flesh and soft curves. He felt the comfort she gave, the consolation, the hope, and his body came alive as never before. Buried inside her, deep and deeper still, he felt fulfillment even as he hungered for more.

She climaxed with the catch of her breath and a soft cry.

He lingered, reluctant to leave her. In time, he

slipped to his side and drew her close, but he didn't speak. He kissed her softly and tucked her against him, thinking that he could be perfectly happy lying still like this with Lily Blake for the rest of his life, then rethinking that moments later when his penis thickened. And she was ready. She welcomed everything he did, then and in the hours that followed, and the initiative was far from one-sided. Her hands weren't knowing, but they learned. Her increasing boldness was an aphrodisiac in itself, feeding his arousal.

Eventually exhaustion caught up, and John finally let go. Safe in Lily's bed, warmed by the heat of their bodies and the scent of sex, he sank into a sleep so deep that he didn't hear a thing.

I'm at the cider house. Will be done at four.

Lily propped the note on her pillow, then took it back and drew her initial couched in a swirl that could have been a heart if John woke up in a mood to see hearts. She wasn't used to mornings after. She had no idea how he would wake up, or when. But she had promised Maida she would work today, and besides, she needed space.

Sheltered by a hooded raincoat, rubber boots, and gloves, she got it. She thought about the night that had been, and the night before that. She thought about the *week* that had been, and the week before that, and tried to reconcile them all, but it felt as though she had been through a lifetime of events and emotions. So many unresolved issues. How to sort through? How to *deal*?

Maida made sandwiches for lunch and served them on the porch. She didn't ask about the day before, not about Gus or John or Terry, but the noon hour was misty and calm, a cat with sheathed claws, and Lily welcomed the break. She returned to the cider house for the afternoon's work, feeling her body now in ways she hadn't earlier, and working harder to limber it up.

Quitting time approached. She had taken off her rubber clothing and was spraying down the cider house floor when John appeared at the door. He looked tentative. Sharing the feeling, unsure about what to say and do after the night, she finished quickly, washed up, and met him outside.

He had his hands in the pockets of his jeans and wore that same hesitant look.

But they were lovers now. At some point during the day, Lily had accepted that. She could agonize all she wanted about whether she was crazy to trust him with her emotions, but that didn't change the fact that she cared deeply for him.

"Walk with me?" she asked with a small smile.

His features relaxed so quickly that it was almost comical. Almost, but not quite. It was actually quite endearing, Lily thought as she gestured toward the orchard. Minutes later they were walking on a hard-packed dirt road past row after neat row of apple trees. She picked a row that looked less worked and led him off onto the grass. Even without the sun, which was still hidden by mist, the apples gave off a sweet scent.

"What kind are these?" he asked as they walked.

She pointed. "Cortland. Macoun. Gravenstein. McIntosh."

"Mixed together?"

"They have to be. Blossoms have to receive pollen from different varieties to be fertilized. Cortland can't pollinate Cortland, or Mac pollinate Mac. Unfortunately, bees don't know that. But they do move from tree to tree. So we mix varieties this way."

"What variety goes into cider?"

"Varieties, plural. There's a mix. Each orchard has its own recipe."

"What's yours?"

"I don't know. Mom does. She has it down to a science. I do know that Delicious apples make thin cider."

"Not so good?"

"Nope." She went to a tree, studied the apples within reach, and picked two deep in her palm, stem intact, as she'd been taught long ago. She passed one to John and looked around. Wooden ladders leaned against a few trees, crates sat under others. "Another two weeks and the harvest will be done. Apples going to market will be at the packer. Apples going for cider will be in our vaults with reduced oxygen to prevent spoilage. We'll take out only as much as we need to produce however many gallons of cider each week. The fresher the better."

She gestured him toward one of the older, wider trees. Slipping down, she sat against its trunk. He joined her there.

For a time they munched in silence. Then, quietly, John said, "I wanted you when I woke up."

She looked his way, but he was studying the trees. "When was that?"

"Noon."

"What did you do then?"

"Went into town. Made funeral arrangements."

"When is it?"

"Tomorrow morning."

She studied his face. Even in pain, it was strong. She had kissed those eyes closed and kissed that mouth open. He had taught her those things by example.

He met her gaze. "It was the bastard thing. I always thought he felt unwanted. What he felt was unworthy."

"I'm glad he told you. It helps."

"Helps me. Not him."

"Are you sure?"

He looked at her, then tipped his head back and studied the tree overhead. He was quiet for so long that she gave up the wait. Then he lowered his head and smiled. "Pretty smart for a cabaret singer," he teased. Snagging her neck inside the crook of his elbow, he pulled her close.

Lily didn't know whether it was the smile, the praise, or the closeness, but she felt warmed all the way to her toes.

And then some.

Oh yes.

And then some. Her hand lay on his chest, covered by a shirt now, as it hadn't been last night. He wasn't as hairy as some men. Smooth skin stretched over ropey pecs. There was a dusting of hair on his upper chest, a larger patch above his navel, a denser one at his groin.

He pushed to his feet, pulled her up, and walked her back to their cars. "I'll follow you home," was all he said, but there was an intimacy to it, a promise.

By the time she had driven around the lake and parked at the cottage, she was as aroused as when John had first pulled her close in the loft. No—more aroused. She knew now what his beard felt like against her breasts, how his muscles tightened and his body shook. She knew what his skin smelled like after a shower, and again after sex. She had touched him when he was fully aroused.

They didn't reach the bed this time, but made love at the top of the stairs, with only enough clothing removed to make it possible. Afterward, he held her close until their bodies had calmed. Then he put his forehead to hers.

He didn't speak. The voice she heard was in her head. It offered up a range of possibilities—the need for life in the face of death, the need for a friend in unfriendly times, even purely, simply, lust. It could also be love—an interesting thought, a *frightening* thought. So she pushed it from her mind.

He held her there on his lap until darkness settled in around the cottage, and he did stay the night. By the time Lily awoke the next morning, though, he was gone.

★   ★   ★

The funeral was held in the church at the center of town. The service was brief, a simple send-off for a complicated man, but the hall was full. Most of the Ridge was there to bury one of its own, but there were enough others to suggest that they had come out of respect for John.

As she had when she attended the service the Sunday before, Lily slipped into a back pew and sat with her head bowed while the minister talked. She would have stayed out of sight at the graveyard, too, if John hadn't caught her hand and drawn her into step with him behind the casket on his way out of the church.

She was trapped. Unable to pull away without hurting him and making a scene, she went along. He held her hand as he had before, as though she were a mooring, the only thing keeping him steady. But it was different now. It was public now.

Unsure about how that would play in Lake Henry, Lily kept her eyes low. After a few prayers, the casket was lowered into the ground. She could feel the tension in John then, and wouldn't have dreamed of stepping away, but again she was trapped, wanting privacy but denied it. Mourners passed John with a brief word, the shake of a hand, the touch of an arm, and always their eyes caught hers. There were faces with names—Cassie; the senior and junior Charlie Owenses; Willie Jake and his Emma; Allison Quimby; Liddie Bayne—and faces without. Lily nodded awkwardly, swallowed often, and thanked her lucky stars that she didn't need to speak. She was neither here nor there, in nearly every respect.

But she didn't leave until John did, which was only after the grave diggers had finished filling the grave with dirt. By then the townsfolk had left, and there was no one to express curiosity or disapproval.

That was small solace for Lily. She couldn't help but fear that she and John had opened a whole new can of worms.

John didn't think so. He liked the idea of extending his protection to Lily. If the respect that the townsfolk felt for him spread to her, it would help. The more they warmed, the more welcome she would feel; the more welcome she felt in Lake Henry, the more she might consider staying.

He wasn't thinking of his book. He felt uncomfortable when he did that—felt as though it cheapened what they had shared. His wanting her to stay was totally independent of the book.

But she wouldn't stay unless things were resolved. The scandal had placed her in limbo; she was here, but the trappings of her life—apartment, clothes, piano, car—were in Boston. The paper wasn't printing a retraction, and after doing all the law allowed, Cassie had to wait for a response. It promised to be a slow, painful process.

John only had to remember Lily as he had seen her that first Saturday morning—all riled up, dressed in her nightgown and shawl, pointing a gun at his heart—to know she had pride. She wouldn't stay in

Lake Henry by default, wouldn't stay simply because she had nowhere else to go. She had to actively *want* to stay, and she wouldn't do that if she couldn't make peace with Maida. He wanted to help her do that. But digging into Maida's secrets felt intrusive, with his relationship with Lily so new.

Terry was something else. He was fair game, where Lily was concerned. John liked the idea of helping her prove malice. He could do that without any conflict of interest.

So, after spending Sunday on *Lake News* preliminaries, nourished by food delivered in bulk by Poppy's Hospitality Committee, he hit the office early Monday and picked up where he had left off when Gus took ill. For starters, he contacted a church in the Italian section of Pittsburgh and went through two priests before he found one old enough to have known Terry Sullivan. Indeed, this priest knew the name, but only from the recent scandal. He informed John, in no uncertain terms, that Terry Sullivan had never spent time in *his* parish.

So Terry hadn't been a practicing Catholic in Pittsburgh, not in the neighborhood he'd written about.

Backing up a step, John returned to Meadville, but the church there was a dead end. No one in the rectory remembered the family, and though he might have worked his way through lay leaders in the parish, he returned to the same assistant principal he had talked with before. Still eager to help, the man put him in touch with a middle-school teacher, who put him in touch with an elementary-school teacher. The two corroborated each other's stories. Both marveled at Terry's success, given the difficulty of his childhood.

"Difficulty?" John asked each.

"He was different from his classmates," one confided. "Always a little aloof."

The second went a step further. "I can say this now, because I saw him on a talk show just last weekend and he's grown to be solid and good looking, but he was a puny little boy."

"Puny?"

"Small. Skinny. Defensive as all get-out. Poor thing, following in the footsteps of a brother like that."

"Like what?"

"Neil? He was a good-looking child. Sweet, personable, *friendly*. He was a natural leader, even back then. Terry was a better student, but children that age don't care about brains if the rest doesn't work. With Terry, having brains backfired. The kids made fun of him for knowing every answer in class. He didn't have an easy time at home, either. His father was a difficult man."

The first teacher had mentioned that, too. "When we see children like Terry now, we report them as being victims of abuse. Back then, we looked the other way."

"What did you see?" John asked.

"Bruises. Terry was beaten. His father had a temper and a belt."

"Did he hit the brother, too?"

"Lord, no. He didn't dare."

"Why not?"

"His wife would have left him for *sure* if he'd laid a hand on that boy. She worshiped Neil. She had him earmarked for priesthood right from the start."

John's pulse skipped. "Did he become one?"

"He certainly did. We were all proud of him for that."

Was it enough of a connection? Could playing second fiddle to a priestly older brother cause enough hatred for the Church to warrant Terry's malice toward Cardinal Rossetti?

John didn't think so. There had to be a more direct link.

"Couldn't the brother stop the father from beating Terry?"

"No one could stop that man. He was large and strong and angry."

"What about Terry's mother?"

"Oh, she's dead. Died in a car crash a good ten years ago."

John knew that, and that Terry's father was gone, too. "But where was she when her husband was swinging his belt?"

"In the way, I gather. She got it first."

Against his better judgment, John felt compassion. For all the verbal abuse his parents had showered on each other, there had never been physical abuse.

"What was the problem?" he asked. "Did he drink?"

Neither teacher knew for sure, but one gave him

the name of the woman who had lived next door to the Sullivans for all their years in Meadville. She still lived there and had no qualms about speaking her mind. "Did James Sullivan drink? Yes, he drank. He drank because he was insanely jealous. Jean could barely raise her eyes in public without him accusing her of looking at one man or another. He was even jealous of his own *son*. I tell you, James Sullivan was a bad man."

"Why did she marry him, then?"

"She didn't *know* he was so bad. A woman never does. Men don't show their true colors until the deed is done. Well, he didn't wait long, that one. He turned to her on their wedding night, she told me once. Held up a finger, and told her not to even *think* about the past. She swore she never did, but he didn't believe it."

"Was there a man in her past?"

"Oh yes. A longtime sweetheart through high school and college. The love of her life, if the look on her face meant anything. Oh, that look came and went, but I saw it."

"What happened? Why did they break up?"

"I don't know. I asked once, but she seemed sorry she'd said as much as she had."

"Where did she grow up?"

"I don't know. She never said that. I suppose she was afraid."

"Because of the other guy?"

"It's a fair guess."

John's imagination was running wild. He needed more. "Do you know her maiden name?"

"Bocce. Like the game. I remember that from the obituary. I thought at the time it was ironic; here she was like one of those little balls being knocked around."

John knew enough about bocce to get the point. *Bocce, like the game. Like the game played in Italian neighborhoods. Italian neighborhoods like the one where Francis Rossetti had lived.*

Sitting forward, playing a hunch now, he finished the call and turned to his computer, but he had barely reached the Internet when Richard Jacobi called. He had returned from the weekend to learn that Terry Sullivan was trying to sell a follow-up of the Rossetti-Blake story to *People* magazine. John said he doubted they would buy, since Terry was about to be thoroughly discredited as a journalist. Richard pointed out that that wouldn't necessarily hurt sales of the magazine in question—a valid observation, John had to admit. Richard said he was thinking of advancing the pub date of John's book because there were bound to be other stories, other Terrys, and he wanted theirs to be one of the first to hit big. He suggested that if John put his nose to the grindstone, they could have something on bookshelves by March, and that discrediting Terry in his book would make it all the more timely.

John didn't like the word "grindstone." He didn't like the sound of March. He did, however, like the idea of discrediting Terry.

Fast, thorough, and exclusive, Richard reminded him. John asked where his contract was. Richard said it was in the works. John reminded him that he'd said the same thing a week before, and asked how Richard expected him to put together a book in less time than it took to put together a contract; *and* maybe the story was worth more if discrediting Terry was part of the deal. Richard said that they had already agreed on money. John said that nothing was final until the contract was signed. Richard asked if he was getting cold feet. John said absolutely not.

And he wasn't, he told himself as he hung up the phone. He just needed to think. His insides tightened up each time he thought about the book. There had to be a way to reconcile his need to write it and his feelings for Lily. Had to be a way to satisfy them both.

While he thought, he worked. In several clicks he had the name of the high school the Cardinal had attended. In several more clicks, he had a phone number.

He said a bright "Hi" to the woman who answered. "I'm trying to track down an old friend. I think that she went there. Her name is"—he sharpened his enunciation—"Jean Bocce. If my information is correct, she was there with Fran Rossetti."

The woman chuckled. "What a concidence. We have his yearbook right here."

"Had a few calls lately?" John teased.

"You could say that. Bocce, you say?"

He spelled it.

"Alexander . . . Azziza . . . Buford," she read. "Sorry. No Bocce."

"She may have been a year behind. Or in a club with Fran. Music? Debating? French?" John's memory didn't fail. The Cardinal had been in those clubs. "They had to know each other somehow."

"Perhaps from church?"

"Perhaps." But John couldn't see asking the priests at Immaculate Conception about a female friend of the Cardinal. "Huh," he said. "I thought it was there."

"You mayyyyyyyy be right." The woman was suddenly distant, thoughtful. There was the sound of turning pages. Then her voice bumped up. "Ah. Here we are. It was the select chorus. There she is, second row up, third one in from the left. Very pretty. Actually"—she was distant again—"familiar. Hold on."

John wasn't going anywhere.

Her voice came back with a smile. "Well, well. Here she is again. I may be wrong. There are no names, just a lineup of three couples, but the face, the hair, the smile is exactly the same. It looks like she was Fran Rossetti's senior prom date."

John could have jumped for joy. But he wasn't risking anything. "Are you sure?"

The woman was mildly defensive. "I know faces. Her name is right there on the chorus picture. I'll send you photocopies of each, if you'd like."

John gave her his address. "It's not that I don't trust you," he teased. "Just that, what with all that's gone on, I'd be insulting the Cardinal if I approach him about this and then find it's the wrong woman."

"I see your point. But here. Let me see if I have any current information on Jean Bocce."

John could barely restrain himself long enough to carry the charade to its end. On his feet now, he practically danced while he waited, and had to pretend disappointment when the school had no current address. If he was a bit fast thanking the woman and ending the call, he figured it was better than giving a whoop. He did that the second he hung up the phone.

Seconds after that he was surfing the Internet for information on celibacy and priestly vows. It didn't take long to find what he wanted. Then he called Brian Wallace and said, "I just learned something that you ought to know."

Brian sighed. "Why do I get the feeling I don't want to hear this?"

"Because your instincts are good, but you were taken in, pal. Terry Sullivan had good cause for wanting to smear Rossetti. Did you know he was an abused kid?"

"Ah, Christ. That's old hat, Kip. If you're gonna say he was another altar boy—"

John cut in. "It's better than that. Terry's father beat him, usually at the same time he beat Terry's mother. It turns out the guy was insanely jealous of the *real* love of her life, someone the mother was with for years before she married him. Three guesses who that was."

There was a long silence.

"There's a picture of them together at Rossetti's senior prom," John said. "It's in his high school yearbook."

"That's no proof he was the love of her life."

"A neighbor who knew her said she was with the same guy through high school and college. The picture would have been taken right in the middle of that time."

Brian sounded skeptical, even scornful. "You said she was 'with' him. What does that mean?"

"It means whatever it meant to kids in those days."

"You think they had *sex?* Forget it, Kip. Rossetti's a *priest.*"

"Yeah, that's what I thought at first, but I just did some research. Priests don't have to be virgins. Once they are ordained, they have to be celibate. There's a difference. Apparently, there are many priests out there who know what it's like to be with a woman, and they make some of the best priests. They understand their parishioners. They're better at marital counseling."

"You're pushing it, John."

"Am I? You can't picture Rossetti being a stud? Come on, Brian. The pieces fit. Terry is repeatedly beaten, probably defending his mother, who is beaten because she's in love with Fran Rossetti, who was probably a live *ghost* in that marital bed. So Terry grows up despising Rossetti, writing essays condemning the church in that Italian neighborhood where his mother grew up, which just happens to be the same one where Rossetti grew up. Rossetti is elevated to Cardinal—a move that is anticipated long enough for Terry to stew. He looks for legitimate dirt, finds none, so he produces it himself."

"Did the mother confirm this?"

"She's dead."

"Then it's all speculation. I still have that tape."

"Test it."

John could have left it at that. But he hadn't even mentioned the brother—Neil Sullivan, the priest.

If that brother had been favored over Terry—if he had been loved more than Terry, beaten less than Terry, and held up to Terry ad nauseam as an example of everything Terry wasn't—Terry's resentment would be understandable. It didn't take a genius to guess that Terry might equate his brother with the Church and hate the two. Nor did it take a genius to wonder whether the mother's adoration of this first child, this marked-for-priesthood child, had something to do with Fran Rossetti becoming a priest.

All things considered, John had a good case. But the journalist in him didn't want a good case. It wanted the *best* case.

So he set about locating that brother.

Chapter 24

Hannah's birthday was Tuesday. Lily had arranged to leave the cider house early so that she could shower and change, then drive over and help Hannah dress. They were picking up her friends at four, heading to a movie and dinner.

Lily was startled to find Hannah alone. It seemed that Rose had dropped her home after school and taken off with the younger girls. "I told her to go," Hannah said. "Emma and Ruthie had gymnastics. I told her to take them. I don't need her help getting dressed."

Lily knew that, but it would have been nice if Rose had chosen to stay. Again she feared that she might have made things worse between mother and daughter. But it was done.

Hannah was newly showered and draped in a huge towel that was knotted over a flat chest and held in place by the press of pudgy arms. Her hair was dripping down her back in unkempt twists. But she was waiting with a face full of excitement.

There was something to be said for that, Lily decided, and pushed qualms about Rose aside. Playing the beautician, she sat Hannah on a stool in the bathroom and blow-dried her hair until it was glossy and smooth, with only the slightest curl at the end, per Hannah's wishes. Discovering bangs she hadn't realized were there, she blew them out, even cut a few more to produce a full, flattering set. She helped Hannah pull on the green tights, dashed a spritz of her own toilet water behind her ears, then helped her into the Black Watch plaid dress. When it was fastened and straightened, Lily put the ribbon in Hannah's hair, drawing the sides back and up and draping the tails of the bow along the graceful fall at her shoulders. She turned Hannah to face her, thinking to rub her cheeks for the tiniest bit of color, but the color was already there, a soft pink on flawless ivory skin. Hannah was Rose's daughter, indeed.

"You look," Lily said with a satisfied breath as she turned her niece to the mirror, "absolutely beautiful."

Hannah seemed to grow an inch taller, right before her eyes, and the height made her look all the more slim. It was an auspicious start for an auspicious event, the most surprising part of which, for Lily, was Hannah's friends. They were delightful. Shy at the start, even with Hannah, they quickly warmed. Opening gifts in the car was a perfect icebreaker. Once they were on the road, Lily, listening from behind the wheel of the Blake Orchards van, heard repeated comments on Hannah's awesome dress, awesome hair, awesome shoes, all woven through a conversation that was increasingly easy.

Hannah was lovely and poised, holding her own in looks and sociability with the other girls. More than once Lily wished Rose, Art, Maida could see her. In their absence, she felt pride enough for four.

Since Hannah had a wonderful time, Lily did, too. She suspected she was predisposed to it, being in a fine mood from the start. What John had learned about Terry changed the picture. The newspaper hadn't yet agreed to test the authenticity of its tape, but it hadn't refused. Cassie thought that was a good sign. She was hopeful that if the tape was found to be suspect, a settlement would follow fast.

Lily didn't want money. She wanted a public apology, and she wanted it with as much fanfare as there had been when the story first broke. She would never forget the humiliation of having her private life bared for all the world to see. Nothing that happened in Lake Henry could compensate for the unfairness of that. The pain of it rushed back every time she thought about returning to Boston.

That said, any fears she had about being recognized with Hannah and her friends proved groundless. She didn't know whether people had forgotten, or fewer had seen her picture than she thought, or her shepherding of five young girls had simply thrown them off the scent, but she saw no one she recognized, and no one who recognized her.

The whole outing went perfectly, and after the last

guest was dropped home, Hannah scrambled into the front seat and, on her knees, leaned over the gear shift and wrapped an arm around Lily's neck. "Wasn't my party wonderful?" she cried with all the glee of a child.

Lily smiled as she drove. "It was."

"Didn't I get neat presents?" Hannah asked and gave an avid commentary on each. She went on for a while about the movie. Then she said, "I liked dinner even better—and not because of the food," she quickly added, "but because my dress was pretty and I was with my friends."

"Your dress was pretty, but the girl in it was beautiful."

"They kept saying that, didn't they?" Hannah asked, beaming.

"They certainly did."

"Oh. Look, Aunt Lily. You missed the turn to my house."

"Want to stop quickly at Gram's? Tell her about the party?"

"Yeah!"

But Maida wasn't alone. Rose was there with Emma and Ruth, both of whom were in their pajamas and ready for bed. Hannah thought this was the greatest thing, her mother being right there when she stepped triumphantly from the van. All Lily could think was that if she hadn't decided to stop here first, Hannah would have gone home to an empty house.

Not an empty house. Art was probably there. But Art wasn't Rose. Hannah needed her *mother* to see her.

She needed Rose to tell her how pretty she looked, needed Rose to see that she wasn't all bad.

But Maida was the one to come forward first, her eyes large with surprised pleasure. "Look at *you*," she said with genuine enthusiasm. Holding Hannah's shoulders, she looked her up and down. "You're *gorgeous*. But where's the little girl? This one's so *grown-up*!"

"It's me," Hannah said with a shy smile. Her eyes went to her mother.

"How was the party?" Rose asked, and for a minute the night's silence was broken only by the chirp of a cricket that the day's sun had revived.

Maida glanced at Rose.

"It was neat," Hannah told her mother; then she told her sisters, "I got presents," and they ran forward to see.

Fearing she would say something ugly to Rose, Lily went into the house. She settled in behind the baby grand, lifted the lid, and stroked the keys. It didn't take long for her anger to fizzle. Simple arpeggios did that. She moved on to something classical and slow. As she relaxed, she played more current songs. They were smooth and slow, easy, sweet. She sang when the words came, hummed when they didn't. Increasingly, she was drawn into the music, absorbed by it, so that she didn't hear Maida arrive. She didn't realize she was there at all until she ended a song, rolled her head back and around to stretch her neck muscles, and happened to pass the doorway with her eyes.

She stopped and righted her head. "Have they left?"

Maida nodded. She was standing just over the threshold, with her hands in the pockets of a pair of soft, slim pants. Despite the pose, she seemed tense. "Do you miss playing?"

Lily nodded. She moved her hands over the keys but didn't know what song to play.

"They could use you at the academy," Maida said.

"Here?"

"You could do what you did in Boston."

"Don't they have someone?"

"He isn't very good. The head of the school is my friend. I could put in a word."

Lily didn't know what to say. It was a high compliment. But she didn't know how long she was staying—and Maida was suddenly frowning.

"Is history repeating itself?" Maida blurted out.

Lily didn't follow. "What?"

Maida's expression deepened. Lily would have said she was angry, but the word "tormented" came to mind first.

"Rose. Just now," Maida said. "Is that what I did to you?"

Lily's heart began to pound. Not wanting to argue, she looked down at the keys.

"Tell me, Lily."

She raised her head. "Different circumstances—"

"But the same effect."

Lily paused, then nodded.

Maida folded her arms on her chest. She raised her eyes to the ceiling. Astonishingly, they were lined with tears.

Lily felt awkward. She didn't know her mother this way. Putting her hands in her lap, she tried to rein in her heart.

In time, Maida's eyes met hers. "I'm sorry," she said and swallowed. "That was wrong of me."

"It's okay," Lily rushed out. "You had other things on your mmm-mind. You were busy with Daddy and the clubs and three kids; and anyway, I had Celia."

"It was *wrong* of me." There was a challenge in it now, a demand—and just enough of an edge in her voice to catapult Lily back in time.

That quickly, the hurt was brand new. "Then why did you do it?" *Tormented.* Yes, indeed, that was the look Maida wore, but Lily raced on. "Because of my stutter? I don't do that on purpose."

"I know."

"Was I so hard to love?"

Maida's eyes went wide. "I loved you. I do."

"You never said it. You never showed it. You were glad when I left."

She lifted a shoulder. "It seemed the right thing to do after . . . that incident."

"I didn't steal any car."

"I know."

"But you wanted me gone."

Maida shook her head, then stopped, seeming to realize that she was contradicting herself. She pushed her fists deep in her pockets and pressed her arms to her body.

"Why?" Lily asked.

Maida shook her head.

Lily wanted to ask what that meant, but she suddenly wanted something else more. Maida didn't have to answer. All she had to do was to cross the room and take Lily in her arms. If she had done that, Lily might have forgiven her anything.

But she didn't come forward. She stood at the door wearing that same tormented look. After a bit, she averted her eyes, bowed her head, and left.

"I may skip work tomorrow," Lily told John that night. They were lying in her bed, face-to-face in the reflected light of a harvest moon. A pair of loons chorused on the lake. It should have calmed her, but there was a thread of fury deep inside that wouldn't go away.

"How come?" he asked.

"My mother takes me for granted."

"Did you have a fight?"

She said a terse "No."

"Then a polite difference of opinion?" he teased.

Grumpy, she tugged his beard. "I'm not telling you. You'll put it in your book."

"Uh-uh. The deal is that I can't use anything unless you say it when you're fully clothed."

Yes. That was the deal. And she did trust that he would keep it. "She apologized."

"For what?"

"The past."

John raised his head. "Well, that's something, isn't it?"

Lily felt another twist of anger. "Yes."

"But?"

"It's not enough."

He stroked her hair. It calmed her some. Gently, he said, "You're very demanding."

"Yes." A month ago, an apology would have been fine. But a month ago, Lily had been in Boston. She had no interest in a life in Lake Henry. Now, here, suddenly—she needed more. "She was awful to me. She made me fff-feel unwanted and unloved and ugly."

"You were never ugly."

"Ugly inside. Like there was something wrong with me. Know who finally got me feeling better about myself?"

"The Cardinal."

"He taught me that we all make mistakes. Well, the whole world knows mine. I want to know hers. I want her to *talk* about what she felt for me and why she felt that way. I need her to say it wasn't me."

Lily did go to work on Wednesday. After venting to John, she slept well. She was mellow and rested by the time morning came.

Maida wasn't. She looked tired. For the first time, Lily thought about widowhood and what it meant to a woman like her mother. Maida had lived with George for nearly thirty-three years, overseeing the house while he oversaw the business. Now she did both, and she did it alone. There was no one to turn to at night, no one to give the kind comfort John had given Lily.

But Maida did have a business. From what Lily

could see, aside from one backhoe that needed replac-
ing and two workers with broken bones, she was running it well.

Lily had to admire her for that—and to feel compassion when Maida took a break from culling apples
to rub her lower back. When they broke for lunch,
Lily waited for her. They walked down to the house
together.

"Is your back bothering you?" Lily asked.

"A little. It's a muscle. Nothing important."

"Can you rest it?"

"In January. Not much to do here in January."

"You pull too much weight getting the crates on
the lift."

"Someone has to do it."

"Oralee could."

"Oralee's too old."

"I could."

"You're too young."

Lily didn't say anything.

They were nearly at the house when Maida said a
tentative "You could."

They changed places that afternoon—just an experi-
ment, both agreed—but it worked well. Maida layered
racks and cloths and let Bub do the pulling and pushing. Lily got crates on the lift, dumped apples in the
bath, culled out bad ones, adjusted pulleys, and raised
and lowered the press. She drove the loader when it
was time to bring more apples in from the yard, and
shimmied under the press when one of the drainage

tubes popped a leak, and she loved it all, because she could *do* it all. She hadn't felt such a sense of accomplishment since . . . since she couldn't *remember* when. And contentment. That, too. There was something about putting in a full day's work at a place with her family name on the sign.

Chapter 25

Father Neil Sullivan, Terry's brother, lived in Burlington, Vermont. When he wasn't at his church, Christ the King, he was counseling college students at a guidance center in town, or teaching at their school. John would have saved himself the trip and simply called on the phone if he had thought the man would talk, but reason said that he wouldn't. Terry hadn't betrayed him; he wouldn't betray Terry.

John did call the church beforehand to make sure that Father Sullivan was in town and not off somewhere in another part of the country. The secretary at the rectory said that he was at St. Michael's College, teaching a course. St. Michael's was in Colchester, the town abutting Burlington. That was all John needed to know.

Having arranged for one of his correspondents to distribute *Lake News,* he left Lake Henry as soon as he finished wiring the paper to the printer. Burlington was a five-hour drive. Assuming, optimistically, that he would spend a few hours with the priest, it would be late when he was done. Barring anything so unpleasant as to put him on the road sooner, he figured he would stay the night.

John knew Burlington. For five years running, dating back to his days with the *Post,* he had participated in a journalism seminar at the University of Vermont. He liked the city—liked the way it rose on a hill overlooking Lake Champlain, liked the aura of energy and excitement that came from six colleges, with sixteen thousand students milling about. Though fall had well passed its peak here, the late-afternoon sun more than compensated with color on both lake and sky.

At Christ the King, John learned that Father Sullivan was at the guidance center, which he drove to in no time. It was located on the second floor of one of the Federal-style buildings that overlooked the waterfront, and consisted of a comfortably furnished, if magazine-and-Styrofoam-coffee-cup-strewn reception area and several offices off a long hall.

The reception area was empty. The doors of two of the three offices were closed, though the fluorescent lights blazing through glass panels high above suggested they were in use.

John wandered down the hall to the open door. The office was empty. He was about to return to the reception area to wait when a woman appeared at the far end of the hall, on the threshold of what looked to be a small kitchen. She was of average height and build, with long hair center-parted and wire-rimmed glasses. John figured her to be in her late thirties. Between that and the tailored look of her sweater and slacks, he guessed she wasn't a counselee.

"May I help you?" she asked in an authoritative voice.

"I'm looking for Father Neil Sullivan."

She came down the hall, pointing at one of the closed doors as she passed. "He'll be done shortly. Do you have an appointment?"

"No. I thought I might catch him at the end of the day."

"For . . . ?"

"Just to talk."

"About . . . ?"

John debated lying. If this woman was as controlling as she sounded—and if she knew anything about the priest's personal life—she might send him packing. But the priest was nearby. John could wait either inside the center or out on the street. He wasn't leaving until he talked with the man.

Evasion seemed pointless. "About his brother."

The change in her expression was subtle, but John was looking for it. Oh yes. She knew about Terry.

Slipping her hands into the pockets of her slacks, she leaned against the wall. "Why?"

He shrugged, held up his hands, then extended one to shake. "John Kipling."

She removed a hand only long enough to meet his. "Anita Monroe. I'm the director here." The hand returned to her pocket. She was keeping her distance. "Are you with a newspaper?"

"A small one in New Hampshire. I used to work with Terry in Boston."

"Lucky you," she said with another subtle change of expression, but before John could explore it, a door opened behind her. A young man came out first. His age and worn backpack said he was a student. Eyes lowered, he slipped past them and hurried out.

John looked at the man in the clerical collar who was watching from the office door. There was a family resemblance, though John couldn't quite pin it down. Neil was clearly older than Terry, with graying hair and creases in his forehead and cheeks. He wasn't as tall or as lean, though he held himself as straight. The mouth might have been the same. But Neil's was bare and gentler. Same with the eyes. Neil looked far more friendly and warm than Terry ever had. He was approachable. Smiling now, he was even inviting. John could easily believe all the good things he'd heard about the man.

Anita cut right to the quick. "Father Neil, meet John Kipling. He wants to talk with you about Terry."

Father Neil inhaled sharply and tipped his head back as if to say, *I'm found out.* His smile was wavering by the time he righted his head, but the handshake he offered was warm. "Lots of Sullivans in the world. I was wondering when someone would make the connection. How'd you do it?"

"An old neighbor in Meadville said you were in Vermont. The local diocese did the rest. I've known Terry for years. We went to college together."

"And worked together," Anita put in.

The priest smiled sadly. "I'm afraid you know him better than I do, then. There were seven years between us growing up. We were never close."

"Aren't you in touch with him at all now?"

"No. We've taken different roads. So I'm not sure what you're looking for, and if you've come a distance, I'm sorry. But I really have nothing to say."

John might have been sly. He might have gotten the priest talking about other things and slipped into his confidence that way. But—totally aside from Anita standing guard—that didn't feel right. So he explained his quest by telling of his friendship with Lily and of the losses she had suffered since being implicated in the scandal. "She's trying to fight her way back. I want to help her. We're trying to understand why Terry hated Fran Rossetti enough to go after him and ruin an innocent woman in the process. I know that your mother and Rossetti were sweethearts, that your father was jealous of that, and that Terry was physically abused. I know that you were immune from much of it."

There was pain. John could see it in Neil's eyes. Quietly, the priest said, "If you know all that, why do you need me?"

"You're the only one who can pull it all together. We can speculate on his motives, but we need to have someone confirm it."

"For publication." With that same sad smile, the priest shook his head. "I'm sorry. I can't do that. He's my brother."

"He slandered a Cardinal. He ruined an innocent woman."

"He's still my brother. You'll get your information one way or another, but not from me."

"I want the information to be correct. You're the only one who was there."

"But I wasn't really. As I said, I was seven years older. That's a world away when you're a kid."

"Was Rossetti at the root of the family problems?"

Neil took another one of those breaths with his head tipped back. It seemed enough to shore up his resolve. "You'd have to ask my parents that."

"They're dead."

"Yes." He went silent.

The silence lengthened.

John tried, "Were you surprised that it was Terry who broke the Rossetti-Blake story?"

There was another sad smile, but patience. "I won't answer that."

"Doesn't it bother you that Terry has caused so much harm?"

The priest thought about that one. Still patient, still sad, he said, "It bothers me that the press has the power to cause so much harm."

"It has to stop somewhere," John said, thinking of Terry.

Neil was clearly thinking of John. "You're right. That's one of the reasons why I won't talk to you."

It was a point well taken. John felt a stab of guilt. It quickly turned to envy. Neil was very sure of himself, but without arrogance. There was calm and the kind of confidence that came with believing in something very much.

Realizing that, John doubted he would be moved. But he made a final stab at it. "What if I promise complete confidentiality." He was willing to do that. It felt right.

"No matter," Father Sullivan said in the same quiet voice. "He's my younger brother. It's not my place to betray him."

"Even knowing the harm he has done?"

"It isn't my job to judge. God does that." Again, he grew silent. Again, the silence lengthened.

John sought Anita's help. "Can't you see this from Lily's point of view?"

Anita surprised him by saying, "I can. If I were her, I'd want to learn everything I could. But I'm not the one whose brother it is."

"Can you convince him?" John asked, tipping his chin toward Neil.

"No," Neil said with finality. "She can't."

John knew when to quit. "Okay," he said. "That's honest enough. Tell you what. I'm taking off now, but I'll be spending the night at the Inn on Maple. If you change your mind, will you call me there? By tomorrow afternoon, I'll be back in Lake Henry." He took a business card from his wallet. "Here's my home number."

The priest tucked the card in his pocket without a glance.

John was discouraged. He had known that getting the priest to talk was a long shot, but after meeting the man, he wanted it more than ever—actually, wanted it on a personal level that had nothing to do with Lily. Neil Sullivan was insightful. He had to be, given his line of work. John wanted to know how *he* lived with the knowledge that he hadn't been there for his younger brother.

But Neil hadn't shown a moment of doubt. He wouldn't talk. John was so sure of it that he debated returning to Lake Henry that night. But the drive was long, he was exhausted, and—even if hoping was futile—he had told the priest he would be at the Inn.

So he ate dinner on the waterfront and wandered through lively downtown blocks wishing Lily were with him. Convinced that the priest wouldn't call, he stayed out late walking, and returned to the Inn tired enough to fall quickly asleep. He slept soundly and late, and woke up with barely enough time to make breakfast. There was neither a call nor a message.

As he entered the mansion's dining room, he was thinking that he could live without the priest's help and that he missed Lily and just wanted to be home— when he spotted Anita Monroe. She sat with a cup of coffee at the most privately situated of three small tables. Her eyes held his.

John helped himself to coffee from an urn on the sideboard, filled a small plate with pastries, and joined her. He kept the coffee on his side and put the pastry dish between them.

"You're not the one whose brother it is," he reminded her.

Her voice was softer than yesterday, but just as

sure. "No. But I'm the one who has watched the one whose brother it is suffer the guilt and regret."

Guilt and regret. Strong words. "Does he know you're here?"

"Yes. We talked it out last night."

"He sent you?"

"Not explicitly. But he knew I would come, and he didn't ask me not to. I took Lily's side in the discussion." She smiled. "You pushed the right button. If this can help her, then he needs to do it. The thing is, though, I need a guarantee of confidentiality. Neil thrives on anonymity. He doesn't want the press rushing here. And he won't have Terry hurt by his hand."

"It'd be yours," John reminded her, then quickly reached out and caught her wrist when, stung by either his bluntness or what she thought might be smugness, she started to rise. "Please," he said humbly, desperate in his way. "Nothing you say is for public consumption. None of it will appear in print. I need my conclusions supported, that's all."

"For Lily."

"Yes."

Slowly she sat down. She studied him, looking torn.

"And for me," John added honestly. "I need to understand."

Her eyes fell to her cup and stayed there another minute. Finally, she raised them. "Neil was the privileged child. He wasn't lying when he said he and Terry weren't close. He was only marginally aware of what was going on in that house."

"How could he not see?" John's own excuse was distance. He had been physically gone when Donny had acted up.

Anita became the therapist, perceptive and patient. "Neil saw what he could bear to take in. The rest went past him. He's seen more in hindsight in recent years, and even more since the Rossetti scandal broke."

"Was Rossetti the problem in the Sullivan marriage?"

"Yes. Jean—Neil's mother—knew that Rossetti planned to enter the seminary, but she thought she could change his mind. Obviously, she couldn't. They were together for more than eight years, and then he was gone. It was like she was widowed, or jilted. Lots of conflicting emotions. Very unsettling. She turned around and married the first guy who came along."

"On the rebound."

"Apparently. There was little love there. James had a drinking problem and, yes, a jealousy problem. Worse, he was a devout Catholic."

"Why worse? Wouldn't that have helped? Given them something in common?"

Anita shook her head. "It made him more conflicted. He hated Rossetti for all he was worth, but he couldn't lift a hand against Neil. Neil was going to be a priest. That made him untouchable. So James had huge amounts of negative energy that had nowhere to go, and every blessed time he looked at Neil, he thought of Rossetti."

"Because of the priest thing?"

"And the timing. Neil was born nine months into

the marriage. James was convinced he was Rossetti's son."

Whoa! John thought. An interesting twist. "Is he?"

"No. Absolutely not. Rossetti was out of her life two months before Jean married Neil's father. Neil was barely seven pounds at birth. No eleven-month baby, that one."

"Why the problem then?"

"Jealousy isn't always rational. James convinced himself that the baby was Rossetti's. He even went so far as to report it to Church authorities. Fifty years ago, people didn't do DNA testing, but the math spoke for itself. The Church dismissed it, but James didn't. And Jean? She would alternately admit it and deny it."

"Admit it? Why would she do that?"

"Wishful thinking. From what I gather, from what Neil said, she grew delusionary as the reality of her life and her marriage set in. Part of her *wanted* to think Neil was Rossetti's son—wanted to believe she had a little bit of him with her forever. So there you have Neil, whose presence aggravated his father, and you have the father, who wouldn't take it out on him but took it out on Jean."

"And on Terry."

"And on Terry," Anita admitted, sounding resigned. "Neil coped by focusing on life outside the home. He was forever doing things at school or spending time with friends. When he left for college, he left for good."

That sounded familiar. John left for good, too—or

so he had thought. "Didn't he try to help Terry? Or his mother? Couldn't he get someone else to help? Report it to someone at school? *Demand* that his father lay off them? Physically put his body between the father and them?"

"He was a *kid,*" she said with conviction. "He wasn't God or a saint, much as Jean wanted to think it. He was a kid whose own life at home wasn't as perfect as the story sounds."

John let out a breath. He could identify with that. He felt soothed hearing Anita say it.

But she wasn't done. "You're a guy. Imagine having a mother who made you the substitute for a lost love. Imagine the responsibility of that. Imagine the hovering and the doting. Imagine the *smothering*. There wasn't anything sexual in it, but it was oppressive. She fawned over him. And what could he do? He knew it was sick. He wanted to rebel. But she had so little pleasure in life, and she took that belt for him. She was his mother and he loved her. So he tried to please her. Tried to be perfect. Tried to emulate Rossetti." She took a breath and straightened. "If you don't think he resents Rossetti even a little himself, think again."

When it was explained that way, John figured he would. "Then it didn't bother him when Terry broke the scandal."

"Not at first. He could easily buy into the idea of Rossetti having a woman. It infuriated him that Rossetti would take up with another woman after he had broken Jean's heart, but he believed it was possible. So here's a priest doubting a Cardinal, and he felt guilty for that. Then came the official apology, and hours of soul searching and prayer for Neil. Gradually he felt sorrow, then shame."

"Not enough to speak up when the papers kept going after Lily," John charged, because his compassion for the man had limits. Neil led a sheltered life.

But Anita was suddenly fired up. "Wait a minute. What about the Cardinal? Did he speak up? No, he didn't. He didn't want to open himself up to speculation about lovers and illegitimate children, and with good cause. Can you imagine the field day the press would have had with that? Can you imagine the *havoc?* It would have been disproven, but the stench would have lingered, and Neil would have been right in the middle."

John couldn't argue with that. As angry as he was at Rossetti for abandoning Lily, Anita had a point.

She grew beseeching. "So now you know. That gives you power over us. You can turn around and use what I've told you"—she held up a hand—"even though you promised not to, or you can respect Neil's privacy and the privacy of his family. He's a good man. He may not have been there for Terry, and he'll carry the guilt of that to his grave, but he's helped countless other kids who've gone through nightmares of their own."

She sat back and lifted her coffee cup.

That gives you power over us. John kept hearing that sentence. It made him feel dirty. Not that he was sorry she had told him what she had. Here was motive reinforced. He couldn't wait to tell Lily. And he wouldn't put this into print. *That* would be dirty. It would be against everything he was trying to do with his life. But Anita didn't know that.

"Why have you told me all this?" he asked.

She set down the coffee cup and took a deep breath. The therapist was gone. There was a naked look in her eyes now. "Because I've watched him suffer. I've watched the secret swell up in his throat until he comes close to choking on it. I like him—okay, love him. If he weren't a priest, I might do something about that. Since he is, I'll sleep alone. But I want him happy. If this gives Lily Blake a better understanding of why Terry did what he did, some of the burden will be lifted from Neil's shoulders. That's it. That's all. That's what I want."

Chapter 26

Lily's muscles had ached the night before, but after one hot bath then and another in the morning, she was ready to go again. Maida was amenable. Oralee didn't blink at the change. Bub readily deferred to her. The apple pickers coming from the orchards gave her their tallies, since she was the one in the yard.

When Maida drove off that afternoon to bid at auction for a backhoe, Lily was in charge. She handled things in the cider house and, when they finished for the day, used the phone in Maida's office to track down a late shipment of plastic bottle caps.

All in all, it was a grand, proud, Sousa afternoon. No matter that the foliage color had crested and was starting to fade; the lowering sun set off sparks on the tips of die-hard maples and birches. She drove home with the radio blaring and a sense of satisfaction in her bones. Her pleasure doubled when she saw John's truck parked at the cottage. She had missed him.

He was sitting on the tailgate and jumped off when she pulled up. "You're late," he said, but he was smiling.

She smiled back. "Lots to do at the old homestead. So?" She had to know. "How'd it go?"

"It went . . . great." As they walked toward the porch, he told her about Father Neil Sullivan, the therapist Anita Monroe, and more than she had ever thought to know about Francis Rossetti.

"They thought Neil was his *son?*" she asked.

"Terry's father did. His mother sometimes did. No one else seriously believed it, but Anita was right. There'd have been hell to pay if the press had gotten wind of it. So even if he wasn't being fair to you, I can almost understand why Rossetti stayed in the background once the *Post* issued its apology. He didn't want more attention drawn to himself."

More attention, Lily mused. It was remarkable, really. "He was covered in such depth after his elevation. How could they not have found this?"

"Easy. Who knows about it? James and Jean Sullivan are dead. Neil wasn't talking. Terry wasn't talking. Church officials James might have talked to once are either dead or not talking."

Lily looked out at the lake, trying to digest it all. "At least there's a reason why he's been so silent. John?"

"Hmm?"

"We can't tell."

"I know."

"I'm sorry. I don't mean to kill your excitement. But we can't put this in print."

"I know. Besides, it isn't excitement."

She studied his face. "Then what?"

He frowned, but the frown didn't hold. Brow furrows faded and smoothed. When he looked at her, his face held a startling calm. "Relief. Peace."

"Understanding," she added.

He nodded. "It doesn't mean we can't use the rest. None of that has to do with Neil or with Rossetti. Just Terry. Poor guy. He won't be pleased."

"No," Lily said and felt a germ of regret. "He wants fame. He wants a name for himself."

"He's manipulative and possessive."

"Controlling. Like his father?"

"Probably."

"I can empathize," she said. When John looked puzzled, she explained. "Needing his mother's love and going without. I had my dad, at least. Terry had neither. So he's run through three wives. Desperate for love, but can't sustain a relationship."

"You aren't having second thoughts about exposing him, are you?"

"No," she said without pause. In a split second, she could refocus on what Terry had done to her. "I need my name back. I need my freedom."

John hugged her then, and she smiled. She had missed this last night—the closeness as much as the sex. She had so much more than Terry Sullivan ever would. All things considered, she was a lucky woman.

"Hungry?" he asked.

She nodded against his chest. She was ready for lightness. After a long day of work, food would do it.

"Let's go to Charlie's."

She stopped smiling, drew back, looked up. "Us?"

John glanced around. No, no one else was there.

"Uh, I don't know," she said, unnerved.

"You survived Gus's funeral."

"That was different. I didn't have a choice."

"Now you do," he said and waited.

Thursday nights were big at Charlie's, second only to Saturday nights in terms of the crowd. The first public singing Lily had ever done outside of church had been on a Thursday night in Charlie's back room. She hadn't been there since she was sixteen, five days before she had gone in a car with Donny Kipling.

"Is it the same?" she asked John. Back then, Charlie Senior had run the show. Thursday nights, the podium had always been reserved for the new, the young, the up-and-coming.

"Pretty much," John said.

Curious in spite of herself, she asked a cautious "Who's playing?"

"A group from Middlebury. Two guitars, a violin, and a cello. They're folk with a pop twist."

Lily liked folk. She liked pop. With a little anonymity, she would have been game. But this was Lake Henry. Even apart from any scandal, there was no anonymity here.

"People will talk," she said.

"Does that bother you?"

The question was absurd. Aside from Poppy, who was her sister and didn't count, John was her best friend in Lake Henry. She saw him every day, had slept with him for six of the last seven nights. He was smart, personable, and handsome. Except for his occupation, she loved everything about him. Did she mind being seen with him?

She threw the question right back. "Does it bother *you*?"

He didn't blink. "Not one bit."

The back room hadn't changed much in the eighteen years since Lily had been there last. Café tables and chairs had replaced benches, and there looked to be a new sound system, with speakers mounted high in the eaves. But the small, raised stage was the same, as were the potbelly stove and the ambience, which was low key and laid-back. Not that much in Lake Henry wasn't. But Thursday nights at Charlie's back room took the cake. No one rushed. No one talked business. No one wore anything dressier than jeans. And perfume? A no-no. The place smelled of old barn board, fresh coffee, melting chocolate, and fun.

It was all instantly familiar, but Lily didn't know what to expect. There were no outsiders here. The audience was wholly Lake Henry. She feared she would be the butt of whispers and stares, as she had been that first Sunday in church.

But Poppy was there, so she spent a while talking with her, and with Marianne Hersey, who stopped by, and with Charlie Owens. The rules held. No one talked business, not even Cassie, who arrived with her husband and pulled up a chair. Coffee arrived, along with the same warm, melt-in-your-mouth chocolate chip cookies that the Owens family had served at the back room for three generations running. By then the place was packed, and the band had begun, giving people something better to look at than Lily.

Slowly she relaxed. She hadn't been on this side of the stage in years, and the energy the band generated was infectious. After several songs she was tapping her foot along with the rest of the crowd; after several more she was humming along. If people were aware of her presence, they didn't make anything of it. For all intents and purposes she was just another Lake Henryite, kicking back on a Thursday night.

Toward evening's end, the band took requests. Most were for songs from the seventies and eighties, and the mood grew nostalgic. It was particularly so for Lily, who had spent much of her career doing Simon and Garfunkel, the Eagles, Carole King, Van Morrison, even the Beatles, and she felt a sudden ache to do them again.

The combination of guitar, violin, and cello were perfect for songs like "Yesterday" and "Desperado," and she wasn't the only one to think it. Hearty applause brought reprise after reprise, then similarly effective versions of "Bridge Over Troubled Water" and "Into the Mystic."

She was into it big-time when, suddenly, Charlie was on his haunches beside her chair. "They do a great 'Tapestry.' " He held a cordless mike her way. No doubt what he had in mind.

"Oh, nn-no," Lily whispered, horrified. "I couldn't."

But there was a sudden, familiar wolf whistle—Poppy urging her on—and the start of a rhythmic clapping from other parts. The sound grew. Lily looked at John, who looked nearly as frantic as she felt. Odd, but that did it. She was an entertainer by trade. She had sung dozens of times before strangers, often in far larger numbers. If she had done that, she could do this—if not for herself, then for John.

Taking the mike from Charlie, she went to the stool that had been added onstage. Bowing her head, she blocked the audience out. Of Carole King's songs, "Tapestry" was one of her favorites. She closed her eyes when the guitars began, and focused on the sound when violin and cello joined in. When the introduction approached its end, she took a deep breath and raised the mike. Eyes still closed, thinking about the words now, she began to sing.

The words flowed, one after the other, and it was easy. She had done this too many times for it not to be, but she hadn't expected the relief. It was like breathing after days underwater, like seeing again after days in the dark. Her voice was an old alto friend that came smoothly, faultlessly. She rode its crest as the tempo picked up, one line leading to the next, the melody growing fuller, if sadder, with the story of a life at its end, but by the time the last words were sung, Lily was going strong. Eyes open, she faced the band more than the audience. It was only natural to segue into "You've Got a Friend."

Lily was in her element. She had always loved Carole King, and the band knew her music well.

"You've Got a Friend" segued into "So Far Away," which segued into "Will You Love Me Tomorrow." She was so comfortable, so oblivious of her audience, that she might have been alone in a small studio with four musicians who shared her passion. She tapped the mike to her chin and grinned at them when they played the opening bars of "A Natural Woman." By the time she sang the last chorus, she practically shook with the beat.

The strings went on for a minute's conclusion. Invigorated, exhilarated, momentarily sated, Lily put down the mike and beamed at the players, but they were motioning for her to acknowledge the audience. It was only then that she heard the rousing applause. With a sheepish smile she turned and bowed low.

Poppy pulled up at her house shortly after ten. It was another few minutes before she was in her chair and out of the van, and another after that before she was inside. Annie Johnson, who had covered the phones, met her in the hall.

"I thought I heard the van," she said, pulling car keys from her pocket. "There's a call for you, still on the phone. A guy with a *great* voice."

Griffin Hughes. Poppy stayed calm.

"Anything else?" she asked, but Annie was already at the door.

"Nope," came the call back. "Quiet night." The door banged shut.

Poppy wheeled herself to the phone bank and, leaving the headset on the desk, picked up the receiver.

"Willie Jake is sound asleep. The man is seventy. Did you really think he'd be available at this hour?"

"No," came the good-natured response. "That's why I called you directly."

Poppy looked down at the bank of buttons and blushed when she saw where the little green light was. "How did you get my number?" She would *kill* Willie Jake—or Emma, for that matter—if either of them had given it out.

"Directory assistance," Griffin said in that same good-natured way.

"Oh."

"Am I calling at a bad time?"

"No."

"Were you out?"

"Yes. It's Thursday night."

"Yes?"

"I was at Charlie's."

"Who's he?"

"It's not a *he*. It's an *it*. A store. Actually, the back room of a store. There's live music there on Thursday nights." She told him about the group that had performed that night, minus Lily's role at the end.

"Sounds like fun," Griffin said.

"Nah. Very small-town. You're New Jersey. You're used to New York. You'd be bored."

"That's a generalization if ever I've heard one, Poppy Blake, and it's wrong. I live in Princeton. It isn't a big place, but I choose to live here because it has a small-town feel. I haven't been to New York in months. There's no need."

"Not even for work?"

"No. Not with telephone, e-mail, and fax."

"Do you teach at the college?"

"No. I just write."

"And you're still calling me for information on Lily? Aren't you anxious to get this article of yours done? Don't you need the *money*?"

Quietly but factually, he said, "No. I'm independently wealthy. Like you. And I'm not calling for information on Lily."

That stopped her short, tied up her tongue. When she didn't say anything, Griffin laughed. "Got you there, didn't I?"

"Why are you calling, then? There must be lots of pretty little coeds in Princeton."

"Coeds are too young."

"Then grad students."

"I like older women."

Poppy smiled. "Flattery will get you nowhere. I don't fall for deep, dark, sexy voices. They're usually tied to frogs."

"I'm not a frog."

No. She didn't think he was.

"Want to see in person?" he asked.

"Hah! Wouldn't you like me to say that I would. You'd come up here with a bona fide invitation and spend the whole time digging up stuff for your piece. I know your type, Griffin. I'm not inviting you here. I don't have time to show you around town."

"Why not? What do you do, other than work?"

"I have friends. We do things."

"Couldn't I tag along?"

She sighed. In a calm voice, she said, "I'm not inviting you."

"Is there someone else?"

She contemplated lying. It would be the easiest thing. End it now. Clean and simple. But she liked dreaming about Griffin Hughes. If dreaming was all she had . . .

"No," she said. "There's no one else." She grew beseeching. "I like talking to you. You sound like a great guy. This is fun. But don't push it. Please?"

Chapter 27

John was so gone he didn't know what to do. He had already fallen for Lily the cook, Lily the friend, Lily the gun toter, even Lily the singer-with-loons. Watching her at Charlie's Thursday night, he fell for Lily the seductress, and it was bad. She was wearing plain jeans and a turtleneck shirt, and no makeup to speak of, and was in either her own world or one with the band, but his heart ached with awe. He hadn't experienced anything like that with Marley, hadn't experienced anything like it watching Meg Ryan in every blessed one of her films—three times. He actually felt shy when Lily returned to their table, and was absurdly pleased when she spent the whole of the drive back to Thissen Cove crowded close to him on the bench seat of the truck. But she did. For all outward appearances, she seemed gone on him, too. At least, that was the message that came through in the minutes before they fell asleep.

By the time he woke up, she was off to work at the

cider house, but he felt her presence in the cottage, along with that same achy awe. This time it had to do with the larger picture of his life—with long-range wants and needs, even dreams. He thought about those as he sat out on her dock shivering in an October drizzle. The moisture made a tapping sound as it dripped through crisp leaves on the shore. There were no boats in sight. Most were out of the water, shrink-wrapped for the winter. In another few weeks Lily's dock would have to come in, too. If the pilings were squeezed by ice, they would snap.

Winter had its big toe on the threshold. The air was raw, the sky like steel. There were no loons in sight. John didn't know if they were still around, but if so, it was only a matter of days before they left. The cold and the wet said it was time to move on.

It was time for him to do it, too. Time to fish or cut bait. The next step of his life was waiting. If he was writing a book, he had to get to it.

So he went to the office Friday morning with a sense of resolve. He hadn't been there for more than five minutes when Brian Wallace called.

"I thought you'd want to know," he said matter-of-factly. "We got the report. The Blake tape was spliced. Terry's been fired."

John waited for the rest.

"Isn't that what you wanted?" Brian asked. "You've hated Terry's guts for years. For what it's worth, you aren't the only one. There'll be joy in the old newsroom tonight."

A month ago, John would have felt it, too. But a month ago he hadn't been part of Lily's cause. "And?" he prompted.

"He's cleaning out his desk as we speak. He claims he has plenty to do without busting his butt for us, but that's a load of shit. He's done for around here."

That wasn't what John was waiting for. "Forget Terry. What about Lily?"

"What about her?"

"Is the paper doing a story?"

"Nah. Terry's firing is a postscript. It's irrelevant."

"Excuse me?" John was incredulous. "An innocent woman was skewered by your paper based on a tape that you refused to authenticate until I gave you grounds for malice on Terry's part—and you don't owe her anything?"

"What would you have us do?" Brian asked, sounding annoyed.

"Her lawyer demanded a retraction."

"Oh please. Gimme a break. We didn't do anything wrong. We acted in good faith. We believed the story to be legitimate based on research—"

"Based on an edited tape."

"Based on a tape we thought was real. Christ, Kip, what would you have us *do*? Test every goddamned tape for authenticity?"

"No," John said slowly. "I know reporters on your staff who are above that, but Terry isn't one, and you knew it. You knew it, Brian, and you knew that this story had the power to hurt. Face it. You went with it because you knew it would sell papers, and it did. You guys made out like bandits. So now you've moved on to blood and gore in the Back Bay. What's the problem with printing a retraction on this?"

"The problem," Brian said with surprising candor, "is that we pride ourselves on being better journalists. Apologizing to the Cardinal was bad enough. Why rub it in? Everyone knows we blew it. Apologizing to Lily Blake is overkill."

"Overkill?" John echoed, lobbying now. A retraction might take some of the punch from his own work by making Lily less wronged, but he wanted that for her. "An innocent woman is ruined, and making things right is *overkill*?"

"Overkill, in terms of our eating crow. Why are you bugging me about this? Terry's the villain here."

"You allowed it. You let it go on and on. If you'd acted sooner, you'd have been able to make a story out of Terry's sins. You'd have done right by Lily, the press world would think better of you, and the whole thing would be done."

Brian yelled, "The whole thing *is* done! *Listen* to me, John! We are not *groveling*!"

John was livid when he hung up the phone, but he knew a dead end when he heard one. Brian was only an editor. There were levels of management above him, people better positioned to order a retraction. John considered calling one of those. Then he reconsidered.

Lily needed closure. She needed a public apology and the restoration of her name that that would bring. She needed justice.

Terry being quietly fired wasn't justice. It was the smallest admission of wrongdoing. No one but insiders at the *Post* would know it had happened. John would even bet that the *Post* was counting on Terry saying that he'd quit. He would get another job and start right in again with barely a blip in his career. That wasn't justice.

So John could threaten to make the firing the lead story in *Lake News* if the *Post* didn't issue an apology. Armand would be in his glory. He would phone everyone he knew in New York, and reverberations would be assured.

Oh, yes, John could threaten that. And the *Post* might issue a retraction. But it would be buried as far back and inconspicuously as possible. No one would see it.

Lily had been destroyed on page one. She deserved vindication on page one.

Unfortunately, a front-page vindication wasn't in his own best interest. Any revival of the story in the mainstream media, especially a story that focused on Terry, introduced the risk that another curious reporter would discover what John had. If that happened—if another writer stole his thunder after he had done the grunt work—John could kiss his book deal good-bye.

Would that be so terrible?

He'd had four reasons for wanting to write a book: fame, money, Gus's approval, and the justification for leading a small-town life.

Fuck the fame. He didn't need that. Lily made him feel important.

Fuck the money. He could live without that, too. Lily wasn't a grubber. She made him feel like a million.

And his lifestyle? If he didn't care about fame and money, his lifestyle was just fine.

That left Gus's approval, which was still wanting, even with the man dead. It boiled down to conscience and self-esteem.

So, did he write a book, or not? He had to decide and decide soon.

Lily was as distracted as John over the weekend. With the *Post*'s refusal to issue a retraction even in spite of the test results on the tape, she had to face the reality of a court case that would be long and drawn out. Already the paper's attorneys had asked Cassie for sixty days to consider the initial suit.

"It's a typical stalling tactic," Cassie said.

"Can't we say no?" Lily asked.

"We can, but it's not strategically wise. If we refuse them the time, if we demand an immediate response, they may be annoyed enough to file a motion to dismiss in state court. We'll win that one for sure. The problem is time. If they file a motion to dismiss now, the hearing date could be as late as February."

"What's to say they won't file the same motion sixty days from now?" Lily asked.

"Nothing," Cassie conceded. "If they want to be bastards, that's just what they'll do."

"Did they sound like bastards?"

"No. But that wouldn't have been strategically

wise for them. The lawyer who called was humble and courteous. Fake as hell, but humble and courteous. I recommend we be good guys and give them thirty days. That doesn't set us back too much in the overall scheme of things."

Lily went along, but she wasn't happy. Thirty days meant a whole other month in limbo. She was feeling an urgency that went beyond loose ends in Boston. She was starting to make a life in Lake Henry. There were still things to work out with Maida if she hoped to stay long, and she was afraid to think too far ahead about John, but a resolution to the scandal was a sine qua non. None of the others would fall into place until it was settled.

John took Lily to church Sunday morning. He took her to brunch at Charlie's afterward, and for a ride in the hills. He took her to the *Lake News* office and gave her the packet of articles from the academy, and when she had picked three, he set her up with Quicken and let her do the dozen small checks that went to town correspondents, miscellaneous freelancers, and Jenny Blodgett each month.

She was delighted to help, which pleased him immensely. Being hooked on the paper was akin to being hooked on him—not to mention that her help was badly needed. He was getting little of his own work done.

Forget writing a book. *Lake News* had to be done. But he was having trouble drumming up enthusiasm for an upcoming intertown soccer tournament, much less dummying up the week's pages. One layout was wrong, another was worse. His heart just wasn't in it.

After a while, pleading the need to air out his mind, he left Lily at the computer, walked up past the post office and across the street to the graveyard beside the church. He stood first at the plot where Donny was buried, and felt the pain he always did. Like Neil Sullivan, he would carry regrets to his grave, but Anita's words helped. *He was a kid,* she had said in defense of Neil. *He wasn't God or a saint. He was a kid whose own life at home wasn't as perfect as the story sounds.* She might as easily have said it in defense of John. It didn't take him off the hook with regard to Donny, just made the hook a little less sharp.

He turned to the patch of earth beside Donny's. Gus's grave. There was no grass here. Grass would have to wait for spring. But there were leaves that had blown off the trees and drifted over the dirt, a dusting of pale yellows, faded reds, muted browns.

It was quiet here—peaceful, as eternity was—because John did believe that his father was in heaven. A man who had suffered so much deserved that.

It was me who let you down. Me who failed. Me who was never good enough. Not for your mother. Not for Don. Not for you.

Sad that that should be a dying thought. Sad that worthiness had been so important to him. A man without a conscience had it easy, John decided. A man without a conscience didn't have a worry in the world.

Gus had a conscience. So did John.

Gus wanted to be worthy. So did John.

Gus built beautiful stone walls. John wrote beautiful articles. But neither was enough to guarantee worthiness.

It was simple, really. Building walls and writing articles was fine. But the essence of worthiness had to do with people.

No, Lily did not want to think about what she felt for John, but those feelings weren't going away. Ideally, she would settle the scandal, then settle with Maida, and *then* think about him. But life was never ideal. Her heart insisted on squeezing and tugging whenever he came to mind.

This Sunday, she felt his distraction and feared he was having second thoughts about their relationship. Unable to ask it lest he say that he was, she helped out at the office as best she could, then made dinner back at the cottage, trying to please him that way. He smiled, ate every last bite, and thanked her more than once. But she turned back from the sink when the dishes were done to find him outside on the dock. Pulling on his sweater, and a jacket over that, she followed him out.

It was downright cold. A wind was up, rippling over the water as it had rarely done the month before. October was in full gear. November would bring snow.

Her sneakers made a muted sound on the planks. John looked up and smiled. Taking her hand, he drew her down and settled her between his legs, facing the lake, with his cheek against her hair and his arms holding her close.

Those arms didn't feel like they were having second thoughts. She was momentarily content.

"Listen to the water," she whispered.

"Mmm-hmm. Lapping up a storm. I've been trying to hear loons."

"Any?"

"No. They may be out there. We'll hear if they call. It's hard to spot them with rough water and no moon." His mouth touched her temple, the gentle brush of his beard. "Warm enough?"

"I am."

"I love you, you know."

Her heart bumped.

"Is it mutual?" he asked, sounding endearingly unsure.

She was totally crazy. Since when could she trust a newspaperman? "Very."

She felt him relax some. When he said, "I want what's best for you," she believed him. More, she believed what she heard in his sudden somberness. The cause of his distraction wasn't their relationship. It was the other mess.

She was relieved, frightened. "What are my choices?"

He breathed in the sigh of one who had examined each in depth. "You have three," he said on the exhalation, still warm and close. "First, you can take the legal course. Hunker down, let Cassie pursue the case, get what remedy you can that way."

"Hunker down" was the operable phrase. That choice would take time.

"Second," he said, "you can say it all in my book. Jacobi wants to put it out in March. I'd rather a few extra months to write it well, but I can do it for March. That would bring quicker results than a lawsuit."

You can say it all in my book. Not, *I can say it all.* It felt like a joint endeavor. That was something.

"Third," he concluded, "we can make headlines this week. I can devote the week's *Lake News* to the scandal. Blow the whole thing wide open. Armand will make sure that the mainstream press picks it up. You'd have your forum."

She swallowed. She would have her forum, at that. She would have exposure, which she hated. But this time there would be headlines, sure vindication, the final revenge.

"If I do," she pointed out, "you won't have your book."

He was silent for a long time. When he spoke, the words held a certain resignation. "It may be that you need this more than I need my book."

She was more touched than she could believe.

"It's your choice," he said.

"But you wanted that book." She knew how much. They had talked about his dreams. She wasn't even as threatened anymore. Not really. It was the trust thing.

"I can still have the book."

"It won't be as strong."

"Maybe not. But right now you need headlines. You need flash."

"I hate flash."

He turned her around and looked her in the eye. "You may hate it, but damn it, it works. Flash took your jobs, your home, your reputation. Do you want those back?"

She remembered the pride she had felt at the Winchester School when her a cappella groups had performed, and the pleasure of playing favorite songs at the Essex Club for people like Tom and Dotty Frische. She remembered the satisfaction of walking through the Public Garden and down Commonwealth Avenue to the place she had made her home out of sheer hard work and determination. Her reputation had been key in all of those things.

"Do you?" John asked.

"Yes."

"Do you want vindication?"

Did she want the world to know that she had never had an affair with Francis Rossetti? Did she want an acknowledgment of the horror that had been made of her life in Boston? Did she want an apology for having been singled out for humiliation and derision?

"Yes!"

"Do you want to punish the people who did this to you?"

So many people who should be ashamed, so many people behind the scenes letting it happen—where to begin? There was Justin Barr, whose lying mouth had painted her a Jezebel across the airwaves, and Paul Rizzo, who had followed her and harrassed her and never once, never *once* given her the benefit of the doubt. But Terry Sullivan was the worst of the bunch. He had dreamed up the story in the first place. Did she want him punished?

Did she ever.

John spent the night at Lily's, but he was the first one gone in the morning. He stopped at Charlie's for coffee and the out-of-town papers, and went straight to the office.

He never did open those papers. He had plenty to write without, and the words came in an effortless flow from his brain, through his fingers, to the screen. On occasion he thought to hold back. There was more than enough news here; he could yet have his book.

But there was Lily, working at the cider house because she had been deemed unfit to teach kids, and Gus, paralyzed by the belief in his own unworthiness.

Was John worthy, or not? Was he decent, or not?

Lake News took on greater import as the hours passed. He wanted this issue to be the best thing he'd ever done. Holding back wouldn't do. This was breaking news. Journalistically speaking, it was John's dream. Lingering thoughts about writing a book took a backseat to the idea of getting justice for Lily.

In a moment of what John now knew to be cynicism born of frustration, Gus had said that journalists reported the news because they didn't have the brains to make the news. Well, John had the brains. He had followed a hunch, done his homework, and found new information to recast an old story.

No, a journalist's job wasn't to make the news. He had learned that years before. But nothing he did or thought or imagined now told him to turn back. He had uncovered the truth and was making it known. That didn't feel at all wrong to him.

Tuesday morning, when Liddie Baynes arrived with Armand's column, John was at the door to greet her. "For your better half," he said, handing her a large envelope as he took her small one. "How's the boss?"

"Crotchety," Liddie said, but with affection. "His new hip isn't working like it would if he were twenty."

John grinned and gestured toward what he had given her. "This should cheer him up."

It took Liddie five minutes to drive home, and Armand another five to see enough of what John had sent to react. His call came within a minute of when John had put down his pen in anticipation.

"What the *hell* is this?" Armand barked into his ear. "Where did it come from? How long you been nosing around? Do you know the *implications* here? Christ, John, why wasn't I told? I'm the publisher. When were you going to clue me in?"

"It was a last-minute decision," John said, knowing Armand was more excited than angry. "I've been digging for a while, but I wasn't sure what I'd find. So. What do you think?"

"What do you *think* I think? I'm . . . I'm *psyched*!"

John grinned. "There's still time to rework the issue if you don't want to run it," he teased.

"I want to run it, all right. The question is, what do we do with it once it's run?"

John cleared his throat. "I have ideas. But I'll need your help."

"That's good. Shut me out at this point and you're fired."

Timing was everything. The key was to get people curious, without allowing them to look into the story themselves. It was tricky with journalists. They were addicts. One whiff of something new and they hit the ground running.

John and Armand made their separate lists and cross-checked them to eliminate duplications. The plan was to spend Tuesday evening making calls to those reporters who would need extra travel time, and Wednesday morning for those within easier reach.

It was something of a game for John, calling old friends in the media, asking enough questions about the validity of the Rossetti-Blake story—and how it had played in their neck of the woods—to arouse suspicion, then confiding that Lily Blake was indeed home, that *Lake News* had a scoop, that yes, there would probably be a news conference at press time, and yes, he supposed the big guns would be there.

"Supposed" was a fair enough word. He knew how press people worked. They wouldn't take the chance of ignoring a tip, lest a rival follow it up and hit gold. He didn't earmark Terry; didn't have to. The people he called were insiders who knew Terry's connection with the story. It helped that they respected John. One after another he heard murmurs and the rustle of paper for making notes when he said that if a press conference materialized, it would take place in the church in the center of Lake Henry Wednesday at five.

That was the earliest John figured he could get *Lake News* back from the printer. It meant that Lily could finish up at the cider house, do what she had to do at home, and join him in town. It also meant that the story would break in time for the evening news.

John didn't spend Tuesday night at Lily's but stayed at the office making calls until midnight, then worked on the rest of *Lake News,* local things that he had neglected, things that had nothing to do with the scandal but that were important, very important, to his readers. He was on the phone again by eight in the morning, made the last of his calls by eleven, put the finishing touches on the paper, and sent it to the printer just minutes before noon.

That was when Richard Jacobi called. The grapevine was active. Richard had heard the words "scoop" and "press conference." He wasn't happy.

"How much are you telling?" he asked.

"Not much. Just one piece of the puzzle."

"It must be a hefty piece if our papers are heading up there. Listen, John, I have your contract here on my desk ready to be mailed, but if you're telling everything now, what's to tell later?"

"Details," John said. "Depth."

"That's just fine if you're David Halberstam, but you're not. You're a newspaper guy who's forte is breaking news. I was counting on this book to be a shocker. That's what the money's for."

"I thought the money was for the inside story. The story behind the story. Nothing's changed about that."

"The deal was for an exclusive. If you run the story in your weekly, that breaks the deal. Hell, John, this is a business. Details and depth are fine and good, but they don't have half the sales potential as shock. I was paying for that. I imagined prepub hype that would have bookstores and readers champing at the bit. Marketing is already on it. So's Publicity and Art. The package was going to be great, and *then* we'd launch with a press conference. You do that now and the deal is off. Hell, maybe this isn't a good match."

"Maybe it isn't," John agreed, because what Richard was describing didn't jibe with his dream. He might *not* be David Halberstam. But the whole point of his doing this book was to prove his worth as a writer.

At least, that had been the dream once. It wasn't now. He wanted to prove his worth as a person. He was doing that just fine without a book.

"Tell you what," Richard said in what he must have thought was a conciliatory tone, "I'll hold this contract here. Give me a call after your press conference, and we'll see where we stand."

John hung up the phone doubting he would make that call, and not feeling disappointed in the least.

Chapter 28

Lily spent Wednesday morning feeling as jittery as she had those last few days in Boston. Seeking relief in routine, she devoted herself to the cider making, working the racks and cloths with a fever, but the sense of anticipation never left her for long. Each time it returned, her emotions swung wildly—excitement to fear to satisfaction to embarrassment to anger. One thing, however, remained constant: she did want justice.

The irony was that Terry Sullivan had given her the tool to get it. He was the one who had put her name on the map. John barely had to breathe it to his media friends and they were on their way to New Hampshire. Once they were all in Lake Henry, the limelight would shift to Terry. As the saying went, he would be hoist by his own petard.

Thinking about that gave her deep satisfaction.

Thinking about the crowds, about other questions

that might come, about a renewal of media attention on her even for a short time made her queasy. But she couldn't have one without the other.

"Something's on your mind," Maida remarked.

They were walking down to the house for lunch. The day was clear but cold. Lily had her hands tucked up into the sleeves of her jacket. Now she tucked the sleeves under her arms.

Maida would have to know. The press might be arriving en masse that afternoon. Or no one might come. John had said it was possible. Not probable but possible. In that case, Maida *didn't* have to know.

In either case there would be a gathering at the church. Lily wanted to tell Maida about it and about the thinking behind it. She wanted Maida to say they were doing the right thing. But Maida wouldn't do that. She didn't want the press around. She made that clear when Lily had first returned.

"Does it have to do with John Kipling?" Maida asked now, holding open the door. The phone was ringing inside, but with Poppy to pick up, she didn't hurry to get it.

Lily followed her into the kitchen, frantically wondering whether she'd heard or guessed, and if so, how much she knew. "Why do you ask?"

The phone rang again. Ignoring it still, Maida draped her jacket over the back of a chair. With a hand on the refrigerator door, she sent Lily a disbelieving look. "I'm not stupid, Lily. Nor am I deaf. Even if I managed not to hear the calls you make, even if you hadn't told me yourself that you were with him the whole time Gus was dying, then again at the funeral, even if I hadn't seen you with him at church, I'd have heard it from friends. They said you were quite a hit at Charlie's Thursday night."

"I didn't plan that," Lily said quickly. "It ww-was a spontaneous thing. Charlie came over and asked. I just did a couple of songs."

Maida took a pot of soup from the refrigerator. She put it on the stove and lit the gas. "Are you serious about John?"

On a serious scale of one to ten, professions of love ranked up at the top. But Lily didn't know where it would go from here, and she couldn't get a handle on Maida's feelings about John. So she said, "I'm not sure."

"He's a Kipling."

"He didn't have anything to do with the car business. And Donny and Gus are both gone."

Maida lifted the lid and stirred the soup with undue force. "Did you *have* to go to the funeral?"

There it was. Disapproval. But at least it wasn't outright condemnation of John. Lily was grateful, but she wasn't cowed. She said a quiet "Yes. I did."

When Maida didn't respond but stayed with the soup, Lily went to the cupboard for dishes. The table was nearly set when the phone started ringing again. Her eye flew to the instrument, but Maida was already there.

"Yes," she snapped into the receiver.

Lily heard threads of an excited voice at the other end of the line. Maida looked sharply back at her. She put her free hand on her waist and her eyes on the wall. As she listened, her shoulders grew stiff.

Lily had a sinking feeling. When Maida hung up and turned, she braced herself.

"That was Alice," she said, looking pale, sounding worse. "She says phones are ringing all over town. Something about a press conference."

"Yes."

"Something about John and you. About reporters coming *today*?"

What could Lily say? "Yes."

"*Why?*"

"Because we have information on Terry Sullivan that proves—"

"I don't care about Terry Sullivan," Maida cried, looking betrayed. "I care about *us*. Everything had quieted down. The press lost interest. It was over and done." She grew pleading. "We were doing just fine, you and I. Weren't we?"

If Lily could have turned back the clock in that instant and vetoed the idea of a press conference, she might have. Maida was right. They were doing just fine.

But life wasn't about doing just fine.

Softly, she said, "This isn't about you and me."

"It *is*," Maida argued. Her hands were on her hips one minute, on the counter behind her another. "It's about respect," she said, raising both hands to the back of her neck. "It's about respect, which you have never once shown me. Singing at church wasn't good enough. You had to sing at Charlie's. You had to sing and dance on Broadway. You knew I'd hate it, but you did it anyway."

"It was what I did well."

"And then the business in Boston." Her hands were back to her hips. "Well, that was over and done, and now you've revived it. Couldn't you have let it *rest?*"

Lily had asked herself that a dozen times. Now she sighed. "No. I couldn't. He's taken ss-something from me. I need to try to get it back."

"What did he take? An apartment that was too expensive to begin with? A nightclub?"

"My name."

"Your name is perfectly good here. Isn't that what Thursday night at Charlie's was about? Why do you always need *more?*"

"Not more, Mom. Different."

"But you're *not* different," Maida shouted. She snatched up a dishcloth and began wiping perfectly clean, dry hands. "You're not *any* different. You let people take advantage of you, just like I did—let people *use* you, just like I did. Donald Kipling—Terry Sullivan—*John* Kipling now. He's not doing this for you," she cried in disdain. "He's doing it for *him.* So don't you stand up there on your high horse and say we're different. You're not any better than me. If there's any difference at all, it's that I had the sense to put it behind me once and for all."

With a cry of dismay she tossed the dishcloth on the counter and stalked out of the house.

*   *   *

Lily didn't eat lunch. She turned off the flame under the soup pot and waited in the kitchen for Maida to return, but there was no sign of her when time came to go back to work. So Lily walked up to the cider house alone. As she neared, her apprehension grew, but she needn't have worried. Maida didn't show up for the afternoon shift.

Lily called in one of the pickers to work the racks and cloths with Bub while she took Maida's part, but she didn't feel exhilaration or pride now. She did what she had to do, and she was distracted, but not by the prospect of the press coming to town. Her heart was heavy wondering where Maida was, what she was thinking, whether they could patch things up. She didn't know why Maida was still so upset about things that had happened so long ago. She didn't know why she should *care* so much what her mother still felt. But she did.

Tears must have come to her eyes once too often, because they were barely into the afternoon shift when Oralee shooed her off. With three hours to go until the press conference, Lily debated returning to the cottage or driving straight to the newspaper office. Maida would calm down in time. She always did.

Yes. She always did. She calmed down, the upset passed, and things were never discussed or resolved.

But things were different this time. The press conference loomed. Lily was unsettled enough about that not to want things with her mother up in the air. She had to talk with Maida. She hadn't explained her feelings as well as she might have, and wanted to try it again.

The kitchen was empty. Likewise the office. Lily guessed that Maida might be upstairs, but she couldn't go up there. It had been a long while since she had lived in this house, a long while since she'd had cause to climb those stairs. And to Maida's bedroom? It seemed an invasion of her privacy.

So Lily sat at the piano and began to play. A Chopin étude, a Liszt sonata—she moved from one to the other without finishing either. At that moment in time, loose ends seemed the story of her life.

And when hadn't they? When had she been more settled? She thought about it for a minute, before conjuring up the image of singing in church when she was ten. Life had been simpler then. Maida had been proud.

Without conscious thought, she began playing the hymns she had sung. She played "Onward Christian Soldiers" and "Faith of Our Fathers"—both to completion, because they did calm her. She was halfway through "Amazing Grace" when Maida appeared at the door. She looked tired, older than her years, defeated almost. Lily stopped playing.

"You think that I'm wrong," Maida said in a reed-thin voice. "You don't understand why I like living my quiet life here and why this whole business with the Cardinal is so upsetting to me, but there are things you don't know." She wrapped her arms around her waist.

Lily started to shake. It was subtle, way deep inside, but it held a foreboding. "What things?"

"Things I did before I met your father."

Lily's heart pounded as she waited for Maida to go on.

"Did you never wonder why I never talked about my childhood?" Maida finally asked.

"All the time. I asked you about it. You would never say. There were no pictures, nothing. When I asked Celia, she smiled and said that there was nothing worth repeating."

"There wasn't until now. But if they come here and see us and start digging again . . ." Her voice trailed off. She pushed a shaky hand into her hair.

Lily started to get up, then stopped herself and stayed put. The piano was a buffer between them. It made the unfamiliar less frightening.

"My father died early," Maida said. "There was other family in Linsworth. Celia had four brothers."

Lily had thought there were three—and that, only from pictures she had found in a drawer after Celia passed away. Growing up, she had assumed there was no one at all in Linsworth to contact. After finding those pictures, she had tried to remember who might have been standing at the back during Celia's funeral, but she had been too wrapped up in her own grief at the time to notice.

Maida spoke softly. Her eyes were distant, stricken. "The brothers were all younger than Celia, the last one by twenty years. He was more my generation than hers. He was a friend, a baby-sitter, a brother, a lover."

Lily could barely breathe.

Maida's eyes filled with tears. "He used to sneak in at night when everyone was asleep. He taught me about my body and about love. He was handsome and sweet and smart." She brushed at the tears with the back of her hand, and looked away. "When I was sixteen, they found out about us and sent him away."

Sixteen was the age Lily had been when she was caught joyriding with Donny Kipling in a stolen car. Lily could only begin to imagine the sense of déjà vu Maida must have felt.

But Maida wasn't thinking about that now. The soft light of the piano lamp picked up the tears on her cheeks, but she was looking straight at Lily, daring her to be revulsed. "They said it was all his fault, that I was too young to understand, but I understood. I wanted what happened. To this day it's my only bright memory from those years. Call me immoral or depraved, but you didn't live there. You didn't know what it was like. We all lived together in a small place. Families did that then. My father worked with Celia's brothers, and Celia had always been a mother to them, so it made even more sense. We were poor. We pooled our resources. When the men hunted, it wasn't for sport but for food. I was the only girl, so I had my own room. There was a lumpy mattress on the floor and a little place to stand. That was all. It was cold and dark. Phillip was my warmth and my light." Her chin trembled. "I loved him. What he did felt good to me. He was the only luxury I had."

"Wasn't *Celia* a luxury?" Lily cried, more offended by that than the other.

"You didn't know her then," Maida scoffed. "She was different from the person you knew. She was busy all the time, and she was hard. After my father died she had the responsibility of her brothers and me. She ran the house and earned the money."

"Didn't the brothers work?"

"They didn't earn much, and most of it went for drink. Phillip went along, but not all the way. He stashed away enough for me to have when I needed to leave. There was a note saying where it was and what it was for. It was in his hand when he died."

Lily caught her breath.

"He killed himself," Maida told her. "Two months after he left. Nowadays he'd have been in jail, but the law never knew about him. He had been wandering around the whole time, not knowing what to do with himself. Friends had seen him in towns as far as thirty miles away, but his body was found in the woods less than a mile from us."

She pressed a hand to her middle, seeming in pain. Lily was up from the piano bench in a flash, but Maida held up a hand to hold her off. Her lips were as close to pursed as they could be and still allow for talk. "There's more." She gathered herself. "You wanted to know, you can hear it all."

Lily felt pain and confusion. She felt shock and sorrow enough to bring tears to her eyes. But Maida wouldn't let her close. So she leaned against the piano.

"We buried Phillip in the family plot. The people of Linsworth said he shouldn't be anywhere near good folk, but Celia wouldn't have him anywhere else. She had loved him, too. She blamed herself for what happened. She still had the responsibility for all of us, and then the weight of that on top of it. She and I grew closer, because we shared the grieving and I wanted to help her. So I dropped out of school and went to work in the logging office where she worked."

Her eyes and voice grew distant again. "It wasn't easy. Everyone in town knew what had happened. Except for Celia and me, the logging operation was all men. Whenever I walked out of the office, men stared at me. Some of them made comments. They touched me whenever they could, like it was a game to see how much they could get. They asked me out, and I refused every time, but that made it worse. If I'd paired up with one of them, there might have been protection. But I was trying to do the right thing, so I was fair game."

She wilted a little. "It became clear to us that I couldn't stay there. Not in that office, not in that town. We were trying to decide where to go and what to do when George showed up one day wanting to buy equipment from my boss. He spent long enough talking with me for us to know that he wasn't married, but we figured that if he stayed around long, he'd learn enough to decide he didn't want me at all. So Celia and I went out and bought me some nice clothes with the money Phillip had left"—her voice caught on the last thought—"and Celia managed to get me sent to Lake Henry with the deliveries. I went back to hand deliver a bill, and back again to deliver a receipt. It was a long trip, over more backroads than you'd drive in a month around here. Took the better part of a day."

The memory lifted her some, pride showing its face. "I acted a part then, acted better than *you've* ever acted, because my life depended on it. I created a woman who was intelligent and poised, who knew how to keep house and balance books, and yes, please a man. She was a woman with a clean past, and she did things right. *All the time* she did things right. Your father fell in love with that woman. She's the one I've been ever since."

Jaws tight, she fixed her eyes on Lily. "I knew what it was to be stared at, and there you were, singing in public, welcoming those leering eyes. How do you think I felt when you got caught with Donny Kipling? Don't you think a part of me worried you were getting in the same situation I'd been in? Only, you didn't find your George. You went to New York, and that was worse. But I didn't have to see it, until this. How do you think I felt when the newspapers started digging up dirty little things from your past? How do you think I felt wondering when they'd dig a little deeper, just a little deeper, and find out about me? No one here knows. When Celia moved here, she started new, too. We never talked about the past. We just erased it from the slate."

"No one will find out," Lily vowed.

"I have a life here. I have a good life here. I have friends and a business. I have a name."

"No one will find out," Lily repeated.

"How do you *know*?"

"Because this isn't about me anymore. It's about Terry Sullivan."

Maida started to pursue the argument. She opened her mouth, closed it, then put a hand up to keep it that way. Lily's first thought was that she was paralyzed thinking about what the town might learn. But it was horror on her face, not fear. Horror.

Because her daughter now knew.

"It's all right," Lily whispered, starting forward, but Maida stepped back with a frantic shake of her head.

Lily felt a greater need to touch than ever. Starting forward again, she said, "It doesn't change my feelings—"

But Maida had turned and, with her hand on the back of a bowed head now, was hurrying up the stairs.

Lily followed her as far as the newel post, wanting to follow farther but afraid. "It was a long time ago," she called. "You've mm-ade up for it ten times over. You were a good wife to Dad, and a good mother to us, and look at you nn-now. You're running Dad's business almost better than *he* did."

But Maida was gone.

Lily knew she would carry Maida's look of horror with her for the rest of her life. It marked the moment when parent and child changed places in the approval game, the moment when, as human beings, they became equal. It was the startling moment when she realized that her mother didn't have any more answers to some things than she did.

She stood at the banister for what had to have been twenty minutes, then she sat down on the bottom step. She wanted to go up, wanted to thank Maida for sharing what she had, because it explained so much. She wanted to thank her for trusting her, wanted to assure her that she was worthy, that no one but her would ever know, that she would make sure nothing, absolutely *nothing* came even remotely close to this at the news conference. She wanted to go up but didn't dare, and she hated herself for that. There was still that fear—always that fear of rejection.

But the clock was ticking. It was nearly four. She had to shower, change, and get to John's office.

She drove back to Celia's with her heart in her mouth, aching for Maida, frightened of what was coming—then positively *terrified* when it struck her that John might know Maida's secret. Lily hadn't seen *Lake News*. She had trusted that he would be writing about Terry. She had *trusted* him on that.

She tried to call, but Poppy picked up and didn't know where he was. So she rushed in and out of the shower, tried the office again—then realized that she didn't dare say anything on the phone. Cell phones were far from secure, and hadn't her supposedly secure line in Boston been tapped into not so long ago? Lord knew whether John's was or not.

She hurried with her makeup and hair, pulled on that lone pantsuit of hers, and drove the old Ford wagon as fast as she dared around the lake to the center of town.

There were cars there. Cars and vans. Vans with satellite dishes on top, the names of local stations and national affiliates in large letters on the sides, and reporters flanking them testing cameras and mikes.

Lily's stomach began to churn.

Doing her best to look like a nobody, she turned in at the post office, but she had to pull up on the grass beside the yellow Victorian, because there were cars there, too—and reporters. She was barely out of the wagon when they spotted her, and suddenly the feeling of being hunted was back, as strong as it had been in Boston.

She ran toward the side door. They fell into step.

"How long have you been here?"

"Have you talked with the Cardinal?"

"Would you comment on the lawsuit?"

John opened the door when she reached it and closed it the instant she was inside. She was shaking badly. He held her, but the shaking didn't stop.

"It's starting again," she whispered, panicky.

But John's voice was calm. "Only because they have no one else to chase. Wait fifteen minutes. It'll be a different ball game then."

She looked up at him. "Where's the paper?"

"Across the street in the church. Willie Jake's guarding it."

"Is there anything in it about Maida?" she asked, searching his face for signs of betrayal, but he looked more puzzled than anything.

"No. I talk about what you went through in Boston. Mostly it's about Terry."

She was weak with relief.

"Did you and she talk?" he asked.

Lily nodded. She wanted to tell him. Wanted to tell him. Wanted to, but couldn't. The trust she felt was still too new.

He held her back. His eyes were the deep brown that she loved, but stripped bare now, naked and honest. "I traced Maida back to Linsworth, but I couldn't get myself to poke around. If something happened there, it's her business. If she chose to tell you, I'm glad, but you don't have to tell me. There's nothing I need to know that I don't already." He brushed her cheek with the back of his fingers. "There are things I begrudge about Maida, like how she treated you when you were growing up, even how she looks at me now, but she's a good person, Lily. A decent person. She gave your father many happy years, and she's kept the business going. Whatever may have happened in Linsworth doesn't matter. As far as I'm concerned, she is who she is today. Period."

In the final minute that his eyes held hers, Lily loved him as much for respecting Maida as for not making Lily betray her.

He checked his watch. "Are you ready for this?" he asked softly.

It was a minute before she shifted gears, but the answer to his question came quickly. Was she ready? She was not. She had visions of John presenting his case and the press rallying around Terry as one of their own, in which case the entire effort would backfire.

Then again, it might not.

Was she ready? She nodded.

"Want to go?"

She did not. She wanted to go home and hide in the safe little cocoon she had made for herself. More than that, though, she wanted vindication.

She nodded again.

John straightened and took a deep breath. Lily was thinking that as he stood there wearing a blazer, shirt, and tie with his jeans, he had to be the most beautiful man in the world. Then he opened the door.

Chapter 29

The meeting hall was full. Lily saw it the instant John led her in from a side door. Every pew was taken, many with people holding equipment. Floodlights, mounted on high poles, glared down on television reporters who stood in the aisles adjusting earpieces and feeding preliminaries to their stations. Townsfolk filled the back of the hall and the small balcony. The low drone of talk was joined by the click and whirr of cameras, evoking memory enough to make Lily's heart pound.

A long table had been set up at the front. A gaggle of microphones, held together with duct tape, was already mounted there, with a snakepit of wires spilling out across the floor.

Lily took the seat John indicated. He had barely taken the one on her right when Cassie slipped into the one on her left, leaned in close, and explained her presence in a whisper, "Just in case someone tries to trip you up."

John leaned in from his side. "The elderly couple in the front row are Armand and Liddie. You know them, don't you?"

Lily did, but she hadn't seen them in years. Armand looked frighteningly frail, though there was a spot of high color on his cheeks and a definite gleam in his eye.

"Armand rarely leaves the house," John went on. "The group to his right is from New York; to his left, Washington. The pair behind him are from Springfield. I see Chicago, Kansas City, Philly, Hartford, and Albany, and that's just the first few pews. The New England media are behind them—Concord, Manchester, Burlington, Portland, Providence."

Lily spotted baby-faced Paul Rizzo several rows from the front. "Did you invite Rizzo?"

John shook his head, but his eyes twinkled. He was clearly delighted that Rizzo had come.

She spotted other faces she remembered from the pack that had followed her in Boston, and familiar faces that were more friendly—Charlie and Annette Owens, Leila Higgins, Alice Bayburr and her family. Poppy's friends filled one pew, with Poppy in her chair at the end of a row. When their eyes caught, she gave Lily a thumbs-up and a grin. It calmed her a bit.

"See the homely guy about halfway back on the left?" Cassie whispered.

Lily searched, found, nodded.

"Justin Barr."

"Omigod."

John's voice came again, still soft but filled now with barely bridled excitement. "Check the guy at two o'clock, way over there on the end."

Lily caught her breath this time. There was no mistaking that mustache. She felt revulsion, then absolute glee. Looking at John, she whispered, "What's he *doing* here?"

"Must think he's getting stuff for his piece."

"Doesn't he *know?*"

John smiled. "I didn't say." The smile faded. "Ready?"

John couldn't have been happier with the turnout. He had expected the New England contingent, plus a handful of other stalwarts, and had assumed that the hall would be comfortably filled. Packed was a treat. The fact of Sullivan, Rizzo, and Barr being there was a triple treat. Though he hadn't invited any of the three, he wasn't surprised they had come. They would be there to defy him. Arrogant people were predictable.

Clearing his throat, he leaned toward the microphones, and in a voice that would have carried even without amplification, began by thanking everyone for coming. He gave a short history of *Lake News*—a little self-promo, but what the hell—and credited Armand with its success. Then he drew up the paper's new issue.

Having gone through the speech dozens of times in his mind, he spoke without notes. "Last month I followed the story about the alleged relationship between Cardinal Rossetti and Lily Blake with interest, in part because Ms. Blake was from Lake Henry, in part because I used to work with the reporter who broke the story, Terry Sullivan. I had doubts about the story's validity from the start, so I wasn't surprised when the Vatican cleared Cardinal Rossetti and the *Boston Post* had to issue him an apology. But then I had to stand by, as did Ms. Blake and her family, and watch the papers blame her for the scandal."

He felt Lily's leg shake and pressed his thigh to hers to steady it. He didn't blame her for being unsettled. The faces out there were hungry. Add to that the hum of video cameras, the snap of cameras, and the rustle of notepaper, and the setting was far different from her usual gigs. Likewise the stakes.

Feeling the responsibility of that, he spoke clearly. "Everyone who knew her here vouched for Ms. Blake's reasonableness, her competence, and her stability. Not a single person voiced anything remotely consistent with the kind of unbalanced condition the papers reported. To us, it sounded suspiciously like the *Post* trying to justify publishing a bad story. The question is why that bad story was written in the first place." He held up *Lake News*. "This new issue addresses that question. You'll all get copies, so you'll be able to read the details. I'd just like to summarize them."

That was all he wanted—to summarize his findings before a captive audience. Calling a press conference—making reporters and journalists travel—created an event. That maximized the odds that the story would be covered well. Looking out at the audience, which was captive indeed, he felt good. Glancing at Terry, he felt even better.

Terry appeared complacent. Without quite staring, John kept tabs on his expression. He wanted to see the minute it changed. And it would. Oh, it would.

"From the start, this story was Terry Sullivan's. Once it hit the air, others jumped on the bandwagon, but he was the one who thought it up and pushed it through. He lobbied for it even when his editors at the *Post* were wary. They resisted printing it until he produced a tape in which Ms. Blake's own voice confirmed an affair with Cardinal Rossetti."

Worried that Lily would be uneasy with those words, he pressed his thigh to hers again. *Wait,* it told her. *Just wait.*

"That tape was illegal," he said. "Ms. Blake didn't know it was being made. Last week, that tape was also proved to be bogus." A murmur slipped through the crowd.

Terry's features tightened, but he remained composed. John marveled at the conceit that kept him from squirming, marveled at the cockiness that made him so blind he couldn't see—couldn't guess, couldn't *dream*—where John was headed.

John went on. "Those of us who know how Mr. Sullivan works urged the *Post* to examine the tape for authenticity, but they refused. It was only after evidence emerged pointing to malice on his part that they acted. Their own experts found that the tape had been cut and spliced, which is consistent with Ms. Blake's story. All along she has said that Mr. Sullivan led her into a hypothetical dialogue and then rearranged her words for his quotes."

Terry was slowly shaking his head, suggesting something pathetic about John's attempt to discredit him.

"Last Friday," John said, "the *Post* fired Mr. Sullivan."

Terry actually rolled his eyes. But John saw surprise on a face or two.

"It was done quickly and quietly," he went on, "the whole thing swept right under the rug, with Ms. Blake left as the villain of the piece. The real villain is what this week's *Lake News* is about. Mr. Sullivan was the force behind this scandal. He pushed for the story even when his superiors discouraged it. He went to the extreme of falsifying evidence to make it happen. Common sense said he had a reason for doing that. *Lake News* discloses that reason."

Lily watched and waited. It was the moment. Terry had gone still.

But something drew her eye farther back in the hall—something, someone. Maida was there. She seemed lost in a large black jacket, but it was definitely her. Lily tried to catch her eye, but it was riveted on John as he went on.

"Mr. Sullivan grew up in Meadville, Pennsylvania. An essay of his that was published in the local paper when he was a teenager suggests that even then he held a grudge against the Catholic Church, and no wonder. Sources in Meadville confirm that his father used to beat his mother and him. Why? Jealousy. His mother came to that marriage loving someone else, someone she had been with through high school and college, but who had left her to enter the seminary. That man was Fran Rossetti."

A murmur rose. Terry slid from his pew and snaked toward the rear, but the wall of townsfolk tightened and wouldn't let him through. The audience turned, searching him out as he tried to escape. Cameramen focused in. Strobes flashed.

An eye for an eye, Lily thought in a moment's perverse rage. *People in glass houses. Do unto others.*

Unable to get through, Terry turned and drew himself up. Looking straight at Lily, he said in a loud voice, "This is a classic case of shooting the messenger when you don't like the message."

John was on his feet so fast that Lily didn't even feel it coming. His voice boomed. "Wrong. It's a classic case of the misuse of power."

"Exactly," Terry shouted back. "You're trying to turn this story around for the sake of a book. Let's talk about that hefty contract you have."

"There's no contract," John said. "There's no book. Anything that might have been in it"—he held up *Lake News*—"is here."

"That paper is filled with slander," Terry charged. "I hope you're prepared for a lawsuit, because that's what you're getting." Indignant, he swung his arms around and forced an opening in the crowd.

Lily remembered doing much the same thing in Boston when she'd had to fight her way through the streets. She hoped Terry was feeling even a tad of the same humiliation, the same helplessness, frustration, and fear. She wanted him to think twice before inflicting it on others again. She wanted his colleagues to learn from his example.

Two photographers, one reporter, and a cameraman followed him out, but the rest of the audience turned back to John.

Maida was sitting straighter. Lily didn't know whether it was anger or pride. She prayed that her mother was understanding more about the situation now, even feeling an iota of satisfaction on her behalf.

Composed again, John sat down. "That's all I have. If there are questions, we'd be glad to answer them."

Hands shot up, voices rang out.

"Was the Cardinal involved in your investigation?"

"No."

"Do you have proof of a connection between Mr. Sullivan's mother and the Cardinal?"

"Yes. There's a senior prom picture in the Cardinal's high school yearbook, and numerous people able to verify it." He wasn't mentioning Terry's brother. It wasn't his intent to sic the press on the priest. Nor did he want to make trouble for the Cardinal. A high school relationship was perfectly acceptable and would be easily explained on Rossetti's part. John said only what he had to to bolster Lily's case. Vindicating her was the thing.

"Does the Cardinal know about the connection to Mr. Sullivan?"

"I don't know."

"Has the *Post* issued an apology to Ms. Blake?"

"No."

"Will you demand one?" a reporter asked Lily.

Cassie leaned toward the microphones. "A lawsuit is pending. Ms. Blake has no comment at this time."

The next question came to John. "You've tried and convicted Mr. Sullivan. Isn't that an abuse of your own power?"

John couldn't believe the man's stupidity. "Excuse me," he said to the reporter who asked. "Would you identify yourself."

"Paul Rizzo, *Cityside.*"

"Paul Rizzo. Ahhh." Utter *stupidity*. John was thrilled. He couldn't have hoped for better if he had scripted the scene himself. Paul Rizzo had just put himself on the witness stand. He was fair game now. "What qualifications do you have to be in this room?"

There were a number of confused looks in the audience, not the least of which belonged to Paul. "I've been on the *Cityside* staff for seven years."

"Before that?" John asked. *Lake News* didn't cover this. It focused on Terry's malice and the harm done to Lily. But a golden opportunity was looking him in the eye. "What's your educational background?"

Rizzo glance uneasily around. Tightly, he said, "That's irrelevant."

"Is it? You pride yourself in saying you have an undergraduate degree from Duke and a graduate one from NYU. That's what your *Cityside* bio says. I assume that's what you told them when you applied for the job. I've heard you refer to those degrees, myself. The thing is, they don't exist. According to the records at Duke, you flunked out after two years. NYU doesn't have a record of your being there at all. So that's misrepresentation. If you lie about those things, can we trust what you write?"

Lily actually felt sorry for him. Being humiliated publicly wasn't fun, and two wrongs certainly didn't make a right. But John wasn't a cruel man. If there had been another way, he would have taken it.

Besides, painful as the lesson might be for Paul Rizzo, there was a moral to the story. She held her head higher. She could have sworn Maida gave a small smile.

"Justice" was the operable word. John told himself that as Rizzo sputtered, "Your information's wrong. Besides, where I went to school is *my* business."

"That's right," John said. "Like where Ms. Blake shops is her business. Like where she eats and vacations is her business."

"You're avoiding the question."

"Since *you* aren't valid, that question isn't," John said and pointed at another reporter. "Yes?"

"Rizzo's question is fair," that one said. "You pulled strings to get us up here for a press conference. Isn't that an abuse of power?"

John might have been guilty of using people at

earlier times in his career, but not now. There wasn't the slightest pulse of a tic under his eye. He was confident.

"I didn't force anyone here. There was no false pretense. I said I had new information. I invited you here, and you came. I've now given you that new information."

Another reporter asked, "What about the issue of trying and convicting Mr. Sullivan?"

"This isn't a trial. It's investigative journalism. I've simply printed the results in my paper."

"How does that differ from what he did to Ms. Blake?"

"He fabricated. He falsified. He invented. What's in *Lake News* is fact."

"You didn't have to call a press conference for that."

"Yes, I did. This is a new development in a case that kept you all going for days, but you're tired of it now. You've moved on to other things. You wouldn't have reprinted anything I wrote in *Lake News* if I hadn't gotten you here."

"How do you know we'll report it now?"

He grinned. This was safe ground. He knew the media mind. Hell, wasn't his one? "Look around. There are quite a few media outlets here. Can you take a chance that one or more of the others will run the headline and get the coup, and you'll have dropped the ball? Ms. Blake was smeared on the front page. She deserves to be exonerated the same way."

"Sullivan will be smeared in the process. But he's been fired. Isn't that punishment enough?"

"It would be. But the *Post* wants this kept quiet. They don't plan to tell people he was fired, because it implies bad judgment on their part. They'll sit there smugly, keeping their mouths shut when another paper signs him—and hey, that's okay by me. The guy has a right to earn a living. I just think the public ought to be warned. His credibility should be seen for what it is." He pointed at another raised hand.

"Ms. Blake, you're an entertainer. Do you anticipate that this notoriety will give your career a boost?"

Lily felt her heart pounding again. John had talked. Cassie had talked. It was her turn.

She took a minute to make sure that her tongue was relaxed, but it took little effort. She was feeling surprisingly strong when she leaned toward the mike. "I'm a teacher. I lost my job because of the charges made in the *Post*. I'm also a pianist. I lost that job, too, because the . . . notoriety . . . was bringing the wrong kinds of people to listen." She paused and collected herself. "This has been a very negative experience. I don't know that I'll ever want to be in that kind of limelight again."

"Would you comment on the car theft conviction?"

Cassie leaned forward before she could. "I'll comment on that, since I've seen the court file. There was no conviction. Ms. Blake didn't know she was in a stolen car. Since she was a juvenile without any prior record, the judge continued the case without a finding. The charges were subsequently dropped and the file was sealed. Ms. Blake's civil rights were violated when Mr. Sullivan printed information from that file. He'll have to answer to that."

A homely man halfway back on the left rose. Lily felt a qualm when he addressed John. "Is it, or is it not true," Justin Barr asked in a self-righteous voice, "that you hold a grudge against Terry Sullivan?"

"That's an understatement," John declared, emboldened. He hadn't asked Justin Barr to put himself in the limelight any more than he had asked Rizzo to do it. It was another gift. Lily Blake was going to be remembered for far more than a trumped-up relationship with any Cardinal.

He experienced a moment's doubt when he glanced at Lily and saw her queasy look. She knew what was coming and regretted it. Hell, so did he. But Justin Barr was no innocent. He used people. He took potshots for the fun of it. Being shot at in turn was the price one paid for that.

Praying that Lily would understand and forgive what he was about to do, he looked out at Barr. Did John hold a grudge against Terry Sullivan? "I loathe the man."

"Then you have cause to smear him, just as he had cause to smear Cardinal Rossetti."

"I'm not smearing him. I'm simply presenting facts about his childhood and family that shed light on what he did to Ms. Blake."

"What is Ms. Blake to you?" Barr asked smugly.

John didn't blink. "An innocent victim. My turn, Mr. Barr. There's a high-priced call girl in Boston by the name of Tiffany Coupe. What's she to you?"

Barr said, "I don't know anyone by that name."

"No. But Jason Weidermeyer does. There are checks signed by him, made out to Ms. Coupe. His name is on ledgers covering a period of eight years. Jason Weidermeyer. Isn't that your real name?"

"There are other Jason Weidermeyers in the world," Barr said, but the crowd was tittering. In making himself a celebrity, Justin Barr had gloried in giving interviews. His standard line, spoken haughtily, was how determination, diligence, and an impeccable sense of morality had turned Jason Weidermeyer from a nobody into the renowned and respected Justin Barr. Jason Weidermeyer. Jason Weidermeyer. Jason Weidermeyer. Everyone who knew of Justin Barr knew of Jason Weidermeyer.

The tittering went on. Barr had few friends here. Beside John, Lily seemed to release a breath and relax. He felt her understanding and her forgiveness, felt her letting go of last bits of anger, and in that instant more than any other, he knew that the day had been a success.

Barr raised his voice, once again the prince of bombast. "Who are *you* to accuse me of that? And who are *you* to question Mr. Rizzo's credentials? You couldn't make it in Boston, so here you are editing a two-bit backwoods weekly. Who are *you* to snoop into people's lives?"

John stood again. "I'm a concerned citizen. Lily Blake's life was destroyed for the sake of selling newspapers—or in your case, boosting ratings. You excoriated her on your show, Mr. Barr. You made her out to be wicked and depraved. So let's talk about wicked and depraved. How do whips and leather fit in with that? Or handcuffs and chains? You want to point a finger at people, Mr. Barr, you'd better make sure there's nothing for them to point back at." He looked away. "Other questions?"

Lily felt the stunned silence and half expected that no one would *dare* speak up, lest John have something on them, too. One reporter finally did. She was a timid type who might not have been heard if the others hadn't been still.

"Will Ms. Blake be writing a book?" she asked.

"No," Lily said, shuddering at the thought.

There was a brief silence. Then, from somewhere in the hall came a defensive "We're not all bad."

She knew they weren't. John had taught her that. She wanted to think there were more than a handful of good people out there—and thinking that, she felt another little boost inside. It was nice, so nice, to trust again.

John was quieter, but no less impressive. "I know. That's why I'm counting on you to cover this story the way you covered the original scandal. Reporters who make up facts dirty the rest of us who don't. We need to put a lid on commentators who shoot off their mouths for the sake of self-aggrandizement. They give us all a bad name. I don't know about you, but I'm tired of that."

He sounded tired. Leaning down to the mikes, he said to the gathering as a whole, "That's it. Thank you for coming."

He turned to Lily, bent over, and said softly, "I'd give you a hug here and now, except I don't trust that that won't be what they report. So, consider yourself hugged."

Lily did. Incredibly. She also felt overwhelmed with emotion—relief, triumph, satisfaction, love. Appallingly, tears came to her eyes.

She looked at the spot where Maida had been sitting, but she had to blink before she could see clearly enough, and then she was suddenly surrounded by people—technicians removing microphones, photographers snapping pictures, reporters asking final questions. Other reporters were facing their own cameras, some broadcasting live. She craned her neck in an attempt to find Maida, but bodies got in the way.

"Are you returning to Boston?"

"Will you try to get your job at the Essex Club back?"

"Has the Cardinal called?"

Having bared enough of herself to last a lifetime, she held up a hand and turned away.

"That's all," Cassie told the crowd. With an arm around Lily's shoulders, she drew her away from the crowd that surrounded John.

When they had sufficient privacy, Lily asked, "What do you think?"

"John did good. They'll report what he said. If you don't get front page, you'll come close."

"Will this affect our suit?" Lily wanted that settled. Other loose ends were being tied up. She wanted this one done, too.

Cassie grinned. "It sure ups the ante. The AG will be looking for Terry once he reads about the tape, and I figure that once the *Post*'s lawyers look at their own case vis-à-vis that tape, they'll be wanting to settle fast." She chuckled. "Max Funder, eat your heart out."

"It's not about the money," Lily said. She wanted no part of the money.

"If it comes, you'll donate it somewhere. But if there isn't a penalty for libel, what's the incentive not to do it again?"

Lily barely heard the question. With the crowd thinning, she spotted Poppy, who was looking at her with such pride that her eyes again filled with tears.

Even through the blur, though, she saw Maida. She was closer to the front of the hall than she had been, but she stopped walking when Lily caught her eye.

"Excuse me," Lily whispered to Cassie.

With reassuring freedom, she moved past the reporters who lingered with John. Maida stood about a third of the way back, with her hand on the end of the pew. She looked like she wanted to flee but couldn't, like she wanted to cry but couldn't, like she wanted to crumble but couldn't.

Lily started toward her. Oh yes, there was the fear of rejection, but the need she felt overcame it. She went the rest of the way, slowing as she neared, stopping when she was right there, less than an arm's length away.

What to say? What to ask? Or beg?

Maida took a deep, shuddering breath. She raised a tentative hand to Lily's cheek. Just shy of touching, it settled on her shoulder. It was light, awkward, testing.

"Forgive me?" she whispered.

Lily didn't know whether Maida wanted forgiveness for things she had done in her own childhood, or in Lily's, or more recently, but there was never any doubt in Lily's mind. Where the Sullivans, Rizzos, and Barrs of the world were involved, Lily needed justice. Where her mother was involved, she needed . . . she needed . . .

Maida's arms were unsteady, but they reached in the right direction. Lily went into them with a sense of relief so great that she was suddenly sobbing, holding on for dear life, finding the comfort she had wanted so badly when she had been alone in Boston.

She wasn't alone now. She had friends here now. She even had someone she loved. But Maida was her mother, which made what she offered very special.

Poppy wasn't prone to tears, but watching Lily and Maida, she came close. She knew all too well that some things in life couldn't be changed. Others could. Grateful that this one had been, she wheeled her chair around and headed for the back of the hall. She was thinking about the improvement this would bring to Maida's life, thinking about how much better Lily would feel and how much happier holidays would be, thinking that Lily really ought to stay in Lake Henry and marry John and how nice it would be to have her here, thinking about everything but where she was headed, when she turned the corner at the back of the hall and found herself face-to-face with a man she had never met—at least, not in the flesh.

But she knew who he was. He wore jeans, a sweater, and a fleece jacket. The jacket was a royal blue that picked up the blue in his eyes and was a perfect foil for hair that was thick, well styled, and red.

Where to go? *Turn back!* Where to hide?

But too late. *He knew.* She could see it in his eyes.

In the few seconds that it took him to approach, she felt guilty for not having told him, disappointed that the fantasy would end, dismayed that she was what she was when she wanted to be something so different.

He hunkered down so that his eyes were on level with hers. "Did you honestly think I'd care?" he asked so gently that, for the second time in as many minutes, Poppy nearly cried.

But Poppy Blake didn't cry. Crying accomplished nothing. She had decided that twelve years before.

So she lashed back at his gentleness with the bleak truth. "I can't run. I can't ski or hike. I can't work in the forest the way I was trained, because I can't get around in a chair on rutted dirt. I can't dance. I can't drive a car unless it's been specially adapted. I can't pick apples or work the cider press. I can't even stand in the shower."

"Can you eat?"

Gruffly, she said, "Of course I can eat."

"Can I buy you dinner?"

Her heart lurched. She fought the pull. "Yes, but if you think I'm talking about my sister, the answer is still no."

"I don't want to know about your sister. I want to know about you." He stood, briefly studied the handles of her chair, then looked at her with such endearing helplessness that she was smitten. "I'm a quick study," he said. "Tell me what to do."

Poppy had strong arms. They were used to propelling her and her chair through almost any wheelchair-accessible area, and the church had a very fine ramp.

She prided herself on being independent.

But her friends did push her chair when they were out together. They said it made them feel like they were walking in step with her.

Wanting to walk in step with Griffin Hughes, Poppy said, "I point, you push."

She pointed, he pushed, and off they went.

The celebration was spontaneous, a gathering of friends—then more friends, then *more* friends in Charlie's back room. When reporters tried to join in, Charlie turned them away. "Sorry. Private party," he said as he and his kids passed through the door loaded down with trays of the best the kitchen had to offer.

Lily didn't sing. It was even better than that. She talked and laughed and was part of something she hadn't known to miss but wouldn't have given up for the world. She half imagined that she knew what it felt like to win the lottery. Mixed in with joy was the fear that something so wonderful couldn't be real.

But it was. John was real; he rarely left her side. Maida was real; she smiled each time she caught Lily's eye. Lake Henry was real; it had come through for her when she needed it most. She couldn't remember a day when she had felt so strongly that every element in her life meshed so well.

Then the Cardinal called. She had just walked into the cottage when the cell phone rang. She assumed it was Poppy.

"Hey," she said, a bit breathless, "was that *fun*?"

"Hey, yourself," he said, playfully sober.

She caught her breath. "Father Fran!"

"Your sister gave me this number. I'm off to Rome tomorrow, but I wanted to talk with you first. You're the only loose end I haven't tied up."

"There's nothing—"

"There is." His voice was as heavy as she had ever heard it. "I owe you an apology, Lily. I knew who Terry Sullivan was. I didn't know him personally, but I knew the name. When he broke that story, which was clearly so wrong, I guessed that he knew about his mother and was getting back at me for hurting her. I didn't know about the beatings until tonight when the first call came after your press conference."

"They called you?" Of course they would. "I'm so sorry—"

"Don't be," he scolded gently. "It's easily handled. I have no problem confirming that relationship. Jean and I were sweethearts, but I never hid from her the fact that I wanted to be a priest. My conscience is clear on that score, but not on the matter of what Terry suffered because of it, and not on the matter of you. If I had acknowledged the connection, the whole thing might have stopped sooner, and you wouldn't have lost so much. I'm sorry, Lily. That was wrong of me. You deserve better."

Yes. She did. She could be angry at the Cardinal for that, even for simplifying the story of his relationship with Jean. Knowing what he had left out, though, she understood. Knowing the predatory nature of the media, she *doubly* understood. Another person in her situation might have said that the Cardinal's apology came too late. But Lily wasn't another person. She was gentle, and she was forgiving.

"For what it's worth," he said, "of all the doubts I've had about my worthiness since I was named a Cardinal, a great many of them relate to this mess."

"Oh, no. That shouldn't be."

"There's no place for pride in my work. Or for dishonesty by virtue of omission."

"But the world *needs* leaders like you."

"It isn't my job to cause suffering."

"But I'm home," Lily insisted. How to resent *anyone* when her life was this full? "So maybe the suffering had a purpose."

He paused then. The tide of the conversation seemed to turn. "Are things working out for you there?"

"Very much. I think I've found me."

"Ahhh," he said. From the sound of it, he was smiling at last. "That does my heart good. It doesn't forgive my selfishness—God will have to forgive that—but it does make me happy. Not surprised, mind you. I always said you were strong."

She was smiling now, too. "You did."

"You finally believe it, then?"

"I'm . . . getting there."

"Will you keep me up on the progress?"

"That depends," she said. "Will Father Mc-Donough put me through?"

The Cardinal chuckled. "You bet. Peace be with you, Lily."

"And with you," she said and, ending the call with a sense of warmth, realized that a loose end had been tied up for her, too.

Chapter 30

They had to be crazy, coming out on the lake. The night was stark, and in the third week of October, the air too cold for canoeing, but Lily wouldn't have been anywhere else. The past hours had been chock full of so many different emotions that she was on overload. Now, here—even in a chilling breeze—things were simpler.

There was no moon. The spot where it would have been was obscured by thick clouds. Farther west, the clouds were spotty. They were moving at a clip, judging from the appearance and disappearance of stars.

"Winter's coming," John said. "You can smell it."

Lily smelled wood smoke from a chimney on shore, and the piney clean scent of John, against whom she nestled, but the leaves were too dry and cold to exude a scent, and the predominant aura on the lake was of something else. "Snow?" she asked.

"Soon. Then comes ice. In another month, there'll

be a skim coat. A month after that, it'll be more'n a foot thick. We're a small body of water. When it happens, it happens fast."

The canoe rose and fell with the wind on the lake. They were thirty feet out from the island in whose shallows John's loons lived. Lily searched the darkness for the birds.

"I can't see them."

Gently he cupped her head, wool hat and all, and turned it left. "There. Those moving things."

She was a minute separating reflection from wind waves from loons. Then she saw, but only two. They floated close together, finding solace in each other, she fancied. In the next instant she understood.

"Mom and Dad have left," John confirmed. "Headed south."

"Will these two ever see them again?"

"Not for three years, at least. That's when they return here to mate. Whether they return to our lake or to another one in the area remains to be seen. Whether they'll recognize their parents, and vice versa, is anyone's guess."

"Sad," Lily said. She was thinking about Maida, and about how . . . *rich* she felt now that they had bridged a gap.

"Let's be honest here," John chided. "These guys may be whizzes at survival. They have to be, to have made it for so many million years. But sensitive? Sentimental? I don't think so."

"No? Aren't you the one who said they came out to see you all the time?"

He mocked himself with a chuckle. "Yeah, well, I liked to think that, but the truth is if you wait here long enough and invisibly enough, they just float into range."

She tipped her head back. Even in the dark, with just the outline of windblown hair on his brow, a straight nose, and a square jaw gentled by just beard enough to cover it, his face was handsome. Taking care not to tip the canoe, she shifted sideways so that she was cradled in the crook of his arm and could more comfortably look up. "I like the other explanation. I think you do, too. You're sensitive. You're sentimental." Then, because she had been wondering for hours, she asked, "Did you mean what you said about not writing a book?"

John didn't have to give it much thought. As no-brainers went, it was right up there. He was perfectly comfortable, entirely confident, saying, "I meant it."

"No book at all?"

"Not on this topic. Enough of the Blake story's been told as I want to tell."

"What about Terry's story?"

"*Lake News* covered it."

"Someone else will do it in depth."

"That's okay by me."

"What about money and fame?"

Looking at her as she lay so trustingly in his arms, John couldn't even *spell* the words, much less crave either one. "Funny thing about money and fame. They can't go canoeing with you in the freezing cold or

warm up in bed with you afterward. They can't talk.
They can't *sing*. They can't have kids."

Her eyes went a little wider. The darkness couldn't
hide that. He hadn't meant to throw it out yet, but
there it was. Must have been tucked away more shal-
lowly than he thought.

"I can have kids," she said.

"I know you can, but you gotta want them."

"Why wouldn't I?"

"You wouldn't if you were still hoping to go back
to Boston; at least, you wouldn't want to have them
with me, because I really don't think I want to leave
here. So. Do you?"

"Do I what?"

"Still want to go back to Boston?"

Lily hadn't made a conscious decision, but that didn't
mean the decision wasn't made. It was made. It was
easy. "What in the world is back there for me?" she
asked, unable to think of a single thing that mattered
more than what she had right here.

"Your car. Your piano. Your clothes."

"Funny thing about that," she said. "A car can't go
canoeing with you in the freezing cold. A piano can't
warm up in bed with you afterward. Clothes can't talk
or sing or have kids."

"But they're your things. They stand for something."

She wasn't letting his eyes go, not for a minute.
"So do moving companies. Besides, how can I be with
you in Boston, if you won't leave here?"

"But I shouldn't be the reason you decide to stay here."

"Why not?"

She had him there. He opened and closed his mouth several times, then finally left it shut and just grinned. The grin warmed its way through her.

"Lest your ego get too big," she cautioned, "there are other things keeping me here. There's Maida." She broke eye contact with him to look out toward the part of the lake where the orchards would be. "She hadn't worked a day in her life until Daddy died. Now look."

"She doesn't like me."

Lily looked back at him. "She doesn't know you. But she has an open mind. She proved that today. So there's Maida, and Poppy. And Hannah. Maida is on her side now, but if Rose doesn't come around, I want to be there, too."

"If you stay, what'll you do?"

"I could teach." Maida had said that the academy needed someone. "I could work for *Lake News* so that the editor-in-chief has more free time." She liked the idea of working with John. "I could see if there's a chamber music group in Concord in need of a pianist." There were choices.

"You won't miss Boston?"

"What I have here is better. Did I tell you how good you were today?"

John didn't mind hearing it again. He was human, and male. "Was I?"

She grinned. "Masterful."

"I think I got my point across."

"Totally." She touched a mittened hand to his cheek. "Thank you for doing that for me."

"I did it for me, too. It felt good saying those things. They've been eating at me for years."

"Gus would have been proud."

John wanted to think it, though he didn't know for sure. "Hard to tell with him. But we were on the right side today, Lily. We may not have changed a damn thing. Chances are good those reporters will do what they've always done."

"Not all of them."

"No matter. I feel better about myself right now."

Lily was looking at the sky. "Here come the stars. He's up there. He knows. He agrees."

"God?"

"Gus."

John wanted to laugh away the possibility, only the laugh didn't come. Looking at Lily, feeling her goodness and her love, he suspected she might well be right.

Barbara Delinsky recently took time from working on her next book to talk to us. Here are the highlights of that conversation.

Q: How did the writing of *Flirting with Pete* differ from the creation of your earlier novels?

A: It differed in several ways. First, the plot actually came to me nearly ten years ago. Prior to then, I had always written about functional characters, but I wanted to do something different—I wanted to explore the games the human mind plays when pushed to emotional extremes. Jenny Clyde evolved, neither smart nor successful nor physically adept, and her mind did indeed play games when pushed to extremes. The writing was an unbelievable experience for me. By the end of the book, I felt I had created my strongest work.

But it was a novella, and therein lay the second difference between *Flirting with Pete* and my earlier work. I knew that I would have to expand upon it to satisfy the expectations of my publisher and my readers—particularly given its ending, which was very, *very* different from anything I had written. I knew I would have to alter that too, but I wasn't ready. So I put *Flirting with Pete* aside and wrote a handful of other books. But Jenny remained with me, patiently awaiting her turn. When the time was right, she gave me a nudge. It was one of those visceral things.

Q: If *Flirting with Pete* is about Jenny Clyde, where did Casey Ellis come from?

A: Casey came from my need to keep Jenny's story intact. Casey gave me a context in which to view Jenny. She provided an environment more typical of my books, and while her story doesn't exactly parallel Jenny's, there are strong analogies. Both women are haunted by their fathers and irrevocably affected by the relationship between their parents.

Q: Are you a gardener?

A: Aha. You're wondering about Casey's town house and that gorgeous garden hidden behind brick walls. Truth be told, I have a brown thumb. But I do love looking at flowers, and I know how to do research. I have to confess that there were times when I was overwhelmed trying to remember which flowers and shrubs grow in sun and which in shade, which bloom in spring and which in summer or fall. I made elaborate charts. I think I got it right.

Q: Casey is a social worker, and you are schooled in psychology. Was this a case of writing about what you know?

A: No. I never did therapy, as Casey does. But I do love people. I've always been attuned to feelings and motivations. Plus, I have a daughter-in-law who is a therapist. She tutored me in the art. I learned a lot.

Q: You must like that—learning. You have written too many books to always write about what

you know, which raises a whole other issue. What's this we hear about lobster trivia?
A: (Smile.) Well, it isn't exactly trivia, since much of it is serious stuff to do with the daily life of a lobsterman. It all has to do with my next book, *The Summer I Dared*.

Q: Which is about lobstering?
A: That's the backdrop—lobstering off the coast of Maine. The story is about three people who survive a horrific boating accident that claims the life of nine others. Julia Bechtel is a wife and mother from New York, Noah Prine is a lobsterman, and Kim Collela is a young woman with a secret. The lives of the three are deeply entwined in the aftermath of the accident.

Q: Which did you pick first—lobstering or the plot?
A: The plot. It's the issue of random tragedy, such as the deaths of September 11, 2001. How to explain those? How to deal with being in the wrong place at the wrong time? Conversely, how to deal with walking away unscathed from something like that? The tragedy that opens *The Summer I Dared* has nothing to do with terrorism, but the questions are the same. I warrant a guess that most of us looked at our lives differently after September 11. Likewise, Julia, Noah, and Kim are irrevocably changed by the accident they survive. Each faces the dilemma of how to reconcile these changes with the lives they've known.

Q: Is the accident the focal point of the story?
A: No. It's simply the catalyst. Honestly, I don't think I could dwell on a tragedy like that through nine months of writing a book. What happens to the characters after the accident—how they deal and adjust and grow—is far more interesting to me.

Q: Can you give an example of this growth?
A: Not without giving away too much of the story. I will say that my main female voice is that of Julia, who has been the obedient daughter, wife, and mother. Following the accident, she wonders if obedience is enough, and whether she owes it to those who died to learn to be proactive.

Q: Why Maine?
A: I like to rotate my settings among the six New England states, and I hadn't done Maine since writing *For My Daughters* in 1994. Not only was it time for Maine in that sense, but I'd been *pining* for Maine. I spent all my summers there as a child. My mother's family came from Portland; I visited my grandfather there many times. He owned a barrel business on the waterfront. It was housed in a cavernous stone building, and produced wooden barrels with metal stays and rims. In recent years, the waterfront of Portland has been transformed into a charming area called the Old Port. I imagine that embedded somewhere among the restaurants and businesses there is an old cornerstone with the name *Finn & Sons* on it.

Q: Getting back to lobster trivia, though, it goes beyond the book, doesn't it?

A: Yes. I had done tons of research on lobstering in preparation for writing *The Summer I Dared,* far more than I ever used in the book, and it seemed a shame to simply file all that way—particularly since I hadn't found such a collection of little bits of information in one place anywhere else! So I gathered it all, put it into a cohesive form, and had it printed. It's not for sale. At this point I'm simply sending it to the people who've been involved in the publication of *The Summer I Dared.* This version will never be for sale, unless it's in exchange for donations to breast cancer research. That can be done through my website.

Q: And if some of your readers hate lobster? What then?

A: I invite them to vent. My web address is www.barbaradelinsky.com, and in addition to all sorts of news and offers and book summaries and reviews, there's the Post Office, through which notes to me can be sent. I can also be reached the conventional way, through P.O. Box 812894, Wellesley, MA 02482-0026. I receive all notes, and answer as many as possible.

Scribner
Proudly Presents

THE SUMMER I DARED

Barbara Delinsky

Now available in hardcover

**Turn the page for a preview of
*The Summer I Dared. . . .***

Prologue

The *Amelia Celeste* was born a lobster boat. An elegant lady, she ran a proud thirty-eight feet of mahogany and oak, from the graceful upward sweep of her bow, down her foredeck to the wheelhouse and, on a straight and simple plane, back to her stern. True to the axiom that Maine lobstermen treat their boats with the same care as their wives, the *Amelia Celeste* had been doted on by Matthew Crane in much the same way he had pampered the flesh-and-blood Amelia Celeste, to whom he had been married for forty years and on whose grave every Friday he continued to lay a dozen long-stem roses, even twelve long years after her death.

Matthew had the means. His grandfather had made a fortune logging, not only the vast forests of northern Maine but the islands in its Gulf that bore trees rather than granite. He had built the family home on one of those evergreen islands, aptly named Big Sawyer. Two generations later, Crane descendants were equally represented among the fishermen and the artists who comprised the core of the island's year-round residents.

Matthew was a fisherman, and for all his family money, remained a simple man at heart. His true delight, from the age of sixteen on, had been heading out at dawn to haul lobster traps from the fertile waters of Penobscot Bay. A purist, he continued to use wooden traps even when the rest of the local fleet had switched to ones made of wire mesh. Likewise, he would have died before trading in his wood-hulled boat for a newer fiberglass one that would be lighter and faster. Matthew didn't need speed. He lived by the belief that life was about the "doing," not the "done." As for gaining a few miles to the gallon with a lighter boat, he felt that in a business where no two days were alike, where the seas could change in a matter of minutes and abruptly unbalance two men hauling loaded traps up over the starboard rail, the stability of the *Amelia Celeste* was worth gold. And then there was the noise. Wood was a natural insulater. Cruising in the *Amelia Celeste* was quiet as no fiberglass craft could be, and quiet meant you could hear the gulls, the cormorants, the wind and the waves. Those things brought him calm.

Reliability, stability, and calm—good reasons why, when Matthew turned sixty-five and his arthritis worsened enough to make his hands useless in the trade, he fitted the vessel with a new engine and tanks, rebuilt the pilothouse with permanent sides to keep out the wind, polished the mahogany to an even higher sheen, installed a defogger on the center window and seating for passengers in the stern, and relaunched the *Amelia Celeste* as a ferry.

During the first few years of this incarnation, Matthew skippered her himself. He made three daily runs to the mainland—once early each morning, once around noon, and once at the end of the day. He didn't carry cars; the ferry run by the State of Maine did that. Nor did he publish a schedule, because if an islander had a special need, Matthew would adjust his schedule to meet it. He charged a nominal fee, and was lax about collecting it. This wasn't a job; it was a hobby. He simply wanted to be on the boat he loved, in the bay he loved, and if he made life easier for the local folk, particularly when the winter months imposed a craze-inducing isolation, so much the better.

On that Tuesday evening in early June, however, when the idyll went tragically awry, Matthew—to his deep regret—was not at the helm of the *Amelia Celeste*. She was being piloted by Greg Hornsby, a far younger cousin of his who had spent all of his own forty years on the water and was as skilled a fisherman as Matthew. No, there was no shortage of experience or skill. Nor was there a shortage of electronics. As a lobster boat, the *Amelia Celeste* had been equipped with multiband radios, fish finders, and radar. As a passenger-toting vessel, she had the latest in GPS navigational systems along with the rest, but none of it would help that day.

Riding low in the water as lobster boats did, the *Amelia Celeste* left Big Sawyer at six in the evening carrying the photographer, art director, models, and gear from a photo shoot done earlier on the town docks. The sun had come out for the shoot, along with a crowd of locals wanting to watch, but the water remained cold, as Atlantic waters did in June, and by late afternoon, the approach of a warm front brought in fog.

This was no problem. Fog was a frequent visitor to the region. The lobsterman who let fog keep him ashore was the lobsterman who couldn't pay his bills.

Between the instruments at hand and Greg Hornsby's familiarity with the route, the *Amelia Celeste* deftly skirted lobster buoys clustered in the shallows leading to inlets at nearby Little Sawyer, West Rock, and Hull Islands. After taking on a single passenger at each pier, she settled into the channel at an easy twenty-two knots, aimed at the mainland some six miles away.

Fifteen minutes later, the *Amelia Celeste* docked at Rockland and her passengers disembarked with their gear. Eight others were waiting to board, dressed not in the black of that city crew, but in the flannel shirts and hooded sweatshirts, jeans, and work boots that any sane islander knew to wear until summer truly arrived. These eight all lived on Big Sawyer, which meant that Greg would have a nonstop trip home, and that pleased him immensely. Tuesday was ribs night at the Grill, and Greg loved ribs. On ribs night, the wife and kids were on their own. His buddies were saving a booth; he'd be joining them there as soon as he put the *Amelia Celeste* to bed.

He took two bags and a large box from Jeannie Walsh and stowed them under a bench while she stepped over the gunwale. Her husband, Evan, handed over several more bags and their one-year-old daughter, before climbing aboard himself. Jeannie and Evan were sculptors; their bags held clay, glazes, and tools, and the box a new wheel, all purchased in Portland that day.

Grady Bartz and Dar Hutter, both in their late twenties, boarded with the ease of men bred on the water. Grady worked as dockman for Foss Fish and Lobster, the island's buyer and dealer, and was returning from a day off, looking only slightly cleaner than usual. Dar clerked at the tackle and gear store; once in the boat, he reached back to haul in a crate filled with stock, set it by the wheelhouse wall, and moved down to the stern for a seat.

It was a wise move, because Todd Slokum was the next to board. Thin and pale, Todd was the antithesis of a seafaring man. Even after three years on the island, he still turned green on the ferry to and from. Local gossip had never quite gotten a handle on why he had come to Big Sawyer in the first place. The best anyone could say was that Zoe Ballard was a saint to employ him.

Now he stumbled over the gunwale, hit the deck on rubbery legs, and tripped toward the nearest bench as he darted awkward glances at the others already there.

Hutchinson Prine was only a tad more steady. A life-long lobsterman, his aversion to talk hid a wealth of knowledge. Nearing seventy, he still fished every day, though as sternman now, with his son at the helm. Hutch wasn't well. He had been in Portland seeing doctors. The scowl on his face said he didn't like what they had told him.

"How's it goin'?" Greg asked, and got no answer. He reached for Hutch's elbow, but the older man batted his hand away and boarded the *Amelia Celeste* on his own. His son Noah followed him aboard. Though Noah was taller, and even smarter and better looking than his father, he was just as silent. His face, at that moment, was equally stony. But he did reach to untie the lines.

The *Amelia Celeste* was seconds shy of pulling away from the dock when a pleading cry came from the shore. "Wait! Please, wait!" A slender woman ran down the dock, struggling under the bulk of heavy bags that bounced against her body. "Don't leave!" she cried beseechingly. "I'm coming! Please wait!"

She wasn't a local. Her jeans were very dark, her blouse very white, her blazer stylishly quilted. The sandals she wore wedged her higher than any islander in her right mind would be wedged, and as if that weren't odd enough for the setting, fingernails and toenails were painted pale pink. Her hair was a dozen shades of blond, fine and straight, blowing gently as she ran. She was simply made-up, strikingly attractive, and married, to judge from the ring on her left hand. The large leather pouch that hung from her shoulder was of an ilk far softer than that worked by local artisans; same with a bulging backpack.

Big Sawyer often saw women like her, but not in early June, and rarely were they alone.

"I have to get out to Big Sawyer," she begged, breathing hard, addressing Noah first, before realizing her error and turning to Greg. "I had my car reserved on the five o'clock ferry, but obviously I missed that. They said I could park back there at the end of the pier for a day or two. Can you take me to the island?"

"That depends on whether you have a place to

stay," Greg said, because he knew it was what everyone on board was wondering. "We don't have resorts. Don't even have a B and B."

"Zoe Ballard's my aunt. She's expecting me."

The words were magical. Noah took her bags and tossed them into the pilothouse. She passed him the backpack, then climbed aboard on her own, but when Evan Walsh rose to give her a seat, she shook her head, and, holding the rail that Matthew had installed when he had turned the *Amelia Celeste* into a ferry, worked her way along the narrow path to the bow.

Noah released the stern line and pushed against the piling of the pier. He said something short to his father, but if there was an answer, Greg didn't catch it. As he edged up the throttle, Noah stalked past the wheelhouse. Stationing himself on the far side of the bow from Zoe Ballard's niece, he folded his arms and stared into the fog.

Quiet and graceful for a boat that was broad in the stern, the *Amelia Celeste* slipped through the harbor at headway speed. Although two hours remained yet of daylight, the thick fog had drained the world of color. Only the occasional shadow of a boat at its mooring altered the pale gray, as did the clink of a hook the silence, but these were quickly absorbed by the mist. Once past the granite breakwater, the waves picked up and the radar came on, little green dots marking the spot where a boat, rock, or channel marker would be. Painted buoys bobbed under the fog, signalling traps on the ocean floor. The *Amelia Celeste* gave these as wide a berth as possible, throttling up to speed only when she was safely in the channel.

The chop was fair to middlin', not overly taxing to the boat, even riding low as she was. In turn, she elicited little noise beyond the soft thrum of her engine, the steady rush of water as the point of the bow cut through the waves, and an occasional exchange of words in the stern. Nothing echoed. The fog had a muting effect, swallowing resonance with an open throat.

Far to starboard, a hum simmered in the thick soup before growing into the growl of a motor. In no time, it had grown louder and more commanding, belying the soundproofing of the fog, just as its owner meant it to do. That owner was Artie Jones, and he called his boat *The Beast*. Infamous in an area dominated by the boats of working fishermen, it was a long, sleek racer of the alpha-male type, whose aerodynamic purple body shot over the surface of the water driven by twin engines putting out a whopping 1100 horses. It was capable of going seventy-five without effort, and from the rising thunder of those twin Mercs, it was approaching that now.

Noah shot Greg a *What the hell?* look.

Bewildered, Greg shrugged. The fog yielded no sign of another boat in the area, but his radar screen painted a different picture. It showed *The Beast* tracing a large arc, having sped from starboard to a point astern of them now, crossing through the last of the wake left by the *Amelia Celeste* and heading off to the north. The rumble of the racer's engines faded into the fog.

One hand on a bronze spoke of the wheel and one on the throttle, Greg kept the *Amelia Celeste* aimed at the island. Dreaming of ribs, he forgot about Artie Jones until the sound of *The Beast* rose again. No mistaking the deep chain saw growl that came from the monster engines in the tail. The racer was headed back their way. Radar confirmed it.

He picked up the handset of the VHF, which was preset to the channel the local boaters used. "What the hell are you doing, Artie?" he called, more in annoyance than anything else, because he didn't care how macho it was, no man in his right mind would be playing chicken this way in the fog.

Artie didn't answer. The roar of those twin engines increased.

Greg sounded his horn, though he knew it didn't have a chance of being heard above the noise. His eyes went back and forth, from the radar screen, which pinpointed the racer, to the GPS screen, which pinpointed the *Amelia Celeste*. It occurred to him that if he didn't do something, the two boats would collide. For the life of him, though, he didn't know what to do. Artie wasn't behaving rationally. The radar screen showed him cutting through prime fishing grounds, plowing past buoys at a speed that was sure to be destroying the potwarp tied to hundreds of traps. If he was aiming at the *Amelia Celeste,* playing some kind of perverted game, he had the speed to follow wherever she turned.

"Artie, what the *hell*—throttle down and get out of the way!" he shouted, uncaring that he might alarm his passengers, because what with the way they were all staring wide-eyed into the fog in the direction of the oncoming howl, they were already highly alarmed.

He sounded the horn again and again, to no avail.

What to do, with the island barely a mile away, the responsibility of nine people in his hands, and Artie Jones a loose canon in his muscle boat, capable of calling on all those horses, shooting off like a bullet with his bow in the air, propelled who knew where in the fog at a speed faster than the *Amelia Celeste* could ever hope to move?

Studying the radar screen for a final few seconds, Greg tried to guess where *The Beast* would go based on where it had been and what it could do. Then he made a judgment call. Unable to outrun the powerful boat, he yanked back on his own throttle to let *The Beast* pass.

It would have worked, had *The Beast* continued along its established arc. What Greg couldn't possibly have known, though, much less plugged into the equation, was that Artie had been hugging the wheel of his beloved machine at the moment his heart stopped, and was slumped against it, unconscious during much of the last arc—but that at the same moment the *Amelia Celeste* made her defensive move, his lifeless body began to slide sideways, pulling the wheel along with it.

Matthew Crane knew what had happened the instant he heard the explosion. He had been in his usual spot on the deck of the Harbor Grill, nursing a whiskey while he waited for the *Amelia Celeste* to emerge from the fog and glide to the pier. His ear was trained to catch the drone of her engine, distant as it was at the mile point, and he hadn't been able to miss *The Beast*. He had plotted its course in his mind's eye, had foreseen bisecting paths and felt the same sense of dread he had known when his flesh-and-blood Amelia Celeste had been admitted to the hospital that final time. The horrific boom had barely died when he was hurrying down the steps and across the beach. Scrambling onto the dock, he ran waving and shouting toward the handful of men who had just returned from hauling traps, and who were themselves staring into the fog in alarm.

Those men set off within minutes, reaching the scene quickly enough to fish the first two survivors from the water before they were overcome by smoke from the fire or cold from the sea. The third survivor was picked up by another boat. None of the three suffered more than minor bruises, a true miracle given the fate of the rest.